Praise for *Feverborn*

"[Karen Marie] Moning's world-building is extensive and inspired, and she never fails to keep the action fast and the stakes high. . . . The heroes' shared danger, victory, loss and turmoil translate into emotional intensity and sexual tension."

—*The New York Times Book Review*

"Karen Marie Moning is back, burning up the pages with scorching tension, gasp-out-loud surprises, unshakable danger and unexpected feels. *Feverborn* is simply impossible to put down. . . . I'm not sure how Moning is able to do it after eight books, but each novel proves more exciting than its predecessor as she continues to raise the stakes in this ongoing, exhilarating saga. *Feverborn* is a fight between ancient magic and renewed determination, a duel between old wounds and deep-seated love. Once again, you won't be able to put this book down."

—*USA Today*

"*Feverborn* is at once the most gratifying and infuriating (in the best way possible) volume in the series yet. Moning's proclivity for passion, emotion and shocking twists is showcased in breathtaking clarity. . . . I can damn near guarantee that fans of the series will be panting, both with heat, and a frenzied need to know what happens next."

—*PopWrapped*

"*Feverborn* is a masterpiece of epic proportions. With this book, Karen Marie Moning shows us exactly why she is such an indispensable writer in the genre."

—*Under the Covers*

BY KAREN MARIE MONING

THE FEVER SERIES
Darkfever
Bloodfever
Faefever
Dreamfever
Shadowfever
Iced
Burned
Feverborn
Feversong
High Voltage

GRAPHIC NOVEL
Fever Moon

NOVELLA
Into the Dreaming

THE HIGHLANDER SERIES
Beyond the Highland Mist
To Tame a Highland Warrior
The Highlander's Touch
Kiss of the Highlander
The Dark Highlander
The Immortal Highlander
Spell of the Highlander

FEVERBORN

FEVERBORN

A Fever Novel

KAREN MARIE MONING

DELL
NEW YORK

2016 Dell Mass Market Edition

Published in the United States by Dell, an imprint of Random House, a division of Random House LLC, a Penguin Random House Company, New York.

DELL and the HOUSE colophon are registered trademarks of Random House LLC.

Originally published in hardcover in the United States by Delacorte Press, an imprint of Random House, a division of Random House LLC, in 2016.

This book contains an excerpt from the forthcoming book *Feversong* by Karen Marie Moning. This excerpt has been set for this edition only and may not reflect the final content of the forthcoming edition.

ISBN 978-0-440-24643-5
Ebook ISBN 978-0-440-33982-3

Cover design: Eileen Carey
Cover photographs: © Elena Alferova/Trevillion Images (woman), © andreiuc88/Shutterstock (background)

Printed in the United States of America

randomhousebooks.com

9 8 7 6 5 4

Dell mass market edition: December 2016

In loving memory of

Anthony Ronald Augustus Moning

1935–2015

Rest in peace, Dad

I'll see you in the slipstream.

Dear Reader,

If this is the first book you've picked up in the Fever Series, at the end of *Feverborn* I've included a guide of People, Places, and Things to illuminate the backstory.

If you're a seasoned reader of the series, the guide will reacquaint you with notable events and characters, what they did, if they survived, and if not, how they died.

You can either read the guide first, getting acquainted with the world, or reference it as you go along to refresh your memory. The guide features characters by type, followed by places, then things.

To the new reader, welcome to the Fever World.

To the devoted readers who make it possible for me to continue living, dreaming, and writing in this sexy, dangerous world, welcome back and thank you!

Karen

Part I

Appearances to the mind are of four kinds. Things either are what they appear to be; or they neither are, nor appear to be; or they are, and do not appear to be; or they are not, and yet appear to be. Rightly to aim in all these cases is the wise man's task.

—Epictetus

. . . then She Who Came First gave the Song to the darkness and the Song rushed into the abysses and filled every void with life. Galaxies and beings sprang into existence, suns and moons and stars were born.

But She Who Came First was no more eternal than the suns, moons, and stars, so she gave the Song to the first female of the True Race to use only in times of great need, to be used with great care for there are checks and balances, and a price for imperfect Song. She cautioned her Chosen never to lose the melody for it would have to be gathered from all the far corners of all the galaxies again.

Of course it was lost. In time enough, everything is lost.

—The Book of Rain

PROLOGUE

Dublin, Ireland

The night was wild, electric, stormy. Unwritten.
As was he.

An unexpected episode in what had been a tightly scripted film.

Coat billowing like dark wings behind him, he walked across the rain-slicked roof of the water tower, dropped to a crouch on the edge, rested his forearms on his knees, and stared out over the city.

Lightning flashed gold and scarlet, briefly gilding dark rooftops and wet-silver streets below. Amber gas lamps glowed, pale lights flickered in windows, and Faery magic danced on the air. Fog steamed from cobblestones, mincing through alleys and shrouding buildings.

There was no place he'd rather be than this ancient, luminous city, where modern man rubbed shoulders with pagan gods. In the past year, Dublin had transformed from an everyday urban dwelling with a touch of magic to a chillingly magical city with a touch of normal. It had metamorphosed from a thriving metropolis bustling with people, to a silent iced shell, to its current incarnation: savagely alive as those who remained struggled to seize control. Dublin was a minefield, the balance of power shifting constantly as key players were eliminated without warning. Nothing was easy. Every move, each decision, a matter of life and death. It made for interesting times. Small human lives were so limited. And for that very reason, so fascinating. Shadowed by death, life became immediate. Intense.

He knew the past. He'd seen glimpses of many futures. Like its unpredictable inhabitants, Dublin had fallen off the grid of expected trajectories. Recent events in the area had not transpired in any future he'd seen. There was no telling what might happen next. The possibilities were infinite.

He liked it that way.

Fate was a misnomer; an illusion erected and clung to by people who needed to believe when things spun out of their control there was some grand purpose for their fucked-up existence, some mysterious redemptive design that made it worth the suffering.

Ah, the painful truth: Fate was a cosmic toilet. It was the nature of the universe to flush sluggish things that failed to exercise free will. Stasis was stagnancy. Change was velocity. Fate—a sniper that preferred a motionless target to a dancing one.

He wanted to graffiti the side of every building in the city: IT ISN'T FATE. IT'S YOUR OWN STUPID FUCKING FAULT. But he knew better. Admitting there was no such thing as Fate meant acknowledging personal responsibility. He wasn't about to ante up on that hand.

Still . . . every now and then one came along like him, like this city that defied all expectation, owned every action, flipped Fate the bird at each opportunity. One that didn't merely exist.

But lived. *Fearless. No price too high for freedom. He understood that.*

With a faint smile, he surveyed the city below.

From the tower he could see all the way to the choppy whitecapped sea, its black and silver surface shadowed by the hulking shapes of abandoned ships and barges, and sleeker vessels bobbing on the storm-tossed waves, white sails snapping in the chilly gale.

To his left rooftops stretched, another shadowy rain-pelted sea, sheltering what humans had survived the fall of the ancient walls that had kept the Fae hidden for millennia.

To the right, tucked down a quiet cobblestone street of pubs and upscale shops—easy to identify by the floodlights blazing on the rooftop and the vast section of forsaken city beyond it decimated by the bottomless appetites of the Shades—was that peculiar spatially challenged place known as Barrons Books & Baubles, which was so much more than it appeared to be.

Somewhere down there where gutters routed streams of water to a vast underground drainage system riddled by long forgotten catacombs, Fae walked the streets both openly and hidden, and neon signs cast fractured rainbows on the pavement, was the prior owner of that bookstore, if such a place was ever owned; his Machiavellian ruthless brother; and an invisible woman who, like the building to which she now laid claim, was far more than she appeared to be.

Farther to the left down winding rural roads, if one traveled a solid hour of stark desolation through a second hour of Faery-lush vegetation, was another of those ancient places that could never be owned and the brilliant, powerful woman determined to command it.

Barrons, Ryodan, Mac, Jada.

The possibilities were enormous, dazzling, and he had a fair idea how things would go . . . but these moments were unpredictable, unscripted.

He threw back his dark head and laughed.

As was he.

I

"It's the end of the world as we know it . . ."

I grew up believing in rules, thanks to my parents, Jack and Rainey Lane. I didn't always like them and I broke them when they didn't work for me, but they were sturdy things I could rely on to shape the way I lived and keep me—if not totally on the straight and narrow, at least aware there *was* a straight and narrow I could return to if I got to feeling lost.

Rules serve a purpose. I once told Rowena they were fences for sheep, but fences do more than merely keep sheep in a pasture where shepherds can guide them. They provide protection in the vast and frightening unknown. The night isn't half as scary when you're in the center of a fluffy-butted herd, bumping rumps with other fluffy butts, not able to see too much, feeling secure and mostly normal.

Without fences of any kind, the dark night beyond is clearly visible. You stand alone in it. Without rules, you have to decide what you want and what you're willing to do to get it. You must embrace the weapons with which you choose to arm yourself to survive.

What we achieve at our best moment doesn't say much about who we are.

It all boils down to what we become at our worst moment.

What you find yourself capable of if . . . say . . .

You get stranded in the middle of the ocean with a lone piece of driftwood that will support one person's weight and not a single ounce more—while floating beside a nice person that needs it as badly as you do.

That's the moment that defines you.

Will you relinquish your only hope of survival to save the stranger? Will it matter if the stranger is old and has lived a full life or young and not yet had the chance?

Will you try to make the driftwood support both of you, ensuring both your deaths?

Or will you battle savagely for the coveted float with full cognizance the argument could be made—even if you merely take the driftwood away without hurting the stranger and swim off—that you're committing murder?

Is it murder in your book?

Would you cold-bloodedly kill for it?

How do you feel as you swim away? Do you look back? Do tears sting your eyes? Or do you feel like a motherfucking winner?

Impending death has a funny way of popping the shiny, happy bubble of who we think we are. A lot of things do.

I live in a world with few fences. Lately, even those are damned rickety.

I resented that. There was no straight and narrow anymore. Only a circuitous route that required constant remapping to dodge IFPs, black holes, and monsters of every kind, along with the messy ethical potholes that mine the interstates of a postapocalyptic world.

I stared at the two-way glass of Ryodan's office, currently set to privacy—floor transparent, walls and ceiling opaque—and got briefly distracted by the reflection of the glossy black desk behind me, reflected in the darkened glass, reflected in the desk, reflected in the glass, receding into ever-smaller tableaus, creating a disconcerting infinity-mirror effect.

Although I stood squarely between the desk and the wall, I was invisible to the world, to myself. The *Sinsar Dubh* was still disconcertingly silent, and for whatever reason, still cloaking me.

I cocked my head, studying the spot where I should be.

Nothing looked back. It was bizarrely fitting.

That was me: tabula rasa—the blank slate. I knew somewhere I had a pen but I seemed to have forgotten how to use it. Or maybe I'd just wised up enough to know what I held these days was no Easy-Erase marker of my youth, scrubbed off by the gentle swipe of a moistened cloth, but a big, fat-tipped Sharpie: black and bold and permanent.

Dani, stop running. I just want to talk to you . . .

Dani was gone. There was only Jada now. I couldn't unwrite our fight. I couldn't unwrite that Barrons and I moved those mirrors. I couldn't unwrite the choice of mirrors Dani made that took her to the one place too dangerous to follow. I couldn't change the terrible abusive childhood that fractured her, with which she dealt brilliantly and creatively in order to survive. Of them all, that was what I really wished I could erase.

I felt immobilized by the many ways I could screw things up, acutely aware of the butterfly effect, that the tiniest, most innocuous action could trigger unthinkable catastrophe, painfully evidenced by the result of my trying to confront Dani. Five and a half years of her life were gone, leaving a dispassionate killer where the exuberant, funny, emotional, and spectacularly uncontainable Mega had once stood.

Lately I'd taken some comfort in the thought that although Jericho Barrons and his men were way the hell out there on the fringes of humanity, they'd figured out a code to live by that benefited them while doing modest damage to our world. Like me, they had their inner beasts but had spawned a set of rules that kept their savage nature in check.

Mostly.

I'd settle for mostly.

I'd been telling myself I, too, could choose a code and stick to it, using them as my role models. I snorted, morbidly amused. The role models I had a year ago and the ones I had now were certainly polar opposites.

I glanced up at the monitor that revealed the half-darkened stone chamber where, on the edge of that darkness, Barrons and Ryodan sat watching a figure in the shadows.

I held my breath waiting for the figure to once again lumber forward into the pallid light streaking the gloom. I wanted a second thorough look to confirm if what I suspected at first glance was true.

When it shuddered and stumbled to its feet, arms swinging wildly as if fighting off unseen attackers, Barrons and Ryodan uncoiled and assumed fighting posture.

The figure exploded from the shadows and lunged for Ryodan's throat with enormous taloned hands. It was rippling, changing, fighting to hold form and failing, morphing before my eyes. In the low light cheetah-gold irises turned crimson then blood-smeared gold then crimson again. Long black hair fell back from a smooth forehead that abruptly rippled and sprouted a prehensile crest. Black fangs gleamed in the low light, then were white teeth, then fangs again.

I'd seen this morphing enough times to know what it was.

The Nine could no longer be called that.

There were ten of them now.

Barrons blocked the Highlander before he reached Ryodan, and suddenly all three were blurs as they moved in a manner similar to Dani's freeze-framing ability, only faster.

Make me like you, I'd said to Barrons recently. Though in all honesty I doubt I'd have gone through with it. At least not at the moment, in the state I was in, inhabited by a thing that terrified me.

Never ask me that, he'd growled. His terse reply had spoken volumes, confirming he could if he wanted to. And I'd known in that wordless way he and I understand each other that not only did he loathe the idea, it was one of their unbreakable rules. Once, he'd found me lying in a subterranean grotto on the verge of death, and I suspect he'd considered the idea. Perhaps a second time when his son had ripped out my throat. And been grateful he'd not had to make the choice.

Ryodan however *did* make that choice. And not for a woman, fueled by the single-minded passion that drove the Unseelie king to birth his dark court, but for reasons unfathomable to me. For a Highlander he barely knew. The owner of Chester's was once again an enigma. Why would he do such a thing? Dageus had died or at the very least was dying, lanced by the Crimson Hag, battered and broken by a horrific fall into the gorge.

People die.

Ryodan never gives a bloody damn.

Barrons was furious. I didn't need sound—although I sure would have liked it—to know down in that stone chamber something primal was rattling in Barrons's chest. Nostrils flared, eyes narrowed, his teeth flashed on a snarl as he spat words I couldn't hear and they attempted to subdue the Highlander without using killing force. Which I suspected was more a damage-control technique than a kindness, because if Dageus died he would come back at the same place they do when reborn. Then they'd have to go wherever that was to retrieve him, which would not only be a pain in the ass but make a tenth person who knew where the forbidden spot was—a thing not even I knew.

I frowned. Then again maybe I was making assumptions that didn't hold water. Maybe they came back wherever *individually* they died, which would put Dageus somewhere in a German mountain range.

Whatever.

Like Barrons, I was pissed.

If Ryodan broke rules with impunity, how was I supposed to figure out where to draw my own lines? What were lines really worth if you just crossed them whenever you felt like it?

My role models sucked.

I circled the desk and perched on Ryodan's chair, staring up at the LED screens lining the perimeter on the opposite wall, wishing I could read lips.

Dageus convulsed and collapsed to the floor. He shuddered and jerked as his beast tried to claw its way from inside his skin in a vicious battle for control of the vessel they shared. It wasn't lost on me that Dani and I waged a similar war—she against Jada, I against a Book. I wondered if that was just what happened to people who served on the front line of the world's battles, who as Dani would say lived large: they got taken by some kind of a demon eventually. I'd seen my share of Veterans back home in Georgia that had that look in their eyes, the one I saw in my own lately. Was it inevitable for people who walked too long in the dark night beyond fences? Maybe that was the price for not staying with the sheep. Maybe that was why the stupid sheep stayed.

Maybe they weren't so stupid after all.

Then again, what happened to me occurred before I'd

even been born. It wasn't as if I'd had any say in the matter. Psychopaths were born every day, too. Perhaps inner demons were nothing more than the luck of the draw. I also drew Barrons, the best wild card a woman could hold in her hand. Inasmuch as that man could be held.

After what seemed an interminable spell of painful morphing, Dageus crawled back to the shadows, dragged himself up onto a stone ledge and lay there shaking violently.

I wondered what he was in for. Were the Nine like vampires, consumed by mindless bloodlust when first transformed into whatever the hell they were? I wondered if he was even capable of thought or if his body was undergoing such traumatic changes that he was a blank slate like me. I wondered how they planned to explain this to the other MacKeltar, to Dageus's wife. Then I realized they obviously didn't intend to since they sent the Highland clan home with what must have been someone else's body to bury.

What a mess. I didn't see any way this situation could turn out good. Well, except maybe for Chloe, if she was eventually reunited with her husband. I had no problem with Barrons's inner beast. In fact, the more I saw of it, the more I liked it. More than the man at this moment, because he hadn't come back to me first but at least now I understood why.

The door to the office whisked open and Lor stood framed in the entry. I glanced down to make sure the chair I was sitting in was actually visible and swallowed a sigh of relief. Apparently it was substantial enough that my sitting in it didn't make it vanish. I eased out of it carefully, so slowly it made the muscles in my legs burn, as I tried to keep it from squeaking or shifting even slightly and betraying my presence. I inched around the side and backed against a wall.

Belatedly I realized the two previously hidden panels on Ryodan's desk were now in plain view and the monitors that had been showing public parts of the club were showing things I wasn't sure Lor knew. Private was too mild a word for Barrons and Ryodan. Stay-the-fuck-out-of-my-business was their shared surname. I had no idea if they'd told Lor I was currently invisible, but if they hadn't I meant to keep it that way.

Lor glanced over his shoulder, up and down the hall, to ascertain whether he was unobserved, then stepped quickly into the office as the door whisked closed behind him.

I raised a brow, wondering what he was up to.

He walked straight for the desk but drew up short when he saw the hidden panel had slid out.

"What the fuck, boss?" he murmured.

He headed for the chair and drew up short again when he saw the panel behind the desk was also exposed. "Christ, you're getting sloppy. What the fuck sent you outta here so fast you couldn't close things up?"

His assumption worked for me.

Shaking his head, Lor dropped into Ryodan's chair and slid the hidden panel out farther than I knew it went, revealing two small remotes. I eased near, peering over his shoulder, then drew back sharply when he dropped the chair back into recline and kicked his boots up on the desk with a wolfish grin. He fiddled with the remote, seemingly unaware that the monitors he was preparing to watch were already on.

I inched forward again.

He hit Rewind for a few seconds, punched Play, then looked straight up at the monitor I'd watched him and Jo having sex on no more than ten minutes ago.

Was he kidding me? He'd come up here to watch the sex he just had with Jo? Freaking men!

I refused to watch it twice. Once had been bad

enough. I closed my eyes, waiting for him to notice what was playing on the monitors next to the one he was watching. It didn't take long.

"What the bloody fuck?" he said in a near-whisper. I heard the sound of something breaking, bits of plastic hitting the floor.

Yep. He definitely didn't know.

"Fuck," he barked, staccato sharp.

After a moment, he growled, "Fuuuu-*uuuck*."

Then, "Aw, fuck, fuck, FUCK."

Lor seemed to have gotten stuck on the word he likes the most. No surprise there.

I opened my eyes. He was standing behind the desk, ramrod straight, legs spread, arms folded, muscles bulging, tense from head to toe. The remote was on the floor in pieces.

"Bloody fucking fuck, are you fucking crazy? Have you lost your motherfucking mind?"

I'd been wondering the same thing.

"We don't do this shit. That's rule the fuck number one in our motherfucking universe. Not even you can get away with it, boss!"

While I found it oddly reassuring to know there were repercussions, I found it equally disconcerting. The last thing our world needed on top of all its other problems was war breaking out among the Nine. Rather, now . . . the Ten.

"Sonofamotherfuckinggoddamnbitch! *Jay*sustittyfuckingChrist!"

That was Lor. Man of few words.

He seized the second remote, punched a button, and the office was filled with harsh groans of pain. The Highlander was curled in a tight ball on the stone ledge. I glanced at Barrons and Ryodan, now sitting in stony silence, watching the Highlander. Apparently they were done arguing. Figured once we had volume they were no longer speaking to each other.

My gaze lingered on Barrons, savage, elegant, despotic, and enormously self-contained. I recognized that shirt, open at the throat, cuffs rolled back. I knew the pants, too, so dark gray they were nearly black, and his black and silver boots. Last time I'd seen him, he'd been gutted on a frigging cliff again—me, Barrons, and cliffs are a proven recipe for disaster—and his clothes were bloody and torn, which meant at some point he'd stopped at his lair behind the bookstore for a change of clothing. Tonight, after I'd left? Or days ago, while I'd tossed and turned on the chesterfield in a fitful sleep? Had he walked through the store? How long had he been back? His senses were acute. He knew I was invisible. If he'd bothered walking through the store while I slept, he'd have seen my indent on the sofa. Had he looked for me at all?

"You fucking turned him," Lor growled. "What the fuck is so special about him? And you killed me just for getting a little uninterrupted time in the sack and fucking Jo!" He snorted. "Aw, man, this is gonna go tribunal. You should have let him die. You know what the fuck happens!"

What was tribunal? I knew what the word meant but couldn't fathom who might serve as the Nine's court of law. Did this mean they'd turned humans in the past? If so, what had the tribunal done with them? It wasn't as if they could be killed. At least not until recently. Now there was K'Vruck, the ancient icy black Hunter whose killing blow had laid Barrons's tortured son to rest. Would they locate him and try to get him to kill Dageus? Would they expect me to help coax the enormous deadly Hunter near? Had Dageus been saved from one death only to die a more permanent soul-eclipsing one?

Barrons spoke and I shivered. I love that man's voice.

Deep, with an untraceable accent, it's sexy as hell. When he speaks, all the fine muscles in my body shift into a lower, tighter, more aggressive gear. I want him all the time. Even when I'm mad at him. Perversely, maybe even more so then.

"You violated our code. You created an untenable liability," Barrons growled.

Ryodan gave him a look but said nothing.

"His loyalties will always be first and foremost to his clan. Not us."

"Debatable."

"Our secrets. Now his. He'll talk."

"Debatable."

"He's a Keltar. They're *nice*. They champion the underdog. Fight for the common good. As if there is such a bloody thing."

Ryodan smiled faintly. "Nice is no longer one of his shortcomings."

"You know what the tribunal will do."

"There will be no tribunal. We'll keep him hidden."

"You can't hide him forever. He won't agree to stay hidden forever. He has a wife, a child."

"He'll get past it."

"He's a Highlander. Clan is everything. He won't ever get past it."

"He'll get past it."

Barrons mocked, "Repetition of erroneous facts—"

"Fuck you."

"And because he won't get past it, you know what they'll do to him. What we've done to others."

How many others? I wondered. What had they done?

"Yet you have Mac," Ryodan said.

"I didn't turn Mac."

"Only because you didn't have to. Someone else extended her life. Giving you the easy way out. Maybe our code is wrong."

"There are reasons for our code."

"That's a fucking joke, coming from you. You said yourself, 'Things are different now. We evolve. So does our code.' Either there are laws or there aren't. And if there are laws, like everything in the universe, they exist to be tested."

"That's what you're after? Establishing new case precedence? Never going to happen. Not on this point. You want to turn Dani. Assuming she's ever Dani again."

"Nobody's turning my fucking honey," Lor muttered darkly.

"You took the Highlander, as your test case," Barrons said.

Ryodan said nothing.

"Kas doesn't speak. X is half mad on a good day, bugfuck crazy on a bad one. You're tired of it. You want your family back. You want a full house, like the old days."

Ryodan growled, "You're so fucking shortsighted, you can't see past the end of your own dick."

"Hardly short."

"You don't see what's coming."

Barrons inclined his head, waiting.

"Have you considered what will happen if we don't find a way to stop the holes the Hoar Frost King made from growing."

"Chester's gets swallowed. Parts of the world disappear."

"Or all."

"We'll stop it."

"If we can't."

"We move on."

"The kid," Ryodan said with such contempt that I knew he was talking about Dancer, not Dani, "says they're virtually identical to black holes. At worst, consuming all objects within to oblivion. At best, from which there is no escape. When we die," he carefully enunciated each word, "we come back on this world. If this world doesn't exist, or is inside a black hole . . ." He didn't bother finishing. He didn't need to.

Lor stared at the monitor. "Shit, boss."

"I'm the one who's always planning," Ryodan said. "Doing whatever's necessary to protect us, ensure our continued existence while you fucks live like tomorrow will always come."

"Ah," Barrons mocked, "the king wearies of the crown."

"Never the crown. Only the subjects."

"What does this have to do with the Highlander?" Barrons said impatiently.

Exactly what I was wondering.

"He's a sixteenth-century druid that was possessed by the first thirteen druids trained by the Fae—the Draghar."

"I heard he was cured of that little problem," Barrons said.

"I heard otherwise from a certain walking lie detector who told Mac his uncle never managed to exorcise them completely."

I scowled, pressing my fingers to my forehead, rubbing it as if to agitate my memory and recall exactly where I'd been when Christian told me that—and if there had been any damned roaches around. That was the problem with roaches: they were small and could wedge themselves into virtually any crack to eavesdrop unseen.

"You know what Christian told Mac when you weren't present?" Barrons said softly.

Ryodan said nothing.

"If I ever see roaches in my bookstore . . ." Barrons didn't bother finishing the threat.

"Roaches?" Lor muttered. "What the fuck's he talking about?"

"The Seelie queen is missing," Ryodan said. "The Unseelie don't give a shit if this world is destroyed. They aren't bound to this planet like we are. Fae magic is destroying the world. It may be the only thing that saves it. The Highlander wasn't supposed to die on that mountain. It wasn't part of my plan. I don't know about you, but I don't want my fucking vagina to be inside a black hole."

That was certainly a visual.

"Me neither," Lor muttered. "I like my vaginas pink and smaller. *Much* smaller," he added. "Like way the fuck tight."

I rolled my eyes.

Ryodan said, "This could be the end of us."

The end of the Nine? I'd always kept in the back of my mind that if things got really bad on this world, I'd just grab everyone I love, along with everyone else we could round up, and travel through the Silvers to another planet. Colonize, start fresh. Unfortunately, erroneously, I'd only been thinking if things on this world got "really bad," assuming there would still be a dangerous planet the Nine would certainly be able to battle their way off of again. I'd never considered that there might be a time this planet didn't even exist. I knew the black holes were a serious problem but I hadn't fully absorbed what the small tears in the fabric of our universe really signified and what they might do long term. I'd overlooked the ramifications of the Nine being reborn on Earth.

And if Earth was no longer . . .

"We've got to fix those fucking holes," Lor growled.

I nodded vehement agreement.

"Your plan?" Barrons said.

"We conceal his existence," Ryodan said. "We push

him through the change. Get the best minds on the problem and fix it. Once it's resolved, the tribunal can do whatever the bloody hell they want. Like give me a fucking medal and the free rein I deserve."

"Jada," Barrons said.

"And the kid because he gets physics, which, while no longer accurate, may help us understand what we're dealing with. Mac. She's got the bloody Book. Between her and the Highlander, we may just have more Fae lore than the Fae."

But I can't read it, I wanted to protest. What the hell good was it?

I shivered again, this time with a much deeper chill. I knew something with sudden, absolute certainty.

They were going to want me to.

"Fuck." Lor was back to his one-word assessment of life, the universe, and everything.

Fuck, I agreed silently.

2

"Seasons don't fear the Reaper . . ."

Inverness, Scotland, high above Loch Ness.

Christian had once believed he'd never set foot there again except in half-mad dreams.

Tonight was madness of another kind.

Tonight, beneath a slate and crimson sky, he would bury the man who'd died to save him.

The entire Keltar clan was gathered in the sprawling cemetery behind the ruined tower, near the tomb of the Green Lady, to return the remains of Dageus MacKeltar to the earth in a sacred druid ritual so his soul would be released to live again. Reincarnation was the foundation of their faith.

The air was heavy and humid from a nearby storm. A few miles to the west, lightning cracked, briefly illuminating the rocky cliffs and grassy vales of his motherland. The Highlands were even more beautiful than he'd painstakingly re-created them in his mind, staked to the side of a cliff, dying over and over. While he'd hung there, the long killing season of ice had passed. Heather bloomed and leaves rustled on trees. Moss crushed softly beneath his boots as he shifted his weight to ease the pain in his groin. Parts of him were not yet healed. He'd been flayed too many times to regenerate properly; the bitch had scarcely let him grow new guts before taking them again.

"The body is prepared, my lord."

Christopher and Drustan nodded while nearby, huddled in Gwen's embrace, Chloe wept. Christian was amused to realize he, too, had nodded. Say "my lord" and every Keltar male in the room nodded, along with a few of the females. Theirs was a clan of all lairds, no serfs.

It seemed a century ago he'd walked these bens and valleys, exhilarated to be alive, riveted by his studies at university and his more private agenda in Dublin: keeping tabs on the unpredictable, dangerous owner of Barrons Books & Baubles while hunting an ancient Book of black magic. But that was before the Compact the Keltar had upheld since the dawn of time had been shattered, the walls between man and Fae had fallen, and he himself had become one of the Unseelie.

"Place the body on the pyre," Drustan said.

Chloe's weeping turned to quiet sobs at his words, then a wild guttural keening that flayed Christian's gut as exquisitely as had the Crimson Hag's lance. Dageus and Chloe had fought impossible odds to be together, only to end with Dageus's pointless death on a cliff. Christian alone bore the blame. He didn't know how Chloe could stand to look at him.

Come to think of it, she hadn't. She'd not once focused on him since they brought him home. Her swollen, half-dead gaze had slid repeatedly past him. He wasn't sure if that was because she hated him for causing her husband's death or because he no longer looked remotely like the young human man she'd known, but the worst of the dark Fae. He knew he was disconcerting to look at. Although his mutation seemed to have become static, leaving him with long black hair, strangely muted tattoos, and, for fuck's sake, wings—bloody damned wings, how the hell was a man supposed to live with those?—there was something about his eyes that even he could see. As if a chilling, starry infinity had settled there. No one held his gaze, no one looked at him for long, not even his own mother and father. His sister, Colleen, was the only one who'd spoken more than a few words to him since his return.

What remained of Dageus's body was positioned on the wood slab.

They would chant and spread the necessary elements, then burn the corpse, freeing his soul to be reborn. When the ceremony was done, his ashes would drop into the grave below, mingle with the soil and find new life.

He moved forward to join the others, shifting his shoulders so the tips of his wings didn't drag the ground. He was getting bloody tired of having to clean them. Although he threw a constant glamour to conceal them from the sight of others, unless making a show of power, he still had to look at them himself, and he preferred not to walk around with pine needles and bits of gorse stuck to his fucking feathers.

Feathers. Bloody hell, he hadn't seen that one coming when he'd considered his future. Like a goddamn chicken.

The clan surrounded the pyre somberly. He hadn't expected to attend tonight, much less be involved, but Drustan had insisted. *You're Keltar, lad, first and foremost. You belong here.* He seemed to have forgotten Christian was a walking lie detector who knew the truth was that Drustan didn't want to be anywhere near him. But then, he didn't want to be near anyone, not even his wife, Gwen. He wanted to disappear into the mountains and grieve for his brother alone.

Once, Christian would have argued. Now he said little, only when necessary. It was easier that way.

As the chanting began and the sacred oil, water, metal, and wood were distributed east, west, north, and south, the wind whipped up violently, howling through rocky canyons and crevices. Thunder rolled and the sky rushed with ominous clouds. Grass rippled as if trod by an unseen army.

Look, listen, feel, the storm-lashed grass seemed to be whispering to him.

In the distance, the rain across the valley turned to a deluge and began moving rapidly toward them in an enormous gray sheet. Lightning exploded directly above the pyre and everyone jerked as it cracked and spread across the night sky in a web of crimson. The pungent odor of brimstone laced the air.

Something was off.

Something wasn't right.

The powerful words of the high druid burial ceremony seemed to be inflaming the elements. They should have been softening the environment, preparing the earth to welcome a high druid's body, not chafing it.

Could it be the Highlands rejected an Unseelie prince's presence at a druid ceremony? Didn't his Keltar blood still define him as one of Scotia's own?

As Christian continued chanting, restraining his voice so he wouldn't drown out the others, the sky grew more violent, the night darker. He studied his gathered clan. Man, woman, and child, they all had the right to be here. The elements had been chosen with precision and care. They were what had been used for generations untold. The pyre was properly constructed, the runes etched, the wood old, dried rowan and oak. The timing was correct.

There was only one other variable to consider.

He narrowed his eyes, studying Dageus's remains. He

was still pondering them a few minutes later when at last the chanting was done.

"You must set him free, Chloe-lass," Drustan said, "before the storm prevents it."

He always believed he was the rotten egg of the two of us, Christian had overheard Drustan saying to Chloe earlier that evening. *When the truth of it is he gave his life to save others not once but twice. He was the best of men, lass. The best of all of us.*

Chloe jerked forward, carrying a torch of mistletoe-draped rowan that flickered wildly in the wind.

"Wait," Christian growled.

"What is it, lad?" Drustan said.

Chloe stopped, torch trembling in her hands, not bothering to glance at either of them. All life seemed to have been stripped out of her, leaving a shell of a body that had no desire to continue breathing. She looked as if she might join her husband in the flames. Christ, didn't anyone else see that? Why were they letting her anywhere near fire? He could taste Death on the air, feel it beckoning Chloe with a lover's kiss, wearing the mask of her dead husband.

He pushed between his aunt and the pyre to touch the wood upon which the bits of his uncle were spread. Wood that once had lived but now was dead, and in death spoke to him as nothing alive ever would again. This was his new native tongue, the utterances of the dead and dying. Closing his eyes, he went inward to that alien, unwanted landscape inside him. He knew what he was. He'd known it for a long time. He had a special bond to the events occurring tonight.

The Unseelie princes were four, and each had their specialty: War, Pestilence, Famine, Death. He was Death. And Fae. Which meant more attuned, more deeply connected to the elements than a druid could ever be. His moods affected the environment if he wasn't careful to keep tight rein on them. But he wasn't the cause of the night's distress. Something else was.

There was only one other thing present whose provenance might be questioned.

None but a Keltar directly descended from the first could be given a high druid burial in hallowed ground. The cemetery was heavily protected, from the wood of sacred, carefully mutated trees that grew there to ancient artifacts, blood, and wards buried in the soil. The ground would expel an intruder. Perhaps Nature herself would resist the interment.

Was it possible what remained of the Draghar within Dageus marked him as something foreign?

Christian had heard the truth in his uncle's lie at a young age. At first, Dageus told Chloe and the rest of the clan that the Seelie queen had removed the souls of the Draghar and erased their memories from his mind. Sometime later, to aid Adam Black, Dageus had come clean with the truth . . . at least part of it, admitting he still retained their memories and could use their spells, though he maintained he was no longer inhabited by the living consciousness of thirteen ancient sorcerers.

Christian had never been able to get a solid feel for just how much of those power-hungry druids still lived within him. His uncle was a proud, intensely private man. Sometimes he'd believed Dageus. Other times—watching him while he thought himself unobserved—he'd been certain Dageus had never stopped being haunted by them. The few times he'd tried to question him, Dageus walked away without a word, giving him no opportunity to read him. Typical of his clan. Those aware of Christian's unique "gift" were closed-mouthed around him, even his own parents. It had made for a solitary childhood, a boyhood of secrets no one wanted to hear, a lad unable to reconcile the bizarreness of others' actions with the truths staring him in the face.

He eyed Dageus's remains, casting a net for possibilities, considering all, discarding nothing.

It was possible, he mused, that they had the wrong body. He couldn't fathom why Ryodan might give them the savaged pieces of someone else's corpse. Still, it was Ryodan, which meant anything was possible.

Hands resting lightly on the pile of rain-spattered timber, he turned inward, wondering if he might use his lie-detecting ability to discern the truth of the remains, or if his new talents might aid him.

An immense wind gusted within him, around him, ruffling his wings, dark and serene and enormous. Death. Ah yes, death, he'd tasted it countless times recently, come to know it intimately. It wasn't horrific. Death was a lover's kiss. It was merely the process of getting there that could be so extreme.

He harnessed the dark wind and blew a question into the bits of flesh and bone.

Dageus?

There was no reply.

He gathered his power—Unseelie, not druid—and shoved it into the mutilated body, let it soak into the remains and arrange itself there . . .

"Bloody hell," he whispered. He had his answer.

Thirty-eight years of human life lay on the slab, terminated abruptly. *Pain, sorrow, grief!* But not by the lance of the Crimson Hag. *Make it stop!* A poison in the blood, an overdose of something human, chemical, sweet and cloying. He stretched his newfound senses and sucked in a harsh breath when he felt the dying, the moment of it, rushing like a glorious wave over (him!) the man. It had been sought, embraced. Relief, ah, blessed relief. *Thank you*, was the man's final thought, *yes, yes, make it all stop, let me sleep, but let me sleep!* He actually heard the words in a soft Irish burr, as if frozen in time, rustling dryly from the remains.

He opened his eyes and looked at Drustan, who fixed his deep silver gaze on a spot slightly above and between his brows.

"It's not Dageus," Christian said, "but an Irishman with two children who were killed the night the walls fell. His wife perished from starvation not long after as they hid from Unseelie in the streets. He tried to go on without them until the day he no longer cared to. He met his death by choice."

No one questioned how he knew it. No one questioned anything about him anymore.

Chloe staggered and melted bonelessly to the ground, her torch tumbling forgotten to the wet grass. "N-N-Not D-Dageus?" she whispered. "What do you mean? Is he alive, then?" Her voice rose. "Tell me, is he still alive?" she shrieked, eyes flashing.

Christian closed his eyes again, feeling, stretching, reaching. But life was no longer his specialty. "I don't know."

"But can you feel his *death*?" Colleen said sharply, and he opened his eyes, meeting her gaze. To his surprise, she didn't look away.

Ah, so she knew. Or suspected. She'd stayed with the *sidhe*-seers, searching their old lore. She'd come across the old tales. How had she decided which one he was?

Again, he slipped deep, staring sightlessly. It was peaceful. Quiet. No judgment. No lies. Death was beautifully without deceit. He appreciated the purity of it.

In the distance, Colleen tried unsuccessfully to turn a gasp into a cough. He was fairly certain she wasn't looking at his eyes now.

That eerie Fae wind gusted and blew open the confines of his skull, leveled barriers of space and time. He felt a soaring sensation, as if he'd taken flight through a door to some other way of breathing and being: quiet and black, rich and velvety and vast. *Dageus*, he murmured silently, *Dageus, Dageus*. People had a certain individual feel, an essence, an imprint. Their life made a ripple in a loch of the universe.

There was no Dageus ripple.

"I'm sorry, Aunt Chloe," he said quietly. Sorry he couldn't say yes. Sorry he'd dragged them into his problems. Sorry he'd gone bugfuck crazy for a time, for so damned many things. But sorry was worthless. It changed nothing. Merely coerced the victim to offer forgiveness for what you shouldn't have done to begin with. "He's dead."

On the ground near the pyre, Chloe wrapped her arms around her knees and began to keen, rocking back and forth.

"You're absolutely certain it's no' him, lad?" Drustan said.

"Unequivocally." The owner of Chester's had packed them off with another man's remains, intending for them to bury it and never know that somewhere out there a Keltar body rotted and a high druid soul was lost, denied proper burial, never to be reborn.

Knowing Ryodan, he'd simply considered it a waste of his precious time to make the hard hike down into the gorge and search the darkness for remains when there were so many more easily available in any city he'd driven through on the way back to Dublin. Coming by Keltar plaid wouldn't have been difficult. The entire clan had been living for a time at the fuck's nightclub.

"You can't bury that man here," Christian said. "He must be returned to Ireland. He wants to go home." He had no idea how he knew that the corpse didn't want to stay here. It wanted to be in a place not far from Dublin, a short distance to the south where a small cottage overlooked a pond smattered with lily pads, tall reeds grew, and in the summer the rich baritone of frogs filled the night. He could see it clearly in his mind. He resented seeing it. He wanted nothing to do with the last wishes of the dead. He was not their keeper. Nor their bloody damned wish granter.

Drustan cursed. "If this isn't him, then where the blethering hell is my brother's body?"

"Where, indeed," Christian said.

3

"These iron bars can't hold my soul in,
all I need is you . . ."

The cavernous chamber was well-sealed against human and Fae with magic not even he understood. Fortuitously, he didn't need to.

He was neither human nor Fae but one of the old ones from the dawn of time. Even now, his true name forgotten, the world still regarded him as powerful, indestructible.

Nothing will survive nuclear holocausts save the cockroaches.

They were right. He'd survived it before. The acute burst had been an irritant, little more. The lingering radiation had mutated him into more than he'd ever been.

He partitioned himself, separated and deposited a tiny segment of his being on the floor near the door. He despised being the insect beneath man's feet. He coveted the life of the bastards that reviled and crushed him at every opportunity. He'd believed for a long time the one he served would eventually grant him what he sought. Make him what he'd observed with crippling envy, a tall, unkillable, unsegmented beast. The glory of it—to walk as man, indestructible as a cockroach!

He'd lived with the threat of the one weapon that could destroy him for too long. If he could not be one of them, at the very least he wanted that weapon back, buried, lost, forgotten.

But stealing from the one who'd stolen it from its ancient hiding place had proved impossible. He'd been trying for a small eternity. The beast that would be king made no mistakes.

Now there was one he believed just might be more powerful than the one he served.

As he slithered flat as paper and pushed his shiny brown body into a crack too small for humans to see, he knew something had changed before he even passed beneath the door and crossed the threshold.

He despised the way his mind instantly went into information-gathering mode, trained—he, once a god himself—*trained* to spy on fools and heathens.

They were the bugs. Not he.

This was *his* mission. No one else's. Yet he'd been conditioned to collect bits of knowledge for so long, he now did so by instinct. Engulfed in sudden rage, he forgot about his body for a moment and inadvertently wedged his hindquarters beneath a too-narrow rough-hewn edge. Seething, he forced himself forward, sacrificing his legs at the femur, and half scuttled, half dragged himself into the room silently, unseen.

The one they called "Papa Roach" in their papers sat, rubbing his antennae together, thinking. Preparing for his new venture.

He'd been duplicitous in the past, playing both sides against the middle, but this was his greatest deceit—informing Ryodan the chamber beneath the abbey was impenetrable.

He wanted it—and its occupant—off Ryodan's radar.

This potential ally, this opportunity was his alone.

He hissed softly, rustled forward on his front legs,

dragging his cerci uncomfortably, until he stopped at the edge of the cage.

It was empty, two bars missing.

"Behind you," a deep voice echoed from the shadows.

He startled and turned awkwardly, hissing, pivoting on his thorax. Few saw him. Fewer still ever saw him as more than a nuisance.

"You have been here before." The dark prince was sprawled on the floor, leaning back against a wall, wings spread wide. "And I have seen you in Chester's, in Ryodan's company more than once. Don't look so surprised, small one," he said with a soft laugh. "There's a decided dearth of events in here. A bit of stone dust crumbles. Occasionally a spider passes through. Of course I notice. You are not Fae. Yet you are sentient. Make that sound again if I am correct."

The cockroach hissed.

"Do you serve Ryodan?"

He hissed again, this time with eons of hatred and anger, his entire small body trembling with the passion of it. Antennae vibrating, he spat a chirp of fury so hard he lost his balance and floundered wildly on his belly.

The winged prince laughed. "Yes, yes, I share the sentiment."

The cockroach pushed up on his front legs and shook himself, then tapped the floor with one of his remaining appendages, rhythmically, in summons.

Roaches poured beneath the door, rushing to join him, piling on top of one another until at last they formed the stumpy-legged shape of a human.

The Unseelie prince watched in silence, waiting until he'd carefully positioned the many small bodies to form ears and a mouth.

"He dispatches you to check on me," Cruce murmured.

"He believes I can no longer enter this chamber," the glistening pile of cockroaches grated.

"Ah." The prince pondered his words. "You seek an alliance."

"I offer it. For a price."

"I'm listening."

"The one who controls me has a blade. I want it."

"Free me and it is yours," Cruce said swiftly.

"Not even I can open the doors that hold you."

"There was a time I believed nothing could weaken the bars of my prison save the bastard king. Then one came, removed my cuff and disturbed the spell. All is temporary." Cruce was silent a moment, then, "Continue taking information to Ryodan. But bring it to me as well. All of it. Omit nothing. I want to know every detail that transpires beyond those doors. When the chamber was sealed, I lost my ability to project. I can no longer see or affect matter above. I escaped my cage yet am blinder than I was in it. I must know what is happening in the world if I am to escape. You will be my eyes and ears. My mouthpiece when I wish. See me freed and in turn I will free you."

"If I agree to help you, I do so of my own accord. You neither own nor order me. But respect me," the heap of cockroaches ground out. "I am as ancient and venerable as you."

"Doubtful." Cruce inclined his head. "But agreed."

"I want the blade the moment you are free. It will be your first action."

Cruce cocked his head and studied him. "To use or destroy?"

"It is not possible to destroy it."

The dark winged prince smiled. "Ah, my friend, anything is possible."

4

"But I never got between you and the ghost in your mind . . ."

I buzzed the foggy, rainy streets of Temple Bar like a drunken bumblebee, darting between passersby who couldn't see me, trying not to bash them with my undetectable yet substantial umbrella. Navigating a crowded street while invisible takes a great deal of energy and focus. You can't stare someone down and make them move out of your way, a trick I learned from watching Barrons and had nearly perfected prior to my vanishing act.

Between ducks and dodges, I was startled to realize how much the post-ice/apocalypse city resembled the Dublin I'd fallen in love with shortly after I arrived.

Same neon-lit rain-slicked streets, same fair to middling fifty-five degrees, people out for a beer with friends, listening to music in local pubs, flowers spilling from planters and strings of lights draping brightly painted facades. The big difference was the lesser Fae castes mixed into the crowds—many walking without glamour despite the recent killing rampage Jada had been on—being treated like demigods. The commingling of races had spilled over from Chester's into the streets. Ryodan permitted only the higher castes and their henchmen into his club. The lowers stalked their dark desires in Temple Bar.

I recognized few faces in the pub windows and on the sidewalks, mostly Unseelie I'd glimpsed at some point. I hadn't made friends in this city; I'd enticed allies and incited enemies. Dublin was once again a hot spot for tourists, immigrating from all over, drawn by word there was food, magic, and a wealth of Fae royalty to be found here. Possessing power to grant wishes to a starving populace and slake a burgeoning addiction to Unseelie flesh, Fae were the latest smart phone, and everyone wanted one.

It was disconcerting to walk invisible through my favorite district. I felt like a ghost of who I'd once been: vibrant, angry, determined—naïve, God, so naïve!—storming into Dublin to hunt Alina's murderer, only to learn I was a powerful *sidhe*-seer and null, exiled shortly after birth and possessed by enormous evil. I'd been weak, grown strong, grown weak again. Like the city I loved, I kept changing and it wasn't always pretty.

There was a time I'd have given anything to be invisible. Like the night I sat in a pub with Christian MacKeltar, on the verge of discovering how he'd known my sister, back in those innocent days he was still a sexy young druid with a killer smile. Barrons had interrupted us, phoning to tell me the skies were filled with Hunters and I needed to get my ass back to the bookstore fast. As I'd left Christian with a promise to meet again soon, I felt like (and was!) a giant walking neon sign of an X. I'd gotten cornered in a dead-end alley by a giant Hunter and the superhumanly strong, decaying citron-eyed vampire Mallucé.

If I'd been invisible then, I would never have been abducted, tortured, beaten so near death I had to eat Unseelie to claw my way back.

Halloween. That was another night being invisible

would have been a blessing. After watching the ancient Wild Hunt stain Dublin's sky from horizon to horizon with nightmarish Unseelie, I might have descended the belfry, stolen from the church and avoided the rape of four Unseelie princes and the subsequent Pri-ya-induced madness that possessed me. Would never have been forced to drink a Fae elixir that had altered my mortal life span in ways yet unknown.

On both those horrifying, transformative nights it was Jericho Barrons who saved me, first by a brand he'd tattooed on the back of my skull that allowed him to locate me hidden in a subterranean grotto deep beneath the desolate Burren, then by dragging me back to reality with constant reminders of my life before All Hallow's Eve and providing the incessant sex to which the princes had left me mindlessly addicted.

If either of those events hadn't transpired, I wouldn't be who and what I was now.

If I liked who and what I was now, it would make both those hellish times worth it.

Too bad I didn't.

A faint, dry chittering above me penetrated my brooding. I glanced up and shivered. I'd never seen my ghoulish stalkers fly en masse and it wasn't a pretty sight. It was straight out of a horror flick, black-cloaked cadaverous wraiths streaking beneath rain clouds, cobwebs trailing from their gaunt forms, the silvery metallic bits of their deeply hooded faces glinting as they peered down into the streets. There were hundreds of them, fanning out over Dublin, flying slowly, obviously hunting for something.

Or someone.

I had no doubt who they were looking for.

I ducked into the shallow alcoved doorway of a closed pub, barely breathing, praying they couldn't suddenly somehow sense me. I didn't move until the last of them had vanished into the stormy sky.

Inhaling deeply, I stepped out of the niche and pushed into a dense throng of people gathered at a street vendor's stand, holding my umbrella as high as I could. I took two elbows in the ribs, got both my feet stepped on and an umbrella poked into my tush. I broke free of the crowd with a growl that turned quickly to a choked inhale.

Alina.

I sprouted roots and stood, staring. She was ten feet away, wearing jeans, a clingy yellow shirt, a Burberry raincoat, and high-heeled boots. Her hair was longer, her body leaner. Alone, she spun in a circle, as if looking for someone or something. I held my breath and didn't move then realized how stupid that was. Whatever this illusion was, it couldn't see me anyway. And if it could see me, presto—proof it wasn't real. Not that I needed any.

I knew better than to think it was actually my sister. I'd identified her body. I'd made her funeral arrangements when my parents had been immobilized by grief. I'd slid the coffin lid shut myself before her closed-casket funeral. It was indisputably my sister I'd left six feet under in Ashford, Georgia.

"Not funny," I muttered to the *Sinsar Dubh.* Assuming Cruce, with his proclivity to weave this particular illusion for me, was still secured beneath the abbey, it could only be the Book torturing me now.

A pedestrian crashed into my motionless back and I stumbled from the sidewalk out into the street. I flailed for balance and barely refrained from plunging headfirst into the gutter. Standing still in a crowd while invisible was idiotic. I composed myself, or tried to, given the image of my sister was now only half a dozen feet from me. There was no reply from my inner demon but that didn't surprise me. The Book hadn't uttered a word since the night it played genie, granting my muttered wish.

I glanced over my shoulder to watch for impending human missiles. "Make it go away," I demanded.

There was only silence within.

The thing that looked like Alina stopped turning and stood, cocking a tan umbrella with bold black stripes at a better angle to survey the street. Confusion and worry puckered her brows, creating a deep furrow between them. She bit her lower lip and frowned, the way my sister did when she was thinking hard. Then she winced and brushed her stomach with her hand as if something hurt or she was feeling nauseous.

I caught myself wondering who she was looking for, why she was worried, then realized I was getting sucked in and focused instead on the details of the illusion, seeking mistakes, while jogging from side to side and stealing quick glances around me.

There was the small mole to the left of her upper lip that she'd never considered having removed. (I zigged to the left to make way for a pair of Rhino-boys marching down the sidewalk.) The long sooty lashes that, unlike mine, hadn't needed mascara, the dent of a scar on the bridge of her nose from crashing into a trash can when we'd leapt off swings as little girls, which crinkled when she laughed and drove her crazy. (I zagged to the right to avoid a stumbling drunk who was singing off-key, loudly and badly, that someone had *wreh-ehcked* him.) The Book had her down pat, re-created no doubt from memories it sifted through and studied while I slept or was otherwise occupied. I'd often pictured her this way, out for a night on the town. In fact, pretty much every time I walked through the Temple Bar district thoughts of her took foggy shape in the back of my mind. But I always pictured her with friends, not alone. Happy, not worried. And she'd never worn a sparkling diamond ring on her left ring finger, glinting as she adjusted her umbrella. She'd never been engaged. Never would be.

As usual the Book couldn't get all the details right. Squaring my shoulders, I stepped forward, drew to a stop with a mere foot of space between us and risked standing still, wagering people would give the image at least that much personal space—assuming they could see it and it wasn't simply my own private haunt, or hey, who knew? Maybe the vision had its own secret force field. I was instantly enveloped in her favorite perfume and a hint of the lavender-scented Snuggle she used in the dryer to make her jeans soft.

We stood like that for several long moments, face-to-face, the illusion of my sister looking through me as it searched the streets for who knew what, me staring at every inch of its face, okay, reveling in staring at every inch of its face because even though it was an illusion, it was a perfect replica and—God, how I missed her!

Still.

Thirteen months and the deep wound of grief remained open, salted, and burning inside me. Some people—who haven't lost someone they love unconditionally and more than themselves—think a year is plenty of time to get over the trauma of their death and you should have fully moved on.

Fuck you, it's not.

A year barely makes a dent. It didn't help that I'd passed large chunks of that year during a few hours in Faery or a sex-crazed stupor, lacking the mental faculties to deal with my grief. It takes time to condition your brain to shut down rather than remember them. You can hold on to them in memories that slice like cherished razors. You can fall in love again; most people do—but you can never replace a sister. You can never rectify the many regrets. Apologize for your failings, for not figuring out something was wrong before it was too late.

I wanted to take her in my arms, hug this illusion. I wanted to hear her laugh, say my name, tell me she was okay wherever it was the dead go. That she knew joy. She wasn't trapped in some purgatory. Or worse.

One look at this facsimile of Alina reawakened every bit of pain and rage and hunger for revenge in my heart. Unfortunately, my thirst for revenge could be directed at no one but an old woman I'd already killed, and was sadly tangled around a girl I loved.

Was that why the Book was doing it? Because it had weakened me with invisibility and feelings of irrelevance and now it sought to twist the knife, showing me what I might have back if I would only cooperate? Too bad I'd be evil and not at all myself once I had her back.

"Screw you," I growled at the Book.

I lunged forward to push through the illusion and slammed into a body so hard I rebounded off it, crashed into a planter that caught me squarely behind my knees and sent me flailing backward over it. I rolled and twisted in midair and managed to splash to my hands and knees in a puddle, umbrella sailing from my grasp.

I jerked a glance over my shoulder. I'd forgotten how good the Book's illusions were. It really felt like I'd collided with a body. A warm, breathing, huggable body. Once, I'd played volleyball and drank Coronas on a beach with an illusion of my sister who'd seemed just as real. I wasn't falling for that again.

It was standing up from the sidewalk, brushing its jeans off, eyes narrowed, rubbing its temple as if struck by a sudden headache, looking startled and confused, searching the space around it as if trying to decipher what weird thing had just happened. An invisible Fae had collided with it, perhaps?

Right. Now I was reading illusionary thoughts into the illusionary mind of my illusionary sister.

Only one thing to do: get out of here before I got sucked in further while yet another of my weaknesses was exploited by the Book's sadistic sleight of hand.

Clenching my teeth, I dragged myself from the puddle and pushed to my feet. My umbrella had vanished beneath the feet of passersby. With a snarl, I yanked my gaze away from the thing that I knew full well was not my sister and marched without a backward glance out of Temple Bar, into the fog and rain.

At the end of the block, Barrons Books & Baubles loomed from the Fae-kissed fog four—no, five—stories tonight, a brilliantly lit bastion of gleaming cherry, limestone, antique glass, and Old World elegance. Floodlights sliced beacons into the darkness from the entire perimeter of the roof, and gas lamps glowed at twenty-foot intervals down both sides of the cobbled street, although beyond it the enormous Dark Zone remained shadowy, abandoned, and unlit.

In the limestone and cherry alcove, an ornate lamp swayed in the wind to the tempo of the shingle that swung from a polished brass pole proclaiming the name I'd restored in lieu of changing it to my own. Barrons Books & Baubles was what it was in my heart and all I would ever call it.

The moment I turned the corner and saw the bookstore, towering, strong and timeless as the man, I nearly burst into tears. Happy to see it. Afraid one day I might turn the corner and not see it. Hating that I loved something so much because things you loved could be taken away.

I would never forget staring down from the belfry on Halloween to find all the floodlights had been shot out.

Then the power grid went down, the city blinked out like a dying man closing his eyes, and I'd watched my cherished home become part of the Dark Zone, felt as if part of my soul was being amputated. Each time the bookstore had been demolished by Barrons—first when I vanished with V'lane for a month, then after I killed Barrons and he thought I was fucking Darroc—I'd not been able to rest until I restored order. I couldn't bear seeing my home wrecked.

God, I was moody tonight. Invisible, lonely, being hunted by my ghouls (at least there were none perched on BB&B!), I couldn't go kill anything, the *Sinsar Dubh* wasn't needling me, and purposeless downtime has always been my Achilles' heel.

Ice that unpalatable cake with a vision of my dead sister and I wanted nothing more than to smash it into a ceiling and storm off. Unfortunately I'd be right there wherever I stormed off to. With the same vile cake dripping on my head. The thing I wanted to escape was myself.

Seeing the Alina-illusion had rattled me to my core. I had a secret I'd told no one, that I kept so deeply buried I refused to even acknowledge it unless it slammed me in the face unexpectedly like tonight. The vision had cut far too close to it, uncovered it in all its unholy horror, dicked with my head in a way that could completely unravel me. Be seen as proof of my problem. Or not. Or maybe. The jury was still out. Which was precisely the crux of the problem: my jury—the part of me that judged and decided rulings—had been on long hiatus. Far longer than I'd been invisible. Since the night we'd taken the *Sinsar Dubh* to the abbey to inter it. I hadn't been myself since that night. Wasn't sure I ever would be again.

I caught myself sighing, terminated it halfway through and forced myself to smile instead. Attitude was everything. There was always a bright side or two somewhere: I could light the gas fires, dry off, prop a book on a pillow, sprawl out on the chesterfield with my favorite throw and lose myself in a story, knowing Barrons was back, would return at some point, and my mind would soon be fully occupied figuring out how to keep them from trying to make me open the *Sinsar Dubh* while coming up with some other way to get rid of the black holes.

A breath of contentment feathered the knot of anxiety in my stomach, easing it a bit. Home. Books. Barrons soon. It was enough to work with. All I could do was take one moment at a time. Do my best in that moment. Pretend I was fully invested when I wasn't sure I'd ever be able to invest in anything again.

I was just unlocking the store, about to step inside, when I glimpsed a sodden *Dublin Daily* plastered up against the door. Propping the door open with a boot, I ducked to fetch the rag.

That was when the first bullet hit me.

5

"And walked upon the edge of no escape,
and laughed 'I've lost control'. . . "

To be fair, I didn't actually know a bullet had hit me. All I knew was my arm stung like hell and I thought I'd heard a gunshot.

It's funny how your mind doesn't quite put those two things together as fast as you'd think it would. There's a kind of numbing of disbelief that accompanies unexpected assault, resulting in a moment of immobility. I vacillated in it long enough to get shot a second time, but at least I was rising from my crouch, slipping sideways through the door, so it grazed my shoulder blade rather than puncturing one of my lungs or my heart.

A third bullet slammed into the front of my thigh before I got the door closed. I heard the rat-a-tat-tat of automatic fire hitting the inside of the alcove before a spray of ammo blasted the glass in the door and both sidelights. Above my head the lovely leaded glass transom exploded. The antique panes in the tall windows shattered, spraying me with slivers and shards.

I threw myself into a somersault, tucking my head, extending my wounded arm to guide me through with each rotation, and rolled across the hardwood floor, wincing with pain.

Who was shooting at me?

No. Wait. *How* was anyone shooting at me? I was invisible!

Wasn't I?

No time to check.

Men were yelling, footsteps pounding, more bullets.

I scrambled behind a bookcase, frantically trying to decide what to do next.

Run out the back?

Trash that idea. More footsteps and voices coming from that direction, too.

I was trapped. Apparently they'd been lurking in shadows, surrounding the store when I'd sauntered up to it, without noticing. I wasn't keeping watch for humans. I was so accustomed to being invisible, I wasn't watching for much of anything.

I nudged a sliding ladder to the left with my foot, bounded up it, kicked it away and vaulted four feet through the air to land on top of a tall, wide bookcase.

I flattened myself on my stomach and snatched a glance at my hand.

Still invisible.

Then how were they shooting at me? And why? Who knew I was invisible? Who could possibly have any reason to *shoot* at me? What had they done—hidden outside and waited for the door to open by an unseen hand then started firing blindly?

Grimacing with pain, I reared back like a cobra on its belly and stared down.

The Guardians.

Were shooting at me.

Spilling into my bookstore by the dozens.

It didn't make any sense.

Two officers burst into the room from the rear. An auburn-haired man near the front door barked, "She's in here somewhere! Find her." He began shouting orders; dispatching men to sweep the main room, others upstairs, and more to my private quarters in the rear.

They didn't just search, they wrecked my home. Needlessly. Swiping magazines from the racks, toppling my cash register from the counter, smashing my iPod and sound dock to the floor.

I was growing angrier with each passing moment. And worried.

I was a sitting duck.

I tallied my tactical advantages primarily by their dearth: no spear, no gun, the only weapon on my body was a single switchblade. I wasn't carrying because I was invisible and had the cuff of Cruce on my wrist. I didn't fear humans. Jada's *sidhe*-seers had been leaving me alone. I only worried about Fae, and with the cuff I was supposedly untouchable.

I couldn't achieve my normal agility at the moment because, damn it, bullets hurt! I might be hard to kill, healing even as I lay there, but it was still painful as hell. The store wasn't warded against humans, only monsters. How else would I sell books?

I searched the cluster of angry men for Inspector Jayne. There were about thirty Guardians in the store, all wearing the recently adopted uniform of durable khaki jeans and black tee-shirts, draped in guns and ammo, many toting military backpacks.

Where was Jayne? Had he sent them here, and if so, why? Had he finally decided to come after my spear in force? Was he prepared to kill me for it? I'd heard he'd taken Dani's sword when she was down, so I guessed I couldn't put it past him.

Too bad I didn't have the spear. Jada did. And how did he know I was—Oh God, had Jada told him? Would she betray me like that? Send someone else to eliminate me because she wasn't feeling up to it, or didn't want the blood of both Lane sisters on her hands? Maybe she just didn't feel like wasting her or her *sidhe*-seer's time on such a pesky detail.

"Find the bitch," the auburn-haired man growled. "She killed our Mickey. Left him in a fucking pile of scraps. Find her *now*!"

I frowned. How did they know I'd killed one of their own? Had someone been watching me the day I'd slain the Gray Woman and inadvertently taken the life of a human in the process? Then why wait so long to come after me?

"Brody," another man called, and the red-haired man's head whipped in his direction. "There's blood here. We hit her. I *knew* we did."

I froze, staring down at the floor where the man was pointing. I'd left a trail of blood along with a long smear of water as I rolled across the hardwood floor. The trail ended where I'd leapt to my feet about ten feet from the bookcase upon which I was perched. I eased my hand to my thigh to see if I was still bleeding. It came away dry, thanks to whatever elixir Cruce had given me that made me regenerate. Shit. I had a bullet in my thigh. How was I going to get it out? Had I bled down the side of the bookcase before the wound closed? I inched my hand across the top of the bookcase. It was wet. I eased my fingers over the side.

Dry.

I felt my hair, wet from the rain but not dripping. Same with my clothes.

I bit back a sigh of relief and assessed the room. There were Guardians between me and both front and rear exits. Even if I managed to somehow silently descend the bookcase—which seem highly improbable, given that I'd shoved the ladder away—I'd still have to dodge a cluster of rampaging men. The odds of crashing into one of them or being struck by a flying piece of furniture were high.

"She couldn't have gone far. She's still in the room. There'd be a trail of blood if she'd left," Brody said.

Apparently they didn't know about my Fae-bequeathed healing ability. That was an advantage. A little Unseelie flesh might make me capable of kicking their asses, or at least outrunning them.

Too bad they ate it, too, and all my stock was spilling out of the overturned fridge one of them had ripped out of the wall. Again, not carrying. Not afraid of Fae.

That was the dangerous thing about thinking you understood your parameters. The "impossible" was nothing more than all those nasty things at the outer limit of your imagination, and unfortunately the universe has a much more creative imagination than I do.

At least my invisibility was still working, casting that same mysterious cloak over me that had prevented even Barrons and Ryodan with their atavistic senses from being able to sniff me out. The moment I thought that, I wondered if the *Sinsar Dubh* would seize this golden opportunity to uncloak me, try to force me to open it or die.

I extended my hand in front of me, watching it anxiously. Still invisible. What was my inner demon doing? This protracted silence between us was frazzling my nerves. At least when it was talking, I felt like I was keeping some kind of tabs on it. Probably not true but that's how it felt.

I narrowed my eyes. Right. And now the Guardians were just being *mean*, kicking and slashing things.

Not the chesterfield!

The bastard, Brody turned his automatic on my cozy sitting area. Tufts of leather and down flew, books imploded, and my favorite teacup shattered.

I gritted my teeth to keep from screaming. Demanding they stop, leave. With absolutely nothing to back it up.

One of the men abruptly shouldered off his backpack, ripped it open and began tossing cans to the men. A second and third man ripped open their packs and soon all were holding multiple identical cans.

Of what? What were they up to? Were they going to gas me? I didn't see any gas masks being yanked from packs. Would gas work on me?

"Fall in!" Brody roared, and the Garda moved into sleek formation, shoulder-to-shoulder, in a line that spanned the room from side to side. Then he barked, "Don't leave a thing untouched. I want that bitch visible!"

I watched in horror as they began storming my beloved bookstore.

Methodically spraying everything in sight with garish red spray paint.

Twenty minutes later there wasn't a square inch of the first-floor, patron-accessible part of BB&B that wasn't dripping red.

My counter was a slippery crimson mess.

Every chair and sofa drenched. Barrons's rugs—his exquisite treasured rugs—had been soaked with red paint that could never be removed without destroying the fragile weave.

My bookcases, books, and magazines were all graffitied. My lovely lamps were broken and bleeding. My pillows and throws were a soggy mess. They'd even spray-painted my enamel fireplaces, the mantels, and gas logs.

My inner *Sinsar Dubh* had remained silent throughout the assault. It hadn't taunted me once with the temptation to stop them. I wouldn't have used it anyway. I hadn't used it to save myself. I certainly wouldn't use it to save my store, no matter how much I loved it.

The massive bookcase on which I sprawled was fourteen feet tall. Once they'd begun spraying, I retreated to the center of the large flat top, squeezing in on myself as small as I could be, praying their spray wouldn't reach that high. I peered down at my side.

Shit! There was a fine mist of red paint all down my right leg! Had my head gotten glossed, too? Did I dare poke it up to sneak a look below?

I lay motionless. Maybe they would just leave now. Stranger things had happened.

"Second floor, Brody?" one of the Garda asked eagerly. Pricks. They were getting off on the destruction, just like so many people had on Halloween, before they'd become prey. Rioting begets violence begets rioting. I sometimes think the entire human race is comprised of barely restrained animals, avid for any excuse to tear off their masks of civility. And here I am, always trying desperately to keep mine on.

If they went upstairs, one of them would certainly glance over the balustrade and spy the vaguely outlined red-misted form of my body stretched on top of the bookcase.

But wait—this was an opportunity to escape!

I tensed, preparing to take a bone-jarring leap from the bookcase and make a mad dash for the door the moment they topped the stairs. I'd strip as I went so they couldn't follow my spray-paint-misted clothes and hope the rain would take care of whatever was anywhere else.

Brody jerked his head toward the front. "Three of you block that door. Three more at the back. Nothing gets in or out."

Fuck.

"Then start climbing the ladders. I want every inch of this place covered. She's got to be here. Check everywhere, she may be hanging off a railing, hiding beneath something. There's no way she got out."

Double fuck.

As the Guardians moved toward both exits, a voice bellowed from the alcove, "What the bloody hell do you think you're doing?"

I knew that voice. I dared a peek over the edge.

Inspector Jayne exploded into the room, shaking off rain. A big, burly Liam Neeson look-alike, the ex-Garda dripped no-nonsense authority and command. I'd never been so glad to see him in my life. If he hadn't authorized this maybe he'd stop it.

He took a long look around and snarled, "Fall in!"

No one moved.

"I said fall the fuck in! Or are you answering to Brody now?"

"The bitch killed our Mickey," Brody growled.

"You aren't in charge of our force. I am," Jayne said flatly.

"Maybe some of us don't like the shots you've been calling."

"Maybe some of you are just bored and looking for a little action. Felt like letting off steam. Tired of Fae you can't kill so you turn on a human. A human *woman*. Who taught us to eat Unseelie? Who showed us what was going on in our city? She's been out there killing Fae."

"She slaughtered Mick!"

"You don't know that."

"Everyone's saying it."

"And since everyone's saying it, it must be true," Jayne mocked. "Without concrete proof we don't move against anyone. And never without my explicit orders."

"They say she's possessed by the Book—"

Who says? I wondered.

"The Book was destroyed," Jayne snapped.

"They say there's another one!"

"They say," Jayne echoed. "Are you so easily persuaded? If there was a second copy of the *Sinsar Dubh* and she was possessed by it and actually here, do you really think you wouldn't be dead right now? It kills. Brutally. Without hesitation. You've seen what it does. We all have. It wouldn't cower and hide while you destroyed its home."

Faulty logic but I wasn't about to argue. Too busy cowering and hiding.

"You wanted an excuse to raise hell and you dragged good men into it with you. Brody O'Roark, I said fall the fuck in!" Jayne roared.

This time, ten men moved toward the good inspector, forming up.

Brody stood unmoving, legs wide, hands fisted. "She has the spear. *We* should have the spear and you bloody well know it."

"We don't kill humans to steal their weapons."

"You took the sword from the kid."

"At an opportune moment, without hurting her."

I wasn't sure Dani saw it that way.

"We don't cry sentence on any human until we've examined the evidence," Jayne continued. "And we sure as fuck don't slaughter people—*any* people—on the unproven word of an unvetted source."

Two more men moved toward their barrel-chested commander.

I like Jayne. He's a good man. Flawed like the rest of us but his heart is in the right place.

I'd give my bullet-pierced right arm to know who their unvetted source was.

"They were right about her being invisible," Brody growled.

"That doesn't mean they're right about everything. And until we've investigated, we take no action," Jayne said. "Besides, do you know whose store this is? Who she belongs to? Are you bloody daft? You want to bring his vengeance crashing down on us? Who the fuck do you think you are to make that decision and jeopardize every man on our force?"

"It's war, Jayne. He's not on our side. He's on no one's side but his own."

"In war, a wise man makes alliances."

"Ballocks. You blow up bridges so the enemy can't come across."

"You didn't blow up a bridge. You invaded his home. Wrecked it. Hunted his woman. Now he'll hunt us for it."

Eight more men joined the inspector's ranks.

"Clean this place up," Jayne ordered.

Everyone just stared at him, including me.

"It's oil-based, Inspector," one of the younger Guardians protested. "There's no cleaning it up unless we slosh the place with—"

"Petrol," Brody said with a savage smile. "We'll burn it down. Then he'll never know."

I jerked.

"The fuck you will," Jayne exploded. "You'll haul your bloody arses out of here now and hope to hell she's not here to tell him who the fools were that did this. Move it, men! Fall in!"

I didn't breathe properly until the last man had marched out the front door, with hostile, battle-ready, pyrodickhead Brody at the rear, glaring back at the room over his shoulder as he left.

I lay there another ten minutes, shaking off the trauma. I'd read in one of my books that most of the time animals didn't get the human equivalent of PTSD. They shook violently after a horrifying incident, their body's way of processing and eliminating the tension and terror. I embraced the involuntary trembling until at last my body was still.

If not for Jayne, they'd have found me. They'd wanted to burn my cherished bookstore. Gut it. Leave it a smoking ruin.

Screw patrons. There hadn't been more than a paltry handful for a long time anyway. I wanted this place warded against humans. I wanted steel shutters on the windows so no one could throw a flaming projectile through. I wanted the entrances changed to bank vault doors. BB&B was more than my store, it was my home.

I dragged myself off the bookcase, dropped over the edge and hit the floor hard, wincing with pain. I smeared wet red paint everywhere as I slipped and slid across the floor to the bathroom.

A half hour later I was sitting naked on a towel in the bathroom, a bottle of rubbing alcohol in one hand, switchblade in the other.

I might have healed, but two bullets were still inside me in highly inconvenient places. One would think, I mused sourly, that regeneration might include a tidy little ejection-of-foreign-objects-in-the-process caveat. Really, if you're going to get some kind of magic fix-it, it should be comprehensive.

The bullet lodged in my arm was either on or partly in a tendon and excruciatingly painful each time I flexed my arm. The one in my leg was in the middle of my quadriceps and burned with each step. Muscles weren't meant to host foreign metallic objects. Especially not hollow points that expanded on impact. Besides, if they weren't iron, they were lead, and lead was toxic. I could end up walking around with a mild case of heavy metal poisoning for the rest of my Fae-extended life. This rapid healing/immortality thing with which I was afflicted came with a whole new set of challenges. I guess if someone stabbed me and I couldn't pull the knife out for some reason—like I was tied up or something—I'd just grow back together around it.

Cripes. Really sick things could be done to me. The more invulnerable I got, the more vulnerable I felt.

Ergo the switchblade and alcohol. I was naked because my clothes were covered with wet paint that was getting on everything I touched, and I refused to go upstairs for clean ones until I had these bullets out. They hadn't gotten that far with their spray paint and I wasn't about to mess up any more of my home.

The problem was, I couldn't see my leg. I splayed my hand over my thigh trying to feel the precise location of the bullet. It was no use. The muscle was too dense. But from the pain deep in my quad, I had a fair idea where to make the incision.

I'd have to be quick.

Slice, dig, wrestle it out, retract blade.

I cocked my head, thinking. I could always smear paint on myself before I cut, but then I still wouldn't be able to see inside my leg, and I really didn't want to use one of the spray paint cans they'd dropped to highlight the inside of the wound. Not only would it probably sting like hell, I wasn't sure I'd have enough time to cut, paint, slice, dig, paint some more before my stupid body started healing. My right arm wasn't working well at the moment. Besides, I might end up getting tattooed by the paint as I healed around it. Never in the mood for a sloppy, random tattoo.

What if I passed out when I sliced myself? Or while digging? I'd probably heal before I regained consciousness.

Surely I was tougher than that.

Clenching my teeth, I sliced.

Moaning with pain, I dug.

I passed out.

The last thing I did before losing consciousness was hastily retract the blade with my thumb.

I woke up to a healed leg.

Bugger.

I could always get Barrons to dig it out. I could spray paint while he cut. Or use flour or something my body would absorb. Well, until I passed out. No telling when he'd be back. Or how many necessary tendons, muscles, or veins he might slice. Besides, I was sick of not taking care of things myself. This was my problem. I was going to fix it. I was tired of being saved by others or, as in this latest case, by divine Jayne intervention. It chafed.

I needed a higher pain threshold. Not that mine was low to begin with.

I had no intention of eating Unseelie again.

I'd eaten it three times to date—after Mallucé had tortured and beaten me to the edge of death, in the middle of the riots on Halloween, and eight days ago when I'd descended the cliff to save Christian. Each time I'd eaten it, I'd been painfully aware that I had no clue what the long-term ramifications were. Christian told me it was the combination of dark magic gone awry plus eating Unseelie flesh that turned him into one of the dark princes. I figured I already was a bang-up candidate to turn Unseelie princess.

Then again, Christian had only eaten it one time and I'd eaten it three so far. The damage was probably already done.

At least that's the excuse I gave myself, rationalizing that the temptation of recent withdrawal had nothing to do with my current need-based decision to partake. After the rape, I'd despised the idea of having anything Unseelie in my mouth ever again. Then I had to eat it on the cliff and remembered how it felt and, oops, well, no longer suffering that revulsion.

It was a painful hike to the spilled contents of the fridge and back. I made it wearing only my boots so I wouldn't get paint all over my bare feet, pausing to nudge them off before I reentered the clean part of the bookstore.

Once back in the bathroom, I dropped back down on the towel and leaned against the wall. I wiped off the lid of the baby food jar and unscrewed it. Without allowing myself time to reconsider, I tossed the contents into my mouth.

It was as disgusting as ever.

The taste of the gray, gristly, pustule-laced flesh was straight out of a nightmare. It was rotten eggs and castor oil, maggoty flesh and tar.

It wriggled in my mouth, tried to escape from behind my clenched teeth. I froze like that for a moment, with jumping beans of slimy Unseelie on my tongue, refusing to open my mouth yet unable to quell my gag reflex.

I pounded the floor with a fist to distract my recalcitrant throat muscles and swallowed. After a few moments icy heat flushed my body and a burst of power hit my heart like a shot of adrenaline.

Abruptly all my muscles slid smooth and sure and sexy beneath my skin, my spine straightened to perfection, my shoulders drew back, my breasts went out, my hips canted in, my stomach smoothed. It was like having all the tiny niggling imperfections of humanity ironed out of my body. If this was how Fae felt all the time, I envied it. I may have been given an elixir that changed me, but, unlike Fae, I still suffer everyday aches and pains, still need to sleep and eat and drink.

The squirming flesh wriggled all the way down to my stomach, where it fluttered like a flock of maddened moths determined to flap their way to freedom.

My heart thundered, my brain felt as if a vacuum had

sucked it clean of all confusion and fear, my body was a live wire.

It was exhilarating.

It was sexy as hell.

I stretched euphorically, drunk on Fae power. Wondering how I'd been living without it since that night on the cliff. Really, I was probably already as altered as I was going to get from the stuff, wasn't I?

Then I realized I had an entirely new problem.

I could no longer feel the bullets. And now I had only a vague idea where to dig.

I have no clue why what happened next did.

Since a wish was what had started it all, maybe I was wishing it so hard the Book finally decided to humor me.

Or maybe the *Sinsar Dubh* didn't like the idea of me cutting myself up.

Or maybe it knew something I didn't, and I really could die and was about to kill myself by slicing a necessary vein.

Whatever the reason, I was abruptly visible.

I gazed down at my body, so happy to see myself that I didn't move for a few seconds. Then I stretched a leg and admired it. Flexed my toes. Examined my fingernails. They were a mess. Short, ragged, and unpolished. Criminy. I needed to trim. And my skin was dry. How could my skin be dry when it rained all the time here?

Okay, so maybe I was postponing my barbaric surgery a bit by reveling in the lovely vision of my badly groomed body. I'd *missed* me.

God, it was good to be back!

I studied my thigh clinically, with a complete absence of fear, pain, or really any kind of concern at all, made a deep surgical slice and started digging around. Blood pooled, evaporated, pooled.

Wow, it was rather interesting in there. I'd never looked at myself on the inside before. What a miracle the body was. What a shame the composition was organic and stamped with such a finite expiration.

But not me, I marveled as I dug. For the first time since learning I'd been tampered with via an unidentified Fae elixir, I felt a small flush of pleasure at the prospect of a longer life. Hated the things that might be done to me in my enhanced condition, loved the idea of more sunrises, more nights with Barrons, more time to try to figure life out.

"Focus, Mac," I muttered. The bullets were only my most immediate problem. I had a whole list of others, the least of which was discovering who'd ratted out all my secrets.

My skin was already trying to close around the blade. With Unseelie flesh in me, I was healing even faster than I had before. I realized I had to keep slicing while I had the knife in there, moving the blade back and forth. It was curiously like operating on someone else's body. I barely felt it.

It took me two tries to get the bullet out of my thigh. Three to get the one in my arm out.

Of course, that's how he found me.

Sprawled on the floor with a couple of chunks of misshapen metal nestled in the valley between my leg and hip, a switchblade in one hand, alcohol which I hadn't had time to use in another, a feral look of triumph on my face. I might have even been laughing a little.

Butt-ass naked.

6

"Remember when I moved in you and
the holy dove was moving, too . . ."

I felt drugged. I *was* drugged, high on my victory over the bullets, blood pounding with immortal strength, stamina, and lust.

My mind registered Barrons, my body said: *Let's get down and dirty. I'm in the perfect condition for it.* Last time I'd eaten Unseelie flesh, he'd been killed a few minutes later. I'd suffered both the high and withdrawal alone. Had endured most of the high getting home from Germany, trying not to think or feel too much.

How long had it been since we'd devolved into an animalistic, no holds barred fuck-fest? What in the world had been wrong with me?

I knew the answer to that question. It was the thing I was keeping to myself, cocooned inside, a voracious worm in the rotten apple that was MacKayla Lane O'Connor.

Now, with the impunity and belligerence of an Unseelie-flesh high riding me, Barrons standing there looking half savage, half man, and no immediate threats to my existence, I had a single imperative. I was clarified—the Mac I used to be, back in more ways than one. Maybe this was what I needed to do to get through the days until I'd sorted out my many messes. Become an addict.

I'd never had sex with Barrons while I was amped up on Unseelie but I'd enormously wanted to. The small taste I'd gotten in Mallucé's grotto had infiltrated my dreams, tantalized me, goaded me to indulge again. Priya was horrific. It made you mindlessly insatiable, little better than a puppet.

But an Unseelie-flesh high was fully aware unquenchable lust—with an unbreakable body. If we fucked too hard, so what? My skin would heal even as we were doing it, letting me have more and more. We could do that thing I loved to do so much, that drove Barrons absolutely bugfuck crazy, with no repercussions.

I shivered with lust, suddenly understanding the See-you-in-Faery girls more than I wanted to.

Our eyes locked and I jerked.

Fucking river of blood in my House.

I actually saw the capital H in his eyes and knew Barrons's House was whatever he'd claimed as his own, and nobody, but nobody, shit in it. There would be hell to pay, and I wasn't certain I wouldn't steer him in Brody's direction before the night was through. I've learned a thing or two during my time in Dublin: when you let the bad guy walk, he comes back. Until you don't let him walk.

Paint, I corrected. But his primal senses had told him that before he'd even walked in the front door. The man could smell if I was having my period. Or even just close to starting it.

Barrons snarled, black fangs flashing, and I realized walking through the bookstore in its current condition must have awakened a memory from another time when he'd stalked a battlefield of blood, wondering what he would find. Most likely discovering everyone he knew—with the exception of his immortal companions—dead.

I wondered how long he'd had to live before he quit letting himself have one ounce of interest in a human. How it must have felt to lose everyone around him like I'd lost Alina. Oh, yes, easier not to care. To ultimately let oneself revile.

Barrons's beast is always close to the surface. I sometimes wonder if one day he won't simply change, lope away, and never walk as a man again. Go be pure in the form that makes the most sense to him, on some other world, in a skin that's much harder to kill and, for him, much easier to live in.

His dark eyes flashed. *Fuck. Didn't know what I'd find. There are still some things that can kill you. Hate that.*

Ah, so he'd considered the possibility Dani had come after me with my own spear. *Fuck. Didn't know if you'd come back.* To me, I was quick to chew off. *Hate that.*

He smiled but it vanished quickly. His lips tightened, his mouth reshaped in a way I knew well. He was thinking about what he'd like to be doing to me with it. And it wasn't talking. Barrons doesn't waste time on the mundane. Another man might have said, "Gee, how are you visible again?" Or, "What the hell happened to my bookstore?" Or, "Who did this and are you okay?"

Not him. He scanned me, made sure I was in one piece, and got down to what really mattered.

Me. Naked.

He stripped.

Muscles rippled in his shoulders as he yanked off his shirt. When he kicked off his boots, jerked his belt from his pants and let them fall, I swallowed hard. Barrons is a commando man. I love his dick. I love what he does to me with it. I adore his balls. They're smooth and silky and there's this seam down the center that I love to lick before I close my mouth over his dick, and just when I know he's lost in the sleek warmth of my tongue moving slow and easy, swirling, sucking him in with thinking it's going to be sweet, I lock my mouth down hard, cup his balls in my hand and jerk harder than I should, and it undoes him every damn time. I'm obsessed with his body and the way it responds to my touch. He's my mountain of man I get to play on, experiment with, and see how high I can make him fly.

Not a single tattoo marred his recently reborn skin. He was dark, muscled, sleek perfection. I was halfway to orgasm just from watching him strip. Well, that, my hand between my legs, and his intense gaze fixed on the movement. Pri-ya, I'd done this a lot, and while I'd sprawled on the bed, he'd sat in a chair next to it, watching me with heavy-lidded lust and fascination and often a flicker of something that looked a lot like jealousy. Then he'd knock my hand away, stretch himself over me, and drive home hard. *You need me for this* his eyes would say. *If for nothing else, at least this.*

He was right. There was masturbation.

There was sex with Barrons.

And there was abso-frigging-lutely no comparison between the two.

I pushed up from the floor, bullets dropping forgotten from the cradle of my hip. My spine fluid, my body strong, I pulsed with desire that rode the razor edge of violence. I don't understand why that happens to me with him. It never happened before with any other guy. With Barrons, I get turned on and I get hostile. I want to have violent sex, I want to smash and break things. I want to push him, I want to force myself into his head. I want to see how much he can take. I want to see how much I can get.

Got something you want to say, Rainbow Girl?

I knew what he wanted. What he always wants from me: to know that I'm aware and I'm choosing and I'm one hundred percent committed, to him, to life, to myself, to the moment, which doesn't sound like so much but it's a damn tall order. And he wants his name in that sentence somewhere.

I tossed my head and shot him a savage look. *Fuck me, Jericho Barrons.* You're my world, I didn't add. At least I hope I didn't. I let my lids flutter at the end, half closed, shielding my heart.

Then he was on me and I was crushed back against the wall, my bare feet dangling above the floor and he was sliding me up it, big hands splayed on my hips. His physical strength is surreal, an indisputable bonus when it comes to sex.

When he buried his face in my thighs, I wrapped my legs around his head, arched my back to push against his mouth, and fisted my hands in his thick, dark hair. When a fang grazed my clitoris, I pulled his hair—hard—and he laughed because, like me, when we're having sex, drugged or not, there's no such thing as pain. We did everything possible when I was Pri-ya. I became conditioned to him in that state. It's all sensation. And it's all good.

I let my head fall back against the wall, lost myself in the bliss of his hot mouth on me, his tongue moving inside me.

I arched my neck and roared when I came. Damn the man, he touches me and I explode and just keep moving in a red-hot haze of lust from one orgasm to the next until at last he stops touching me. He knows exactly how to work my body. It's incredible. It's frightening.

In desire, in lust, Barrons and I are perfect together. In everyday life, we're porcupines who must navigate the circumference of each other's existence carefully because one poke and either of us might bare our teeth and scuttle off. Not because the needles hurt but because we're both . . . volatile. Temperamental. Proud.

Obtuse as hell. It makes for difficult days and incredible nights. I can't change. He won't. It is what it is.

Here, now, in lust, we unite, bond in a way that makes the days work fine. I realize as I explode again and hear him make that low, raw sound in the back of his throat that makes me crazy, vibrates into my pelvic core, spreads in a rumbling purr through my body, enhancing my orgasm to exquisite proportions, that this is essential to us, to our ability to stay together.

I don't dare not fuck this man frequently because this is the glue that holds us, the tie that binds, the only tether, collar, leash either of us can permit, the place where everything else falls away and we become something more than we are alone. I get now why he fucks with the single-minded devotion of a dying man hunting God. Sex with him is the closest thing to holy I've ever known. Barrons is my church. Every caress, each kiss, a hallelujah.

Burn me in Hell if you have a problem with that.

He'll be there with me.

We won't care.

As the orgasm ebbed, flashed red-hot then ebbed again, he leaned back and slid me down the front of his body, eyes glittering crimson, face half transformed into beast. He was two full feet taller than he had been before, shoulders massively wider, skin darkened to burnished mahogany. I could feel talons on my skin. Low humps of horns were sprouting on his skull.

I was shaking with aftershock, and still, fresh lust blazed through me, sanctifying my blood, opening a floodgate I'd not even realized I'd closed. I was breathless for a moment, stunned by the sudden unsought awareness that I'd once again been repressing all emotion for months. Every single bit of it. Just like I did after I believed I'd killed him on a cliff with Ryodan. Skimming the surface, a flat stone skipping across a bottomless loch, grateful to be a dispassionate observer, the invisible narrator of everyone else's life. I'd *hungered* to be unseen. I'd wanted to disappear long before it happened. I have a critical fault line of a defect and it's not the Book inside me. And it's not something I can fix. At least not any way I've been able to figure out. The relentless, unsolvable clusterfuck in my own head made me choose to deaden myself rather than contend with the uncontendable.

Yet one carnal touch from Barrons and I was alive again. Awake and so very damned alive. And my problem that couldn't be fixed would be as ever present and unmanageable as always when we were done. May as well savor the now.

He dropped his dark, misshapen head forward and long matted hair brushed my back. "I taste Unseelie in you," he murmured thickly into the hollow of my neck around teeth much too large for a human mouth. I felt his tongue trace my jugular. Felt my heartbeat in my neck, pulsing against his fangs. His next words were guttural, violent, barely human, "Just how hard do you want to play?" He shook me a little then, like a dog with a rabbit in its teeth.

"How hard can you take it?" I purred into his chest.

He raised his head and looked down at me and laughed like I've never heard him laugh as a man. Oh, yes, Barrons prefers the beast. There's something so sure and uncomplicated in that form. As if there, a prehensile creature, he's free in a way I can't begin to understand. I want to explore what he feels wearing that primal ebon skin, how life tastes to him on those killing fangs, cozy up to the basest he has to offer, meet it in kind.

I slammed my palms into his chest, knocking him backward. He crashed into the wall of the bathroom so hard his head went down, and when it whipped back, his smile was feral, exultant. “You want to fight or fuck, Mac?”

I bounced from foot to foot, wired with fury and sexual energy. I may never understand why I always feel them together around him but I sure as hell can enjoy it. “Both.”

“Think you can take me?”

“Going to damn well try.”

“Think you’ll survive it?”

I stabbed a finger in his chest and smiled up at him. “I think I’m gonna own it. Jericho.”

He growled low in his chest. “Bring it the fuck on, Mac.”

I brought it.

7

"I'm gonna walk before they make me run . . ."

I stretched, supremely satisfied, rolled over on my side, and looked at Barrons. He was in human form again, flat on his back, chest not moving, and I knew if I lay my ear against his skin, I'd hear no heartbeat thudding behind his breastbone.

Barrons doesn't sleep. He drifts and was in what I'd learned to recognize as a deep meditative state. It wouldn't be long before he disappeared into the night to do whatever he does that makes his body electric and his heart pound again.

I raked a hand through my hair, trying to push the wild mess out of my face, and succeeded only in getting my fingers tangled in knots matted with spray paint. I gave up and shoved it to one side. We were both smeared with oil-based lacquer and if I wasn't . . . enhanced, and he wasn't . . . whatever he was, I'd worry about all those nasty chemicals on our skin. We'd slipped and slid all over the store, thrown each other around in the wreckage, painted our skin crimson, not all of it paint, some of it blood.

We were currently wedged between half a shot-up broken chesterfield and a shattered bookcase, I had hard-cornered books digging into my ass, was using a crushed lamp shade as a pillow, and one of the many baubles in the store was gouging the small of my back.

I felt incredible. Released. Open. I made a mental note to jump on him the next time I found myself feeling uncertain or shutting down. Barrons is antitoxin for the venom poisoning me.

I tipped my head back and looked around the room.

If the bookstore hadn't been completely decimated before, it certainly was now. Something bizarre had happened to us while we were fighting and fucking, taking out everything we felt on each other's bodies because words don't work for either of us anymore. As if possessed by a unified prime directive, we'd abruptly stopped having sex and devoted our focus to finishing what the men had started. We smashed, slashed, and crushed.

Those few things the Guardians had left unbroken we'd destroyed ourselves. My iPod had actually still been working in the sound dock. It wasn't now, ground to smithereens beneath a heel. The rugs shredded by Barrons's talons. Bookcases that had been standing were now on the floor, contents dumped across the garishly stained floors.

I understood on an intuitive level. Someone else had desecrated our home. By participating in its destruction, we'd said goodbye to its current incarnation. We'd given the bookstore a proper burial. We'd grieved in fury. We'd torn down the Phoenix to ash so it could rise again.

We would start over. Barrons and I would always start over. Longevity requires it.

As I lay there, considering how I would redecorate—and yes, I still love decorating, as a brilliant, half-mad king likes to say more often than I like to hear it: can't eviscerate essential self—my eye was caught by the piece of paper I'd been stooping to collect outside the bookstore when I'd been shot. It had traipsed in stuck to someone's boot, evidenced by a large red heel print and was stuck by yet more paint to the broken arm of the chesterfield.

I reached over Barrons to snag it. Smoothed it out and turned it over.

Between splatters of paint, my name screamed from the page.

I began to read. Stopped. Cursed. Read and cursed some more.

The Dublin Daily

August 2 AWC

EMERGENCY ALERT!
BREAKING NEWS GOOD PEOPLE OF NEW DUBLIN!

MACKAYLA LANE

is under control of the deadly Book of black magic known as the *Sinsar Dubh* and is on a rampage in New Dublin! She's been committing HORRIFIC MURDERS of INNOCENTS and will DESTROY OUR CITY if she isn't KILLED immediately! Her latest victim was a good man who worked for the New Guardians in a tireless effort to PROTECT us! Mick O'Leary was ripped to pieces by the SAVAGE ANIMAL **MACKAYLA LANE**.

See photo of Lane below! She usually has blond hair but may color it, don't be deceived by one of her SLEAZY disguises!

If you see her, DO NOT approach! She's a KILLER, PSYCHOTIC, and EXTREMELY DANGEROUS!!!

Notify WeCare with any news of her location!

She used to reside at BARRONS BOOKS & BAUBLES but hasn't been spotted there for some time.

It's rumored the Book can make her INVISIBLE, exponentially increasing the DANGER she presents!

Help us PROTECT New Dublin!

Join WeCare today!

Sleazy. I scowled, offended. There was nothing sleazy about me. Well, recent activity aside and that wasn't sleazy. That was freedom.

I smiled grimly. "Jada" hadn't needed to raise a finger against me. All she'd had to do was rat out my *Sinsar Dubh*–compromised state, my invisibility, and location to WeCare to place me squarely in the crosshairs of every vigilante, Fae, and nut job in Dublin. Thanks to Dani's past papers, in which she'd kept the city informed of every detail of the threats she deemed important, including the *Sinsar Dubh,* the world was fully aware of the astronomical power it contained. Some would hunt me to kill me, others with the futile hope of controlling the iconic, deadly Book. Rather than telling WeCare I was the Book, she'd made them think I *had* a copy, which made hunting me all the more desirable for those who wanted to possess its power.

I wasn't psychotic and she knew it. I was holding my own pretty damned well. I'd only killed a single person.

By accident. And I regretted the hell out of it. Would give a great deal to be able to undo it.

I was fuming again, all that lovely hostility I'd managed to vent on Barrons's body flooding right back into my veins like someone had turned on the mother lode of spigots inside me.

This was bullshit. I'd been betrayed to the entire city and I was visible. There would be no more sneaking through the streets to get where I wanted to go. No more evading the searching ghouls in tonight's sky. It struck me as incalculably odd they'd been hunting for me on the precise night I'd become visible again. Could they sense me so easily?

Not that I wanted to be invisible again, I appended mentally, hastily. If the *Sinsar Dubh* was listening, and I was sure it was, I was not making wishes. No wishes. Not a single one. "You hear that?" I muttered. "This is me, Mac. Not wishing."

There was no answer but apparently we were on the outs, the Book and I. Or it was merely intensely occupied doing something nefarious, underhanded, and evil that was requiring all its attention, the results of which would soon bite me in the ass with vicious little teeth. I may as well enjoy the silence and lack of teeth in my ass. Occupy my time with something much nicer in it.

I glanced hungrily at Barrons. Sex on an Unseelie-flesh high was every bit as phenomenal as I'd thought it would be. Eating Fae makes a normal human existence seem a shadow of what life really should be. It enhances all your senses, taste, touch, sound, smell. Sex had been even more mind-blowing than usual with Barrons, each nerve exquisitely sensitive. My orgasms had gone on and on, one barely sputtering out before the next had set me on fire. Oh, yeah, eating Unseelie twice in eight days was probably a really bad idea.

I resolved to think about that in a few days when my high wore off.

Barrons's eyes opened slowly, heavy-lidded. Lust in those ancient eyes always sparks mine, goads my inner savage. I trailed my fingers up his body, from his stomach to his jaw, savoring each ripple, each hollow. I get off on touching this barbarian, seeing him gentled before he retreats into his hard, controlled, distant shell.

He cupped my chin and brushed his thumb across my lower lip. "Jayne shot at you," he said, executioner-soft, and I knew he could smell the inspector in the ruined store and that Jayne would be a dead man before dawn.

"Jayne stopped the men who were shooting at me," I corrected. "A Guardian named Brody instigated it. Red hair. Probably around thirty-five, a little over six foot." I gave him ample description to find him, should he choose to. He would choose to. "The others were following his lead. He's the only one I consider a liability among them. He wanted to burn my store," I said. "The rest will obey Jayne once Brody is gone."

He smiled faintly at how calmly I spoke of a human's pending demise. "Good to see you back." *In more ways than one,* his eyes added.

I handed him the *Dublin Daily.* " 'Jada' outed me."

He scanned it then rose and stalked naked to the shattered counter upon which my lovely antique register used to sit, silver bell tinkling as I rang up orders. Whatever he was looking for wasn't where he'd left it. He rummaged beneath wreckage then returned with another piece of stained, crumpled paper.

I smoothed it out.

The Dublin Daily

August 3 AWC

EMERGENCY ALERT!
NEW DUBLINERS BE ON GUARD!

We've just received confirmation that there are TWO deadly copies of the PSYCHOPATHIC, EVIL *Sinsar Dubh* in Ireland!

One has possessed MACKAYLA LANE. The other has possessed

DANI O'MALLEY

who now calls herself JADA. See photos below.

MACKAYLA LANE and JADA are under full, terrifying MIND CONTROL of the deadliest books of black magic that have ever existed! They CANNOT be saved.

They're PSYCHOTIC AND DANGEROUS!

They must be KILLED to be stopped!

Contact WeCare if you have information on their whereabouts. DO NOT APPROACH THEM YOURSELF!

Help us PROTECT New Dublin!

Join WeCare today!

I frowned. "Wait, what? This doesn't make any sense. She's not, right?" Surely in the past few days she hadn't released Cruce and fallen under his control.

"Not that I'm aware. Ryodan's been keeping close tabs on her."

"Who would print this and why?"

He cocked his head, studying me intently.

"You thought she posted the first one and I printed this in retaliation."

He shrugged. "If someone throws you to the sharks, drag them in with you. Makes two of you against the sharks. With few exceptions, humans will unite to defeat a common predator before resuming their personal vendettas, creating multiple opportunities for escape."

I loved his logic, clean, simple, and effective. "I probably would have just protested my innocence. Printed a *Daily* of my own denying it all." Rather than turn on Dani, even if she *had* turned on me. I would never admit to anyone that I'd killed a Guardian. I hated myself for it, hated the idea someone may have watched me do it. I wanted a name. It's creepy to think someone knows something terrible about you and you have no idea who they are.

"Reason never works. There's an inherent bias in the system. The attacker has the offense, which makes the defense appear defensive, therefore guilty. If neither you nor Dani printed these, someone wants both of you targeted, on the run or dead. And with two simple pieces of paper, achieved their aim. These are posted all over the city. I saw a small mob forming outside Dublin Castle, demanding the Guardians take action."

Which is why he'd thought it was Jayne who came after me. The castle had been commandeered after the walls fell to house Guardian garrisons and what passed as the city's only hospital. "But why would anyone believe this? WeCare didn't offer a shred of proof. Besides," I groused, "their writing is positively juvenile."

"Fear, boredom, and a sense of helplessness have bred many a witch hunt. He who controls the presses . . ."

"Controls the populace," I finished. "Don't they realize we have far bigger problems? Like the fabric of our planet being destroyed?"

"They're blaming the black holes on you and Dani. The mob was ranting that the magic you're using is so destructive it's tearing the world apart."

"And you don't worry they might be on the way here right now?" I said tartly. To further damage my home. My hands fisted.

"I might have sidled into that mob and let it drop that I saw two young women dancing naked around a glowing book in a cemetery on the edge of town."

I snorted. "And it worked?"

"The promise of naked women and violence has always been irresistible bait for frightened men. Still, it's only a matter of time before they come."

He pushed up like a graceful dark panther, muscles rippling. He didn't look as forbidding when his body wasn't covered with black and crimson tattoos. I rarely saw him with his skin unblemished. Beautiful naked man. My skin smelled of him. I didn't want to shower it off but the paint had to go.

He offered his hand, pulled me to my feet. At the last moment his head fell forward and he inhaled. I smiled. We smell good to each other when we fuck. People should always smell good to each other when they fuck or they're fucking the wrong person.

"I have work to do," he said, and I caught the hint of regret that we couldn't just forget the world, stay devolved. Life was so much simpler when we ignored everything but each other.

"*We* have work to do," I corrected. I wasn't sitting on the sidelines anymore.

"I. Get cleaned up. We leave within the hour."

Before I could even open my mouth to argue, he was gone, vanishing in that fluid way of his, either too fast for me to see or blending into objects like a chameleon as he moved from one to the next.

A disembodied voice said, "I'll ward the store against humans. You'll be safe here until I return, Ms. Lane."

I bristled. I'd been "Mac" to him for the past hour, deep inside his skin, taken him deep inside mine.

With two tiny words he'd erected that formal wall between us again.

"Ms. Lane, my ass," I muttered. But he was gone.

Precisely one hour later we left by the back door, stepping into the alley between BB&B and Barrons's garage. I loathed leaving the store with all the windows shot out but Barrons assured me no harm would come to it.

While showering I'd realized something I'd overlooked when reading the *Dublin Daily* earlier: Today was August third—exactly one year to the day I'd first set foot on Irish soil. So much had happened. So much had changed. It was still hard to process the existence-altering vagaries of my life. Now that I was visible again I wanted to talk to Mom about some of my problems, get swallowed in one of my daddy's big bear hugs, but our family reunion would have to wait.

I shivered in the chilly damp air. My hair was still wet, blond streaked with crimson. The lemon oil I'd used to break down the spray paint had softened and separated the matted areas but hadn't eradicated the scarlet stain. Just another bad hair day in Dublin.

My wet hair wasn't the only reason I was shivering.

An icy Hunter crouched in the back alley, restrained by symbols Barrons had etched on its wings and the back of its head. It was the same Hunter I'd ridden the day we tried to track the *Sinsar Dubh* and were deceived by the Book, scattered like frightened mice. The day the ancient Hunter, K'Vruck, had sailed alongside me, admonishing me for not flying on him and warming me with his "old friend" greeting.

I have an enormous sappy-sweet spot for the largest, most ancient Hunter whose name is synonymous with death and kiss so final it eradicates the very essence of the soul. No poodle girl here. Not even a pit bull. My chosen beast is the happy odd finality that is K'Vruck. I wondered where he was and if he might join us again in the sky tonight.

I shuddered at the thought. If so, I'd drive him away. I didn't want him near Barrons. Ever.

He wasn't my only problem in the skies. Now that I was visible, I wondered how long I had before I was smothered in noxious ghouls. It seemed like all I ever did was swap one complication for another.

This evening's conveyance was a fifth the size of its gargantuan brother. I wondered why we weren't taking one of Barrons's cars; they'd certainly outrun anything else on the road. The Hunter's leathery skin was the absence of all color, inkier than midnight in a dark grotto, swallowing what light hit it as if it had ducked into a cosmic bathroom and powdered itself with black-hole dust. Wings at rest by whatever charm Barrons used that could control such creatures, its body steamed like dry ice in the drizzly night.

I shivered again. Riding one of these great beasts was like stretching yourself across a glacier. And if you're damp anywhere and touch it with bare skin, you stick like a tongue to a metal post on an icy morning. I'd gotten conned into accepting such a dare on a rare wintry morning in Georgia, waiting for the school bus with friends. "I need to grab more—"

Barrons silenced me by tossing me a bundle of clothing: gloves, a scarf, and a thick, lined bomber jacket. The man is always prepared.

The Hunter chuffed irritably in my mind, *Remove his marks. They chafe.*

I was startled to hear its voice in my head. Eating Unseelie flesh deadens all my *sidhe*-seer senses until the high wears off. I'd assumed I'd be unable to mentally communicate with it.

Not you that possesses power to hear. I possess power to be heard, it rumbled. *Wipe off.*

I'll consider it, I lied, tucking my gloves into my sleeves and wrapping my scarf securely around my neck.

Its amusement tickled the inside of my head, and I suddenly knew two things: it knew I was lying and the Hunter was not restrained in any way. It was pretending.

Were you ever?

Unrestrainable. All is choice. Stop your kind from shooting at us in the skies. We are benign. The marks chafe. Remove them.

It shifted its enormous hind flanks ponderously, impatience evident.

If they do nothing, why do they chafe? I asked.

Do you like *those red streaks in your hair?*

A snort of laughter escaped me, and Barrons gave me a look.

Vain much?

Interfere with my vision. Do not trinket us. We will trinket you and you will not like it.

I had no desire to know how a Hunter might trinket a human.

"One must mount in order to ride, Ms. Lane," Barrons said dryly.

"I think I just demonstrated my understanding of that sequence of events back in the bookstore," I said just as dryly. "It's talking to me. Don't you hear it?"

Not even I communicate with that one, the Hunter murmured in my mind. *There are doors. He has none.*

What do you mean?

I said.

Huh?

I do not clarify, expound, or elaborate. Open your puny mind. If you cannot see, you do not deserve to.

I rolled my eyes thinking it was no wonder the Unseelie king had a special fondness for these creatures. They communicated in a similar fashion.

Barrons sliced his head once to the left, dark eyes glittering, brilliant. He'd fed while out and his big body was thrumming with electric energy. I was looking forward to leaning back into him, astride the Hunter's back.

Since I couldn't use my *sidhe*-seer senses to determine if the Hunter was speaking truth, I listened to my gut instead, stepped forward and smudged my gloved hand against its icy hide, wiping the shimmering symbol from its skin.

"What the fuck do you think you're doing?" Barrons snarled.

"It chooses to be here. It won't harm us."

"You know that because it told you? And you believed it?"

I knew more than that. I knew if I wiped off its symbols, it would cooperate far more fully than if I didn't. Perhaps even tantalize me with an ancient secret of the universe or two, and I'm insatiably curious about what might be out there in the great beyond. Ever since I wandered the White Mansion, that infinite abode of endless wonders, I've suspected I have a bit of Gypsy in my blood. If—no, when—our problems are finally over, I plan to go exploring with Jericho Barrons. Everywhere.

This Hunter was proud, aloof, and accustomed to being utterly without authority. It didn't comprehend the meaning of the word, had to break things down in its mind like the Unseelie king had to split himself into many skins to walk among humans. I wasn't sure it was even alive in the sense we think of things being alive, unless blazing icy meteors or stars are alive. The symbols didn't constrain it. They were pesky flies on its hide and offended it to its core.

"Trust me."

He stared at me, not moving at all except for a tiny muscle in his jaw, which is a full-blown hissy fit for that man.

After a long moment of silence he ground out, "Your call, Ms. Lane."

I circled the Hunter and wiped the other one off its wing. Barrons boosted me when it crouched and I clambered up its icy back, crawled forward onto its enormous head and smudged away the final mark.

As Barrons leapt up behind me and we settled behind its wings, it purred, *Ahhhhh, now we fly.*

The Hunter lunged forward, and when it reached the wide intersection of streets at the edge of the Dark Zone, flapped its leathery sails, churning black ice into a small storm around us. We rose up and up.

I hated leaving the bookstore behind for who knew how long to God knew what fate. I glanced down to watch it grow tiny beneath us and assure myself attackers weren't at this very moment raiding my home, and realized why Barrons wasn't worried.

Black and turbulent, whirling with debris, a tornado encompassed eight full blocks, with BB&B nestled snugly in its eye. We soared straight up from the epicenter. A small mob was stalking a good distance from the perimeter but there was no way in without getting caught up by the cyclone that stretched into the sky.

I glanced back at him over my shoulder. Icy beast beneath me, hot man behind me. "And you did that how?" I said disbelievingly.

"Called in a Fae favor. Climate is one of their specialties."

It was a huge "favor." "Who among the Fae likes you enough to do that favor?" I knew the answer to that. No one.

"The one I didn't kill when I demanded it. After I killed the other two."

I smiled faintly. One word: badass.

I want to be Jericho Barrons when I grow up.

8

"Everybody has a face that they hold inside . . ."

When we landed in a field not far from the abbey to meet Ryodan, who was standing near the Hummer in which I'd spent far too much time recently, I resolved to say nothing of what I'd seen on the monitors at the club, curious to discover if Barrons or Ryodan would volunteer information.

I wanted to know if I was "Mac," a trusted member of our tenuous confederacy, or "Ms. Lane," still on the outskirts of the inner circle. Plus, knowledge was power, and I liked harboring secrets no one knew I knew. Such as Kat training beneath Chester's with Kasteo, Papa Roach serving as Ryodan's spy network, Jada and Ryodan kissing, and Lor carrying some kind of caveman torch for Jo, perfectly willing to piss off his boss to pursue it. Lor, who was indebted to me for a favor no one knew about either. A wise woman indiscriminately picked up all the tools others left lying around. You never knew what kind of wrench or knife you might need, or when.

Barrons and I hadn't spoken since the Hunter had taken flight. Barrons—because he doesn't—and me because I'd been lost in the pleasure of the moment, gliding through a velvety night sky luminous with stars, leaning back against the raw, electric carnality behind me while pondering the intriguingly unfathomable emotions/thoughts/images in the head of the ancient beast between my legs. Thanks to my high, I'd been more attuned to the kiss of the breeze, the beauty all around me, and less attuned to physical discomfort, like the ice beneath my ass.

On the back of a Hunter with Jericho Barrons, I'm free. I'm uncomplicated. Life is good.

It ended much too soon.

Ryodan was walking across the pasture toward us, and despite that I actually like him, my hackles went up. He wanted me to open the *Sinsar Dubh,* he ruthlessly pursued whatever he wanted, and it was never going to happen. That made us adversaries. The Unseelie flesh in my blood might have been amplifying my bristling a bit. It was nice to know if push came to shove, I was currently capable of pushing back.

He didn't say a word. Like Barrons, not a, "Gee Mac, you're visible again," or, "How did you do it?" Or even, "Where are your carrion stalkers?" a thing I was wondering myself, telling myself maybe they'd found some other person to persecute.

Nor did I say, "Gee, who's watching Dageus? Did you leave him to suffer his horrendous transformation alone?"

Ryodan thrust a paper into Barrons's hand.

Cripes, not another paper! What was I being accused of now? I glanced over his arm and read as he shined his cellphone on the words:

The Dublin Daily

August 3 AWC

EMERGENCY ALERT!
BREAKING NEWS GOOD PEOPLE OF NEW DUBLIN!

BEWARE THE NINE!

Nine immortals walk our city in human guise. They are SAVAGES and we have it from trusted sources they plot to seize control of our city, withhold food and MEDICINE necessary for YOU and YOUR CHILDREN, and ENSLAVE US ALL!

They FEED on HUMAN FLESH and BONES and prefer to eat small CHILDREN. They frequent Chester's nightclub but do not engage them there. They are too powerful on their own turf.

Shoot from a distance if you have the opportunity!

See photos below!

Jericho Barrons

Ryodan

Lor

Fade

Kasteo

Daku

(Further names forthcoming)

RETRACTION: JADA is NOT under control of the *Sinsar Dubh*.

Only **MACKAYLA LANE** is.

I bit back a laugh, certain it wouldn't go over well, but really, I was tired of being singled out for persecution and at least now I wasn't the only one. I looked up at Ryodan, arched a brow. "Children? Really?" I said sweetly.

"You fucking believe everything you read."

It wasn't a question but things from him rarely are. "The paper was partly right about me."

"Ditto. Partly."

"Who the bloody fuck," Barrons growled, "is printing these bloody things?"

"Well, now at least we're all outed," I said, "and I'm not feeling so personally persecuted anymore."

"Jada," Ryodan said.

I defended instantly, "I thought so, too, at first but I don't think so anymore."

"There are no contractions in this one, the grammar's superior, and Jada's the only one exonerated," Ryodan said.

Barrons inclined his head in agreement. "And there's no mention of Dani. Jada considers her dead."

Viewed that way, even I was tempted to concur. I couldn't see whoever was behind WeCare retracting the accusation against her, and she certainly had the hyperspeed to get a paper printed and distributed quickly.

"Dani's not dead." A dark head popped out from behind Ryodan's large frame. I hadn't seen him approaching in the twilight.

Apparently, Ryodan wasn't wasting any time getting his "crew" to work on the problem of the rapidly atrophying muscles of the Nine's vagina.

"And I don't believe she printed it. The Mega is massively more colorful and entertaining."

Oh, honey, I thought, are you ever in for a surprise. Jada was icy white and colorless as they came. I narrowed my eyes, studying the young man standing next to Ryodan, and wondered if he wasn't the only one that was going to be shocked when the two met for the first time since Dani had returned.

Even in the pale light of the moon, I could see Dancer was different. He seemed taller, and he'd been tall to begin with at a good six-foot-four. My gaze swept down to his feet. Gone were the usual tennis shoes, replaced by boots similar to those Ryodan and Barrons wore, adding an inch or so of height. Gone was the zip-up sweatshirt, traded for a rugged black military field jacket. His jeans were faded, his shirt a concert tee, but the overall impression he gave was several years older than the last time I'd seen him. The biggest difference was something about his face. I cocked my head, trying to figure it out. Thick, wavy dark hair fell forward, brushing his jaw in a sexy college poet kind of way.

He felt me staring at him and flashed me a grin. "Contacts. Dude, whole world for the taking. Don't know why I didn't do it before. Would've rather had Lasik but haven't found myself a surgeon I trust yet."

That was it! He had gorgeous aqua eyes fringed by thick dark lashes. Before, I'd only seen them through lenses. He looked more athletic without them, more rough-and-tumble masculine.

I smiled faintly. He'd heard Dani was back, older, so he'd stepped up his game, made his intentions clear. Said, "I'm a man and you have choices, Dani." Good for him. Their relationship was the most normal of any she'd had, and Dani had experienced precious little normalcy. I preferred him to the other liabilities she'd once told me she might give her virginity to; Barrons, and V'lane before we'd learned he was Cruce.

She'd been so determined that the loss of her virginity be epic, and while Dancer might not be epic, I wasn't so sure her first time needed to be as much as it needed to be good, caring, honest, and real.

I winced as I realized I was thinking of Dani not Jada, and as if she was still fourteen, innocent in that one remaining way. It was highly doubtful Jada's virginity was an issue. Especially not after the kiss I saw her give Ryodan. Jada was a woman who knew her sexual power. Five and a half years was a long time. Five birthdays. Had anyone celebrated them with her? Or like Barrons, had she come to despise cakes? I wanted to ask Jada if the loss of her virginity had been as stellar as she'd hoped.

Jada would never tell me.

Dancer was watching me, intuited some of my emotion. "She's still Dani," he said.

No she's not, I didn't say. Because I wanted so much for his words to be true.

"Even if, as he says," Dancer jerked a thumb at Ryodan, "she has an alter ego, so what? Some people have too much going on inside to be limited to one mode of being. What was Batman but Bruce Wayne's alter, and the Bat was faster, stronger, smarter, and way cooler. In fact, the case can be successfully argued that Batman wasn't the alter. Wayne was. Batman had evolved, toughened, become superior in every way and occasionally donned the mask of the man to navigate society. Look at Wonder Woman, aka Princess Diana or Diana Prince, different in each situation. Superman became Clark Kent—"

"We get the fucking point," Ryodan cut him off.

"I thought Kent became Superman," I said.

Dancer shot me a derisive look. "Don't you watch TV? You need to read up on your superheroes. He was born Kal-El on Krypton."

"Life isn't a bloody comic strip, kid," Ryodan said coolly.

"Yes it is," he said, "and we get to write our own script, so be epic or vacate the page. You're all taking this way too seriously. Leave it to the Mega to create an alter ego to deal with tough times. Be impressed. Don't rip it. I've got no problem with anyone she wants to be."

"Say that once you've seen her," Ryodan said.

"I will," Dancer said. "She wants to be Jada, I'm fine with it. She wants to be Dani, I'm fine with it. Quit looking at it like Jada killed Dani. Figure out how to appreciate both sides of her personality. Christ, you people have to put everything in neat little boxes, don't you? And if they don't fit, you get your panties in a twist until you pound things back into the shape you want them. News flash: life doesn't work that way."

I blinked, disarmed by his words. Appreciate them both? I might be able to consider that if I'd caught even the tiniest glimpse of Dani since she'd returned.

"Something happened to all your 'dudes,' kid," Ryodan said. "And your clothes. You think Jada might like you more grown-up. News flash: Jada doesn't like anyone."

"Anyone she's seen so far," Dancer replied. "Rule number one about the Mega: you take her as she is or you don't get her at all. Try to cage her with boundaries and she'll go into full battle mode. You of all people should know that."

"What do you mean 'him of all people'?" I said.

"He's supposed to be so bloody smart. He's blind as a bat where Dani's concerned. You all are. Your rejection of Jada stems from how guilty you feel about what happened to her and that's all about *your* hang-ups, not hers. Stop looking at it like it's a bad thing and see what she has to offer. Most of all, give her time. We have no clue what she went through. Dani was gone five years plus change and she's only been back a few weeks. Might take her a few minutes to acclimate. Rush much, folks?" Without another word, he turned and walked back toward the Hummer.

I snorted. "From the mouths of babes."

Barrons laughed softly.

"I should've killed that kid in the alley when I had the chance," Ryodan said.

Arlington Abbey. The place has never been an easy visit for me. The first time I was there, I'd just killed the *sidhe*-seer, Moira, and had a Fae prince at my side for protection and a show of power. Between V'lane and I, we'd pissed off pretty much everyone inside those walls.

I'd endured my second sojourn there in a hellish haze, Pri-ya, locked in a cell in the dungeon.

The third time I'd called on the Grand Mistress, I arrived armed to the teeth and inspired Dani to steal the sword and spear from Rowena, once again alienating my sister *sidhe*-seers.

Honestly, my only decent memory of the place was the night we'd interred the *Sinsar Dubh*, and even that had gone wrong. We'd merely swapped a bodiless Book for an Unseelie prince capable of nearly flawless illusion, adept at calculated, long-term sleight of hand. I didn't think for a minute Cruce was as "inert" as the Book had once been. Nor did I believe the Unseelie king had taken adequate measures to keep him imprisoned. Now that I was wearing his cuff, I doubted it even more. Jada had taken the cuff off Cruce's arm. Had she damaged the bars to do it? Was that why the doors were now closed? Had she managed to get the grid to work? Was he still in his prison or merely sealed in the cavernous room? What risks had she taken in her quest to accumulate weapons? Had she weakened the cage enough that Cruce's escape was only a matter of time?

My fingers curled at the thought, closing on nothing. I hated not having my spear, especially now that I was visible again. I consoled myself with the thought that I'd hated Dani not having her sword nearly as much. After all, she was sitting right on top of his cage. If he escaped, she'd do what she did best—kill. That'd make two Unseelie princes for her tally. The Mega would crow about the spectacular feat from the rooftops. Jada would probably never mention it. But then Jada had no doubt eclipsed Dani's kill count years ago.

As we drove through the open gates, parked near the fountain, and got out of the Hummer, I stood a moment, blinking. The grounds so closely resembled the gardens outside the White Mansion, with the moonlight silvering lush fantastical flowers, illuminating inky megaliths, shimmering dark roses and vines that didn't exist beyond Fae realms, that I had to focus on the gray stone walls of the abbey to convince myself I hadn't somehow slipped inside the Silvers.

On my last visit here Josie had haughtily informed me that Jada was able to stop Cruce's changes. Good thing, or the abbey might have been as lost as Sleeping Beauty's castle, swallowed by a Fae forest of vines and thorns. I took hasty note of the megaliths—still uncapped. They'd not yet been turned into a dolmen, a Fae gate to another realm. I really wanted those stones destroyed or at least toppled.

Dancer let out a low whistle as he exited the Hummer. "Didn't look like this last time I was here," he said.

None of us bothered replying. I moved to a bush covered with enormous velvety flowers that smelled of night-blooming jasmine, plucked a blossom the size of a grapefruit and played its petals through my fingers. It felt every bit as real as the illusion of my sister. I buried my nose in it. The scent was rich, intoxicating, amplified by the Unseelie in my blood. Did Cruce's reach extend all the way to Dublin? Was it he who'd fabricated the illusion of Alina, not the Book? Just what the hell was my Book doing?

Ryodan said, "Mac, confirm Cruce is still contained."

"She can't. She ate Unseelie again," Barrons told him.

"Why?" Dancer looked baffled.

"It gives you superpowers," Ryodan said. "Makes you harder to kill. Stronger. Faster. Guess Dani never shared that fact with you. Wonder why."

"Obviously she didn't think I needed it."

"Or doesn't care if you survive."

"Time will tell, old dude."

"When you're ash. And I'm still here."

"Alone. Because Dani and I will have died, battling a supervillain together, and moved on to the next adventure. Together."

Ryodan said flatly, "Never going to happen," and stalked off toward the abbey.

I shot Barrons an uneasy look. He didn't look any more pleased than I felt. Ryodan's comment had sounded like an insinuation he meant to keep Dani alive at any cost. And he'd already proved he was willing to do what it took.

"And *that's* the thing that's never going to happen," I muttered at Ryodan's retreating back. Dani had already become a bit of a beast as far as I was concerned. No way she was turning into a bigger one.

I narrowed my eyes, looking past Ryodan, absorbing

the abbey as a whole, beyond the overgrown topiaries, the dazzling, trellised gardens, to the structure of the building itself.

It was here that the battle with the Hoar Frost King had been fought and the icy Unseelie vanquished. Unfortunately, not before it had deposited a cancer in our world. I'd missed that fight. Been in the Silvers with Barrons hunting a summoning spell for the Unseelie king. But I'd heard all about Dani and Ryodan saving the day down by the far end of . . . Oh!

I blinked but it was still there. Near the ancient chapel that abutted Rowena's old quarters, where the IFP they'd used to destroy the HFK had been tethered, the night was darker than black.

The absolute absence of light mapped a perfect circle nearly the size of a small car. I pointed it out to the others. "Did either of you know about this?"

Barrons shook his head.

Dancer sighed. "I was hoping we'd killed the Hoar Frost King before it managed to make one of its cosmic deposits, but it fed while we were untethering the IFP. It looks like the flatted fifth we were feeding it was a bloody rich source."

As if we'd needed any reminders why we were here or how dire our situation, hovering near the south chapel, a mere fifteen yards from the wall of the abbey, was the largest black hole I'd seen yet.

"And if it expands enough to reach the wall?" I demanded. I knew the answer. I wanted someone to tell me I was wrong.

"If it behaves like the one we saw beneath Chester's," Barrons said, "the entire abbey and everything in it will disappear."

"Best case scenario," Dancer disagreed. "I've been studying these things, tossing in small objects. Each one I've seen was suspended aboveground. I believe they all are, since the HFK took the frequency it wanted from the air and left its deposit in the same place. Which makes sense because once the sound waves contacted another object, they would no longer have emitted undiluted frequency. Each item I tossed in was instantly absorbed and the anomaly grew slightly. Worth noting, its growth was not proportionate to the mass of the item absorbed."

"For fuck's sake, what's your point?" Barrons growled.

"I'm making it. When the hole beneath Chester's absorbed Mac's ghouls—which glided aboveground, by the way—it sucked them upward and in. Nothing I've tossed to any of the black holes was in direct contact with another object."

Maybe I *didn't* know the answer. Maybe the answer was worse than I'd thought.

"Worst case scenario," Dancer continued, "it'll devour the abbey and everything it's touching, sensing it all as a single large object."

"But the abbey is touching the earth!" I exclaimed.

Dancer said, "Precisely."

"How quickly could it absorb it, if it did?" Barrons demanded.

"No way of knowing. It could be the holes will always suck things upward and in, provided the object is small enough that it doesn't counter the pull of the thing's gravity. It could be very large objects like the earth are beyond their ability to tackle and it would merely take a chunk of the abbey. If it emits inadequate gravitational force, one might assume matter would separate under oppositional tension as competing gravities reach critical inertia. Problem is, I can't confirm they function identical to what we understand as black holes, and frankly that understanding is limited and speculative. Performing an experiment elsewhere might topple an unstoppable cascade of dominoes."

"Sum it up," I said tersely.

"Bottom line: I suggest we don't let the black hole touch the abbey even if it means tearing the place down to get it out of the way."

9

"Out of dark a hero forms, city's knight that serves no throne . . ."

Jada stared into the night, watching through the window as visitors passed from sight beyond the columns of the grand entrance of the abbey.

She'd known they would come. Those who wanted her to be someone she was no longer, someone who would never have survived those insane, bloody years in the Silvers.

They thought she'd stolen their Dani away. She hadn't. They thought she was split. She wasn't.

She was what Dani had become.

Which wasn't the Dani they'd known.

But how could they expect a teenager who'd leapt into a Silver to come out the same five and a half years later, as if nothing had happened to her while she was gone?

It wasn't possible.

Fourteen-year-old Dani was as irretrievable as anyone's youth.

Their desires were illogical. But desires usually were. She had a few of her own that defied reason.

She knew the name she'd taken for herself upset them. But no one had called her Dani for longer than she could remember, and she'd wanted a fresh start to put the past behind her.

She was home.

Life began now.

As she'd learned to live it.

When she realized she'd been gone a virtually insignificant amount of time, Earth-time—a fact nearly beyond her comprehension at first—she'd known those at the abbey would never follow an abruptly older Dani as readily as they would an unknown warrior. Much depended upon the presentation of facts—more so than the facts themselves. Since they'd "met" her as Jada, many of the *sidhe*-seers still had a hard time believing she'd ever once been the rebellious, calamitous teen.

Even if she'd continued calling herself Dani, those people she'd been closest to would have found her disturbing. They would have rejected she'd come back at nearly twenty, under any name—because what they couldn't accept was that she'd lived five and a half years of life without them and was different now.

But not entirely.

Everything she'd done since her return demonstrated who she was, what she believed in, the things she lived for. She'd begun recruiting *sidhe*-seers, rescued the abbey, started training the women to be the warriors they should always have been, as the prior Grand Mistress had unforgivably failed to do. She'd hunted her past enemies, protected her past allies. She'd obsessed over repaying a debt to Christian.

Still, sheep, as she'd once called the willfully blind, perceived things in black and white. Saw only that a fourteen-year-old explosively emotional child who tried to outrun her issues by darting into the Silvers had come back a mature, self-possessed woman and was, in their opinion, the wrong version of her.

They'd rejected her completely.

With the exception of Ryodan, hadn't even recognized her. And he'd rejected her, too. Decided the "other" part of her that was so useful when necessary had taken her over entirely, as if she were that bloody incompetent. Couldn't even see her looking right at him with Dani's grown-up eyes.

Adaptability, he'd said, was survivability, and she'd been listening. Now he condemned her for her method of adaptation without even knowing her challenges or choices.

She found that immensely offensive.

Perhaps a more tactful woman wouldn't have provoked Ryodan with comments that Dani was dead or scorned the teen she'd once been, but just as he had all those years ago, he'd irritated her, offending her even more because she'd believed herself beyond such a response—never a reaction, because reacting could be so deadly.

When she first returned, she *had* been beyond such responses, hardened by savagery and frozen by a glacier of grief in her heart, but day-to-day life in Dublin wasn't the same as battling her way home with a single, consuming purpose. It was more complex, and certain people seemed to possess the ability to bring out the worst in her. She'd forgotten she had those parts. Attachments were chains she'd taken pains to avoid, yet here she was, stuck in the middle of link after link.

Recent weeks had been muddied with emotional humans, both inside the abbey and out, fragments of flawed relationships, subtle traps lurking everywhere she turned, time spent in a Hummer with two of those she'd intended to kill before she reconsidered the timing and perhaps even the intention, a past she'd put away, all of it stirring things in her she'd never wanted to feel again.

She'd survived by not feeling.

Thoughts were linear. Feelings were grenades, pin out.

Thoughts kept you alive. Feelings drove a person to leap into a Silver that took them straight to Hell.

Five and a half years, most of it alone.

Before that, fourteen years, eternally misunderstood.

Back in Dublin, in charge of over five hundred *sidhe*-seers, and growing every day.

Still alone. Still misunderstood.

She turned from the window and glanced in the mirror. Gone was the wild, curly hair that had driven her crazy that first, treacherous year in the Silvers until she hacked it off with a knife. Although it was long again, she'd learned to control it with product and heat. Her sword was the only adornment she wore, breaking the stark black of her attire. She met the emerald-eyed gaze of her reflection levelly before turning away from it and settling in a chair behind the desk, waiting.

She knew what they'd come for, and would work with them because her city was in danger, the world's fate at stake, and she couldn't save it by herself. She knew what she was: one of the strongest, therefore a protector of those not as strong. She would function as part of a team, despite the peril to her inner balance, because the world depended on it.

They'd brought Dancer with them, whom she'd hoped to continue avoiding. She would accept his presence because his mind expanded into unexpected places and in the past he'd grasped things she'd missed. There was no question his inventiveness was a valuable commodity. She understood the danger the black holes presented, and hadn't fought so ruthlessly to get home only to have it stolen from her again.

They'd been young together. Exploding with excitement for the next adventure, wild and free.

He still was.

But she was no longer the swaggering, cocky,

impassioned teen she'd been, and he, too, would despise her for stealing his friend.

They were predictable.

Mac had allowed her to keep the spear, as she'd known she would if she concealed that she had the sword long enough, unable to bear the thought of Dani defenseless. One more thing she'd learned from Ryodan: assess the lay of the land, evaluate the physical and emotional clime, and present the face that serves the immediate purpose.

Pretending not to have the sword, unable to openly slaughter Unseelie, her need to kill had built a fever pitch inside her, and the moment she'd had the spear, she ripped through the streets, venting all those dangerously pent things in an explosion of guts and blood.

Mac felt guilty for chasing her into the hall. That was useful. But Mac had only been chasing her because Dani had run. There were more successful ways to run than with one's feet. If there was blame, Jada had owned it long ago.

Not accepting her for who she was now? That was entirely on Mac's head.

She'd given the spear to her *sidhe*-seers to use as they saw fit, as the prior Grand Mistress should have done. Checks and balances. The *sidhe*-seers would remove more Unseelie from the streets and save more people than Mac would, neutered by fear of her dark cohabitant.

Besides, Mac would be fine, even without the spear. She had the cuff and she had Barrons at her side.

When something like Barrons walked at a woman's side, he walked there forever, and not even death would come between them. He would never permit it.

There was no place Mac could go that Barrons wouldn't follow.

Not even the Hall of All Days.

* * *

"What the fuck is this."

Jada went motionless. It was human nature to tense when startled or afraid. Illogical and self-defeating, as once you stiffened, evasion was more difficult. It had taken her a long time to overcome the instinct, perfect a go-still-and-be-water response. In battle, the combatant who was most fluid won.

Damn the Nine and their inexplicable abilities. She'd not been able to find a single origin myth about them on this world or any other, and she'd searched. She who could destroy a thing controlled it.

Ryodan was in her study, standing right next to her, thrusting a sheet of paper at her, and she'd not even felt his air displacement.

He was good. Moving normally, she could sense him. When he moved in his enhanced, whatever-the-hell-it-was state, she might as well be blind.

She turned toward him, tipped her head back and was momentarily in the past, staring up from whatever hopeless situation she'd landed herself in, an impertinent Batman quip on the tip of her tongue, hoping to see him, praying to see him, towering over her, finally there to get her out of her worst jam yet. They'd fight side by side, blast their way home.

"A *Dublin Daily*," she said without inflection.

"Written by."

"Me, of course. Diversify the pool of the hunted and all. More targets. Less risk. My exoneration."

"You admit it."

"Why wouldn't I?"

"Because you pissed me off and you know what happens to those who piss me off."

"As I said before, I'm all you have left of *her*—the one

you prefer. So fuck you," she delivered in a cool monotone.

He smiled faintly. She had to bite her tongue to keep her features from rearranging into a frown. He wasn't supposed to smile. Why was he smiling? His smiles had always made her uneasy.

"You betrayed those who are mine," he said softly.

She stood slowly, drawing up to her full height of five feet ten inches, faced him and folded her arms. "I'm sure you'll figure it out. You always do. Get to the point. Black holes."

"Nice sword, Dani. Mac knows you have it."

"Jada. She's about to. I hide nothing. I do nothing I need to hide unless I'm concealing or misrepresenting facts to get something I want. Oh, wait, am I you or me?"

He leaned closer until they stood nearly touching but not. "Battle ready, are you, Dani," he murmured. "Feels good, doesn't it. To fight with someone who can take it. Someone who can't be broken. Remember that when you choose your allies in this city. I can't be broken."

"Nor can I."

"You learned how to bend in the right places. The supple don't break."

"Holy astonishing accolades," she mocked, "a compliment."

"Put some fire behind your actions and I might like you again."

"Again." She hadn't meant to softly echo the word, but around him, more than anyone else, her mouth tended to function independent of her self-imposed rules. She suspected it was because she'd talked to him incessantly, those early years in the Silvers. Answered herself back as him. Measured her decisions by whether the great Ryodan would have deemed them useful, wise.

Silver eyes met hers and locked. "I didn't like Dani."

"At least you're consistent," she said coolly.

His silver eyes were ice. "I loved her."

She failed to control it. Every muscle in her body locked. She refused to do what her body was screaming to do, break the lock with motion, turn away, distract her hands with something, evade his much too sharp gaze, which even now was searching her, trying to translate her body language. He'd always seen too much. She willed herself to relax, went fluid. "You don't know the meaning of the word."

"Refusal to permit emotion is a noose with a very short rope."

"Emotion is a noose with a very short rope."

"I agree to disagree. For the moment. Dancer is here. I expect you to—"

"My cooperation has nothing to do with what you expect. Nothing I do has anything to do with what you expect." For years she'd lived precisely that way. "Merely that I will do whatever it takes to save my world."

"Our world." He turned toward the door at the sound of footsteps approaching.

"Is the only thing we'll ever share."

"Careful, Dani. Crow is something you used to like to do. Not eat."

The footsteps sounded wrong to her. People were running, shouting.

Jada darted sideways into the slipstream and blew past him.

If her elbow was slightly out and nailed him in the ribs, it was a matter of haste, nothing more.

10

*"You think you own me,
you should have known me . . ."*

On a tiny world of teleporting trees, Jada encountered a furry creature that could best be described as a cross between a feral lynx and a chubby koala bear, with a feline face, a shaggy silver-smoke pelt, and a fat white belly. Its paws were enormous, with thick, sharp black claws. Its ears were tall and perky and great silver tufts curled out of them.

It was surprisingly agile despite its pudginess, capable of shimmying up trees on the rare occasions they remained stationary long enough, and loping great distances at astonishing speed.

It had morosely informed her it was the last remaining survivor of its race.

Incessantly talkative, cranky, prone to fatalistic commentary on virtually every topic, it had mocked her many bruises from colliding with the impossible to predict, randomly relocating trees, chastised her for no doubt starting a certain apocalypse with her chaotic crashes, and taught her to better navigate "the slipstream."

She wasn't, the little beast told her, sounding enormously cross and depressed for whatever reason he was always spectacularly cross and depressed, picking herself up mentally and shifting sideways, she'd merely managed to hitch a ride through one of the higher dimensions—and *how* was quite perfectly beyond him, considering how primitive and clumsy she was.

She'd asked his name, not surprised they could communicate in the strange fashion they did because by then she'd already seen too many strange things to be surprised by much of anything.

He'd announced with nearly hysterical despair that he had no name but was not averse to being given one.

With tears streaming from enormous violet eyes, he'd told her that his life was without meaning and he preferred to remain in the eighth dimension—which she couldn't possibly understand, seeing how she couldn't even manage the fifth one adequately—where no one could see him because there *was* no one to see him, and when someone is unseen and alone, *nothing* matters, not even matter.

He'd only returned to the third dimension when he'd sensed her there, he'd told her, around great hiccupping sobs, because he thought she might be troubled to finger-comb his matted fur (considering the dirty orange mass of tangles on her own head wasn't a *complete* mess), perhaps trim his nails (though not quite as short and dirty as hers), which were too sharp to chew and getting painfully ingrown.

She'd christened him Shazam!, hoping he would grow out of his brood into the moniker and become an epic companion. She'd later changed it to Shazam, as he favored the wizard more than the superhero.

This was during her first year Silverside, as she called it, before she'd hacked off her hair, when she still believed she might be rescued and was yet willing to risk connecting with the seemingly more reasonable occupants of the worlds she briefly inhabited.

Trapped on the planet Olean, roughly a sixth the size of Earth's moon, for months, she'd traveled the small continents, seeking the way off world with the gloomy, prone-to-vanishing-without-warning, small-cranky-needy-feline-bear thing by her side, absorbing all he had—or was willing—to teach her between his nearly comatose bouts of depression that alternated with alarming binges of eating everything he could get his paws on.

She'd been instructed by her mopey, volatile companion to stop locking her grid down mentally, and instead expand her senses and *feel* for the disturbances looming in her path.

She'd ended up with far more bruises than she'd ever gotten doing it her way.

But one day, blindfolded, aching in every limb, depressed and aggravated by his eternal defeatist commentary on everything from the ominous portent of the angle of the sun in the sky to the certain impending destruction of his world as clearly foretold by the bent of the teleporting tree limbs, she finally began to see what he was saying.

Thanks to Shazam, Jada now freeze-framed effortlessly, sensing all obstacles, impacting nothing, riding the slipstream as smoothly as an unobstructed water-park slide.

Here, now in the abbey, moving in the fifth dimension, she sensed enormous energy ahead. It wasn't Ryodan, she'd left him in her dust in the study.

It was Fae/not Fae. Prince/not prince.

Thirty feet to go and nearing, twenty-five, twenty—

She slammed into a solid wall and bounced off it, exploding out of the slipstream, cartwheeling her arms for balance.

"Ah, Dani," Ryodan said, smiling faintly. "Didn't see you there."

She went still. Her ass, he hadn't. She didn't press her fingers to her cheekbone, which she was certain would soon bruise. She was the eye of the storm, not the storm. Never the storm.

"I realized years ago your vision wasn't as astute as I'd once believed," she said without inflection. He'd been in the slipstream with her and she hadn't even known. She would learn to sense him. She would eradicate that vulnerability.

His smile vanished.

Good. She hadn't reacted. She'd responded. She was Jada. Not the one he remembered. In the periphery of her vision, wings unfurled and she turned to assess the visitor. The last she'd seen Christian, he was unconscious, being transported by his clan back to Scotland, along with his uncle's remains.

Flakes of iridescent ice crystalized in the air and began to fall, dusting the Cruce-gilded floors of the abbey. The temperature dropped sharply and a six-light segment of the hall's torchères went out. The prince in the Highlander was displeased, affecting the environment.

"Jada, he sifted in!" Brigitte exclaimed. Then mouthed silently around his back, *Our wards didn't work, what the fuck?*

"At ease," she told her first in command, which meant "hold your weapons for now." Christian wasn't who or what he'd been before his time on the cliffs. Though he'd been largely unconscious for the duration of the ride back from Germany, she'd seen enough to know something had changed him, tempered his wildness and madness.

There was a sudden commotion as more *sidhe*-seers joined them in the hall. She allowed herself a moment to bask in seeing the corridor of the grand old abbey lined with self-possessed, well-trained, heavily armed women, as it always should have been. Each face was a life, with a family, a vivid story, and she'd already made a significant dent in committing them all to memory.

Christian glided down the hallway toward her, part muscled Highlander, part sleek, dark Faery, majestic black-velvet wings trailing the gold floor, and despite having been trained to stand their ground, a few of her *sidhe*-seers peeled back.

She didn't fault them. He was formidable. She made a point of never underestimating either enemy or ally. His treatment of her now would define which one he was. His transformation seemed to have halted midway, leaving his skin golden, not white-blue, his lips pink, not blue-black, but he had the long midnight hair, muted tattoos, and majestic wings of a hauntingly beautiful, deadly Unseelie prince.

But his eyes! She fixedly avoided staring into them, blurring her focus slightly, absorbing his face as a whole with no clear features. His gaze leaned more toward Fae than human and she knew she would weep blood were she to meet it directly.

In faded jeans and a cabled Irish sweater split down the back to accommodate his great midnight wings that arced high and swept wide, he personified wolf in sheep's clothing. At his throat, a torque writhed, glinting, not an adornment but rather part of his flesh and quite possibly bone.

He'd saved her once from what she'd thought would have been a hellish decision. She'd known nothing of hellish decisions back then.

"Dani, lass," he said quietly.

"Jada," she corrected.

He studied her, from hair to boots and back again but with none of the sexual heat she'd once seen in that sometimes-black, sometimes-whiskey gaze. With her slightly unfocused gaze, she noticed his eyes widen, narrow with anger and that all-too-familiar rejection, then go void of all emotion.

Oh, yes, trapped in unending pain, he'd learned control. Learned to pull his feelings back and box them so they couldn't turn into fuel that would burn a person alive.

One did. Or didn't survive.

"Fair enough," he said. "I bring no quarrel to you or yours. You've my thanks and a favor owed for seeing me off that cliff. I would speak with that one." He jerked his head toward Ryodan.

She inclined her head, granting permission, wondering what had brought him here tonight, if they might work together toward common goals.

Christian stalked past her to the bastard that could still knock her out of freeze-frame. "What the bloody fuck did you do with my uncle?"

Before he'd been captured by the Hag, so many years ago for her, Christian would have stormed these halls and tried to kill Ryodan for the slightest offense, real or imagined. He was now demonstrating forethought and patience.

She didn't tell him to save his breath. Ryodan would never answer. No one interrogated that man, certainly not a walking lie detector.

"Precisely what I said I would do," Ryodan said mildly. "I brought him back."

Christian went still, mining the comment for its true ore. After several moments he growled, "Truth. Yet it was not his body you gave us. Explain yourself."

Ryodan never explained himself.

"There were countless bodies in that chasm. I thought I recognized the plaid," Ryodan said.

She narrowed her eyes. He was behaving uncharacteristically, this man who did nothing without a complex agenda. What was his game?

"It was our tartan," Christian allowed after a pause. "Yet not our kin. Where the bloody hell is his corpse?"

"I have no other knowledge of his corpse. I suggest your clan search the chasm thoroughly. Perhaps I missed something."

Jada studied Ryodan intently. " 'Perhaps I missed something'?" If he had, which she found quite frankly impossible, he would never admit it.

"Did that already. Sifted straight there. None of the bodies belonged to my uncle."

"Perhaps there's a fragment of Faery splintering the chasm. There were many caves and a fast-running river. Perhaps you didn't search well enough."

Nor was he a man who liberally employed the word "perhaps." He was being questioned—*questioned*, mind you, which was only one of several oddities here—by one of the Keltar who, on a good day, got under his skin and on a bad one he wanted to kill, yet hadn't used so much as a single "fuck" or made one aggressive comment. Even his body language was bland, relaxed.

"Did you do something with my uncle's remains?" Christian demanded.

"I did nothing with Dageus's remains."

Jada mentally pinned the elements of their conversation—and absence of elements such as hostility Ryodan should have been exuding—on a structure of sorts in her mind: words here, body language there, subtext sprinkled throughout. Remains, he'd said. Corpse, he'd said. And all his answers were ringing true to the lie detector.

There was a subtle yet significant difference between truth and validity. Ryodan's responses were tallying up on her structure as valid.

But not true.

There was something here . . . she just didn't know what.

She moved to join them, folding her arms, legs wide like them. "Do you know where Dageus is right now?"

Ryodan turned and locked eyes with her. "No."

"Did you do something with Dageus the night we killed the Crimson Hag?" she pressed.

"Of course. I fought beside him."

"Did you do something with Dageus after we left?" she rephrased.

"I tried to bring him back."

She glanced at Christian, who nodded.

Jada understood the art of lying, she'd perfected it herself. Wrap your lie in precisely enough truth that your body presents full evidence of conviction and sincerity, employing sentences vague enough that they can't be picked apart. The key: the more one simplified the question, the greater the odds of isolating the answer.

"Is Dageus alive?" she said to Ryodan.

"Not as far as I know," he replied.

"Is he dead?"

"I would assume so." He folded his arms, mirroring her. "Are you done yet?"

"Not nearly."

"Do you believe he did something with my uncle, lass?" Christian asked. "Something he's not telling us?"

Lass. The others despised who she'd become. The Unseelie prince still called her lass.

"I've been crystal clear," Ryodan said. "I did my best to bring Dageus back. The body I returned to your clan was not his. Everyone makes mistakes."

"Not you," she said. "Never you."

He smiled but it didn't reach his eyes. Then again, it never had. She'd modeled her own infrequent smiles in similar fashion. "Even me."

"Truth," Christian said.

"I believe," she said to Christian without taking her eyes from Ryodan, "that a full-frontal assault never works with this man. You've had all the answers you'll get from him."

"Truth," Ryodan mocked.

At the end of the corridor there was a sudden commotion, sharp cries and a scuffle. "She's here, Jada! The one with *Sinsar Dubh* inside her!" Mia cried.

"Let her pass," Jada commanded. "She's no threat to us at present and there are greater ones that need addressing."

Although her women grumbled and parted only reluctantly, they obeyed the order.

Without another word she slid up into the slipstream and returned to her study, knowing they would follow.

Where one staged one's battles was often nearly as important as how.

11

"Never meant to start a war
I just wanted you to let me in . . ."

I stepped into what had once been Rowena's study and inhaled lightly but deeply, girding myself to interact with Jada.

Differently this time.

I'd been pondering Dancer's words as I hurried through the abbey, trying to refine my emotions and stop seeing Jada as the enemy. Open myself to getting to know the icy stranger. Kicking myself for needing someone else to point out that it was my guilt insisting Dani be exactly the same, because if she was, I wouldn't feel so terrible about chasing her that night.

Dancer was right. My rejection of "Jada" was proportionate to how much I blamed myself, and as he'd so bluntly stated, that had nothing to do with her and everything to do with me.

The problem was, we'd had no warning, no time to adjust. One day Dani had been here, and a few weeks later she was gone, replaced by someone five years older, completely different, and quite possibly an alternate personality.

All I'd known was I wanted Dani back and I resented the one who'd taken her—the new Dani. It had been a gut punch, and I'd reacted instinctively, out of pain and grief.

Here, now, buoyed by the clarity of mind, strength, and energy of an Unseelie-flesh high, I could strip my feelings from the situation and perceive it more clearly.

I had no right to reject "Jada." Whether we liked her personality or not, this *was* Dani.

She'd made it back by hook or crook, battling God knows what for five and a half long years to return to the only home she'd known, and upon finally making it—not one of us welcomed her back or was happy to see her. Her hard-won homecoming had been an epic failure.

If Dani was in there, a repressed personality, our actions were unforgivable. If this was who Dani actually was now? Doubly unforgivable. We'd all changed. Even my mother. But she'd had the rock that was Jack Lane at her side to share her burdens and leaven the pain. What had Dani had? Anything?

I sighed, looking at her, seated behind the desk. *Really* looking at her for perhaps the first time since she'd returned.

Dani "the Mega" O'Malley.

All grown up.

Every bit as beautiful as I'd known she would be. Creamy Irish skin, faint dusting of freckles, long red hair swept up in a high ponytail caught in a leather thong, her gamine features both sharpened and softened, resulting in a finely chiseled, stunning face.

This time, however, as I examined her, I looked for the Dani in Jada without regretting the aspects I couldn't see, focusing instead on the aspects of Dani that still shined through.

Strong. Criminy, she'd always been so strong, and now was even more so.

Smart. Check—fierce intelligence blazed in those slanted emerald eyes above high blades of cheekbones.

Aware. Yes, her gaze was even now skimming the room, taking our measure, missing nothing. It rested briefly on my badly "highlighted" hair. Dani would have burst out laughing. We'd have joked about whether I might add a Mohawk to the mess.

Jada merely noted it and moved on with her assessment.

As did I.

Loyal, she sat in this abbey, training the *sidhe*-seers as the prior headmistress had never been willing to do.

A warrior, like our Dani, she patrolled the streets, tirelessly killing the enemy.

Like Dani, fighting for what she believed in.

I offered her a smile. It wasn't hard. This was Dani. She was here. She'd survived. We could have lost her completely. We hadn't. I would find a way to love this version of her, too. And maybe, one day, I'd get to see more of the girl I'd once known. Dancer's reminder that she hadn't been back long was something to consider. A soldier on the front needed time to decompress from the nightmare. A soldier who'd seen hard battle came back mined with triggers. I knew what those felt like from the rape I endured, the complete and total powerlessness I'd felt. I also knew that every time I'd sensed one of my triggers even potentially being approached, I'd done everything in my power to shut down inside. "Jada." I infused her chosen name with as much warmth as I could.

"Mac," Jada replied coolly. Like Ryodan and Barrons, she didn't comment on my visibility. These were difficult people to surprise. Then she looked past me and her face went stiller than still, as if she'd frozen into a stone statue of a woman.

"Jada," Dancer said happily behind me. "Welcome home!"

I felt like the biggest shit in the world. The one thing none of us had said, Dancer put right out there right away. Saying the normal thing, the nice thing, the thing she'd probably wanted to hear the most. Making the rest of us look like monsters.

Animation returned to Jada's face—well, as much animation as it ever had—and she said, "Thank you. It's good to be back."

A nice normal reply. More than any of us had gotten from her.

"I can imagine," Dancer said. "Actually, no I can't. No clue what you went through, but you kicked its ass, didn't you, Jada? You made it—just like you always do. Good thing, too. We're in a world of shit."

"The black holes," she agreed.

"I've got a ton of stuff to go over with you, when you have a minute. Primarily speculation at this point, but between the two of us, we'll sort it out. I also finished the Papa Roach spray whenever you have a minute to swing by."

"No one's swinging by anywhere." Shooting Jada a pointed look, Ryodan said, "Someone published a rash of dailies that have everyone looking for us."

"I told you, I don't believe Jada published the one about me," I defended again.

"And Jada certainly didn't publish the one about herself," said Barrons.

"She admitted she published the one about us," Ryodan said flatly.

Barrons whipped his head toward Jada, eyes narrowed.

"Well, why wouldn't she?" Dancer said. "More targets dilute the hunt."

"Precisely," Jada said. "I think Ryodan published the first two that betrayed me and Mac."

"It sounds like something he would do," Christian agreed. "Hunted women are easier to control."

"Whoever is behind WeCare is the one who published those dailies," Ryodan growled. "That's who you need to be looking for."

"And who the bloody hell is behind WeCare?" Christian said.

"Don't look at me," Ryodan said.

"Well, it's not me," I said. "Remember, I got targeted."

"Enough!" Jada said, pushing herself up to her full height, which never failed to startle me. She was taller than me now. "We're not devolving into our customary bickering. I didn't fight so hard to get back here only to lose my world. If you are incapable of focus," she gestured at the door, "leave. Now."

I didn't hear a word she said. The moment she'd stood, a glint of silver against the stark black of her outfit had caught my eye. While she'd been seated, I couldn't see it. My tongue was useless for a few seconds, thickened by shock. I was able to focus on one thing only. "What are you doing with the sword?" I demanded.

"The same thing I always did with it. Killing Unseelie."

"You said you lost it!"

"I said no such thing. You said I lost it. I said I knew precisely where it was."

I narrowed my eyes. "You played me."

"You assumed. I didn't correct you. It's not my job to correct you. The spear was useless in your hands. It's useful where it is now."

"You took Mac's spear?" Barrons said. "When you already had the sword, leaving her defenseless?"

"You're talking to Dani, Barrons," Ryodan murmured. "Remember that."

"Really?" I snapped at Ryodan. "Because I thought she was sounding a lot like you."

"I'm Jada," she said to Ryodan. "And don't try to protect me. I stopped needing you a long time ago."

"Stopped," Ryodan echoed.

"Not that I ever did," she corrected.

"I don't care who she is," Barrons growled. "I gave Mac the spear. It's hers and no one else's."

I shot him a curious look. *You didn't like me carrying it. You said so yourself.*

He shot back, *Far more than someone else carrying a weapon that can harm you. While I believe Jada won't use the sword against you, I have no such faith in the* sidhe-*seers. Untenable risk.*

"I gave her the cuff of Cruce," Jada said. "She can also make herself invisible when she so chooses. Clearly, however, she can't color her hair. Still, she is hardly defenseless."

My hand went to my hair. "It's paint," I said stiffly, "because someone printed a daily that set the Guardians on me, shooting at me. They invaded BB&B and sprayed everything with red paint, and no, I can't make myself invisible when I want to. That was the *Sinsar Dubh*, not me."

Jada said acerbically, "So it *is* controlling you."

I snapped, "That's not what I—"

My hair shot straight up as a small tornado blew past me. I was talking to thin air.

Jada was gone. So was Barrons.

I glanced at Ryodan. Then he was gone, too.

I heard a high whining sound as if they were all snarling or shouting much faster than my brain could process as they faded down the hall.

Then silence.

We were alone in Jada's study.

I looked at Christian, who was looking at Dancer. Dancer was staring at the door, looking worried. The three of us stood in silence until Christian said, "I've a corpse to find while that bastard's otherwise occupied," and vanished.

Dancer shook his head and slowly turned his gaze to me. "How do you expect us to save the world if we can't even stay in the same room together for five minutes?"

"We just need to work a few things out first," I said irritably. "We'll get there."

"The black holes don't give a rat's arse about our 'things.' And she's right about the spear. Word on the street is no one was killing Unseelie. Why weren't you out there?"

"That's none of your business."

He smiled faintly but his eyes were sad. "You know one of the best things about Dani?"

The list was long.

"She feared nothing. Do you know what fear fears?"

I inclined my head, waiting.

"Laughter," he said.

"Your point?" I said stiffly, in no mood for more of his cutting insights. We'd accomplished nothing tonight but pissing each other off. Again.

"Laughter is power. One of the greatest weapons we have. It can slay dragons and it can heal. Jada doesn't have it anymore. As long as she doesn't, she's more vulnerable than any of you seem to realize. Stop worrying about your idiotic 'things' and start worrying about her. Make her laugh, Mac. And remember how to do it yourself, while you're at it. Nice hair, by the way."

Then he, too, left.

* * *

Since we were on the first floor, I exited by the window for two reasons. One: I had no idea how long Barrons, Ryodan, and Jada might go at it, but I knew one thing for certain—I would have the spear back before the night was through.

Because I'd eaten Unseelie multiple times, if someone stabbed me with it, I might suffer the same horrific death I'd dealt to Mallucé. I hadn't worried about that quite so much when I was invisible.

Then again, thanks to a mysterious elixir given to me by Cruce, I might survive the wound and shamble around indefinitely, rotting in various places, clumps of my badly stained hair falling out.

Yes, Barrons would definitely reclaim the spear.

I'd never have let her keep it in the first place if I had suspected for one moment Jada might turn my spear over to *sidhe*-seers, who not only didn't know me but knew I harbored their ancient enemy, although they weren't clear on the how.

I'd been willing to give it to *her*, no one else. That weapon was a serious liability, and like Barrons, I didn't know or trust the new *sidhe*-seers, and the original ones had been conditioned with fear and manipulation for too long. It was going to take more than a few weeks for Jada to retrain them.

My second reason for slipping out via the tall casement window was because I wanted a better look at the black hole, and it would have taken me ten minutes to get there if I'd gone all the way around the inside of the abbey to the front entrance then followed the exterior wall to the rear of the abbey again.

I approached the anomaly warily, recalling what Dancer had said about gravitational pull. About fifteen feet in diameter, it hovered some three or four feet above the earth. Directly beneath it was a thick carpet of abnormally lush, tall grass, exploding with large red poppies, bobbing heavily in the breeze, shimmering with leftover droplets of rain. Many of the blossoms were as large as my hand. I inhaled deeply, the air deliciously spicy behind the sprawling stone fortress, and with my temporarily heightened senses, it was intoxicating. The night was hot and sultry as a summer noon in Georgia, the foliage lapping up the heat and humidity as if it were Unseelie-flesh-laced plant food.

I scanned the immediate area. There were no trees near the floating sphere, no jagged trunks or holes in the ground to indicate trees had once grown nearby and been sucked up and in.

Then how had the anomaly gotten so big? I couldn't believe it had been here all this time, so large, and no one had mentioned it. More logical that it began small and grew quickly.

But what was feeding it?

I dropped onto a nearby bench some twenty feet from the ominous vortex, drew up my knees, rested my head on my arms and studied it.

When I'd been this close to the one beneath Chester's, I was assaulted by a melody so wrong, so vile, I'd felt as if my internal cohesion was being threatened, feared I might be torn apart at the core, atoms scattered to the corners of the galaxies.

Yet tonight, gorged on Unseelie flesh, I heard nothing. My human senses might be heightened but my *sidhe*-seer senses were useless. If I came back in a few days when the high wore off, would it sing the same soul-rending song to me I'd heard before?

I narrowed my eyes. The poppies were trembling beneath the weight of glistening, nectar-coated insects I hadn't noticed at first in the pale light of the moon, their soft buzzing engulfed by the nocturnal symphony of crickets and frogs and half a dozen Fae-colored fountains splashing water.

There were hundreds—no, thousands—of sticky bees swarming the poppies, Earth-born creatures gorging on Faery nectar. Flying erratically, with airborne starts and stops and stumbles, buzzing left and right with dizzying speed.

I pushed myself up and moved cautiously nearer.

Ten feet from the black hole, I became aware of a subtle change in the air. It felt . . . thicker . . . almost sticky, as if I was pressing forward into a mild, unseen paste.

If it was affecting me, with my considerable mass, how was it affecting the bees?

I took three more steps and gasped softly. Bee after bee was vanishing into the black hole above. Drunk on poppy juice, disoriented by abnormally dense air, they were being pulled directly into the spherical abyss.

How long had this been going on? Since the night they'd destroyed the HFK? How many tens of thousands of bees?

I sensed motion above and tipped back my head. Not just bees—bats. Was it messing with their echolocation? They were flying straight into it as if lured by a siren song. Was it confusing the birds, too?

"What are you doing?" A voice cut through the night behind me, and I spun around.

Two of Jada's commando *sidhe*-seers stood in the moonlight, watching me with cold calculation. I'd been so lost in thought that if I heard them approach, I'd tuned it out.

"Trying to figure out why you're letting this thing grow unchecked," I said coolly. I didn't like being between *sidhe*-seers that knew I had the *Sinsar Dubh* inside me and a black hole that could swallow me alive in an instant.

I eased to the left. They did, too.

I stepped farther to the left and they moved with me,

keeping me pinned, black hole at my back, a mere seven or eight feet away. I could feel the light inexorable pull of it and shivered.

"Funny. We're trying to figure out why Jada is letting *you* go, unchecked," the tall blonde said icily.

"We have history," I said. "She knows I won't use the Book."

"No one can resist such temptation forever," the brunette said.

Yeah, well, that was pretty much exactly what I was worried about, but there was no way I would admit it, and certainly not to them, so I evaded. "It's sucking in bees, bats, small animals. You've got to stop it from growing. Burn the ground beneath it. Get rid of the bloody flowers. I don't know, put up a wall or something to keep the bats out."

"We don't answer to you," the brunette said.

"If you answer to Jada, you know I'm off-limits. So back off." They were moving closer, threateningly. Both were toned, athletic, draped in guns and ammo. I fervently hoped neither of them had my spear.

"If you're truly no threat, you'll accompany us back to the abbey," the blonde said.

"I told you she was up to no good when she left by the window, Cara," the brunette growled. "She's probably been out here, feeding it."

So that was how they found me. They'd been watching Jada's office and I hadn't come out. "And why would I do that?" I said acerbically.

"Because *sidhe*-seers are the bred enemy of the *Sinsar Dubh* and you want to destroy us," the brunette said tightly. "What better way to begin than by taking the fortress that houses so much knowledge about our ancient foe?"

"If you truly have good intentions," Cara said, "you'll let us secure you, while Jada reconsiders what to do with you. Come willingly, or not. But you're coming." While she was still speaking, Cara lunged for me.

If I hadn't eaten Unseelie flesh, her full frontal charge would have caught me off guard—as it was meant to—but I reacted with inhuman speed, ducking, rolling, gone. To them, it must have seemed I'd freeze-framed like Jada and simply disappeared.

I instantly realized my mistake.

"No, Cara, *no*!" the brunette cried.

I whipped my head around, shoving hair from my face. Cara was on a collision course with the black hole, arms pinwheeling wildly, trying to get her balance back, a look of terror on her face. She hadn't known I'd eaten Unseelie, couldn't have anticipated I'd move as fast as Jada, or that there would abruptly be no object in her way to diminish the velocity of her attack.

The brunette dove for her, and all I could think was, Oh, shit, if she touches Cara while Cara's touching the black hole, they're both dead. I tackled the brunette, taking her to the ground hard, then vaulted over her sprawled body, grabbed Cara's ankle and tripped her.

If not for Unseelie flesh in my veins, I'd never have been able to pull it off. But heightened senses, strength, and speed endowed me with flawless, instant precision. Criminy, I thought, I could get used to moving so fast. No wonder Dani had always hated what she'd called Slow-Mo-Joe walking.

As Cara tumbled to the ground, clearing the edge of the black hole by mere inches, I let out a sharp *whoosh* of relieved breath. One *sidhe*-seer was all I was ever going to have on my conscience. And, although this wouldn't have been my fault, I'd still have added the guilt to the rest of my sins.

"Ow! Shit! Ow!" Cara was lying directly beneath the black hole, slapping at her face, and I saw a cloud of angry bees swarming her, many of them getting even more disoriented, sucked straight up into the sphere.

"Hold still," I snapped. "And keep your fucking head down." There were three feet between her head and instant death.

I crawled forward on my knees and elbows, staying low. The air grew denser, exerting a stronger tug on my body as I approached, and I wondered how much larger it would have to get before people started getting trapped in its event horizon. Twice the size? Three times? And how quickly might that happen? Stretching out long, I snagged Cara's ankle and began scooting us both backward, dragging her from the bee-covered poppies.

We lay on the ground a few seconds, breathing heavily.

Finally, Cara stopped slapping at herself, propped up on an elbow and looked at me in silence. Her face was covered with angry red welts that were swelling fast but she paid them no heed.

I met her gaze levelly. I knew what she was thinking. Had I done nothing, both of them would have vanished into the black hole. No one would have ever known. Our quantum enemy left no evidence. They would have simply disappeared. People did all the time around Dublin.

Jaw set, Cara moved farther from the black hole and stood. As the brunette joined her, they exchanged a look, then Cara gave me a slow, tight nod.

She said nothing but I didn't expect her to. The women Jada had gathered closest to her were some kind of ex-military, and wouldn't easily change their minds about someone they'd decided was an enemy. But they weren't fools either, and my actions had created a question in their minds.

It was enough to work with. One day, I wanted to be

welcomed at the abbey. Not distrusted, as I'd been from day one.

As they turned and stalked off without a word, I dusted myself off and got up. I couldn't tell if the sphere had grown appreciably from the sudden influx of bees.

But at least it hadn't acquired the mass of two *sidhe*-seers.

There was a sudden blast of air, then Jada was standing between the sphere and me.

This was followed by two more rushes of wind behind me. I sensed Barrons's electrifying presence and Ryodan's more controlled one.

Jada's face was disapproving but she extended my spear, handle toward me, blade toward her. "I accept Barrons's reasoning," she said stiffly. "Many of my *sidhe*-seers feel strongly you should be killed. They obey me, still . . . some are young, unpredictable."

Gee, duh, really? I didn't say it. I tensed. With Unseelie flesh in my veins, I was acutely aware of what my spear might do to me. I have a serious love/hate relationship with my weapon. The tip was no longer encased in foil and I wasn't carrying a sheath. I hadn't expected to get it back tonight. "You were young once, too. And unpredictable. Gloriously, I might add."

"And made mistakes, hence my concern about those in my charge. Take the spear."

"Can I just tell you I actually miss your 'dudes' and kind of hate your 'hences.' You did a lot of things right, Jada." I made a point of using her name, underscoring my acceptance of her as she was now.

"Your opinion of the things I did is irrelevant, as is your opinion of my speech. My point is merely that he has a point. And until we've resolved this immediate problem," she jerked her head at the black hole behind her, "we may need you alive."

She thrust the spear out. Had it been tip toward me,

I'd have tested my Unseelie-flesh-fueled speed. I'd considered it back in the abbey when they all freeze-framed out, but opted to leave that particular battle among the three of them, as the last thing I wanted to do was fight any more than I had to with Jada.

Toward that end, I also wasn't ready to take my spear quite yet. She might not be stubborn Dani but she was laser-focus-on-the-point-at-hand Jada, and I suspected as long as she continued holding it, she would remain where she was until she saw her goal accomplished.

"Otherwise you wouldn't care if I remained alive," I said, stating her unstated implication.

"Otherwise it wouldn't signify."

I deflected the pain of the jab, remaining focused on her, realizing I might have a unique insight into Jada. How had I forgotten I'd once gone away and come back different myself? When I believed I'd killed Barrons, grief and rage had turned me into a cold, hyperfocused bitch. Jada might never tell me what she'd gone through in the Silvers but it was a sure thing it hadn't been a walk in the park. How would someone have reached me during those days and nights of unyielding obsession when I'd found it perfectly reasonable to sleep with my sister's lover and plot the destruction of the world? *Could* anyone have? "I know you're not Da—not the person we remember. I'd like to get to know you now."

"Take the spear. I am what you see. There is no getting to know me."

"I'd like to hear about your time in the Silvers." Perhaps the right actions could have thawed me back then. Maybe love, if someone had been able to rattle me enough to feel it. I did recall enough of those dark days to know the last people in the world I'd wanted to see were my parents. Jack Lane would have disturbed me deeply. Staying savage and psychotic would have been extremely difficult around the man who'd taught me to be everything but. What might penetrate Jada's icy façade? "I want to know what your life was like."

"My life is now."

"Jada, I'm sorry I chased you that night. I wish I could do it over again. Keep you from going through."

"Once again implying that I am a mistake. That I came back wrong." She looked at Barrons and Ryodan, who were standing behind me in silence. "How *does* one get her to focus?"

I snatched the spear from Jada's hand. "Bees." I changed the subject that was clearly as dead as a three-day corpse. "And bats. I wasn't out here taking a cheery stroll through your gardens. I was investigating. Figure out how to keep the damn things from getting sucked into that hole or we'll be tearing down the abbey."

"No one is tearing down my abbey. This evening," Jada said. "Galway. Three miles east of town there is one of these anomalies much higher in the air. Bring Dancer. I'll meet you there."

"This evening, Chester's," Ryodan said flatly. "That's where we'll be. Unless you think you can save the world alone."

Jada was motionless a moment, then, "The map I saw—"

"The map Dani saw," he corrected.

"—I assume you've continued tracking the anomalies."

"Every bloody one. And there are more than there were. You're missing information. I have it."

"Tonight, then. Chester's." She turned and freeze-framed out.

Dawn was pressing at the edges of the drapes by the time Jada sought her private quarters to sleep for a few hours. It had been three days since she'd last rested, and she wanted to be sharp for the meeting tonight.

Working with a team was so much more complicated than working alone. But none of the things she'd learned Silverside had the least effect on the growing tears in the fabric of their reality. Closing the doors on Cruce had been difficult but doable. Not a single ward or spell she'd mastered affected the black holes. She'd tested them exhaustively on the smaller, isolated ones.

Long ago she'd have pursued her investigation alone, but she'd lost too much and was unwilling to lose more. The girl she'd once been was impulsive, to her own detriment. Jada had conditioned herself to pause before acting. She was uncomfortably aware that very pause might be why she'd failed to predict the Crimson Hag's moves on the cliff. Intellect and gut were two vastly different things, with disparate strengths and weaknesses.

Imperfect as a child. Imperfect as a woman. But at least she could choose her imperfections.

The Dragon Lady's library in the east wing was her domain, locked, warded, and spelled so nothing could get in or out unless she permitted it. Inside the ornate yet comfortable book-filled chambers was everything she needed to survive. And a few things she'd gathered for no discernible reason.

Seeing Dancer had been uncomfortable. The others she'd managed with nominal discomfort, reminding herself of one past incident or another, mortaring the wall between them.

Not Dancer. They'd had a single argument long ago about boundaries and friendship, about letting each other breathe, but it had steamed off like fog on a sunny morning.

He'd accepted her on first sight, had said, "Jada," letting her know right off the bat they were fine, the same as his hand had always held easy, letting her stay or go.

He'd said, "Welcome home," and meant it, smiled, and it was genuine, with none of the rejection she saw in other people's faces.

Mac, too, seemed different, but Jada had no desire to ponder it.

She moved into the second room of the chamber, draping various bits of shirts and towels and throws over lamps and sconces as she went, dimming the lights. Thanks to Cruce, all lights burned at all hours, and she hadn't yet fathomed how to degrade that particular magic. She no longer feared Shades in the abbey. Her *sidhe*-seers had exterminated the last of them.

When she reached the bed, she rummaged beneath it and removed a small wooden box containing various items she'd collected upon her return to the city. She withdrew a folded piece of paper smudged with chocolate, sat on the bed, undid her hair, and ran her fingers through it.

Time. Both enemy and ally.

They thought she'd lost five and a half years of her life. She hadn't. She'd lived them. *They* were the ones who'd lost five and a half years of her life. And held it against her.

Absurd.

She turned to gaze at handwritten words she knew by heart.

Kill the clocks, those time-thieving bastards
Haunting every mantel, wrist, and wall
Incessantly screaming our time is gone
Marching to war with us all

Kill the clocks, they remind me of people
I once met in passing that pushed me aside
To rush to their train or plane or bus
Never seeing where the true enemy lie

Kill the clocks before they've seduced you
Into existing as they do, in shadows of the past
Counting the days as they slip by us
Boxed into a world where nothing ever lasts

Kill the clocks and live in the moment
No cogs or gears can steal our now
When you laugh with me, Mega, time stands still
In that moment, I'm perfect somehow

She touched the chocolate stain. It was a lifetime ago that Dancer had given her this poem, the same night he'd given her a bracelet she'd lost in the Silvers. Securely tied, it had been sacrifice that or her hand. At one point or another she'd sacrificed most everything.

"What a mess," Shazam muttered crossly. He was sprawled in the middle of the bed, on a mound of pillows, peering over her arm. He yawned, baring enormous teeth and a curled-up black-tipped pink tongue. "Not a bit of it works. It should be 'lay' not 'lie.' What does manage to flow has been bastardized for the sake of the rhyme. *Awkward.*"

"Those who can't, critique."

"As if clocks can be killed, and even if they could I hardly think enlightenment would suddenly descend on such a primitive race, granting the ability to grasp complex temporal truths. Why do you insist on remaining with these three-dimensional people? There's no question one of you will manage to destroy this world. Sooner rather than later. We should move on *now.* Did you bring me something to eat?" he said plaintively. "Something with blood and a heartbeat?" His whiskers trembled in anticipation.

"There are power bars—"

He sniffed. "A misnomer if I ever heard one. Not only don't they confer any appreciable power, I'm quite certain they sap mine. They taste bad and make me depressed." His violet eyes grew dewy.

"Everything makes you depressed. If you ever got out of bed—"

"What point is there in getting out of bed when you make me stay in these stuffy, dirty chambers?"

"I don't make you do anything. I merely asked—"

"Your 'asks,' boulders around my neck," he said woefully. "I'm as unseen as I was on Olean."

"That makes two of us." Refolding the poem along the creases, she tucked it back into the box, stretched out on the bed, sword at her side, and closed her eyes. She didn't undress. She never undressed. Sleeping was dangerous enough. She'd had enough of waking up to battle nude. Although it had certain advantages—blood was much easier to wash off and it often disconcerted the hell out of a human male enemy—she preferred not to.

Shazam got up immediately, turned around three times, lay back down then bounded right back up, bristling so hard the mattress vibrated. "You smell bad. Like a predator. I'm not going to be able to sleep with you smelling up my air. Who touched you? Why did they?"

"I'm not taking a shower," she said without opening her eyes. "I'm too tired. Besides, we've both smelled worse."

"Fine. I'm not cuddling, then."

"I didn't ask you to cuddle. I never ask you to cuddle. I don't even use that word."

"You don't have to. Your expects, bars on my cage."

"I merely suggested in exchange for grooming, since you have all that fur and blaze like a small sun, you might keep me warm. Some of those worlds were cold." And still, she often felt she had ice in her bones.

"It's not cold here. And you haven't groomed me all

day. It was a *long* day. I was alone the *whole* time. Because you make me stay in here."

"You would attract too much attention out there."

"I would stay in a higher dimension."

"Until you thought you might get some attention."

"I *like* attention."

"I don't."

"Did you *ever* like attention?"

"I don't remember."

"You're ashamed of me. Because I'm fat. That's why you don't want them to see me."

She slit her eyes open just barely, lids heavy. "I'm *not* ashamed of you. And you're not fat."

"Look at my belly," he said tearfully, clutching it with both paws and jiggling.

She smiled. "I like your belly. I think it's a perfectly wonderful belly, all soft and round." Yesterday, he'd been convinced his ears were too big. The day before that it had been something wrong with his tail.

"Maybe you're ashamed of yourself. You should be. The fur behind my ears is getting matted."

"You're beautiful, Shazam. I'll groom you tomorrow," Jada said sleepily.

"It's *already* tomorrow."

She sighed and stretched out her hand. Shazam headbutted it ecstatically.

Jada worked her fingers into the long fur behind his ears and began gently detangling. It was beyond her how he got so matted all the time when he slept most of the day and rarely left the bed.

He turned his face up, eyes slanting half closed with bliss, and rumbled in his broad chest. "I see you, Yi-yi."

Yi-yi was what he'd named her that day long ago on Olean when she'd named him. He'd been saying the same words to her every time she awakened or fell asleep for four years, and wouldn't rest until she said it back.

"I see you, too, Shazam."

Sometime later they curled together and slept as they had on so many worlds, Shazam's head nestled on a pillow of her hair in the hollow between her neck and shoulder, one paw wrapped around her arm, one leg sticking straight up in the air, twitching as he dreamed.

Part II

the thing I came for:
the wreck and not the story of the wreck
the thing itself and not the myth
the drowned face always staring
toward the sun
the evidence of damage
worn by salt and sway into this threadbare beauty
the ribs of the disaster
curving their assertion
among the tentative haunters.

–Adrienne Rich

The legend of a monster is invariably
worse than the monster.
Unfortunately the monster is usually
quite bad enough.

–The Book of Rain

12

"Yet it was there I felt the crossroads of time . . ."

Barrons and I landed a safe distance away from the cordoned-off black hole suspended in the air near the underground entrance to Chester's nightclub.

Jayne and the Guardians had been busy, commandeered by Ryodan to secure each and every black hole in Dublin. I glanced over my shoulder at it and shivered. They disturbed me on a cellular level, even with my *sidhe*-seer senses muted. Murder was now alarmingly easy: just shove someone into a floating black sphere, no evidence remained. Not that anyone was prosecuting murders at the moment, or even caring, too busy trying to stay alive themselves. The endless line of patrons waiting to get into the club angled sharply away from the roped-off area, apparently liking it no more than I did.

Barrons slid from the Hunter's back and dropped gracefully to the pavement. It never ceased to amaze me how such a large, massively muscled man could move so lightly, half vanishing into shadow without even seeming to try.

He reached up to help me down, as if my accompanying him was a foregone conclusion.

I had no doubt he planned to head off with Ryodan to do whatever they were going to do about the Dageus situation I'd still not been told about, and I'd be stuck alone at some subclub, sandwiched between black holes above and below, killing time all day, watching various soap operas unfold, waiting for "my man" to come get me and lead me like a dutiful puppet to our next activity.

Not.

Being a woman raised in a rural area of the Deep South—although my mother urged both Alina and me to be independent—I had a tendency to get swept along by a strong man.

Being Barrons, sprung from whatever cataclysm sprung him, he had a tendency to sweep things along without asking—humans falling neatly into the category of "things."

But I've come to understand the difference between nurture and nature, and my nature is vastly different than I once believed. More rigid. Less malleable. More solitary. Less social. It would be easier to embrace what I suspect my true nature is if not for the dark squatter within making me second- and tenth-guess myself.

I'd been invisible and inactive too long. In the streets, I was a target for anyone who'd seen the blasted Dublin dailies. I was considerably less of a target high above them, where those hunting me wanted only to smother me in noxious yellow dust, not control or kill me.

"Go on without me. I want to be in the sky, Barrons." The morning was aglow with the faint pastel promise of a dazzling Fae-kissed sunrise.

"I want you inside Chester's."

"Because you want to keep me safe. The Unseelie king wanted the concubine safe, too. Built a hell of a cage for her." I would feel useless and aggravated in

Chester's. I would feel stupendously alive high above Dublin. No contest.

He went still, and for a moment I nearly lost track of him, standing right there in front of me. Big, dark man turned transparent shadow. "I'm not the Unseelie king," he said tightly.

"And I'm not the concubine. Glad we figured that out." There'd been a time I'd vacillated between thinking we were both one or the other.

"You're being hunted, Ms. Lane."

"What's new?"

"Feeling invincible because you ate a little Unseelie?" Barrons said sardonically.

Feeling alive because sex with him had reminded me who I was, deep down at the core, glued me back together in some intangible way, but I was not about to tell the arrogant beast that. Boundaries were necessary for a successful relationship. Most relationships aborted in the boundary-defining stage. Not because people demanded what they needed. But because they didn't, then got resentful about it.

I wanted to walk beside this man for a long time, and to do that I'd have to be able to be completely myself. I was still discovering what that was. I couldn't say that I'd ever call us a "couple." But we were together. Committed to that togetherness as best as we were both able. I wondered what my rules were. Wondered who the woman was that had once been this man's sun, moon, and stars. If he'd tried to curtail her activities.

"Stay the fuck out of my head, Ms. Lane."

I blinked. I hadn't even been aware I was pressing.

"She was her own woman," he said. "You are, too."

"That's what I wanted to know."

"Ask next time," he said coolly.

I snorted. "You'll answer?"

He turned and walked away. Over his shoulder, he tossed, "Try to stay alive, Ms. Lane."

"You, too, Barrons," I said softly, as the great beast between my legs flapped its wings and rose, carrying us into the rainbow-streaked morning.

If someone had told me, a year and a day ago when I'd stepped off the plane from Ashford after countless, exhausting layovers, that I would one day be flying above Dublin, breathing in the crisp, briny air, on the back of an icy dragonlike creature that wasn't from our world, taking stock of my city, I'd have laughed and pointed them in the direction of the nearest psychiatric facility.

I'd have been really wrong.

I'd been really wrong about a lot of things back then.

The lure of watching the sunrise on a Hunter had been impossible to resist. As we sluiced through wet clouds, I nestled close to the frigid base of its wings, with the hot brimstone of its breath drifting past my face. Clamping the bony ridge between my thighs, I threw my arms wide and trailed my gloved fingertips through crimson, orange, and pink mist. Head thrown back, gazing up at the dawn, I experienced a moment of uncomplicated bliss.

I was just Mac. Not someone's daughter or lover or sister or walking time bomb. Flying alone in the vast morning, I felt connected to everything, simple and good. Sky above, earth below, fire within.

Although I despised the Fae on my world, I had to admit, their presence made it more beautiful. And therein was the deadliness of their race: seduction via beauty, magic, and the power to grant wishes.

Rays of sun slanted intermittently down as we pierced banks of fantastically colored fog, until the Hunter, perhaps intuiting my innate desire to enjoy the sun at any opportunity, soared straight up and broke the dense cover to float lazily above rainbow-hued cumulus and nimbus stretching as far as the eye could see, granting me a clear view of the star I so worship, whose undiluted presence is so rare in rainy Dublin.

For a time, I stretched out, ignoring the ice beneath my back, soaking up the golden rays on my front, basking like a cat at a warm hearth. Who needed a Fae trip to the beach when I could sunbathe in the sky? But it wasn't long before the clouds swirled once again in my mind and I reluctantly refocused, urging my ride to take us low again so I could get a Hunter's-eye view of the city.

We plummeted through mist, dropping down and down until at last I glimpsed rooftops and streets and gas lamps dotting the overcast, cloudy morning that was a typical day in Dublin.

People were out, heading off to help rebuild in exchange for supplies. Street vendors were once again hawking wares at portable stands, including food and drinks. Guardians stood by the fours near each vendor, reminding me it was far from a safe city yet.

Still, I felt a fierce flash of pride and optimism. The walls had fallen. We'd gotten back up. The ice monster had come. We'd survived and the city had recovered. Now we had black holes. We would figure it out.

"Lower," I urged. I wanted a closer look at certain parts of town. I wanted to know if any of the Shades had returned, if there were new castes of Unseelie in town, if we had more black holes of considerable size to worry about. I would have gone on a focused hunt for *all* the black holes, but apparently Ryodan had been keeping track of them for some time now. No point in duplicating our efforts.

As we flew through a whiteout of fog above the docks, circling wide to turn back over the city, I suddenly gasped, "No! Stop! Turn the other way!" A flock of my dreaded stalkers had just materialized directly ahead of us, streaking out from behind a bank of low-slung clouds.

But my outcry came too late. We dove straight into the center of the clutch and I squeezed my eyes shut—remnant of some absurd ostrich instinct that if I couldn't see them maybe they couldn't see me—bracing myself for their sudden cloying presence on all sides.

Nothing.

I sniffed cautiously. No awful stench, no rustle of leathery cloaks, no creepy chittering.

I opened my eyes a slit.

I was still alone on the Hunter's back.

I opened them wide and glanced over my shoulder. My ghoulish stalkers were vanishing rapidly behind us.

"Didn't they see me?" I exclaimed. Was I so small and unexpected astride a Hunter that they'd not noticed me? I nudged the icy beast to get its attention. "Do you know what those things you just flew through are?"

Minions. It spoke in my mind. *To one nearly as ancient as I.*

"One what? A Hunter?"

Collector.

"Collector of what?"

Powerful, broken things. It presumes to fix them. It once tried to fix the one you call Unseelie king. It rumbled with soft laughter.

I couldn't imagine anything trying to "fix" the Unseelie king. What would it change? Where would it even begin? And how powerful was this "collector" if it could actually tinker with something as omnipotent as the King of the Dark Fae? "I take it that didn't go well."

Subjective.

"Was one of the things we flew through the collector?"

That one does not appear until it has decided. Dis-

patches minions to assess. Not all things are deemed fixable.

I bristled. For months now I was being assessed by something's minions? There was an ancient thing out there that had decided I was "broken" and wasn't sure whether it wanted to fix me? That was offensive on too many levels for me to count. I had yet another enemy out there and didn't even know what it looked like.

But it had been watching me.

All this time, through countless hooded eyes. Pressing close to me, sleeping beside me in Chester's, monitoring my every move. And when I'd killed its minions, it had simply dispatched more. Always watching. Until the Book made me invisible and the collector had apparently lost the ability to keep track of me.

I snatched a hasty glance at my hand, fearing the worst. But no, I was still visible. Then why hadn't they noticed me?

"Does it have a name?" I wanted something concrete to call my unknown enemy. Something to research, ask around about. Ryodan had once said my ghouls had attended the Unseelie king in his private quarters. Now I knew why. They'd scouted him, too, in a time long past.

Sweeper.

A simple word but I had sudden chills at the base of my spine. I'd heard it before. The Dreamy-Eyed Guy, one of the Unseelie king's many skins, had recently said, " 'Ware the Sweeper, BG. Don't talk to its minions either." The damn king had known all along I was being hunted by it. And that was all the warning he gave me?

"I really hate the Unseelie king," I muttered.

You are.

"Am not," I groused. I'd laid that to rest. I might have been contaminated by the peculiar half-mad being but I wasn't him.

Were you not, you would not fly.

"Tell me about the Sweeper," I said. "Tell me everything."

It said nothing.

"Have you seen it?"

The Hunter moved its great head from side to side, mouth open, straining wind through its teeth.

"Do you know anyone who knows more about it?"

Perhaps the one that inhaled the child.

"K'Vruck!"

It rumbled again, laughing at me. *Name this. Name that.*

"Do you know where K'Vruck is?"

Nightwindflyhighfree.

"Could you find him?"

I do not hunt for you. Not-king.

I sighed. "If you see him, will you tell him I'm looking for him?"

Again there was no reply. I made a mental note to be more circumspect in the future about telling the Hunters I wasn't the king. If they sensed something in me, they accorded respect, I wanted that respect. And cooperation.

I leaned forward over the Hunter's back. Something had just caught my eye, a thing I couldn't believe we'd forgotten.

"Fly low and land there." I pointed to the center of the city's largest Dark Zone.

Months ago, V'lane/Cruce had rebuilt the dolmen at 1247 LaRuhe in order to help the Keltar free Christian from the Unseelie prison. And there it stood, towering and ominous, behind the uncharacteristically formal house, smack in the middle of the crater left when Cruce had destroyed the warehouse it once occupied. The Highlanders had either neglected to dismantle the stone gate to the prison when they were done with it, or it had been rebuilt again.

I shivered. I'd walked the Unseelie prison. It hadn't been empty. There'd been things lurking in blue-black crevices, terrible things that hadn't ventured forth despite having been granted their freedom.

All portals between my world and Faery: bad.

And if I were successful, I'd have the Hunter fly me to the abbey, where I'd knock down those stones, too. Perhaps I'd be able to convince my ride to assist, lend a massive wing or perhaps char them with its smoky breath.

Nor do I perform tricks for you, it said in my mind.

The Hunter touched down in a wide intersection, flapping debris into funnel clouds with its giant leathery wings, showering the cobbled streets with black ice.

"Stay here until I get back." I stripped off the gloves I was wearing, checked to make sure my spear was tucked into the makeshift holster I'd created with my scarf, and hurried down the street toward what had once been the Lord Master's house.

The estate at 1247 LaRuhe was exactly the same as it had been last time I saw it, extravagant, forgotten, and as out of place in the casually dilapidated, industrial neighborhood as slender Kat had looked in powerful, forbidding Kasteo's subterranean gym.

The first time I'd come here, I was following my sister's last clue, chiseled as she lay dying. I believed it would lead me to the Book she'd wanted me to find, and instead discovered her boyfriend, learned he was the Big Bad ushering Unseelie into our world, and was nearly killed by one of his bloodthirsty companions. Six months later, I'd visited the house again, because Darroc had taken my parents captive and I was hell-bent on freeing them.

It hadn't gone as planned, but few of my ventures in this city had.

Today my plan was simple.

I would skirt the house and head straight for the giant stones of the dolmen to see if my Unseelie-flesh-enhanced strength was considerable enough that, with a chain or rope purloined from a nearby building, I might be able to send the whole thing crashing to the ground.

Or perhaps I'd find one of those little Bobcats in a nearby warehouse I could use to push it over. I could drive anything if there was gas in it.

One less portal.

My plan was *not* to go inside the tall, fancy brick house with the ornate facade and the blacked-out mullioned windows that made me feel as if the bone-pale structure was a bleached skull with creepy shuttered eyes that might pop open at any moment, insanity blazing within.

As I stood at the wrought-iron gate, one hand resting between pointy posts, the dense cloud cover gusted lower, shrouding the eaves, dispatching wispy tendrils down the sides to ghost across the barren yard.

I drew my jacket closer and turned up the collar. No sun penetrated the fog, and the abandoned property abruptly seemed painted in shades of the Unseelie prison, harsh whites, gunmetal grays, and eerie blues.

This particular Dark Zone in heavy fog was *not* one of my better memories of Dublin.

I shook off my chill, opened the gate, and stepped briskly onto the long curved walkway. As I hurried past skeletal trees, the gate screeched shut behind me and latched with an audible *clack*.

One year ago I'd followed the elegant walkway straight to the door and brazenly slammed the ornate knocker against burnished wood.

I'd let myself in and rummaged around, astonished to discover signs of my sister's presence mingled with that of an urbane, Old World man with lavish Louis XIV taste in decor and strikingly Barronsesque taste in clothing.

I'd sat on the bottom stair inside the silent, luxurious home and pored over pictures of Alina I'd taken from an upstairs bedroom. Thumbed through photos of her with her mysterious, handsome lover. I'd glimpsed my first unusual mirrors here, although I'd not understood what they were at the time.

The mirrors. I smacked myself in the forehead. Shit.

I paused a few steps from the porch, wondering if anyone had bothered to smash them, if perhaps Barrons had spelled them shut after I shoved into one six months ago, planning to step out in Georgia, only to end up lost in the Hall of All Days, where—like Dani—I had stared at billions of mirrors, wondering if I would ever be able to find my way home again.

I didn't like the idea of anything I'd glimpsed within those hellish Silvers having access to our world. We had enough problems as it was.

I sighed. There was no way I was leaving today without closing all portals at this location.

I took a step forward. Aware I was trudging a little. There were reminders of my sister here. I didn't want to go inside. But want and responsibility are rarely boon companions.

I took another step.

And froze.

One window on the house had not been blacked out.

The stained-glass transom above the lavishly carved front door.

And somewhere inside that abandoned house, a light had just come on.

13

"Let's imitate reality—insanity . . ."

Spear, check.

Unseelie flesh in my blood, check.

Attitude, check.

I silently ascended the porch stairs and pressed my hand to the door.

Damn. *Sidhe*-seer senses, not a check.

I had no way of knowing if what was within was Fae, human, or perhaps even something else entirely. I took nothing for granted anymore. Whatever it was, it wanted light for some reason. I couldn't envision an Unseelie flipping a switch or yanking a chain. They liked the dark. They'd lurked in it so long their eyes were well-accustomed to gloom.

I tested the knob, turning slowly.

Unlocked.

I took a fortifying breath and nudged the door open as quietly as possible, just far enough to steal a glimpse inside the house.

Nothing. But then, I couldn't see much from this point of view.

I listened intently. Thanks to my heightened senses, I

was able to discern soft footfalls upstairs on thick carpet. One set. There was a single entity moving inside.

I waited, listening to see if more footfalls joined them.

After a solid minute of hearing the sound of only one person/Fae/whatever, I eased open the door, slipped quickly inside and closed it behind me.

I inhaled deeply, mining for clues about the intruder. I untangled various elements: mildew of an old, unoccupied house; an acrid mold from the eternal rain with no heat running in the colder months and no air when it was warmer; something sulfurous that was no doubt escaping from one of the damned mirrors; a touch of wine spilled long ago—perhaps my sister having a drink with Darroc that had ended in impassioned lovemaking and forgotten wineglasses.

A doughnut.

I inhaled again, deeply. Sure enough. I smelled a doughnut. And coffee. The scent of yeast and something sugary was enormously enticing. I marveled that somewhere in Dublin someone was making doughnuts again. My stomach rumbled loudly. I made a mental note to find that vendor. Food had been in short supply for so long I could only give kudos to the black market if they were managing to obtain baking ingredients.

I moved quietly into the foyer, across black and white marble floors, beneath an elaborate crystal chandelier, my gaze focused tightly ahead, skirting a large round table with a dusty vase of silk flowers and pausing at the foot of an elegant, spiraling staircase.

Soft footfalls directly above.

The sound of a drawer sliding open. A muffled curse.

I couldn't make out much. The walls and floors were of solid, hundred-year-old construction and served as sound insulation.

I cocked my head, listening, trying to fathom who might come here and search the premises. Besides me.

For a moment I wondered if that was what I might find, should I ascend those curving stairs, if I'd somehow gotten trapped in a time loop, if the *Sinsar Dubh* was playing games with me.

If I doggedly mounted these carpeted risers, was it *me* I'd find up there?

Like I said, I take nothing for granted anymore. Not a damned thing.

Darroc? Had he truly died?

Some other *sidhe*-seer, dispatched by Jada, to reconnoiter the house?

Nah. *Sidhe*-seers worked in twos or more, not alone. Jada and I were the oddity, not the norm.

I eased my foot onto the first riser, placing it squarely in the middle because stairs always squeak when you're trying to climb them silently. Sure enough, it let out a sullen squeal.

Biting my lip, I eased up, foot sideways, attempting to distribute my weight evenly, moving cautiously.

Above me a door banged shut and I heard another muffled curse, followed by an angry, "Where *are* you?"

I froze. Sniffed the air. Faint, but there. So faint I'd not caught it, but then I hadn't expected to.

Squaring my shoulders, I marched up the stairs, determined to lay this particular bullshit to rest once and for all.

Another door banged, footfalls approached. I stiffened and stopped halfway up the stairs as the intruder burst from one of the bedrooms and stormed toward the very stairs I was on.

No. No. No.

This was wrong. This was so bloody wrong.

Alina stood at the top of the stairs, emotion flooding her beautiful features.

Shock. Astonishment. Joy.

Tears trembling in eyes I knew as well as my own.

Better. I'd looked at her much more than I'd looked at myself in a mirror.

"Mac?" she breathed. "Holy crap, is it you, Jr.? Oh my God, oh my God!" she squealed. "When did you get here? What are doing in this house? How did you even know to look—Oh! *Ahhhhh!*"

She froze, mid-sentence, her joy morphing to pure horror.

I froze, too, midway up two more stairs, boot in the air.

She began to back away, doubling over, hands going to her head, clutching it. "No," she moaned. "No," she said again.

"You are *not* my sister," I growled, and continued bounding up the stairs. I was confronting it this time. Staring it down cold. Proving the truth to myself, even without my *sidhe*-seer senses. My bastard Book, or Cruce, or whoever the hell was behind this was not playing this game with me.

Never this game.

The Alina-thing whirled and ran, hunched in on herself, clutching her stomach as if she, too, felt as kicked in the gut as I did.

"Get back here, whatever you are!" I roared.

"Leave me alone! Oh, God, I'm not ready. I don't know enough," she cried.

"I said get the hell back here! Face me!"

She was sobbing now, dashing through the house, stumbling into walls and crashing through doors. Slamming them behind her and locking them.

"Alina!" I shouted. Even though I knew it wasn't her. I didn't know what else to call the monster. Was my Book projecting an image? Or was the worst I'd feared for so many months now true?

Had I really never stepped out of the illusion that night we'd "allegedly" defeated the *Sinsar Dubh*?

Had it suckered me so completely that I only "believed" I'd been the victor but was in truth living in a matrixlike cocoon, my body in stasis, under complete dominion of the Book, merely dreaming my life? And I could either dream good things or have nightmares?

For months now I'd been crippled by that debilitating fear.

I didn't trust one damned thing about my so-called reality.

"Alina!" I roared again, crashing into a locked door, blasting my way through it. Hall after hall. Door after door.

Until finally she was trapped. She'd locked herself in one of the back bedrooms, one door between us and no way out for her. I could hear her sobbing on the other side.

What the hell was the Book playing at?

I kicked the door in with perhaps more violence than was strictly necessary.

She screamed and wrapped both arms around her head. Rolled over and puked violently.

I took a step closer and she screamed again, as if in soul-rending pain.

I stood and stared, trying to make some sense out of what was happening.

"Please," she whimpered. "Please. I don't . . . want you. I'm not . . . looking for . . . you. I'll . . . go home. I'll . . . leave."

What the hell?

"We're ending this now," I snarled.

"Please," she cried. "No!" She unwound one arm from her head, raised it, shaking as if to ward me off. "Darroc!" she screamed. "I need you!"

"Darroc is dead," I said coldly. "And so are you."

On the floor, huddled in a ball, my sister screamed and screamed.

* * *

I ended up leaving.

I couldn't take it one more second. What was I going to do? Kill the illusion of my sister?

I spun on my heel and stomped down the stairs, hands thrust into my pockets, head down. With the scent of lavender Snuggle sheets in my nostrils.

I grabbed the doughnut on the way out. It was in a bag, sitting near the vase of dusty flowers on the table.

I took the coffee next to it, too.

With the coral-pink lipstick on the rim, precisely the shade my sister wore: Summer Temptress.

I figured I might as well enjoy the happy parts of my madness if I had to stomach the bad.

Munching a soggy cruller (they may have gotten the right supplies but certainly weren't professional bakers—then again, if this was all an illusion, why wasn't my doughnut stellar? Was I so self-sabotaging I screwed up even my own illusory treats?), I ignored the mirrors I passed and forgot entirely about the blasted dolmen until I was nearly back to the intersection where I'd left the Hunter.

Of course, it wasn't there.

I tapped my foot irritably, cracking the thin layer of black ice sheeting the pavement.

And felt utterly lost.

I'd just seen the impossible. Confirming my fear that I might truly be stuck in an illusion I'd never escaped.

But other details, like the imperfect doughnut, the half-warm coffee (with heavy cream, no sugar, just the way my sister liked it), the sheet of ice on the pavement, all hinted at a cohesive reality.

This was what I'd been doing for months now, constantly assessing everything around me, trying to ferret out the Ultimate Truth.

Had Barrons *really* shouted me out of my illusion that night in Barrons Books & Baubles when (I believed) I'd seen through the projection of Isla to the reality that Rowena, possessed by the *Sinsar Dubh,* was trying to trick me into giving her/the Book my amulet by masquerading as my biological mom? Perhaps the illusion the Book had woven for me that night had never stopped.

Had I really helped lay the *Sinsar Dubh* to rest in the abbey, then watched it get absorbed by Cruce, then seen Cruce locked up?

Or had I *never* escaped the Book's clutches?

That was the motherfucking question.

The worm in my apple.

Something had happened to me that night that made me begin to deeply question the nature of my reality. Being deceived so thoroughly—even if only for a finite time—made me wonder if I was still being deceived. Some days I got by fine. Accepted that I'd made it. Saw only consistency in the world around me.

But some nights, especially those nights I dreamed the hellish song I'd been hearing lately, I wondered if something was trying to break out of my subconscious into my conscious mind that I couldn't quite bring to the surface and it—whatever it was—existed on the opposite side of an illusion the Book had woven for me.

Plans kept me sane. Obsessively hunting the Unseelie king to get him to remove his Book had kept me focused.

Focus prevented me from stretching out on a sofa somewhere and just giving up because I couldn't decide upon a satisfactory way to prove to myself that the reality I was living was real.

My fake mom and dad, Pieter and Isla, had seemed utterly real, too.

Now Alina.

But the Alina situation was odd.

With all kinds of wrong details. The glittering diamond on her wedding finger. Sobbing, hiding from me. Screaming if I got too close. Crying out for Darroc.

Alive.

Not.

I pressed my fingers to my temples and rubbed. "Focus, focus, focus," I muttered. "Do not take a single illusion as a sign that everything is. That doesn't necessarily follow. You're in the right reality. You defeated the *Sinsar Dubh*. Alina is the *only* illusion."

But why?

Having something inside me that was capable of weaving the convincing illusion the external Book had crafted, then having it go suddenly silent, was worse than it taking jabs at me and me snapping Poe back at it. At least our inane and bizarrely harmless spats had been something concrete I could hold on to. I'd been almost relieved when it made me kill Mick O'Leary.

Because at least then I'd been able to say: *Oh, so* that's *its game. I'll just never use my spear again. I'm in my reality. This is it. I understand.*

I'd told Barrons none of this. I'd hidden it from everyone.

I'd been grateful to vanish.

I couldn't shake the feeling that even if I was in the right reality, the Book was even now spreading nooses around me everywhere, and the first misstep I made, it would jerk that rope tight.

I stared down the empty street, littered with debris and dehydrated human husks blowing like sad tumbleweeds across the cobblestones.

"Not wishing," I growled. "I don't want to be invisible."

I wanted to feel like myself again. I desperately craved certainty in my soul. I was appalled to realize I'd almost given up. Withdrawing from Barrons, rarely pausing in my search for the king those weeks after I'd killed (or had I?) Rowena, not even to have sex, detaching from my parents.

But Barrons and Unseelie flesh had stirred fire in my belly again. Fire I needed.

I resolved to eat Rhino-boy and fuck constantly until I figured out this crisis of faith.

Toward that end, I needed a sifter.

Where the bloody hell was I going to find a sifting Fae?

"Christian," I said, smiling. "I thought I'd find you here."

"Mac," he said, without lifting his eyes from the cut-crystal glass of whiskey in his hand.

I dropped down on a stool next to him at what had once been the Dreamy-Eyed Guy's bar, then mine for a time.

The Sinatra club in Chester's was one of the quieter ones, where human males gathered to discuss business and, on rare occasion, some freakish Unseelie took a table for a time. This subclub drew a more refined clientele, and the Fae were all about the unrefined. The more brassy, sexual, and desperate tended to catch their eye.

I gave him a once-over. Hot, sexy Highlander with strange eyes I was grateful were currently brooding into his drink, not turned on me. Something was different. He looked awfully . . . normal. "Where are your wings?" I asked.

"Glamour. Bloody women in this place go nuts if I show them."

"You can sift, can't you?"

"Aye. Why?"

"I was hoping you'd take me somewhere."

"I'm not moving from this stool. That fuck Ryodan lied. He said he tried to bring Dageus's body back to us but he didn't. He doesn't know that *I* know the man he brought us was from Dublin, not the gorge at all. He must have snatched a bit of plaid from our rooms upstairs and bloodied it up. Why would he give us someone else's body, Mac?"

I rapped the counter sharply, ordering a drink. I raised my whiskey when it came as if to make a toast. "Sounds like you have a mystery. I've got one of my own. What do you say you help me solve mine and I'll see what I can do about solving yours?"

He turned his head slowly and looked at me.

I dropped my gaze instantly.

He laughed softly. "That bad, Mac?"

I inhaled deeply and snatched a quick glance from beneath my lashes. I'd seen this look before, times a thousand, as I rolled in the Unseelie king's great wings. I lowered my gaze again and steeled myself. Then looked up and straight at him, right in the eyes.

For about two seconds.

"Not bad, Christian," I said, looking down at my drink. "Just different. Intense. Like looking up at stars. We'll get used to it." I paused then added, "You know I can get into more places in this nightclub than you can. I can keep an eye out. Go poking around later tonight, see if I can learn anything about your uncle."

I had no intention of telling him. My loyalty is one hundred percent to Barrons. Period. The end. That is one of the few things I'm absolutely certain about anymore. Our bond. Our two-person religion. But I would certainly see if I could get Barrons to get Ryodan to consider letting Christian know. At some point. I knew what it felt like to lose family. I'd blamed myself a dozen different ways for all the things I hadn't done that might have saved Alina. I could only imagine how badly Christian was blaming himself for his uncle's death.

After a measured pause, he clinked his glass to mine. "Perhaps we can be of use to each other. You should know, lass, I'm far from a pro at it. It was easier before my stay on those cliffs."

"Because you didn't turn full Unseelie?"

"Aye. I suspect. I can do it, but it's more difficult. I tend to give myself a wide margin. Where is it you're wanting to go?"

14

"I am stretched on your grave and will lie there forever . . ."

Ashford, Georgia: population 3,979, covering 8.9 square miles, boasting over 100 original antebellum homes, housing 964 families. It's nestled in the prettiest part of down-Dixie I've ever seen.

Of course, I may be biased.

I love every nook and cranny of my town.

I'd not only toured all the historic homes decorated from pillars to eaves at Christmastime—Alina and I loved the holidays—but we'd practically lived in those atmospheric old homes on sultry afternoons and weekends, hanging out with our friends on bead-board-ceilinged porches with slow paddling fans, on white wicker swings, drinking sweet tea and believing nothing would ever change.

I'd eaten in every quaint restaurant and partied in every bar. I'd attended prom at the local high school and gone to concerts on the square. I knew every shop owner, and was even moderately acquainted with the politics of the region.

Given the size of my town, one would think it boring, filled with average people living moderately, but with its rich history, expensive, sprawling historic homes, and easy access to Atlanta, Ashford drew a lot of high-powered transplants from large, exciting cities—like my parents, who were seeking a simpler way of life yet enjoyed the finer things.

Mom and Dad bought a 1905 neoclassical revival mansion that had fallen into disrepair, surrounded by old, enormous wax-blossomed magnolia trees, and had lovingly restored it over the years. It boasted a typically southern, generous front porch, palatial white columns, an expansive yet warm and cozy sunroom off the back, and, of course, the pool I'd so enjoyed in the backyard. It was an idyllic, happy, safe place to grow up. Crime was virtually nonexistent in our town.

The Ashford cemetery occupied twenty-two acres, with a large Confederate memorial full of unknown soldiers, a few smallish mausoleums, manicured gardens, well-maintained walkways, and a tiered fountain.

It seconded as a park for the locals, with its gently sloping hills, flowering bushes, and crisp, cool lake on the back acreage. On the weekends you could find half the parents in town power-walking through gravestones. Divided into sections: the old cemetery, the new, and the memorial, we'd had Alina interred on the south side, in the modern portion, with a lovely marble marker.

It was late afternoon when Christian and I arrived in Ashford, or rather *near* Ashford. It had taken me hours to sneak back to Chester's dodging every person and Fae I saw, ducking into doorways to avoid Guardians, once, reduced to hiding in a trash Dumpster. Between my recent shock and my face plastered everywhere around the city, I'd been in no mood for confrontation. Near Chester's, though, I'd been unable to avoid it and tested my skill at Voice that Barrons had taught me, for the first time on strangers. It worked beautifully. They obeyed me instantly, turning around and heading the other way. My hastily shouted, *And don't breathe a word about seeing me to anyone. Forget everything about this day forever!* hadn't necessarily been the wisest choice of words, but I was operating on the fly. I hated the thought of people walking around out there with a whole day missing from their memory. I knew what it felt like to lose time, Pri-ya, to question your own mental faculties, and resolved to be more precise in the future.

Christian had been telling the truth about his sifting abilities. I think part of the problem was he'd never been to the States before. The other Unseelie hadn't exactly volunteered information about his new powers. He was an outsider to both races. Everything for him was trial and error. He frankly admitted he had no clue how he was "supposed" to sift. Places he'd been were the easiest. He hadn't yet figured out tracking by person but heard he was capable of it.

We'd had to stop first at BB&B, an easy sift for him, where I rummaged for a map in the wreckage and showed him where I wanted him to take me. As there was no detailed topography of the town—it was far too small for that—we ended up smack in the middle of a cornfield and had to walk twenty minutes to get to the cemetery. By the time we arrived, I was dripping sweat. Just another hot August day in Georgia: sun scorching, humidity thick.

He'd offered to try to sift us closer but we materialized alarmingly near a colossal live oak dripping Spanish moss—as in half an inch from the massive trunk. While *he* might survive manifesting in the middle of solid wood, I wasn't so sure about myself, so I'd opted to use my feet from there. I had a good deal of nervous energy to burn off anyway.

"Why are we here again?" he said.

"I want to check on something," I muttered. I hadn't

bothered to tell him that I planned to dig up a grave. I wasn't entirely certain he would have complied with my request for transport.

I glanced over my shoulder. He was trailing behind, looking at everything.

"Christ," he said, sounding disgusted, "everything is so new here."

I would have laughed if I hadn't been in such a pissy mood. I'd always thought my town dripped history but ours was a few hundred years old, and in Scotland his was a few thousand. I guess when you grow up with prehistoric standing stones in your backyard, American towns seemed prepubescent.

I was pleased to see that V'lane/Cruce's protection of Ashford when the walls had fallen had indeed kept it remarkably unchanged. Lights glowed in windows, there were no wrecked cars blocking the streets or signs of random rioting and carnage. No Dark Zones, no Unseelie lurking in the alleys, not one husk of the dead tumbling down desolate streets.

I supposed it was pretty much the way it had been before the walls fell—my town was too provincial and unexciting to draw the Fae.

It was as if the war between our races had given the place as wide a berth as Sherman's armies when the troops made the devastating march from Atlanta, after burning it to the ground. Although Ashford hadn't been torched by Sherman's marauding army determined to "make Georgia howl," half the town center burned to ash in the late 1890s, and they'd rebuilt it with a plan for revenue, planting a large number of shops and restaurants arranged around an enormous, beautifully landscaped square.

We passed the Brickyard where I used to bartend.

I barely spared it a glance.

My head was jam-packed with images of my dead sister, curled on the floor, screaming. Afraid of me. Crying out for Darroc.

It was too much to deal with. It was one thing to see an illusion of my dead sister, another to see her apparently terrified of me for some reason. That moment when her joy had turned to horror was scorched into my brain, eclipsing all my good mental photographs of her.

What sadistic game was the Book playing?

"See that hardware store?" I said to Christian, pointing. It was open for business, I supposed on the barter system, but I was in no mood to see anyone I knew. "Can you sift in and grab me a shovel?"

He shot me a look that couldn't have more plainly said, *What the bloody hell do you think I am? Your little fetch-it boy?*

"Please," I added. "And make it two."

One brow arched. "You think I'm going to dig?"

"I was hoping."

"You do know I can simply make the earth move, Mac. Even as a mere druid, I had that much skill. What do you want moved?"

"Silly me," I said dryly. I'd not even considered that Christian *was* the *Bewitched* I'd teased Barrons about being. Truth was, I'd rather been looking forward to some physical labor. That damn steam I needed to burn off.

"Come on," I said, sighing. "The cemetery's this way."

"Great. A bloody cemetery," he said, and matched my sigh. "I'm never going to get away from Death."

There were no flowers on my sister's grave. My town puts plastic bouquets everywhere in the cemetery, which is attractive from a distance but I always thought was kind of gruesome close up. Embalmed blossoms for embalmed people.

I paused at the foot of her grave and closed my eyes. It was over a year ago I'd stood here in the pouring rain, matching it tear for drop, trying to make sense of my life, trying to envision a future—any kind of future—for myself without her.

If I'd known back then how much worse it was going to get, I might have stretched on her grave and never gotten up.

I opened my eyes and read the inscription on her headstone, although I had no need. My parents had been too distraught to think, nodding blankly as all their friends murmured sadly and too many times to count, while clutching their children close, *No parent should outlive their child.*

I'd made all the funeral decisions.

Alina McKenna Lane. Beloved Daughter and Sister. And beneath it, in flowing calligraphy: *If love could have saved you, you would have lived forever.*

Beside me, Christian snorted. "You want to dig up your sister's grave?"

"Yes," I said flatly.

"Why, lass?"

"I want to see her body."

"That's twisted, even for you."

"Says the man who's stalking his uncle's corpse. You said you could move the dirt. Can you raise her casket?" I glanced around the cemetery. "And somehow glamour us so those people walking over there, staring at us, don't see what we're doing?"

"Bloody hell, you better find me solid information on my uncle, Mac."

"Do all Fae get testy when humans ask them to perform minor tasks?"

"I'm not Fae," he growled, and moved to stand beside me.

"Ow!" I snapped. "What did you just do?" I'd felt a sharp tug on my hair, as if a cluster of strands had been yanked out at the roots.

"Sorry, lass. My wings. I'm not always certain where they are. Looks like some of that red stuff in your hair is still sticky."

I rubbed my head where it stung. I didn't feel any paint.

Then I forgot all about my hair when the ground in front of me began to tremble and churn, as if something enormous was rising from the bowels of the earth. It shook and shivered and dirt poured up and tumbled away from the burial plot as the casket emerged from the ground.

Christian was pretty darned handy.

"I don't know why you're bothering, Mac," he said irritably.

"I need to see that she's dead."

He gave me a strange look with those strange eyes. "There's nothing dead in there, lass."

"I *put* something dead in there," I snapped. "And it had damn well better still be there."

"Whatever." He shrugged.

When the casket settled next to the gaping hole in the earth, I stepped close and ran my hands over the lid.

Cool wood. My sister's home now.

I dusted it lovingly, brushing away clods of dirt.

Months ago I'd stood with Christian near another casket, both determined to open it and dreading it, just like today. But that had been a coffin of ice, containing the concubine/Seelie queen.

This casket was mortal, not Fae. I remembered the day I'd chosen it, the fancy one with the elaborate inlaid burl, the elegant pin-striped cream silk. Funny how you obsessed over funeral details when you lost someone you loved, as if they might somehow see all the care you were putting into the last things you would ever be able to do for them. I'd chosen the one with the many hidden compartments, into which I tucked treasure after treasure, so she could take them out in Heaven and smile. I know, foolish to an extreme. Assuming there was a Heaven and assuming she went, I highly doubted the coffin went, too. It had been a time of madness. It had cost a fortune. I hadn't cared. Only the best for Alina.

I remembered closing the lid myself, I'd even insisted on turning the crank to seal it. I'd tucked the key into my pocket for some absurd reason. As if I might someday visit her, dig her up, and talk to her or something. That key was in a jewelry box in my bedroom, a mile away.

"I need you to break the seal," I told Christian. "Make it open."

The casket exhaled a soft plosive and the lid shifted slightly.

I stood there every bit as woodenly as I'd stood there a little over a year ago, feeling as cold and hard as her new home. Tears spilled from my eyes.

With shaking hands, I raised the embossed upper panel of the casket.

I shouldn't have been surprised.

By this time I'd thought myself beyond all surprise.

There was nothing inside.

I'd lost my sister.

Now I'd lost her corpse, too.

15

"I came to explore the wreck.
The words are purposes, the words are maps . . ."

I stalked into Chester's in a shit of a mood, leaving Christian at the Sinatra club with yet another whiskey in his hand. He'd declined my invitation to join our meeting. Said he had more immediate problems than the fate of the world and he was sure we'd figure it out, considering how controlling and micromanaging Ryodan was about everything he owned—and as he believed he owned the entire world and everything in it, and could play with it all like his personal chess set—the bastard would surely find a way to patch things up to his liking. He'd added that at least we were now both in the same boat, with missing corpses, and maybe I should ask Ryodan about mine.

I wasn't sure who was pissier, him or me. He was certainly more loquacious about it.

I pushed through the crowd, grateful for the first time that Chester's was off the grid in terms of morality and legality. Although many eyes in the crowd observed me with shock and a good bit of fear, no one tried to mess with me.

I was almost sorry about that.

My sister's casket was empty.

I knew for a fact that I'd buried her.

I knew for a fact it was her.

I knew every inch of my sister. The barely-there stretch marks on the sides of her hips that she'd hated whenever she wore a bathing suit after having lost twenty-five pounds rapidly when she caught mono, then gaining it back again. The birthmark so similar to mine. The funny shape of her second toe, longer than the big one. The fingernail on her right hand that never grew right because she'd gotten her finger slammed in a car door and the nail had darkened with a blood blister and fallen off.

I'd buried Alina.

If I hadn't, nothing in my entire existence was certain.

I slapped my palm to the wall of Ryodan's office and stormed in.

"Ms. Lane," Barrons said.

"I need to talk to you," I snapped. "Alone. Now."

Ryodan said, "We're having a meeting—"

"I. Don't. Give a damn." I said to Barrons, "Now." I forced myself to add, "Please?"

He was on his feet before I even added the please. I turned and stormed back out, down the stairs, through the club, feeling him behind me all the way. I stopped only when I reached the corridor that led to the server's wing. Then I spun sharply to face him. "Do you know where there's a private closet?" I demanded with a touch of hysteria.

"I'm not sure I know the difference between a private closet and a public one, Ms. Lane," he said dryly.

"Someplace there are no bloody cameras!"

He went motionless, swept my body with that dark, inscrutable gaze, and the shape of his mouth changed. "Ah, Ms. Lane, did you pull me out of there to fuck?"

"You bet your ass I did."

"Bloody hell. I don't know what happened to you—"

"I don't want to talk about it! Are you going to cooperate or not?" I snarled.

"—but goddamn, woman. I like you this way."

He shoved me back against a wall, palmed open a door I hadn't even noticed, backed me in, spun me around, and crushed me against the wall, kicking the door shut behind us.

Then my jeans were down and he was inside me with a rough growl, and I was ready for him because I'm always ready for him, pushing deep and hard, and I was flattened against the wall with my hands over my head, shoving back with my ass, and that was all I needed to find a lifeline, to connect, to remain sane.

When we returned to Ryodan's office, I felt remarkably better. I could think again. I wasn't a raw mass of pain and confusion and fear. I'd dumped all that on Barrons's big hard body. I'd turned the savagery I was feeling toward myself and the world on him. I'd nipped and fought and fucked and cleansed.

God, I love that man.

He'd understood exactly what I was doing. No words. No discussion. No pointless questions or offering of empty platitudes about whatever was bothering me.

He'd assessed.

I was pain and violence.

He'd given his body as a Band-Aid for the wound.

I suspected there would be times he would seek the same from me, and I made a promise to myself in that wonderful, fantastic, lovely closet that if I ever sensed in him what I felt myself tonight, I'd rise to his need as willingly and intensely as he'd risen to mine.

He'd taken and given, encouraged and incited . . . and finally soothed my wildness.

Sex is so damned healing.

"Better?" Ryodan said dryly after we walked back in.

My hair was a mess. Barrons's shirt collar was askew. And Ryodan never missed a trick.

"Much, thanks. You?" I said just as dryly.

"Not as good as you," he murmured, silver gaze cool.

"Where's Da—Jada and Dancer?" I said, looking around. I could smell that they'd recently been there. We must have just missed them.

"I saw no reason to waste their time simply because you were wasting mine."

I arched a brow. "And that means?"

"That he sent them off to do something else because he wants to talk to you without them around," Barrons said.

I stiffened, dropping my leg from the arm of the chair where I'd tossed myself in a fairly relaxed position. Sat up straight and folded my arms. Ryodan wanting to talk to me in semiprivate is never a good thing. Private would worry the hell out of me.

"We need to talk about the *Sinsar Dubh*, Mac," said Ryodan.

I blew out a gusty sigh. Recent sex aside, this was not turning out to be a banner day in Dublin. "What about it?" I was irritable all over again.

"Dancer has a theory. He thinks the Hoar Frost King inadvertently deposited the components of a Song of Destruction. He thinks the only thing that will stop the black holes from taking over this world entirely is a Song of Making."

That made two of us. I said nothing.

"The *Sinsar Dubh* allegedly contains parts of that song."

"Allegedly," I underscored. "The truth is, none of us know a damn thing about the Book. It's all legend and myth and supposition."

"Which is precisely why we need you to tell us what's

actually in it. Unless you'd rather we try Cruce," Ryodan said evenly.

Surely not even Ryodan was arrogant enough to try to interrogate Cruce in his prison. "You think you could question a psychopathic Book?"

"I suspect that's not what he is."

"What do you mean?"

"In the past, the Book possessed whoever touched it. That's not what happened with him. He knew the First Language and was able to read it. The spells traveled up his arms, into his body. Did you ever see that happen before when someone handled it?"

I shook my head. It had always seized control of the person, taken them over completely. Never had the Book itself been destroyed.

Yet only a thin pile of gold dust and a handful of red, winking gemstones had remained of the *Sinsar Dubh* on the slab.

"The sentient Book crumbled once he was finished. Legend holds there are two parts to the *Sinsar Dubh*. A Book of words, spells on a page. And a second facet, the thing that evolved into a living, intelligent, hate-obsessed being with far more power than the words it contained. It appeared the sentient *Sinsar Dubh* was destroyed that night, and Cruce merely absorbed the knowledge."

"Oh, God," I breathed. "You could be right." That prick. Had he gotten all the power without any of the price? That would make him pretty much . . . well, nearly the Unseelie king. I narrowed my eyes. "We don't know that for certain."

"But if it's true, we wonder if you could do the same."

"Can you tell us anything, Ms. Lane?" Barrons said.

I swiveled my head to look at him. I'd been "Mac" mere minutes ago. "Why do you do that?"

His eyes said, *Do you really want to call me Jericho?*

I thought about it a minute and was rather startled to realize I didn't. Jericho was . . . intimate. Jericho and Mac were a completely different entity than Ms. Lane and Barrons. They existed in a different place. A freer environ, a sacred one. And I liked that difference. I nodded, smiling faintly. His dark eyes gleamed with something appreciative, and I practically preened.

You continue to evolve, his eyes said. *Keep fucking me instead of worrying.*

"Tell me about the Book," Ryodan said. "I want to understand how it's in you."

I sighed and tried to figure out how to explain it. "I've got this place inside me. I don't know how to say quite where, I think it must be in my head. It's a deep, glassy black lake but it's more than that, too. There are caverns and pebbled shores. Who knows, maybe I've got a whole bloody country inside me. I think the lake is my *sidhe*-seer place. But it was altered by something else inside me and now it's . . . different. If there were boundaries, I can't tell where they are anymore."

"The Book," Ryodan said.

I looked at Barrons. I don't know why. Maybe just to make sure he was there, as he'd been there the single time I dived to the bottom of my dark glassy lake and beheld the *Sinsar Dubh* in all its shining, tempting glory. Just in case talking about it made it do something evil, I wanted to know he was nearby.

"It's there," I said peevishly. "At the bottom of the lake. But I have to swim all the way down to get to it. It's in a black cavern, on a pedestal. Closed." I glared at him. "For good reason." I'd closed it that afternoon, months ago with Barrons. Whumped it firmly shut.

"Have you gone inside your head and looked at it recently," said Ryodan.

"Nope." Not about to either. Knowing my luck, it would be open to an extremely useful spell that I'd begin to think I might want, or need, or possibly not be able to live without.

"I want you to," Ryodan said.

"Are you on board with this?" I fired at Barrons.

His dark eyes flashed. *We all have our inner beasts.*

And you think you can manage mine? I shot back.

I think I do a damn fine job. Images of what we'd just done surfaced in his eyes.

That's different.

We control ours. It took time.

How much time?

We made mistakes, was all he said.

You want me to look.

I want this world. I want you. It may be the only way. I see no other alternatives at present. If there's a way inside you to stop the black holes from destroying Earth, we need it.

I want you. Those three simple words. They undo me. Melt me. Forge me into steel stronger than I am. Barrons's belief in me is pure titanium.

Over millennia, searching for the spell to free my son, I never once caught wind of anything reputed to contain part of the Song of Making aside from the Book I hunted.

Millennia, he'd said. Barrons had lived for thousands of years. It was one thing to suspect it, another to hear him admit it. My lover was thousands of years old. I was twenty-three. No wonder we had issues.

I frowned, recalling something else I knew about that might be of use to us now. A thing I'd seen in the White Mansion when I was hunting with Darroc for the Silver back to Dublin.

But I'd been stoically refusing to think about it ever since I realized what I had inside me, unwilling to let my inner beast catch wind of it, if it hadn't already.

I sighed. "I'll take a look. But if I go batshit crazy down there, don't say I didn't warn you."

"Go?" Ryodan said, his inflection clearly implying he thought I was already there.

I wrinkled my nose at him. "If I'm going to do this, I need a drink first."

"I'll have one sent up," Ryodan said. "Name your poison."

"I want to get it myself," I said coolly, aware I was only trying to stave off the inevitable. But I wanted to walk somewhere of my own volition, feel alive and free for a few more minutes before I risked body and soul.

"We'll all get one," he said, pushing up from behind his desk.

When I walked down the chrome and glass stairs with Barrons on my left, Ryodan on my right, I could have been slain by the daggers of envy shot my way, from every subclub below.

If only they knew.

I would have opted for the Sinatra club but Ryodan saw Christian looming darkly at the bar and steered us away.

To the kiddie subclub where Jo worked, wearing a short, kicky plaid skirt, white blouse, and baby doll heels, looking pretty, her short dark hair highlighted with gold and blond. She came to wait on us with a wary look when Ryodan gestured, but he only ordered three glasses of Macallan, Rare Cask, with the blandest of expressions. As she hurried away to fill the order, I sensed a stir in the crowd on the dance floor.

I looked around, trying to decide what was causing it, and realized the crowd was parting for some reason, allowing someone or something's passage.

Jo deposited two fingers of rare cask scotch in front of

me. I picked it up, swirled it and sipped appreciatively. I watched, waiting, and finally a woman came into view, heads turning as she passed.

Jada.

Abso-frigging-lutely stunning in a red dress and heels. Bare-legged, hair scraped back high from that beautiful face, ponytail nearly brushing her ass as she walked. Her skin was smooth and creamy, her face smoother, her eyes flashing banked heat. I could make out Dancer's head behind her, taller than her, even with her wearing heels. Unlike one of the Nine, he wasn't shadowing her every move, using his body to lead and block. He merely walked with her.

Dani was all grown up, wearing a dress that fit her like a second skin. And that walk! Graceful, long-legged power and heat. Awareness that she was gorgeous.

Dani didn't swagger anymore.

She strutted. She prowled. She stalked, owning the ground she walked on.

And she was setting the men on fire as she passed. Humans and Fae alike watched her go, coveting, lusting. She shined. Even though she wasn't our Dani anymore, there was something utterly brilliant about her, almost luminous. Oh, there was still fire within. I'd bet my sanity on it. Well, wait, that wasn't necessarily a solid bet. I'd bet my right arm.

She wasn't oblivious to the attention. She simply didn't care.

I glanced at Ryodan. I don't know why. I guess I'm always mining for gold where there is none. His face was as smooth as Jada's.

But those eyes, those cool silver eyes, were flashing with a similar banked heat. He looked up. Down. Up again. Lingered. Then sharply away.

I thought for a moment Jada and Dancer were coming

to see us but they detoured and went right instead of straight.

"Odd way to dress for an investigation," Barrons murmured.

"She's not Dani anymore," Ryodan clipped.

"Would you rather she had on jeans and sneakers?" I said.

"I'd rather she had on a fucking suit of armor," Ryodan said coolly.

And a chastity belt, if I could read the look in a man's eyes. And I could. "She's a woman, Ryodan," I said softly. "Get used to it. Dancer was right. We need to accept her."

"Don't tell me what to get used to, Mac. I'm the one that breaks all the rules, remember."

I stared at him.

"This morning, with Christian at the abbey, you were thinking about when you watched us down in the dungeon. You were in my office, watching my monitors."

"Stay the hell out of my head!" I barked. Or had there been a roach or three, lurking beneath his desk, reporting back?

"Don't give it away so easily. You saw the forbidden."

"You *did* the forbidden," I said flatly. "And believe me, I keep quiet about a *lot* of things I see."

He looked at Barrons. "She knows about the Highlander."

Barrons said, "Yet said nothing and could have."

"Did *you* skim it from my head, too?" I asked Barrons sourly.

"I accord you greater respect. And henceforth, Ryodan will, too." It was a warning.

Ryodan said to me, "If you turn invisible again, I'll ward you from my club. Permanently." To Barrons, he said, "I'll break as many rules as you do, brother."

I supposed he also knew somehow that I was aware

they were brothers, since he was no longer hiding it from me.

None of us said anything then. I sipped my drink and glanced back at Jada, but she was gone. "Speaking of the Highlander," I couldn't help but meddle, "you should tell Christian. He may be able to help." I should have left it there, because the only thing that would motivate Ryodan was if there was something in it for him, but I couldn't help adding, "Besides, it's his family. He deserves to know."

"Be wise, Mac. Never mention to me that you know again."

"Fine," I said irritably. Then, "Shit!" The Alina-thing was on the dance floor, turning in a circle, standing tall as if to peer over the sea of heads. Looking for someone. Looking as distraught and worried as she had the first time I'd seen her. Looking as if she'd been crying her eyes out. Looking so achingly like my sister that I wanted to burst into tears myself.

Beside me, Barrons tensed. I glanced at him. He was staring where I'd been staring.

"That woman looks like she could be your sister, Ms. Lane."

He could see the Alina-thing, too?

I was so flabbergasted for a moment that I couldn't draw breath to speak. "Wait, how do you know what my sister looks like?"

"Your albums. The photo you put in your parents' mailbox, Darroc later hung on my door."

Ah, I'd forgotten about that.

"Perhaps a Fae throwing a glamour?" he said, assessing me.

I hadn't thought of that. If he could see her, too . . . well, I'd positively cotton to the idea if I hadn't opened an empty casket in Ashford earlier today.

But . . . maybe it was a Fae and the same Fae had

stolen her body just to play some kind of sick trick on me. Both Seelie and Unseelie could cast flawless glamour. And so long as I had Unseelie flesh in me, I couldn't use my *sidhe*-seer senses to see past it.

Well, damn. That was a darned plausible explanation.

Except, I realized glumly, the first night I'd seen the illusion had been before I'd partaken of forbidden fruit.

I had no idea what to think.

Barrons could see my illusion.

Did Ryodan see it, too? I turned to look at him. He was staring directly at her. "Lovely woman," he murmured.

"Stay away from her," I snapped before I could stop myself. Whatever this thing was, I simply wouldn't be able to stand seeing Ryodan get it on with something that looked like my sister. "I mean," I added hastily, "because we have more important things to do."

"You made time for it."

"A Fae?" Barrons prompted again. Prompting was an unusual demonstration of interest on his part. Uh-oh.

"Who knows? Could be." I shrugged. "Then again, don't they say everyone has a doppelganger somewhere?"

Barrons gave me a level look. *Something you want to talk about?*

Nope. Not a thing, I said lightly.

Another thing I love about the man: he dropped it. That was going to be a hard favor for me to return when it was time.

"I assume you're ready to look in that lake," Ryodan said, tossing back the last of his drink.

I was only too happy to escape the apparently visible-by-all illusion on the dance floor before we collided again, further wrecking my tenuous grasp on reality. Alina was dead. I knew it in my bones. I knew it with utter and complete certainty. And if she wasn't dead, nothing I thought I knew could be trusted. Not one damn thing. Easier to turn away from the illusion than confront it.

I tossed back my drink and stood.

Why not? I thought acerbically. Could things get any worse?

16

"What a tangled web we weave when first we practice to deceive . . ."

I should never think that.

I know better.

Still, I persist, and every damned time the universe seizes the challenge on bullish horns, stomps its hoof, and snorts, "Hey, MacKayla Lane just said she doesn't think things can get worse. We'll show *her*!"

Ryodan took us to the dungeon level I'd glimpsed yesterday on his office monitors. Not to Dageus's cell but to a small stone room down a narrow passageway.

I trailed my fingers along the cool damp stone of the corridor, skimming a marbling of brightly colored moss on the walls. Apart from the nearly iridescent algae staining a strangely luminous skein on the stone, it was gloomy, gray, and cold in the subterranean chamber.

I despise being underground. I wondered if anyone was with Dageus or if they'd left him alone to deal with his transformation. Although I listened intently, I heard no sound, no anguished baying, no tortured groans.

"Uh, Barrons, why are we in the dungeon?" I asked, looking around for ancient manacles bolted into the stone or something of the like, perhaps an iron maiden or a few bloodstained racks.

"Precaution. Nothing more. If you go, as you call it, batshit crazy, there are fewer people to kill down here."

"I'd still leave through the club." Meaning I could still destroy everyone within it. "Maybe we should go out into the middle of a field. Far from any town."

He slanted me a look. *You're not going to lose it. You're not going to open the Book tonight. We merely want to get the lay of your inner landscape.*

I heaved an audible sigh of relief. "Then let's get on with it." I shot Ryodan a look as he closed us in the narrow stone cell. "Since you know I know everything, what the heck is the deal with Kat and Kasteo?"

"Another thing a wiser woman wouldn't mention."

"I'm only mentioning it to *you*, not anyone else," I said. "So, what gives?"

He kicked a straight-backed chair toward me. "Sit."

I clamped my mouth shut on *I prefer to stand*. No point in wasting energy just to vent my dissatisfaction with the current state of my life on everyone around me.

I sat. After a moment I let my lids flutter closed, although I didn't need to. I remembered all too well, during that time I'd been a darker version of myself, letting my eyes go only slightly out of focus to drift into the place of power I called my dark glassy lake. Scooping up runes floating on the surface, power I'd naïvely believed my birthright, some part of my *sidhe*-seer heritage, only to learn they'd been temptations strewn by the *Sinsar Dubh*, gifts to seduce and entice.

Never mine at all.

I wondered, for perhaps the first time with my intellect, precisely where my inner lake actually was. Talking about it to Ryodan made me perceive it differently. Instead of seeming normal, I'd found it peculiar.

Why did I have a lake inside me? Did every *sidhe*-seer? Was it simply my chosen visualization of an inner power source, different for all of us? With constant calamity around me, I'd never gotten time to sit down with the sisters of my bloodline to ask questions, compare notes.

I frowned. Now that I'd added my brain to the mix, trying to pinpoint the metaphysical coordinates of my dark glassy lake—as if I might establish some quantum latitude and longitude—was difficult. The place proved abruptly elusive.

I inhaled deep, exhaled slow, willing myself to relax. *Sink, sink, don't think,* I murmured in my mind.

Nothing.

Not even a puddle in sight anywhere.

I opened my eyes, thinking I needed to refocus and try again. Barrons gave me a look. "Hang on," I said, "give me a minute."

"Don't play games with me, Mac," Ryodan warned.

"I'm not," I said. "It's not easy. I've spent months trying to stay away from the place and now you expect me to dive right in. I've trained myself to never even *think* about it." Although I didn't always succeed.

Letting my gaze shift slightly out of focus, I mentally envisioned a giant lake, glassy and deep. I paid careful attention to the details, the pebbled shore, the faint light from what seemed to be a distant sky. I lavished attention on the sleek black surface. Told myself I couldn't wait to swim, climbed up on a large rock, and when I'd gotten the scene exactly right, closed my eyes, leapt into the air, and dove.

I crashed into the ground, hard.

Not one bloody drop of water anywhere.

"Fuck," I snapped, rubbing my head. It hurt, as if I'd actually hit a rock with it. And my arms felt bruised. I looked at Barrons. "I can't find it."

"Try again," Ryodan ordered.

I did.

And again.

And again and again.

Driving us all crazy with repeated failure.

"You're too tense," Ryodan growled. "For fuck's sake, you don't stalk an orgasm, you enjoy its arrival."

"Bloody talk about bloody orgasms with your own bloody woman, not mine," Barrons said tightly. "You don't know a thing about her orgasms and never will."

Ryodan shot him a dark look. "It was a metaphor."

"I never stalk an orgasm. I don't have to with Barrons," I said.

"Too the fuck much information, Mac," Ryodan said.

"You're the one who brought up orgasms."

"And he never will again," Barrons said pointedly.

"Everybody shut up. I'm trying to concentrate." Now I was thinking about orgasms. I considered Ryodan's advice. Maybe I *was* trying too hard.

An hour later I was dripping sweat, my head was pounding, and my arms felt like I'd been delivering karate chops to brick walls.

"I can't get there," I finally said wearily. "I don't know why."

Ryodan regarded me through narrowed eyes. "You said you thought it was a *sidhe*-seer place."

I inclined my head, waiting.

"Barrons said you ate—"

"Aha! Unseelie flesh!" I pounced on the excuse, enormously relieved. "So it *is* a *sidhe*-seer place and that's why I can't find it! I can't possibly see my lake right now!" I'd begun to fear the *Sinsar Dubh* was so quiet of late because it had been stealthily rearranging my internal furniture, hiding things I might want to use, planting booby traps. Could it do that?

Ryodan rolled his eyes. "Outstanding. Meet Mac, the junkie."

"I am not."

"How many times have you eaten it in the past week," he demanded.

"Twice. But I *had* to the first time because I was going down the cliff, and the Guardians were shooting at me the second time," I defended.

"I'm sure you'll 'have to' the next time, too."

"I am *not* an addict."

"How the bloody hell long does the high last anyway," Ryodan growled.

I shrugged. "Dunno exactly. Three days or so. I should be myself again in a couple of days." Immensely irritable and tired but myself.

He looked at Barrons. "Don't let her eat it again."

"She makes her own decisions," he said. But he shot me a look: *We need information, Ms. Lane. I would prefer you refrain for a time.*

Great. One of my two ball-fortifying techniques that were keeping me strong—sex with Barrons and eating Unseelie flesh—was now lost.

I was just thinking what an anticlimactic night this was turning out to be when Ryodan opened the door.

Christian MacKeltar stood on the other side.

17

"Knows everybody's disapproval,
I should've worshipped her sooner . . ."

Three hours earlier . . .

Jada didn't have to wear the red dress.

It was a choice.

Men on every planet, in every realm, Fae or human, shared inherent characteristics.

They didn't like to kill a beautiful woman.

At first.

They wanted other things. At first.

Beauty was one of many weapons.

It was why she'd abandoned her ragged haircut to grow it long again. But curly and wild, it had been far too easy for an opponent to grab a fistful, a liability in any battle. She'd learned to scrape it back, high, out of her face. Sometimes tuck a low braid into the collar of her shirt.

She didn't have to dance either.

That, too, was a choice.

But when she walked into Chester's, one of the Nine caught her eye across the dance floor and beckoned with such in-your-face enthusiasm and happiness to see her that she couldn't resist.

Lor.

The man was a beast. A primitive caveman who loved being what he was. Blunt, blatantly sexual, with a voracious appetite for rock and roll, brawls, and hot blondes, he was prone to proposition a woman by saying, "Hey, wanna fuck?" and scored a ridiculous amount of the time with his Viking good looks and that hint of something dirty-kinky-raw just beneath the surface, locked, loaded, and ready to blast a woman's inhibitions to dust.

They'd had something when she was younger.

Not *that* kind of something.

A bond that had been innocent yet knowing. An awareness that they were two people who were precisely what they were, no apologies, no excuses.

He'd appreciated who she'd been then, and from the look on his face, he was willing to appreciate her now.

He'd once brought her steak and potatoes. Had trailed her, making sure she stayed safe. He'd offered advice the night Ryodan dragged her off, after she'd defied him and slaughtered half the patrons in one of his subclubs. Helped her escape the room upstairs when the boss locked her in.

He'd encouraged her impulsiveness and belligerence, and for that reason alone, she should avoid him. She'd turned her back on those character flaws years ago.

But the music was seductive and the song playing was one of her favorites, and despite the icy facade she projected, she knew the heat she had inside. She didn't deny it. Denying would have made her weaker.

Heat was strength. It was resilience. She channeled it, shaped it into purpose, like everything else.

Sexuality, too, was power.

Lor moved toward her, pushing through the crowd, completely ignoring the many hot blondes looking his way, his grin wide and only for her.

She approached him, allowing herself a faint smile. They met in the middle of the dance floor.

"Hey, kid," he purred. "Looking good, honey. Nice to see you back."

"You, too, Lor." She could count on two fingers those who'd been happy to see her.

"Fuck, I always look good. I was born looking good. Dance?"

With Hozier inviting his lover to take him to church, she moved into Lor's body with effortless grace, following the tempo of his hips, the muscle of his powerful torso. He danced from the groin, as most powerful, centered men did, easy to match.

On one of the worlds she'd briefly visited, nature itself had danced, sinuous vines, draping from trees, moving to a rhythm she'd not been able to hear. At first she was wary, regarding them as threats, but after nearly a week on that world, she'd seen a slender trailing plant heal a wounded animal with its dance.

And one night, under three full moons, she'd taken off her clothes and gone native, pretended to be part of the vegetation, imitating the sensual undulations until she finally found the rhythm with her body.

It had healed her, too. The wounds on her back had closed, expelling the infection, leaving only scars.

Now, she half closed her eyes and followed the lead of Lor's hips, dropped her head back, arched her neck, and gave herself over completely to the music. The body had needs that couldn't be ignored. It needed to run, to fight, to eat, to breathe, to move. There were other needs, too, which now that she was back on this world, surrounded by so many people with complicated feelings, had been making their presence known. She wasn't yet ready to deal with them.

Nothing, no one, had touched her for a long time. It

was difficult to process Lor's body so close to hers, moving in tandem with her own.

So she pretended he was a vine and she was dancing in a great, dark forest, safer than most places because there were no upright creatures on that world, and the dance was only for her, to let her soul breathe, to revel in being alive one more day. In her mind, moonlight kissed her skin, a gentle, fragrant breeze rippled her hair. Abandoned to the moment, the beat, the freedom of thinking no further ahead or back than now.

"Aw, honey, keep dancing like that, you're gonna get me killed," Lor said close to her ear.

"I doubt that," she said dryly.

"Figure it's worth dying for. If only to get off on the look on that fuck's face."

She didn't dissemble. Didn't ask who. She knew who, and he knew she did. Lor was a hammer. He called it like he saw it, pounded words like nails into conversation and didn't care what anyone thought of him. "And what is the look on 'that fuck's face'?" she murmured. "He's behind me. I can't see him."

Lor laughed and spun them so she could see Ryodan standing on the edge of the dance floor, tall, powerful, dressed in dark slacks and a white shirt, sleeves rolled back, cuff glinting. Watching, thunderclouds in his eyes.

Once she'd seen him laugh.

Once she'd watched him fuck. A lifetime ago.

Their eyes locked. He took two steps toward her and she flared her nostrils, cut him a cool look.

He stopped.

Lor slid an arm around her waist, turned her away.

"Then why didn't he find me?" she said. She wanted to know how hard he'd searched. How he'd reacted. If he'd mounted a rescue and how extensive it had been.

She'd had no one to ask that wouldn't promptly report back to him.

Lor wouldn't carry the tale. They'd shared secrets in the past.

"Aw, kid, he tried. As soon as he heard you were missing. We didn't know you were gone for a coupla weeks. Mac didn't tell Ryodan right away."

Jada cultivated fluidity, resisting the urge to tense. "Mac didn't tell you right away that I went into the hall?"

Lor shook his head.

She was momentarily breathless. She'd believed they were all out hunting for her. Worrying. Moving mountains to find her. She'd waited. Living by WWRD: What Would Ryodan Do.

"Boss said Mac was chompin' at the bit to go after you but Barrons vetoed it. Said if she followed you through you'd just keep running."

True, she acknowledged. She'd been running as if the hounds of Hell were on her heels that night, determined to outrun everything, especially herself. She wouldn't have stopped if Mac had followed her. She'd have leapt into the nearest mirror in the hall. But truth, the pernicious bitch, didn't make her feel better. "Why didn't she tell Ryodan?"

"Dunno. You gotta ask her that. But, honey, it's not like those two get along real well. They sure weren't spending any time together. Maybe she was giving you time to find your way out. Maybe she had her own problems."

Jada did the math. She'd been gone five and a half years and they hadn't even started looking for her until two weeks *after* she'd gotten back. She'd spent those weeks coldly combing the country, amassing her wandering army of *sidhe*-seers who'd come to Dublin for one reason or another, inspiring their loyalty with her strength and laser focus, implementing the plans she'd made wandering through Hell, trying to figure out how to regain what she'd lost by coming home. Years that felt like centuries had passed for her. It had been a single week for those she'd counted friends.

She closed her eyes, finding her center. The place where she felt no pain, only purpose. When she'd fixed herself firmly there, she opened her eyes, kissed Lor lightly on the cheek and thanked him for the dance.

Then she turned to find Ryodan, deliberately late for their meeting.

He was gone.

"I thought we were having a meeting," Jada said as she entered Ryodan's office.

"We are," he said, not taking his eyes from the monitor he was watching beyond her head.

"I'd hardly call the two of us a meeting."

"What would you call us?"

Us, he'd said. With interrogative inflection. As if there was an "us." Once, she'd thought them Batman and Robin, two superheroes, saving the world. "Was that a bona-fide question with proper punctuation?" she mocked.

"Dani needed things to fight. I was the logical choice. Even something so small as improper punctuation kept her distracted."

"What are you saying? That you're not really endlessly irritating—you just irritated me endlessly to keep me occupied?"

"No need to go hunting dragons when the one right next to you keeps yanking your chain. And you had so very many chains to yank back then."

She stared at him, but he still wasn't looking at her. That was exactly what he'd done, kept her racing from one thing to the next, provoking her so incessantly that even when she wasn't with him, she'd been fuming about how much he annoyed her, planning how to one-up him the next time.

Or impress him.

Get him to look at her with respect, admiration.

God, she'd hero-worshipped this man! Constructed endless fantasies around him.

He looked at her then. Sharply. Hard. And she belatedly remembered his ability to skim minds, hoped she hadn't thought that last part loud and on the top of her brain.

On the off chance she had, she tossed him something to throw him off course.

"I hated you," she said coolly.

"You were an explosion of unchecked desires."

"You were a complete void of them." Not always, though. Just around her.

"Now you're an implosion of repressed passion. Find the middle ground."

You're not the boss of me, rose to the tip of her tongue, and she bit it off so hard she drew blood, hating that a mere month in this world could unravel her so much, send her sliding down the slipperiest of slopes right back into who and how she'd once been.

"Never tell me how you think I should be," she said. "You don't know a thing about who I am now. You don't know what I lived through and you don't know the choices I had to make."

He inclined his head, waiting.

"Oh, that's not happening. I'm never going to tell you," she said.

"Never is a long time. I'll be here at the end of it." He stood up, reached in his drawer, pulled out an object, and offered it to her.

She arched a brow. "A phone?"

"I can't track you on other worlds. If you allow me to tattoo you again, and carry the phone always, you will never get lost anywhere I can't find you."

Lost. That was how she'd felt. So damned lost. She'd fallen off the face of her earth. The worlds had been so strange, many of them hostile, with so little food that she'd often had to crawl her way through a Silver to her next hope of a world, too hungry, too fevered, to have a whisper of a prayer of accessing the slipstream, Shazam hovering over her anxiously, cursing, weeping, for a novel change giving up his incessant predictions of doom, to urge her on. "You mean if I'd had this phone and hadn't cut off the tattoo . . ." she trailed off. "Even in the hall?"

"I'd have come for you the moment you called."

"Anywhere?"

"Yes."

"Without limitation at all?" She took pains to mask her incredulity. He was that powerful?

He inclined his head.

"Why the bloody hell didn't you give it to me back then?"

"Would you have carried it?"

Honesty with herself was now part of her spine, her fundamental structure. At fourteen, she'd carried her own cell only for the music and games. She'd have seethed at the mere idea of carrying a phone for Ryodan, considered it just one more way for him to track and control her, another chain draped around her shoulders by adults who didn't understand her—and she'd have laughed from the belly as she flung it in the trash. Then kicked the trash can for good measure and laughed some more.

"Let me tattoo you." He was silent a long moment then said, "Jada."

She went utterly still, not liking him this way, not

trusting this at all. He was being direct, noncaustic. Treating her as if she was exactly what she was—a woman who'd been through hell and made it back by sheer force of will and the skin of her teeth. He was calling her by her chosen name. Asking her to "allow" him to do something. No longer berating her for not being who he wanted her to be. Offering his protection. No longer jabbing at her or giving her anything to fight.

She didn't know how to deal with this man without fighting him. "No," she said.

"At least carry the phone."

She regarded it as if it were a snake that would bite her the instant she reached for it. "It's a little late to start worrying about me."

"I always worried about you."

The door behind her whisked open.

"Hey, guys." Dancer stepped in to join them. He looked at her, did a double take, and said, "Wow. You look amazing, Jada."

She felt suddenly nonplussed, a thing she'd not experienced in years. The faint heat of a blush was trying to stain her skin and she willed her capillaries to constrict and deny it. Once before Dancer had seen her in a skirt and heels, the night Ryodan made her change because her clothes smelled like Christian. She'd felt just as off-kilter with the way he'd looked at her then, with a soft stirring of butterflies in her stomach.

Sometimes she felt as split as they thought she was: a young girl hungry to spend time with a young man that was smart and good and real, a grown woman hungry for a grown man with edges sharp enough to cut herself on.

But hunger, like emotion, could drive a person to do stupid things. And the stupid didn't survive. "It's just a dress," she deflected.

"It's not the dress, Mega," Dancer said quietly. "It's the woman in it."

He smiled at her and she felt herself smiling faintly back. Mega. She should correct him. How young, how naïve, she'd been all those years ago.

She'd had a crush on Dancer. The older, brilliant boy-genius she'd idolized. She hadn't known what to do with it. Hadn't been ready for that kind of thing. She'd had so little childhood that she'd been determined to preserve what remained as long as possible. Sex was an irretrievable step into adulthood. She'd missed him in the Silvers. Had longed for his inventive, brilliant mind and way of making it seem it was the two of them against the world and that was more than enough, because they would win every battle.

She narrowed her eyes, studying him. He looked older now, especially without his glasses. He had beautiful eyes, flecked with every shade of green and blue, like a tropical sea, with thick, long dark lashes. And he was dressing differently than he used to. She was startled to realize he had a man's body beneath his jeans and leather jacket, a man's eyes. Perhaps he'd been dressing younger when she was young, matching her style. Perhaps her fourteen-year-old eyes simply hadn't been able to see the parts of him she'd not been ready to deal with.

She saw them now.

Ryodan dropped the phone back into the drawer and slid it shut. "I want the two of you to gather every bit of information you have on the anomalies and bring it by tomorrow evening."

"Already got it," Dancer said, waving a packet of papers. "Right here."

"I have other things to do tonight."

Jada looked at Ryodan but his gaze was shuttered, distant, as if they'd never spoken before Dancer had arrived.

"You said you had a current map of all the black holes," Jada said. "I want it."

"I'll have copies for you tomorrow night."

"Time is of the essence," she said coolly. Why didn't he want to give her the map? Because he didn't trust she'd come back once she had it?

Dancer said, "The first hole appeared more than two months ago, Jada. They're growing slowly. I can't see that another day will make much of a difference. Besides, the map isn't the most important thing. Knowing their location doesn't tell us how to fix them. I've been working on some other ideas about that."

"Out. Now," Ryodan said flatly.

Once, she would have insisted, argued, perhaps blasted up into the slipstream and raised a ruckus to get what she wanted. Or at least put on one hell of a show trying.

Now, she simply turned for the door, refusing to glance over her shoulder, although she could feel his gaze resting heavily on her.

Still, she heard Ryodan's voice inside her head as clearly as if he'd spoken aloud.

Change your mind, Jada. Don't be a fool. It won't cost you anything. Let me be your anchor. I'll never let you be lost again.

She'd always hated the doors in Chester's.

They couldn't be kicked open and they couldn't be slammed shut.

18

"Ruler of the frozen lands . . ."

I lied to Mac.

Fortunately she isn't capable of detecting lies as well as the Highlander/Fae prince/druid/lie detector that I am.

Besides, she'd been so obsessed with digging up her sister's empty grave that she'd scarcely paid any attention to my small theft. She'd shrugged off the momentary tug she felt at her scalp, embracing my glib excuse and forgetting it.

I know precisely how to sift to a human's location.

I need part of their physical person in my hand to track them, parting space like so many vines hanging from trees obscuring my vision as I isolate the hunted.

Such as the strands of paint-stained blond hair in the pocket of my jeans.

I know where her loyalties lie.

With Barrons.

With all of the Nine. Far more so than with me and my clan.

I don't judge her for that. I understand clan and she's chosen hers. Clan is necessary in times like these.

And so I played performing pony to get close enough

to yank out a few long strands of her hair, then sat at the bar and sipped my whiskey, patiently waiting for a sign that something was going on in the bowels of Chester's, wagering she was indeed in the innermost part of their circle.

Easier than trying to get some of *that* bastard's hair, which, frankly, I'm not sure would even work. Although I can truth-detect with the Nine, if I try to apprehend any one of them as a singular entity, they simply aren't there.

I know death intimately. I know life as well. The Nine register as neither. An hour ago, when Mac had risen, with Barrons and Ryodan flanking her, a severe expression on her face, I'd known something was afoot.

I'd sifted to follow her at a distance, wanting access but desiring not to be seen. I'd cloaked myself in glamour, spreading like moss along the walls, moss she'd touched, causing me to shiver. Moss that had peeled from the walls and coalesced once they entered the room at the far end of the corridor, re-forming as the Unseelie prince/Highlander that I am.

I'd stalked every inch of the dungeon, endless and sprawling. Empty. Utterly empty but for one corridor.

A false corridor.

A wall where in truth there was none. I could feel the invalidity of that stone barricade in every atom of my body.

Still, I couldn't penetrate it. The bastard had powerful wards, designed to repel both human and Fae, and I was both, therefore blocked.

I'd planned to storm the room into which they vanished, thinking perhaps my uncle's body was in that small cell and they were trying to perform some bizarre ritual with his potent druid remains.

It, too, was warded against Fae and human.

I stood outside, waiting for them to emerge with the long patience of an immortal.

Finally, the narrow door swung open.

"Where the fuck is my uncle?" I demanded.

Ryodan said coolly, "I already answered your questions, Highlander. As I'm sure you've seen, there's nothing down here."

I sifted his answer into grains: truth or lie. It told me nothing and made me wonder if somehow the prick had known I'd come hunting and deliberately left parts of the dungeon unguarded, wagering I wouldn't be able to detect the illusionary wall in the north corridor. "Your false wall. Tear it down. Then I'll believe you," I said.

Ryodan's eyes briefly flickered, and I knew I was right. For some reason, my uncle's body was behind that wall.

"Tear it down," I told him, "or I'll destroy every inch of this bloody nightclub, killing everyone within." I summoned the elements, drew them to me, beckoned like a lover, exhaled long and slow, and ice crackled down the walls, erupted on the floor, glazing the stone with thick, slippery black. "Then I'll bring thunder and fire from the sky and burn this place to ash."

Ryodan vanished.

I'd expected no less.

I sifted out, reappearing down the hall. Keeping a careful distance between us. The Nine can kill the Fae. No idea how. No plans to ever let one of them close enough to find out.

Ryodan vanished again.

I sifted and reappeared standing near Mac, with one arm around her throat. She twisted and kicked and growled. She was strong but I'm stronger. She smelled like me, and I knew she'd been eating my race again. I might have squeezed her neck a bit harder than I should have, but bloody hell, her cannibalism needs to stop.

"Let go of me!" she cried.

Barrons vanished.

I sifted out with a struggling Mac, reappeared in the air above them, wings open. "We can do this all bloody night," I said. One more sift and I'd vacate the club for a while. Let them stew in the juice of knowing I had Mac with me, beyond their reach.

Barrons snarled.

"You won't hurt Mac," Ryodan said.

"But I *will* destroy your club."

I dropped lightly to my feet and re-created what I'd watched Cruce do down in the cavern the night we'd interred the *Sinsar Dubh*. I'd felt his spell, absorbed the taste and texture of it, his methods. Gone seeking information in the king's old library. I'd only recently embraced my power. Now, I used it to erect an impenetrable wall around Mac and me. One I'd seen them fail repeatedly to breach, standing in the cavern below the abbey.

"Aye, you could kill me, if you could catch me," I acknowledged the unspoken threat blazing in both their dark gazes. "But you'll never touch me." I smiled faintly and without mirth.

Nor, likely, would anyone else. I hadn't risked fucking since the cliffs, fucking I needed like I needed to breathe. But I had no taste for killing another woman. Such things threatened my Highlander's heart, blackened it.

"Barrons," Mac said urgently, "forge an alliance. We don't want a war with Christian. You've pushed his back to the wall. The two of you would do no less than he's doing, under the same circumstances."

"Alliance, my ass," Ryodan clipped.

"She's right," I said. "We can be enemies or allies. Choose carefully."

Barrons looked at Ryodan. "He could be useful."

I snorted. "There will be many conditions if I agree to

be allies. The first is that you return my uncle's remains."

In my arms, Mac sighed and went supple. "I told you that you should *tell* him," she said to Ryodan.

I angled my head to look at her. "Tell me what?"

"I told them they should trust you. That you had a right to know."

Truth. I relaxed my grip on her and she straightened in my arms but didn't try to break free.

"You wouldn't have done what you did," Mac said to Ryodan pointedly, "if you hadn't been willing to live with the essential makeup of the one you did it to for a very long time. That, more than anything, is a testament to what you think of the Keltar clan. Trust Christian. Make him an ally, not an enemy. We have more than enough enemies out there already."

Ryodan looked at Mac for a long moment then smiled faintly. "Ah, Mac, sometimes you do surprise me."

"I take that as one hell of a compliment," she said dryly. "My point is, yes, you can keep trying to kick Christian's ass. Yes, you could hunt him and, if one day you catch him, kill him. You could all stalk around for a small eternity being the testosterone-laden brutes you all sometimes are."

Barrons and Ryodan shot her a nearly identical look of disgruntlement, and I laughed softly.

She ignored them. "But consider the power he has. Do you really want that turned against us? You, Ryodan, more than most, have the ability to clear a logical path through dense emotions. Think about the potential if you become allies. Think about the grand waste if you become enemies. Three incredibly powerful men stand in this corridor. If you want to brawl, make an alliance, *then* beat the shit out of each other. With limits. No killing. Ever."

Ryodan growled, "You fucking Highlanders. I knew the moment I laid eyes on you that you'd be trouble."

"Friend or foe?" I said.

Ryodan stared at me, unmoving for a long moment. Finally, "There are times I could use a sifter," he allowed.

"You think I would let you that close to me?" I snorted.

"For you to take someone like Dancer or Jada to inspect various places."

I inclined my head. That was easy enough. "There are times I may need assistance as well."

"Such as the cliff we just dragged your ass off of," Ryodan said flatly.

"See how well you've been working together already?" Mac said brightly.

"You will never speak of what you learn tonight," Barrons said.

"I won't agree to that," I said.

"Then destroy my club," Ryodan said coldly. "And I, and all my men, will hunt you until the end of time. Enemy or ally, Highlander. We'd make stupendous ones, either way."

"Pledge your alliance to me. Tell me you will never try to kill me. Say it," I demanded. So I could take fair measure of it. These were men of honor, in the same way I was. Corrupted as we are, there must be a solid core or we become the villains. If Ryodan spoke and it rang true, he would adhere to the letter of the law he'd chosen. As would I.

"I can't guarantee I can make that claim sound like truth," Ryodan warned. "There's a part of me that obeys no one and nothing. And if you focus on that part, no words of mine will ever sound like truth to you."

"Then we'll be enemies. I suggest you convince me."

Ryodan glanced at Barrons and they exchanged a long look. Then Ryodan glanced away as if consummately chafed. "We are allies," he said.

"And we will protect each other and fight together against common foes. Say it."

He repeated it coolly.

I waited.

He looked at me, I at him. I wasn't asking. He knew what I wanted.

"And we will never turn on each other." His words dripped ice. It didn't matter. He'd said them.

I looked at Barrons, who then repeated the same. Both of their voices held the knell of a sacred pledge. Smacked of truth.

Sauntering close to the walls I'd thrown up, locking gazes with me, Ryodan said with silky menace, "And we will guard each other's secrets as our own."

Fucker, I thought. But I knew he'd not seal the alliance without it. And I knew we'd be at an impasse forever if I didn't. Truth was, I preferred them as allies, not enemies. The Unseelie sure as hell didn't have my back.

Barrons echoed it.

"Now you, Mac," I said.

She looked at me, startled, but repeated the entire oath.

I said it with her. All the way through. Right down to guarding each other's secrets as our own. Then I withdrew a blade and cut my wrist.

Barrons and Ryodan exchanged another of those inscrutable glances.

"Blood," I demanded. "Yours with mine. It's a pact ancient and binding, made to an Unseelie prince."

"He's one demanding fuck," Ryodan murmured to Barrons.

Barrons said to me, "Magic doesn't bind us."

"I've heard some does," I said. I'd caught wind of Lor

getting chained up by the Unseelie princess in Ryodan's office.

Barrons gave me a dark-edged smile that disturbed me more than a little. "Have you any bloody idea what you're doing, Highlander?"

"I've no doubt sharing blood with the two of you will screw with me in ways unimaginable and uncounted. Nevertheless, we're doing it." I dropped my walls and released Mac. Moved forward slowly.

The four of us came together in the middle of the corridor, meeting warily.

Only when each of us had smears of all of our blood mixed together on our arms, above an open vein, Mac, too—and she was a bit of a challenge, as quickly as she kept healing—did I relax.

I could see the magic of our sworn oath shimmering on the air around us. Performed properly, by a high druid, oaths have enormous power. It wasn't just the Unseelie blood in me they should worry about.

Barrons was at Mac's side, shooting me a killing look that said clearly, *Never threaten my woman again.*

Those two. Christ.

"Come." Ryodan turned and walked away.

I followed him to the north corridor, my wings canted up behind me, so not to have my feathers serve as a bloody broom and attract every bit of dust and slosh of ice on the floor.

At the wall that wasn't a wall but had been as impenetrable as those of the Unseelie prison, Ryodan stopped and pressed his hands to the air, as if there were indeed a surface there. He murmured softly, touching various places, then traced runes in the air.

A corridor was revealed before us.

From the far end, terrible sounds echoed.

I stiffened. What the bloody hell was down there? But I held my tongue and trod in silence, boots echoing on the stone floors, barely audible above the din.

Ryodan stopped outside a cell, one with a small window and bars in the door. The baying became deafening then abruptly ceased.

I moved forward to join him, wondering what the bloody hell they were doing with my uncle's body. Had they fed it to some creature, thinking it might assuage torture beyond imagining? In olden days, the blood and flesh of a druid was considered sacred, reputed to have enormous healing properties, especially the heart.

"Think before you react," Ryodan warned, stepping aside so I could look in.

I looked.

I blinked and stared.

I shivered and drew thunder from the sky without even thinking. Far above me, it rolled and lightning crashed, followed by screams and something enormous falling, exploding into rubble. I knew it to be a concrete chunk of Chester's ceiling far above, in one of the many subclubs.

"I said bloody *think* before you react! If you intend to be allies, get a goddamn grip on yourself," Ryodan snarled. "And you *will* fix that later."

I turned slowly from the door. Feeling carved of marble, as I once had in the icy prison. Feeling a storm brewing in me, a storm that could rip and crack and tear asunder.

But Ryodan was right. I had to think before I reacted. With my power, I always have to think first. I won't become wanton destruction like my brothers, my dead brothers who will no doubt rise again, inside some other tortured human male. I made that choice on the cliff, dying over and over, carved it into the flesh of my Highlander-druid heart. The heart that I'd refused to let freeze and decay to blackened Unseelie flesh. A heart I'd kept beating with force of will and memory of love. In large part because of the one who lay shuddering beyond the bars of that small window.

With a sigh and enormous inward focus, I filled my veins with the unending summer of the Seelie court. Beckoned into my body a peaceful day, grass rippling, no clouds in the sky.

Not a hint of thunder.

When I had it under control, I opened my eyes and said, "What the bloody hell did you do to my uncle? What is that . . . *thing* in there?"

Ryodan said stiffly, "Dageus is one of us now."

"You fucking turned him into a . . . what the fuck are you anyway?"

"He was dying. There was no other option. Of all possible future scenarios, if I saved him, fifty-two percent of them were favorable," Ryodan said.

"Fifty-two bloody percent? And you thought that was good? Forty-eight percent of the outcomes weren't? Christ, I'd hate to know what a sick fuck like you considers 'unfavorable.' "

"You would," Ryodan agreed.

"So, what was your plan? Send us home with someone else's body and never tell us?" I said.

"He will be incapable of speech for some time. No telling how long," Ryodan said.

"But then—when he could talk—you were going to tell us?"

Ryodan's gaze was shuttered. "If there had been an opportunity that was . . . opportune."

"Christ," I said again, disgustedly. "You weren't even going to let us know he was alive. How the bloody hell did you plan to keep Dageus from telling us? Were you planning to keep him caged down here forever?"

Thunder began to grow in me again. I inhaled deeply, fisted my hands, exhaled slowly, and opened them.

"We were working on that," Barrons said.

"Dageus would never give up Chloe," I said.

I glanced in the door again. Glanced sharply away. My uncle was in the same kind of pain I'd been on those bloody cliffs.

And not human. Not entirely.

Never again entirely.

Changing. Becoming something else. Bile flooded the back of my throat. Now, Dageus, too, was something else, something more. And he'd already been complicated to begin with. "You had no right—"

"Your uncle is alive," Ryodan snapped. "Would you prefer he wasn't? Would Chloe prefer he wasn't? I broke every goddamn code we live by to save that bastard's life. And will pay an enormous price if I'm betrayed."

"Good," I snarled.

"You're being an ass," Mac growled. "And you know it. Ryodan saved your uncle's life. Dageus is here. He's not the same as he was before and he's messed up right now, but in time he'll be just like Barrons and Ryodan."

"Now there's a horrible thought," I said flatly.

She snorted. "That's not what I meant. He'll be capable of living again."

"And what else will he be?" I looked at Ryodan. "What price will he pay for his miraculous second life?"

"He'll live forever," Mac said heatedly. "So will you. That means you'll always have family. That's priceless."

"And the other prices? The ones that cut into flesh and bone? I'm not daft, lass. This kind of thing always has consequences. Terrible ones."

"Perhaps he will choose to discuss them with you. If so, we'll probably have to kill you," Ryodan said.

"We made a pact," I reminded him.

"Does it matter, Christian?" Mac said. "Your uncle

isn't at the bottom of a gorge or buried in the ground. One day you'll be able to talk to him again. He didn't die for you. That must be a weight off your shoulders."

"My clan has the right to know."

"If you tell your clan, the tribunal will hear of it and you'll lose him," Barrons warned.

"What is this tribunal?" I demanded.

Mac perked up beside me, suddenly all ears.

Barrons shot me a look, something ancient and feral moving in his dark eyes. "None of your bloody business. There are terms, Highlander. You may know he's alive. You may be of help to him through what lies ahead. But no one else may know. If word of his existence gets out, you'll only be giving him back to your clan to lose him again. Permanently."

"Our secrets. Yours now. And yours, ours," Ryodan reminded.

"You don't know my secrets."

He smiled faintly. "You might be surprised. We shared blood." His eyes said he knew what that meant. In a druid sense. And that maybe I didn't know what that meant in a whatever-the-fuck-he-was sense. That I was as bound to him as he was to me. And I wondered for the second time if he'd not left most of the dungeon unprotected for a reason. If he'd not perhaps arranged this very scenario, wanting me bound to them. What better way to get help with my uncle, draw another Keltar into the fold? Was he that diabolical?

I dismissed him and weighed Barrons's words for truth. "Your tribunal would take him? It *could* take him from you?"

"Yes. And yes," Barrons said levelly.

"Truth. Fuck."

"He must always remain hidden. You uncle died in that gorge," Ryodan said.

"Chloe."

Barrons said, "Perhaps in time. She, like Mac, would have reason enough to protect his secret. If she passes our tests."

"You would test my aunt." I was incensed.

"You should hope they would," Mac said. "No point in giving him back only for her to lose him again."

"My entire clan can be trusted."

Barrons and Ryodan snorted.

Mac said, "Save your demands for another day, Christian. Deal with today."

I turned to look at Dageus, shuddering on the stone slab. Finally, I said, "What is he going through?"

Ryodan said to Barrons, "I'll take the Highlander from here. Get her out of here." He jerked his head at Mac.

"Oh, come on!" Mac protested. "Don't you trust me by now?"

"Need-to-know basis, Mac. And you don't. But he," Ryodan jerked his head at Christian, "might just prove a grand babysitter while we figure out how to save the world."

Babysitter, my arse.

Mac and Barrons vanished down the hall.

When Ryodan opened the door, I followed him inside, unable to shake the feeling he might just have intended the evening to end this way all along.

19

"It's time to begin, isn't it . . ."

"Have you located the other Unseelie princes?" Cruce asked.

The roach god had to finish molding his many roach parts into the stumpy-legged shape of a human dwarf before he had the mouth to reply.

"All but one have been slain," he said, when he'd completed his tongue. He craned his neck to stare up at the tall prince, roaches scuttling to shift position with his movement. It was complicated to function in this form. It required incessant readjustments, yet it was this mimicry of those around him that had enabled him to strike his first alliance long ago. The more he donned it, the more he despised its limitations, envied those who suffered none.

"Which one remains?"

"He was once a Highlander, now mutated." He shifted slightly, settling the remaining stragglers into place, reinforcing his knees.

"Useless. Who killed my brethren?"

"Ryodan and Barrons." He observed his new ally closely. "I was there, beneath the desk when they placed their heads on it."

The winged prince demonstrated no weakness of rage at the news. He absorbed and moved on. The roach god's satisfaction with his choice of allies increased. Success did not grace the stupidly violent, but the patient, the unseen, those who lurked and bided and seized the correct moment.

"The Seelie princes?" Cruce demanded.

"Dead as well. The last of them slain by the same two."

"The concubine? The female that was in this cavern the night they imprisoned me," Cruce clarified. "The one with the Unseelie king. You were there that night, were you not?"

"Ryodan bade me scatter my parts through the abbey that night, while the wards were down, listen and learn. He misses no opportunity. I've seen no sign of that woman."

"And the Unseelie king?" Cruce said.

He shook his head, masses of roaches swaying and churning, but not one of them slipped. In his upright form, he was cohesive enough to do a few things. Far too gelatinous to do most. He resented that deeply. He was tiny, weak, in a world of giants who crushed him beneath their heels, drenched him with sticky hair spray or canned poisons that made him sick, sick, sick, even flushed him down a toilet as if he were excrement.

"No one leads my race. They are lost. Who do they follow?" Cruce said.

"They scatter, establishing small strongholds, warring among themselves. Most do nothing but feed and slaughter."

Cruce shook his head. "The depths to which my race has descended."

The roach god had studied the world carefully for eons. When the Fae began to walk openly, he had finally been able to show his face, too, as the powerful entity he was. He that knew the world's best-kept secrets could rule it. He suffered no delusion of being king himself. But he intended to be the one who stood beside the king, granted every liberty.

In his estimation, the recently freed Unseelie and the Seelie who now had no ruler were primed to follow any powerful, focused Fae. He told the prince this. "Still," he grated, "I have no way to open this chamber." He measured his next words carefully. "There is an Unseelie princess on this world. She was the one who bargained for the prince's deaths. She would see you slain as well if she knew you existed."

"Is that a threat?" Ice flared out across the floor, instantly freezing his many feet to the hard, cold surface.

He'd not spoken carefully enough. "Of course not. A warning among allies."

Cruce was silent for a time. Eventually the ice beneath the roach god's feet warmed enough that he could shift and free himself. Then the prince murmured, "I believed the bitches destroyed long ago by the king himself. Is there only one?"

"I have only seen one. I've heard of no others."

The prince thought about this, then said, "It must be risked, and if it draws her attention, so be it. How solid is the form you now wear?"

The burn of it. Not nearly solid enough. He'd walked among men long enough to have adopted their expressions, mimicking them when he mimicked their form. Roaches rearranged into a sour look with downturned mouth and narrowed eyes. He couldn't imagine how smoothly such things would occur in a cohesive body.

Cruce read the answer on his face. He stood and plucked a single feather from an enormous black wing, gilded iridescent blue and silver. "Can you carry this out when you leave?"

The roach god nodded, thousands of hard shiny brown shells rustling to perform the simple task.

The prince asked him many more questions about things he would have deemed insignificant, much like Ryodan, but the kind that knit together a much vaster, cohesive view than the roach with his divided parts and eyes. The roach god answered them fully, omitting no detail, however minor, from the recent rash of papers hung on every street corner, to the strange black spheres and the talk he'd overheard about them, to the terror-inspiring walking trash heap he'd seen the other day.

When he was finished, Cruce said, "Find an Unseelie who calls himself Toc." He described him to the roach god. "Tell him Cruce is on this planet and would see the Unseelie united, see them rule. Then tell him this . . ." The winged prince bent low and spoke at length, and the roach god nodded and committed his instructions to his very long memory.

"Before they come," Cruce finished, "I need you to bring the ingredients I've instructed you to ask Toc to prepare. With it, I will make icefire. Once I've finished, you will conceal it where I instruct."

"Will I be able to carry it?"

"That is why I chose it. One drop of Toc's blood added to each drop of icefire will cause flames to explode, which no water can extinguish. It spreads rapidly. How fare you in fire?"

The roach god smiled. He'd survived nuclear fallout. Fire was nothing to him. "Do you really believe this will work? That you'll be free in mere days?" He licked his lips with anticipation, rustling roach against roach. Freedom. So near. He would never be controlled again. And perhaps this new ally could force the gift he sought from his prior master.

Before this great winged prince crushed the arrogant prick like a bug.

Cruce laughed softly. "Not at all. But it will topple the first of many dominos. And once they begin to fall, my freedom is assured. Go find Toc and do as I've told you. And remember, when you next report to Ryodan, you must henceforth omit those areas of information I detailed."

The roach god relaxed and let his body scatter into a horde of shining, virtually indestructible insects. He dispatched several parts of himself to collect the feather that had drifted to the floor of the cavern and scuttled off with it, tugging it into the unseen crack beneath the door.

20

"Life inside the music box ain't easy . . ."

I raked a hand through my hair, stared at my reflection and snorted.

The paint was still visible after multiple oil and shampoo treatments. I'd even tried a stale jar of peanut butter. I'd had no luck salvaging Barrons's rugs either. The problem was the same with both items: employ a chemical harsh enough to remove the oil paint—destroy the wool or hair.

I have a strong desire to *not* be bald.

After trying for over an hour to lift the crimson from my blond, I conceded defeat. It would go away eventually, and I was in no mood to go dark again. I didn't even like the phrase "go dark."

I blew my hair dry the rest of the way, shrugged out of my bathrobe, and glanced around my sixth-floor bedroom for something to wear. The room was a wreck. I hadn't cleaned it in months.

Although it had moved floors again, it had a penchant to remain on the backside of BB&B, overlooking the back alley and the garage where Barrons stored his cars, and beneath which he and I often rested and fucked and lived. When Barrons isn't around, I can't get to our subterranean home beneath the garage. The only access to those lower levels is through the dangerous stacked Silver in his study, and I don't have the power to survive the many traps with which he mined the path. Once, the Book helped me navigate that deadly terrain, but my inner demon no longer offers help.

Ergo, showering upstairs. At least when my bedroom spontaneously relocates, it does so in toto, with all my belongings in it. Unfortunately, it doesn't clean itself in the process.

I rummaged for jeans and a tee-shirt in a pile of clothes I was reasonably certain had been laundered at some point, then preloaded my spear in its holster before positioning it beneath my left arm. Given the amount of Unseelie flesh in my body, I preferred to err on the side of caution.

I'd opted for a double shoulder harness, so I could carry my 9mm PPQ with its sixteen-cartridge magazine beneath my left arm, and tucked an extra magazine in my waistband. I slid dirks into both boots and my Ruger LCP .380 crimson trace—with an eight-pound trigger so I was less likely to shoot myself in the ass—into my rear pocket. I pushed Cruce's cuff farther up my arm so it was snug, then eased a lightweight jacket over it all, zipping it at the bottom. I pocketed two more bottles of Unseelie flesh (for emergency only!) and reached for my backpack, to eliminate the useless and outdated and then restock it with fresh supplies.

When I was invisible I hadn't worried about any of this. Now that I was back to being hunted by most of Dublin, countless creepy wraiths, an entity called the Sweeper that wanted to "fix" me (and I didn't think that meant neuter my female parts, although I did wonder exactly what the hell it *did* mean), and haunted by something that looked like my sister, I wanted all weapons all the time.

I'd left Barrons and Ryodan back in the office at Chester's, bottles of red and black ink on the desk, needles gleaming in trays nearby. I'd never seen Ryodan sporting the same unusual tats as Barrons, but when I'd left, Barrons had been tracing exactly those outlines on Ryodan's back.

Expecting trouble? I'd shot over my shoulder.

They'd raised their heads and given me such an identical look of *You're still here/what-the-fuck, is she asking questions again?/Christ, woman, go home for a while*, that I'd wondered how I could possibly not have realized they were related long before I overheard them talking about it.

After making plans to meet later that night, I'd taken the Hunter that Barrons had summoned back to BB&B and into the funnel cloud. The man has some seriously neat tricks. The Hunters might tolerate me, even cede a degree of respect, but I'd had no luck calling one myself, staring up into the sky.

I dumped the contents of my backpack on the bed. My little pink carry iPod fell out first and I smiled. How long had it been since I listened to a few hours of happy one-hit wonders? I connected it to my dock, only to discover the battery was dead. While I waited for it to draw enough juice to boot up, I rummaged through the other items in my pack, tossing out old water bottles, stale protein bars, dead batteries from my MacHalo I'd not wanted to further litter the streets with, tucked a music box up high on one of my shelves along with a glittering bracelet with iridescent stones and a small pair of jewel-encrusted binoculars, turned to throw my spare-change set of blood-and-goo-stained clothing into what I thought was the dirty laundry pile in the corner—

Music box?

I spun back around and stared at it, nestled on my

shelf, stunned. The sides were elaborate gold filigree, the lid a lustrous pearl encrusted with gems, each winking with a tiny inner flame. It squatted on ornate legs, half the size of a shoe box. More gems were embedded in the sides and each held a small swaying fire. The lid was attached with diamond-crusted hinges. There were no locks, and I somehow knew it had other ways of protecting itself.

How long had it been since I'd completely emptied this backpack?

Bracelet? Binoculars?

Had I ever?

How the hell had the music box gotten in there?

The dirty clothes dropped unheeded from my hands.

I narrowed my eyes, thinking, trying to recall the last time I'd used this particular pack. I hadn't carried it since the night I discovered Barrons had a son, the night I forced my way into his hidden lair and got my throat ripped out by a beautiful young boy. I'd been rummaging for a tarot card the Dreamy-Eyed Guy had given me, remembered touching something that made me shiver, but I was totally OCD that night about finding the card and had ignored the alert of proximity to an OOP. Hadn't bothered to see what it was. I'd had far bigger problems on my mind.

Had I been up here again since then, for longer than to grab something or take a quick shower and hurry back out?

I frowned, thinking that even if I had, I might not have sensed the music box's presence. I almost always had at least one OOP on me somewhere (Cruce's cuff, the most recent acquisition). I sleep and shower with my spear, I keep my *sidhe*-seer senses on low volume pretty much constantly. I wouldn't have picked up on anything else in the room with me unless I'd been actively hunting for it.

Had I really pilfered this OOP that dreamy, numb day in the White Mansion, months ago? I'd thought I left it there on the shelf of the crystal curio cabinet, but I had a dim memory of pocketing various trinkets, objects I'd been certain I simply couldn't live without.

I stared at it on the shelf, horrified that it was here, so close to me when I'd been so strenuously avoiding thinking about it lest the *Sinsar Dubh* catch wind of what I suspected it might be.

I hadn't felt a thing when I touched it this time, but with my current high, no object of power out there could penetrate my deadened senses.

I nosed cautiously around inside myself for my evil inner Book.

Nothing.

When I hunted for my lake last night, I'd not been able to spy even a drop of those still glassy waters. The lake was as gone from me right now as all my *sidhe*-seer gifts.

Did that mean the Book, too, would prove impossible for me to reach and conversely and more importantly, that *it* couldn't reach me right now?

Was I looking at the box that held the Song of Making?

Could the solution to our problem of the black holes be so simple? Had someone, long ago, tucked the all-powerful melody away and concealed it directly beneath the future Seelie queen's nose? If so, why? Assuming the original queen, who'd been alive at the same time as the concubine, wanted to pass the song along, she certainly wouldn't have given it to the king's mistress she'd so despised! Was this the result of some twisted Fae sense of humor? Had the queen concealed that very thing the king had so desperately wanted in the same house with the woman he'd wanted it for?

I scowled. The idea that this box might contain the

song seemed suspiciously serendipitous. The universe didn't work that way. At least not for me. The things that got tucked away in my curio cabinets were psychopaths, not all-powerful songs.

Yet time and again I'd recalled the melody it had played, the power I felt listening to it, and wondered if it might just be. This was the thing I'd been so studiously avoiding contemplating for even a second, grateful it was in the White Mansion, far away from me and my *Sinsar Dubh*, even as I grew increasingly certain we might need it. I hadn't realized how critical our state of affairs was until two days ago when Ryodan pointed out that the black holes could ultimately destroy the Nine.

And here it was. Staring right at me.

I closed my eyes, searching my memory, drifting back to that day in the concubine's house, trying to methodically re-create my steps. My time in there was so vivid, like all my time in Fae, as overblown and sensually saturating as the Fae themselves. And so surreal. Each time I'd been inside the mansion, I'd felt an intense bipolarity. I now understood it was because of the Book's/king's memories inside me, amplified by the residue of their consuming love in the psychically sticky house. It had seemed I'd been the Unseelie king himself, dancing with his concubine, whirling her around the boudoir, clutching her gown. I'd wandered through her private chambers in a daze, found one of her favorite bracelets, the special seeing glasses I (the king!) had crafted for her.

My eyes snapped open. Bloody hell, I *had* picked all three of those things up. Then completely forgotten I'd done it, obsessed with my quest to bring Barrons back to life.

If the music box did contain the colossal song, dare I risk touching it again, knowing the enormous evil I carried inside me? What if the Book took me over like it had the day I killed the Guardian, and destroyed the song?

Could it?

I stood, torn between wanting to tuck the music box into my pack so I could protect it and show it to Barrons, and not wanting it on my person, in case my high wore off and the *Sinsar Dubh* caught on to me.

Although . . . I mused, I'd toted it out of the mansion, which meant the Book had been in close proximity to it once before. And done nothing. But then, we hadn't needed the song back then either. Might it try to hold my soul hostage for it now that we did? Insist I capitulate or it would destroy it? Could it do any of those things?

Why the hell wasn't my Book talking to me anymore?

I cursed. I knew nothing about the *Sinsar Dubh*'s abilities or limits and I wasn't exactly in a hurry to go poking around trying to discover something. And since I knew nothing for sure, not wanting to underestimate it, I tended to pack that abyss of the unknown with fears of potentially greater power than it had. Or not.

I sighed, waffling in indecision. After a moment's deliberation, I stooped and pried up the loose floorboard where I'd stashed my journals, hoping Barrons—the man has an uncanny knack for discovering my innermost secrets—would never find them, grabbed a shirt, used it to pick up the box, tucked it beneath the floor, and replaced the board. Then I scooted a rug over it for good measure.

I'd bring Barrons back to see it later. I'd trust it to him, like the amulet, far sooner than I'd trust myself. Dani—I corrected myself mentally, Jada—and Dancer could investigate it. See if we might really get so bizarrely lucky. The king had been meddling in my life since childhood. I'd never forgotten that my grade school principal and high school gym coach were two of the king's many skins. The Seelie queen was, too. Who could ever guess what Fae were up to?

One day, I vowed, grabbing my pack to take it downstairs so I could restock it with fresh supplies later, I would no longer be afraid of who and what I was. One day I would be unified, suffer no crippling doubts, and make decisions fearlessly.

One day, like the day I first met Jericho Barrons in this very store and refused to give him my last name, I'd be "Just Mac" again. No hitchhikers, no screwed-up hair, and no dead sister look-alikes.

At seven o'clock that evening I deposited my umpteenth box of debris near a wobbly stack of broken furniture by the back door and rummaged for my cellphone to shoot Barrons a text that I needed the Hunter back in twenty minutes to make our meeting on time.

Given Barrons's endlessly surprising resources, I had no doubt he might have coerced one Fae or another to help me restore my store, but I didn't want a magical solution. There was something cathartic about cleaning BB&B myself. No magic. No trade-offs or threats. Good, simple, hard work. Besides, I figured I had another twenty-four hours of Unseelie flesh high and could accomplish a great deal with the extra strength and energy until then.

However, I mused, glancing back through the doorway at the commerce portion, when it came to the floors and furniture, I was definitely going to need assistance. Barter with some local woodworkers, if any had survived the fall of the walls and subsequent ice, learn to run a power sander, stain properly, and make everything gleaming and new again. I liked the idea of refinishing my bookcases, a satisfying nesting task that could be completed without any woo-woo elements.

In the meantime I'd managed to stack an enormous pile of debris in the alley behind BB&B and had no aversion to asking Barrons to somehow make the trash outside disappear. It wasn't as if we had trash pickup anymore.

I opened the back door to toss my last box of junk on the pile and froze. With the funnel cloud whirling around the eight-block circumference of BB&B, the day had been unnaturally quiet. Very little penetrated to the eye of the storm.

Yet now I heard something odd approaching: whirring and clanking, ponderous and large, coming from my left, from deep in the adjacent Dark Zone.

I eased the door shut to the tiniest of slivers, wondering if we'd trapped some gruesome Unseelie inside our funnel cloud with us. Even armed to the gills, I had no intention of bursting out into the deepening gloom of dusk in Dublin, which can slam down hard and fast, to confront whatever it was. I'd let it come to my turf, where lights blazed into the alley from the top of BB&B, and assess it before taking action.

It wasn't long before the thing lumbered into view.

I narrowed my eyes, trying to understand what I was seeing through the gloom.

An awkwardly ambulating trash heap?

I glanced at my newly mounded pile. It didn't appear as if anything had arisen from it.

I glanced back at the bizarre thing.

It whirred and clanked and shuddered its way toward me, made of gears and cogs, wheels and gray hoses and shiny steel boxes and blades. And other things—wet mucosal things that looked like external intestines, looping around it and through it. No discernible face. No mouth or eyes. Fifteen maybe twenty feet tall, it seemed haphazardly slapped together from bits of gristle and guts and odds and ends from a dump.

With a deafening grinding of cogs and wheels, it rolled and clattered my way.

When it passed directly in front of me, within a mere fifteen feet, I froze. I didn't back up, I didn't shut the door. I just went motionless. It wasn't a choice. My body simply stopped obeying all commands issued by my brain. Once before, I'd felt raw, stupefying terror as I cowered before the beast form of the *Sinsar Dubh*, enduring the most excruciating pain of my life, pain I'd not believed it possible to survive. The mere presence of this pile of refuse incited similar terror, and like a deer shocked by blinding headlights, I was incapable of fighting or fleeing.

Run, hide, draw your spear. But I was able to do none of those things. Gripped by panic, I prayed the walking refuse/guts pile never noticed me, and I didn't even know why.

Only that I wanted to pass beyond this thing's regard *forever.*

I stood, not breathing, not sure I could breathe again if it chose to remain in close proximity, while it clattered past my own junk heap, which I'd created that afternoon, rattling like an ancient, badly made machine.

I had no idea if it was alive or fabricated, sentient or programmed. Only that if it had purpose—it was one I never wanted to know.

I gasped softly, finally managing a breath.

Still, I stood motionless in the doorway, trying to shake off the body-numbing terror, until at last it disappeared and my Hunter arrived.

Part III

I shiver. What I need to see is right here in front of me. I can feel it. I'm just not looking with the right eyes, the clear eyes that suffer no conflicts. I need a brain like mine and eyes like Ryodan's. I focus on the backs of my lids, take the grayness of them and cocoon it around me. I make a bland womb where I can begin the process of erasing myself, detaching from the world; the one where I exist and I'm part of reality and everything I see is colored by my thoughts and feelings. I strip away all that I know about myself and sink into a quiet cavern in my head where there is no corporeality. And no pain.

–From the journals of Dani "the Mega" O'Malley

I know that no matter what fecked-up things Ryodan does, he'll never forget me. He's meticulous. There's a lot to be said for detail-oriented. 'Least in my world there is. Especially when I'm one of the details.

–From the journals of Dani "the Mega" O'Malley

21

*"All my tears have been used up
on another love . . ."*

THE JADA JOURNAL

August 5 AWC

NEW DUBLINERS BEWARE!

The Hoar Frost King—the Unseelie that recently iced Dublin and froze people to death—left areas of great danger in our city. These spots appear to be round black spheres, suspended in the air, anywhere from five to twenty feet above the ground.

THEY ARE LETHAL!

Do NOT TOUCH the spheres or disturb them in any way.

The Guardians have been cordoning them off to keep you safe. If you see one of these black spheres that hasn't been cordoned off please

REPORT IT to the Guardians at DUBLIN CASTLE.

These spheres will GROW if you toss anything in,

and pose a GRAVE THREAT to our world if they get bigger.

PROTECT YOURSELVES. PROTECT OUR WORLD.

If you see one near

STEER CLEAR OF THE SPHERE!

Dancer grinned. "I especially like the last part. Nice rhyme."

Jada was far from pleased with the paper. "They 'appear to be round black spheres'? How much more redundant could that be? A sphere is round."

"Some folks don't think like that, Jada. You know you have to spoon-feed when conveying information to the masses. Keep it simple, stupid."

She shot him a cool look.

"I'm not saying you're stupid. Christ, Mega. We both know your brain weighs more than your whole head."

"A logistical impossibility."

"Not with you. Your brain probably exists in a higher dimension than your body. I think the paper's perfect. It communicates exactly what we want to get across in the simplest possible terms. Now freeze-frame me around like you used to so we can slap these things up. It'll be like old times." He arched a brow. "A month ago for me."

Old times. It was difficult for her to wrap her brain

around the fact that she'd lived so much life while he'd lived so little.

"I'll put them up and be back soon."

"Don't do that to me," Dancer said coolly. "Once, you deposited me on the sidelines at the abbey, the night we battled the HFK. Then you got deposited. You know how it feels. We're a team. Even if I'm only fucking human, I've proved useful many times."

She looked at him sharply. There was someone much older than a seventeen-year-old in his eyes. "You're . . . less indestructible than I am. We need your mind on the black hole problem."

"So, you want to park me somewhere to guarantee free access to my brain? Get a clue: 'only fucking humans' have been going to war for this world since the dawn of time. You're not the only one that can make a difference. Your attitude invalidates the efforts of every military man and woman on this planet."

"You could die. Exposing you to risk is illogical."

"We all can. Any time, Mega. Shit happens." He looked at her levelly, with those brilliant aqua eyes. "Bugger it, my whole family's gone and we both know it. You think you're the only one left with something to prove, something worth putting your life on the line for? If we don't work together, I work alone. But I *work*." He gave her a faintly bitter smile. "With or without you. Look at it this way, if you keep me close, you have a better chance of keeping me alive. If you don't, who knows what danger I could get myself into?"

"That's not fair."

"Life isn't."

"You sound just like him."

"Not necessarily a bad thing all the time," Dancer said, intuiting exactly who she meant: Ryodan.

"Trying to rope me—"

"Bloody hell, Jada, I'm not trying to rope you. I'm

trying to work with you. Leave it to you to decide someone helping is a hindrance or a cage."

She went still. This wasn't Dancer. Not the Dancer she knew, the one who always went along with her decisions. Never gave her guff. Well, except for once. "You never used to talk to me like this before," she said coolly.

He snorted. "I was never willing to risk it. You ran at the drop of a hat. My every move was designed to keep the magnificent Mega from dashing off. One wrong phrase, one hint of emotion or expectation, and she vanished into the night. I watched every bloody word. I lived with the constant awareness that if I cared about you and you figured it out, you'd leave. Then you left. Again. For another month. Didn't even tell me you were back. Then I heard you told Ryodan's men you weren't even willing to work with me. Was I dead to you? You shut me out completely and now only spend time with me because you have a mission you need me for. I'm sorry if you don't like what I have to say but I'm not walking on eggshells around you anymore. If you want to avail yourself of my many splendid qualities—and they *are* pretty stupendous," he flashed her a smile, "accord me the courtesy I give you. Take me as I am. A real person, with desires and boundaries of my own."

Jada spun on her heel and began to walk away.

"Great. And there you go. Fine. I'll be fine alone. I'm always fine alone," he shouted after her. "It's just that you're the only person I ever feel completely alive with. You're the only girl that ever gets half of what I say. Do I really have to come up with some fucking superpower just to hang out with you?"

She stopped. Completely alive. She remembered feeling that once. Running the streets of her town with him, laughing and planning and fighting, amazed and thrilled that she got to be alive in such an exciting time.

She remembered, too, the unique feeling of being so easily understood by him. They'd had an effortless rapport.

"Run away," he said, shaking his head. "It's what you do best."

Killing was what she did best. She didn't run anymore. She never ran. She knew the price. She never reacted. Merely divined the logical, efficient action most likely to yield intended results and pursued it.

Was she running?

She went still, sought that cold clear place inside herself, tacked the emotions and elements of their interaction on a truth table of sorts, analyzing her responses. She pinned his words here, overlaid the subtext, her words there, interpreting the subtext. Then in the middle of the whole thing she taped up the question: *What harm if I let Dancer help me hang the papers?*

Absolutely none.

In fact, there was more potential for something to go wrong if she left him behind.

There was an unacceptable amount of "reaction" evident in her actions. She knew better. She who controlled herself, survived.

She turned around. "You may come with me."

"Why do I feel like I just won the battle but lost the war?" he said softly.

The slipstream was beautiful, trailing past them like a starry tunnel. It took thirty minutes to plaster papers around Dublin proper. Hours to return for more at the old Bartlett Building, then dash around the outlying districts, distributing them far and wide, knocking on doors, hanging them on houses with lights on inside when no one answered.

It felt good to be back out, taking care of her city

again. Along the way they tore down every *Dublin Daily* they saw, as they'd been written in a way that imparted no useful news and incited fear. For the dozenth time she wondered who was crafting the slanted things. All they'd done was turn the entire city on her and Mac.

"Holy human surfboards, you caught a perfect wave every time!" Dancer exploded when they paused, back in town, near the River Liffey. "Not one rough start or stop. We didn't hit a bloody thing!" His beautiful eyes were brilliant with excitement. "That was incredible! You've gotten massively better at freeze-framing."

"I learned a few things Silverside." She winced inwardly at his Batman quip. She'd given them up long ago. Shortly after she'd accepted that Ryodan had never read a single comic and had no idea the lengths to which Batman and his fearless sidekick would go for each other.

"No kidding. It felt different. Instead of trying to force yourself into something that didn't want us there, you were in sync with it. One with the force."

She had Shazam to thank. She would never have survived without her cranky, mopey wizard/bear/cat manic-depressive binge-eater.

He was watching her. "Did you meet anyone in there? Did you have friends?"

"A few. I don't want to talk about it." Some things were private. She'd lost too much. She wasn't losing anything else. Feeling suddenly drained, she grabbed a couple of power bars from her pack, ripped them open, dropped down on a nearby bench, and shoved one after another into her mouth. She missed the glistening silvery pods Shazam had encouraged her to eat on the planet with the dancing vines, the ones that had kept her fueled for days. She'd filled her pack with them before she left that world and had been rationing them for herself since. Back on this world, food didn't pack nearly the energy punch as it had on many in the Silvers. Too much processing, not enough purity. Or maybe Earth just didn't have any raw elemental magic in the soil anymore.

They sat in silence for a time, watching the river roll by.

When Dancer touched her hand, she moved it quickly. Nearly stiffened but caught herself.

"Easy, wild thing."

She looked at him. "Is that what you think I am?" Others thought her rigid, passionless.

"I see it in your eyes. Deep. You bank it. Wilder than you were before. And, I have to say I like it. But you're something else, too. Softer in some places."

He was clearly deranged. There was nothing soft about her.

He put his hand on the bench between them, palm up, fingers relaxed, and gave her a look. It was an invitation. His hand would stay or go, as she wished.

How long had it been since she'd twined her fingers with someone's, felt that click as they locked into place, the heat of someone's palm against hers? The feeling that she wasn't alone, that someone was in life with her. Young, they'd raced through the streets, holding hands and carrying bombs and laughing their asses off.

"When we're kids," Dancer said, "we're made of steel. And we think we're invincible but stuff happens and that steel gets stretched and pulled and twisted into impossible shapes. Most people are torn apart by the time they're married and have kids of their own. But some people, the few, figure out how to let that steel heat and bend. And in all the places other people break, they get stronger."

Eyes narrowed, curious, she moved her hand to his, placed it on top, palm to palm. He didn't try to lace their fingers together. Just sat there, her hand resting lightly on his. She suspended the moment, absorbed it, tried to wrap her brain around it. But brains didn't wrap well around hands.

"How did you get wise?" she said. "Nothing ever happened to you. Until the walls fell, your life was charmed." She didn't mean to sound cutting. It was simply the truth. It had fascinated and bewildered the teen she'd been. They'd been so much alike, sprung from opposite sides of a wide track. She'd had a nightmarish childhood, and his had been storybook perfect. Yet they'd understood everything about each other without ever having to say much of anything.

"I've got a bloody IQ through the bloody roof," he said dryly. "Besides, you don't have to suffer what other people have in order to understand. Not if you have half a brain and a willing heart. And where you're concerned, Mega, my heart's always been willing. I hate that you got lost in the Silvers and I didn't even know it. I hate that you suffered. But I can't say I'm sorry you grew up."

She stared out over the water, saying nothing. She had no idea what to say. He wanted to be more than friends. He'd made that clear today. She wasn't there. One day, maybe she could be. In the meantime this was oddly . . . well, odd. And a little . . . nice. She'd known the closest thing to safe she'd ever felt, years ago with Dancer.

But there was something in her that was—as others believed—rigid and unyielding, something that couldn't bear the thought of bending even one inch. And touching and caring meant bending. There was a place inside her where she simply couldn't let go. She'd let go of the wrong things.

They thought she was fearless. She wished that were true. There were things she feared.

She'd thought the day she got back to Dublin would be the best day of her life.

It had been one of the worst. The cost had been too high.

She drew her hand back to her lap.

Dancer stood up. "What do you say we work on our own map of the anomalies? Screw Ryodan and his monopoly on information."

And just like that her sorrow ebbed and she stood like the young, strong woman she was, not the woman handicapped by tears locked in a box deep inside her. Fully aware, as Ryodan had said, that it was impossible to seal away a single emotion. Fully aware the price of no pain was no joy.

Because if those tears ever started to flow, she'd drown.

Jada hurried through the abbey, books tucked beneath her arm. She had two hours before she would head to Chester's. She'd spent the day putting up her papers and mapping black holes around Dublin. On the way back to the abbey, she'd stood outside the funnel cloud that surrounded BB&B, staring up at it, forcing herself to remain cold, logical, an arrow toward the goal. Nothing more.

They had their agenda on Earth. She had her own elsewhere.

She wanted to go back into the Unseelie king's library but wasn't willing to lose more time Earthside. One never knew the price of stepping through a Silver. Besides, until she spoke with Barrons, she had no way of deciding which Silver would take her into the White Mansion. Five and a half years Silverside and she'd never managed to learn a bloody thing about the mirrors that could so dispassionately give or take life.

Penetrating the funnel cloud wouldn't be a problem. She'd mastered that magic year two, Silverside. A few well-placed wards could degrade almost any self-contained Fae storm, allowing passage.

For a month now, ever since she'd arrived back in Dublin, she'd been looking for a ward, a spell, a totem, some way to mark a Silver, embed something on its shimmering surface, something visible from both sides.

Her efforts had yielded no fruit.

Now, as she moved through the corridors of the abbey, she gathered recent news from the *sidhe*-seers and dispatched orders, impatient to be in her chambers, craving Shazam's warm, irascible presence and time alone with him to analyze and refine her plans.

He was slumped in a mound of fatness and foul mood. He didn't even lift his head when she came in.

"I brought you something," she said, removing an oily brown paper bag from her pack. His head shot up. He was insatiably curious.

He was insatiable, period.

His whiskers trembled with anticipation and he burped.

"Have you been eating something while I was gone?" she demanded.

"What do you expect? You didn't leave me anything."

"Technically, you don't need to eat."

"Ever heard of boredom? What am I supposed to do in here all day? Make the bed I never get out of because there's no place I'm allowed to go?"

She assessed the room. Every single pillow was gone.

When he belched again, a feather floated from his mouth.

"They couldn't possibly have tasted good."

"Good is relative when all you have is nothing," he said sourly.

"Soon I'll let you out. Soon you'll be free again."

"Right. And soon sentient beings will stop destroying one another and themselves. Not. We're all going to die. Alone and miserably. With lots of pain. That's the way life goes. People make promises and don't keep them. They say they care about you and forget you."

"I didn't forget you. I never forget you."

She tossed three raw fish on the bed and Shazam exploded upright, straight up in the air, bristling with excitement. He fell on the fish like they were manna from Heaven, slurping and sucking and devouring every morsel until only fine bones remained on the down comforter.

"You are forgiven," he said grandly, settling down to polish his face with spit-moistened paws.

If only she was.

22

"But you, you're not allowed,
you're uninvited . . ."

Jada pressed her palm to the door of Ryodan's office a full hour earlier than she'd been advised to arrive. He might think he'd ordered her to be there, but no one ordered her anymore. They worked with her or against her.

She'd refined her thoughts during her time with Shazam, the two of them deciding her next move would have to be risked, that she'd have to accept the tattoo he'd offered.

So when the door slid aside, before she even stepped in, she said, "I'll let you tattoo me."

Barrons and Ryodan both looked over their shoulders at her, and she was struck suddenly by how . . . inhuman they looked, their faces more savage, their movements more . . . animalistic and sleek, as if caught momentarily off guard, engrossed. But their masks went up the instant they saw her and then they were just Barrons and Ryodan again.

The owner of Chester's was sitting backward in a chair, watching monitors, while Barrons sat behind him, tattooing his powerfully muscled back.

Ryodan reached for a shirt, tugged it on over his head.

When he stood, he and Barrons exchanged a look, then Barrons nodded at her and said, "Jada, good to see you," and walked out.

"You shouldn't cover fresh tattoos," she told Ryodan coolly. "They weep."

He stood legs wide, arms folded, silver cuff glinting, looking down at her. "How would you know anything about tattoos or weeping?"

She was five-foot-ten now, and still had to arch her neck to look at him.

"I've heard," she said. He had a tight-fitting tee-shirt on. Then again probably every tee-shirt he put on was tight because of his sheer width and musculature. She could see the delineation of each muscle in his abdomen through the shirt, the pronounced outline of his pectorals. His lats flared, his biceps were sculpted, his forearms thickly corded. For a moment she was fourteen again, looking up at him. And she finally understood and acknowledged what she used to feel. The teen had suffered an intense crush on Dancer. The superhero had been utterly infatuated with Ryodan. They'd become her world when Mac had turned her back. She'd felt safe being with Dancer. Yet Ryodan had made her *feel* safe.

They stood a long moment, ten feet apart, looking at each other as silence spun out.

"What changed your mind?" he said finally.

"I'm not sure I have fully changed my mind," she said, noting his second use of the interrogative in a single conversation and wondering if he really was done baiting her all the time. "How does it work?"

He sliced his head once to the left. "If you mean the mechanics of it, too bad. Bottom line is this: if you let me tattoo you and you carry the phone, I can find you if you ever get lost again."

"Details."

"There are three numbers programmed in. Mine. You call it, I answer. The second one is Barrons's number. If I don't answer for some reason, Barrons will. The third one is called IISS." He waited.

"I resent being cued. It makes me not want to know."

Tiny lines around his eyes crinkled as he threw his head back and laughed.

Jada fisted her hands behind her back. She hated it when he laughed.

"Good to see you haven't lost all your irrational prickliness," he said. "IISS stands for I'm In Serious Shit. Use it only if you are."

"What will happen?"

"Hope you never find out. But if you'd called it in the Silvers, I'd have been there."

"How quickly?"

"Very."

"What good would that have done?"

"I'd have gotten you out."

"Who can say your way would have been better? Maybe it would have taken us *ten* years with you leading the way."

"Doubtful. Maybe it would have taken ten days. And you wouldn't have been alone."

"Who says I was alone?"

"Do you want it or not."

"Seriously, ten days?" She assessed him remotely, wondering if it could possibly be true. This man had awed her with his unfathomable abilities and strength. She'd never forgotten how he could out-everything her, from spying a drop of condensation on a frozen sculpture she couldn't see, to freeze-framing faster, to always being able to find her no matter what. *I tasted your blood,* he'd said once. *I can always find you.*

She'd believed that. Even Silverside.

He sighed explosively and raked a hand through his short dark hair. "Ah, Dani. It doesn't work in there. Would that it fucking did."

"The tattoo?" she said, refusing to believe he'd just skimmed her mind. "Then you're not doing it. And it's Jada," she corrected. "Every time you call me the wrong name, I'll call you a wrong one. Dickhead."

"That I tasted your blood. It doesn't work in Faery."

"If I don't invite you into my thoughts, stay out of them. It's called respect. If you don't respect me, you don't get to know me." She stepped closer, moving to stand nose-to-nose, staring straight into those cool silver eyes that used to so intimidate her, but she would never have let him know that. They didn't intimidate her now.

He inclined his head. "Understood. I won't do it again. Much. Often, it was the only way I could stay one step ahead of you."

"Why did you think you needed to?"

"To keep you alive."

"You thought I needed a foster parent?"

"I thought you needed a powerful friend. I tried to be that. Are we still talking or are you ready to tattoo?"

"I still don't understand how it works."

"Some things require a leap of faith."

She gave him her back and swept her ponytail aside. "Have at it."

His fingers moved across the nape of her neck, at the base of her skull, lingering. She suppressed a shiver. "How long is this going to take?"

"I can't work with this spot. Too bloody much scar tissue from you cutting the last one off."

"If you tattooed me, why didn't you give me the phone then, too? What was the point of tattooing me at all?"

"We had this conversation. You wouldn't have carried it. You would have believed it was another of my infamous contracts. However, at some point I knew you would. I prepared for that eventuality."

"I'm not an eventuality. Get off my neck if it won't work."

"I'm not touching you," he said. "I touched the scar only briefly."

Still, she felt the burn of his fingers against her skin, the faint electrical charge. She spun to face him. "Where, then?"

He arched a brow. "The second best location is at the base of your spine."

"A tramp stamp?" she said incredulously.

"Its effectiveness increases bound to the base of the spine."

"And I still don't know what that effectiveness is. This could be just another one of your—"

"And that's precisely why I never tried to get you to carry the phone," he cut her off roughly. "For fuck's sake, you vanished and I couldn't find you. Do you really think I'm going to let that happen again? If you believe nothing else, concede it will work for that reason alone. I don't lose things that are mine."

She arched a brow and said coolly, "I'm not yours and never was."

"Tramp stamp or get the fuck out," he said coldly.

She stood motionless, realigning herself deep inside. This day was hands down the most brutal one she'd had since she returned. People had been clawing at her all day with their feelings and demands and expectations. She didn't know how to live in this world anymore. Didn't know how to pass through unscathed, unchanged. It was changing her. She could feel it.

"Fine," she said flatly. Kicking a chair into place, she dropped into it with her back to him, legs splayed around it, stripped off her shirt and leaned forward, resting her arms on the back, stretching long and lean.

"We don't have all night," she said finally, breaking the long silence.

"Ah, fuck," he said softly, and she knew he was looking at the scars.

23

"Pour some sugar on me . . ."

I go looking for Jo, and man, that's one chick I just don't get.

She told me this morning she "doesn't wanna wanna fuck me."

How can that shit even happen in the same sentence? One wanna negating the other wanna makes no fucking sense.

Some things are simple. Leave it to a woman to point a man down a straight path then twist it into a bloody maze before he even takes two steps.

You wanna fuck somebody.

There it is.

Nothing complicated about that at all.

And if you wanna fuck somebody, why would you waste any time thinking twice about it when you could be using that time to fuck them? Do women sit around all day dreaming up bipolar-crazy-ass conversations just to make us bugfuck crazy?

She says, all serious like, *Lor, you're a really sweet guy* (who the bloody fuck is she talking about? I'm looking around the bed but it's only me and her) *but I don't want to do this again* (she announces, with her ass way up in the air, me driving into her dirty-dog-buried-to-the-hilt-and-she's-howling style). *It was wrong from the get-go* (what was wrong was *me* doing a brunette with little tits but you don't hear me complaining), *and I don't want to keep compounding the same mistake* (I don't point out that she seems to be enjoying the hell out of said mistake, if the sounds she's making are anything to judge by, and before she started using her mouth to say such stupid shit it was her idea to use it sucking my dick, but that's me, a paragon of restraint), *so we need to stop this.*

Then she drops the mother of all bombs on the parade of bombs she's already dropped and it's a wonder my dick doesn't go limp from the shrapnel. Well, actually, that's not a wonder.

Naked woman. Hard dick.

She says—and get this nut-job-crazy-bitch-ass-shit that came out of her mouth next, *Lor, I might need you to help me. I might change my mind, and if I do, I need you to say no.*

I stop what I'm doing, grab her by the hair, turn her head toward me and stare at her. "You're saying if you come to me later today, saying 'I want you to fuck me, Lor,' I'm supposed to say no?" I'm having a hard time with the nuances of this.

She's looking all hot and flushed and sweaty, with glazed eyes and kinda panting, and she nods and gasps, "Exactly."

I shove her head back down and get back to business. Which, I might point out, she's loving the hell out of.

Thinking the whole time, I don't get brunettes. It's why I avoid 'em. Never heard a blonde say such a fucked-up thing.

I'm supposed to help a woman that doesn't wanna wanna fuck me but obviously *does* wanna fuck me and sucks dick with the tender aggression and dedicated zeal of a wet, velvet-lined vacuum be strong enough not to fuck me when I thoroughly enjoy fucking her?

Women.

Whose bright idea was it to make them?

No wonder we got booted from the goddamn Garden.

After a few days with Eve, Adam couldn't think straight.

I find Jo in the corridor of the server's quarters. Her eyes flare and she backs away when she sees me coming, thrusting her tray of dirty glasses out at me, like something so puny could keep me from getting what I want.

I don't do the caveman routine. It doesn't work with brunettes. It's why I hate 'em. They take work.

"You said you got a problem with your memory," I say.

She looks wary. "You mean my *sidhe*-seer gift?"

"Sure do, babe. You can't organize it. Wading knee-deep in mental detritus."

She gives me a look when I say "detritus" like all I could possibly know are four-letter words, and I think, Keep thinking that, babe. Lor's just a dumb blond. I'm gonna blow her messy-ass mind and when I'm done maybe it'll be clean enough in there she'll be able to see when you wanna fuck you wanna fuck.

"Lessons start tonight. After your shift."

"I'm not going to have sex—"

"Oh, yes you are. You're gonna fuck me every time I give you a lesson. Ain't no free lunches. And when I'm done you're gonna be goddamn brilliant. And then, maybe, I'm not gonna want to fuck you anymore."

She gives me a skeptical look. "How are you going to help me organize what's in my head?"

"Loci. Latin for 'places.' Mnemonic device for managing memory. Simonides, Cicero, Quintilian all used it. I'm going to teach you to build a memory palace."

"How come I've never heard of this before?" she says suspiciously.

"Probably can't find it in your mess in there. The mess that thinks you don't wanna fuck somebody you wanna fuck."

"A nicer person would offer to teach me, not bully me into trading sexual favors."

"Uh-huh. A nicer person would. And I'd hardly say it's you trading me a favor. Seems damned mutually beneficial to me. You want what you want from me, you gotta give me what I want from you. And hopefully we'll both get so sick of each other by the time it's over, we'll leave each other alone."

She narrows her eyes and I can tell the idea appeals to her. Hell, it appeals to me. The sooner I get her out of my system the sooner my life gets simple again.

"How do you know anything about this kind of stuff?"

"Honey, when you've lived as long as I have, if you don't have a filing system, you're fucked. Besides," I flash her a wolfish grin, "I needed a good way to track my chicks, skirts, and babes through the millennia. Every fuck. All in there. Every last detail."

She gets a weird look, and I think, Aw, shit, Ryodan wasn't as open with her as I thought he was, then it turns into a scoff and I breathe a little easier. "Millennia?" She laughs and says, "Yeah right." She blushes. "I'm in your memory palace."

And she's the one I'd like most to take out with the trash at this point. "Every time you come. Smell. Taste. Sound. Deal or not?"

"I'll try it once," she says. "And if I think you have anything to teach me, we'll continue."

Aw, honey, I think, we're definitely gonna continue.

* * *

I start out simple. I tell her about the London cabbies and the test they have to take called the Knowledge. First thing about mastering any subject is understanding the mechanics of it.

Like the clit.

I've studied it exhaustively, in theory and with a buttload of practical application. It's remarkably like a dick with a foreskin, erectile tissue, and even a tiny little shaft. But it's way better. Women got some eight thousand sensory nerve endings in it. The penis only has about four thousand. On top of that, the clit can affect another fifteen thousand nerve endings, which means a whopping fucking twenty-three thousand nerve endings exploding in an orgasm.

We definitely got the short end of the dick, er, stick.

I also know Marie Bonaparte (one sexually adventurous babe!) had her clit surgically moved closer to her vagina because she couldn't score a Vag-O. Another goddamn brunette, thinking too much, hanging out with Freud. I could've helped her with that problem without moving nothing. Once she did, it didn't work anyway 'cause she didn't take into consideration three-quarters of the clit is embedded in the woman's body and can't be moved.

Then there's the fact that this amazing little clit men got screwed out of actually *grows* throughout a woman's lifetime.

By menopause it's *seven times larger* than it was at birth and fucking-A—there's a reason older women are hot as hell in bed! Can't imagine what kinda nut I'd bust with a dick seven times this size. Not sure there'd be anyplace I could put it, so I ain't gonna bemoan that one. And clits are all different: some are little nubs, some are big, some hide, some protrude, and each one is as unique as the woman attached to it.

"Clits?" Jo says, blinking. "I thought we were talking about cabbies."

"Clits, cabbies, different means, same end. Pay attention. You're getting me off track."

"I didn't say one word about clits," she says, looking pissy.

"You were thinking about them."

She blows out an exasperated breath. "What about this test, the Knowledge? How does this have anything to do with me remembering where I put things in my head?"

"I'm getting to that. Goddamn woman, learn to take your time on the buildup. So the cabbies in London study for years, memorizing the patterns of twenty-five thousand streets, locations of some twenty thousand landmarks, and have to be able to plot the shortest distance between any two areas, including all significant places of interest along the way. Like two or three out of ten actually manage to pass the Knowledge."

"And?"

"Their right posterior hippocampus is seven percent larger than the average person's. Not because they were born that way, babe. Neuroplasticity."

She blinks at me like she's having a hard time understanding English. She mouths the word "neuroplasticity." "You know this how? Why?"

"I drove a cab for a while. Coupla months."

"In London?"

"Why the fuck do you think I'd tell you about a test I didn't take?"

"You took a test? And passed? You drove a cab?" She's looking at me like I'm from outer space.

"Do you know what the babes in London are like? How many wives fly in or out without their husbands from all kinds of international places? Look at me, honey. I'm a walking, talking, fucking Viking that loves to fuck. I had the run of the airport."

"Oh my God. You were a cabbie to get laid."

I wink at her. "Fun times."

"Okay," she says, shaking her head briskly, "we're done with clits and cabbies. What does this have to do with my problem? Are you saying I have to increase the size of part of my brain? How am I supposed to do that?"

"Like the clit, the brain can change. The right posterior hippocampus registers spatial encoding—"

"I'm having a real hard time with your sudden language proficiency," she says, eyes narrowed.

"Babe, I ain't dumb. I'm efficient."

She leans back in her chair, looking at me with a slow smile tugging at her lips, and she's trying not to let it happen but all the sudden she busts out laughing. "I'll be damned," she says when she finally stops laughing, and all the sudden I don't like how she's looking at me. Like she sees something I didn't want her to see. Don't ever want a babe to see. I'm suddenly wondering how smart this arrangement was.

But in for a goddamn penny and all. So I start telling her about the theory of elaborate encoding, embellishing memories and inserting them spatially, tying them to a place, and suggest she use the abbey, because it's so familiar to her. Some folks argue fictional places are superior, but when you already got a great big sprawling fortress you grew up in to use, why do more work than necessary? That's pretty much the motto of my life.

"So you're saying I encode everything I want to remember into various images and tuck them into different places at the abbey in my mind? Sounds like a lot of work," she says.

"Yeah, but you only gotta do it once. And it gets easier when you get the hang of it. You gotta trick it up. Make it funny somehow. I remember this chick, I never knew her name and I wanted to file her and the woman was a serious-ass kink, so I called her Lola, you know, the Kinks—'L-O-L-A low-la.'" I belt it just like Ray Davies, and fuck me they always did put on one helluva show. "I made her a bent paper clip resting in the fold of the sleeve on the Ray Davies statue in my study."

"Paper clip? You have a Ray Davies statue in your study? What else is in your study?"

"Don't be nosy, honey. It ain't attractive. She was twisted. Like a bent paper clip. It worked for me."

She ponders it, worrying that hot lower lip of hers that has some serious suction power. "And this really works?" she says finally.

"It's all about taking control of your inner space, babe."

She stares at me a long moment in silence. She opens her mouth and closes it again, rubbing her forehead. Then, looking like she can't even believe what's coming out of her mouth, she says, "Can we just fuck?"

I'm on her before she even finishes the sentence.

I think I just gave a whole new spin to talking a chick into fucking.

24

"I pushed you down deep in my soul for too long . . ."

"You want me to hunt the woman that looks like your sister?" Barrons said.

I nodded. I was sick of not knowing what was really going on in so many areas in my life. It was bad enough that I had this thing inside me that, if it had rules, I didn't know any of them, but now there was some creepy trash-heap Unseelie out there that had managed to freeze me in helpless horror, even though my *sidhe*-seer senses were currently neutralized, and another unknown entity masquerading as my dead sister.

Two of those three things I could take decisive action about. Starting with the one that posed the greatest threat to my sanity.

"I want you to capture her," I clarified. "And I want you to bring her somewhere I can question her."

"You blew this off in Chester's."

I sighed. "I didn't want to say anything in front of Ryodan. You know he chews a bone until it's nothing but splinters. I didn't feel like being his bone at the time."

"Do you believe it could be Alina?"

"No. I think it's completely impossible. But I want to know what the hell it actually *is*."

"You told me you buried your sister. You were certain it was her. Have you changed your mind?"

"Nope. I buried her." I don't bother mentioning that I also recently exhumed her corpse and it wasn't there. I saw no point in further complicating an already complicated issue. I wanted to examine the Alina-thing first, then I'd disclose all, if necessary, to Barrons.

"I won't be able to bring her to the bookstore," he said.

I nodded. He was going to have to change from man to beast to hunt Alina, and I didn't think for a minute any Hunter would permit the creature Barrons became on its back and fly them over our private tornado. "Do you have another place nearby that's well warded?"

"The basement where you were Pri-ya is still protected."

Our eyes met and we had an intense nonverbal conversation, graphic reminders of sex, raw and aggressive, hungry and obsessive. *You are my world,* I'd said. *Don't leave me.*

You're leaving me, Rainbow Girl, he'd said, and I'd known even then I was under his skin as deeply as he was under mine.

"Is the Christmas tree still up?" I said lightly.

I left it like it was. Best fucking cave I ever lived in, his dark eyes said.

One day, we'll do it again, I sent back. I wouldn't have to fake being Pri-ya. Not with this man.

He stretched and moved, began subtly changing.

"Uh, Barrons, we have a meeting. I thought you'd go afterward."

"Ryodan canceled it," he said around teeth much too large for his mouth. "He's tattooing Dani. Jada."

"She's letting him?" I said incredulously.

"She asked."

I narrowed my eyes, mulling that over. "You were inking Ryodan. Same kind of tats you wear. I never saw those on him before." And I'd seen him naked. "Is he giving her a phone? Will he be able to find her like you found me?"

"Speaking of," he growled, twisting sideways with a series of painful-sounding crunches, "you *do* still carry the cell, Ms. Lane."

"Always," I assured him.

"I'll find this thing you seek, but when I return it's imperative I finish my own tattoos."

"Oh, God," I said slowly. "When you're reborn all your tats are gone. Even the ones that bind us together."

"And until I replace them, IYD won't work. That, Ms. Lane, is the only reason I wanted you to remain in Chester's the other day. Until I finish them."

IYD—a contact in my cellphone that was short for If You're Dying—was a number I could call that would guarantee Barrons would find me, no matter where I was. "I'm not completely helpless, you know," I said irritably. Dependence on him makes me nuts. I want to be able to stand so completely on my own one day that I feel like I measure up to being with Jericho Barrons.

"Head for the basement. I'll see you there. This won't take long." He turned and dropped to all fours, loping off into the night, black on black, hungry and wild and free.

One day I want to run with him. Feel what he feels. Know what it's like in the skin where the man I'm obsessed with feels most completely at home.

For now, however, I'm not running anywhere. I'm flying on the back of an icy Hunter to the house on the outskirts of Dublin where I once spent months in bed with Jericho Barrons.

* * *

Dreams are funny things. I used to remember all of mine, wake up with the sticky residue of them clinging to my psyche, the slumbering experience so immediate and intense that if I was in my cold place, I'd wake up freezing. If I was hearing music, I'd come to singing beneath my breath. My dreams are often so vivid and real that when I first open my eyes I'm not always sure that I have awakened and wonder if "reality" isn't really on the other side of my lids.

I think dreaming is our subconscious way of sorting through our experiences, tying them into a cohesive narrative, and filing like with like in a metaphorical way—so in the waking we can function with a tidily organized past, present, and future we barely have to think about in the moment. I think PTSD occurs when something so shattering happens that it blows everything that's stored neatly into complete chaos, disorganizing your narrative, leaving you drifting and lost where nothing makes sense, until you eventually find a place to store that horrible thing in a way you can make sense of. Like, someone trying to kill you, or discovering you're not who you thought you were all your life.

I have houses in my dreams, rooms filled with similar pieces of mental "furniture." Some are crammed with acres of lamps, and when I dream I'm looking at them, I'm reliving each of the moments that illuminated my life in some way. My daddy, Jack Lane, is in there: a solid, towering pillar of a lamp made from a gilded Roman column with a sturdy base. My mom is in that room, too, a graceful wrought-iron affair with a silk shade, dispersing in her soft rays all the gentle words of wisdom she tried to instill in Alina and me.

I have rooms with nothing but beds. Barrons is in those rooms pretty much everywhere. Dark, wild, sitting sometimes on the edge of a bed, head down, gazing up at me from beneath his eyebrows with that look that makes me want to evolve, or perhaps devolve into something just like him.

I also have basements and subbasements in my dream houses wherein lurk many things I can't see clearly. Sometimes those subterranean chambers are lit by a pallid gloom, other times corridors of endless darkness unfold before me and I hesitate, until my conscious mind inserts itself into the dream and I don my MacHalo and stride boldly forward.

The *Sinsar Dubh* lives in my basements. I've begun to wonder endlessly about it, feeling like a dog with a thorn deep in my paw that I just can't chew out. It manifests often when my subconscious plays.

Tonight, waiting for Barrons to bring the Alina-thing to me, I stretched out and fell asleep on silk sheets in the ornate Sun King four-poster bed in which Barrons fucked me back to sanity.

And I dreamed the *Sinsar Dubh* was open inside me.

I was standing in front of it, muttering beneath my breath the words of a spell that I knew I shouldn't use but couldn't leave lying on the gleaming golden page because my heart hurt too damned much and I was tired of the pain.

I awakened, drenched by an abject sense of horror and failure.

I stood abruptly, scraping the residue from my psychic tongue. In my dream the words I'd muttered had been so clear, their purpose so plain, yet awake, I didn't have one memory of the blasted spell.

And I wondered as I had so many times in recent months if I could be tricked into opening the forbidden Book in a dream.

Like I said—I don't know the rules.

I looked around, eyes wide, filling them with reality, not shadows of fears.

The Christmas tree winked in the corner, green and pink and yellow and blue.

The walls had been plastered—by Barrons months ago—with blow-up pictures of my parents, of Alina and me playing volleyball with friends on the beach back home. My driver's license was taped to a lamp shade. The room held virtually every hue of pink fingernail polish ever made, and now I knew why I couldn't find half the clothing I'd brought with me to Dublin. It was here, arranged in outfits. God, the lengths he'd gone to in order to reach me. There were half-burned peaches-and-cream candles—Alina's favorite—strewn on every surface. Fashion and porn magazines littered the floor.

Best cave indeed, I thought. The room, with the hastily plumbed shower I was certain he'd had to force my sex-obsessed ass into on frequent occasions, smelled like us.

I frowned. What a terrible place to bring the facsimile of my sister. Surrounded by memories of who I was, who she was, how integral a part of my life she'd been.

I cocked my head, listened intently with the last day of my Unseelie-flesh-heightened senses.

Footsteps above, something being dragged, sounds of protest, heated yelling, no male answer. The beast was dragging the imposter of my sister to the stairs. I guessed she'd gotten the screaming out of her system. But then again, if it were a Fae masquerading as my sister, it wouldn't have screamed. There would have been some kind of magic battle. I was interested to learn how and where he'd found it, if it had put up a fight.

I pushed up from the bed and braced myself for the coming confrontation.

* * *

The screaming started in the basement, loud and anguished, beyond the closed door. "No! I won't! You can't make me! I don't want it!" it shrieked.

I kicked open the door, stood framed in the opening and glared at the imposter. It was near the bottom of the stairs, with Barrons blocking the stairwell, it was trying to clamber back up on its hands and knees.

Was it going to pull the same stunt it had at 1247 LaRuhe? Pretend to be so terrified of me that I couldn't possibly interrogate it?

I stalked closer and it curled into a ball and began to sob, clutching its head.

I moved closer still and it suddenly puked violently, whatever it had in its stomach spewing explosively on the wall.

Barrons loped to the top of the stairs, shut and locked the door. I knew what he was doing. Transforming back into the man in private. He would never let anyone besides me see him morphing shapes. Especially not a Fae.

I studied the sobbing form of my sister, filled with grief for what I'd lost and hate for the reminder, and love that wanted to go somewhere but knew better. Such a screwed-up mixture, so poisonous. It lay curled on the floor now, holding its head as if its skull might explode as violently as its stomach just had.

I narrowed my eyes. Something about it was so familiar. Not its form. But something about the way it looked, laying there curled, clutching its skull as if it was—

"What the hell?" I whispered.

Surely it hadn't studied me that closely! Surely it wasn't playing such a deep psychological game.

I began stepping backward, moving away, never taking my eyes off it. Five feet. Ten. Then twenty between us.

The thing that was impersonating my sister slowly removed its hands from its head. Stopped retching. Began to breathe more evenly. Its sobs quieted.

I strode briskly forward ten feet and it screamed again, high and piercing.

I stood frozen a long moment. Then I backed away again.

"You're pretending you can sense the Book in me," I finally said coldly. But of course. Alina—my dead sister, not this thing—had been a *sidhe*-seer and OOP detector like me. If my sister had stood near the *Sinsar Dubh*, like me, might it (me) have made her violently sick?

I frowned. She and I had lived in the same household for two decades and she'd never sensed anything wrong with me then. She hadn't puked every time I'd walked in the room. Was it possible the *Sinsar Dubh* inside me had needed to be acknowledged by me to gain power? That perhaps, before I'd come to Dublin, it had lay dormant within and quite possibly would have remained that way forever if I'd not awakened it by returning to a country I was forbidden to enter? Had Isla O'Connor known that the only way to keep my inner demon slumbering was to keep me off Irish soil? Or was there something more going on? Had there really never been any Fae in Ashford because it was so boring while we'd been growing up? Or had my birth mother somehow spelled our *sidhe*-seer senses shut, never to awaken unless we foolishly returned to the land of our blood-magic?

Oh yeah, feeling that matrixlike skewed sense of reality again.

Why was I even speculating such nonsense? This thing was *not* my sister!

It raised its head and peered at me with Alina's tear-filled eyes. "Jr., I'm so sorry! I never meant for you to come here! I tried to keep you away! And it got you! Oh,

God, it got you!" It dropped its head and began to cry again.

"Fuck," I said. It was all I could think of. After a long moment I said, "What are you? What's your purpose?"

It lifted its head and looked at me like I was crazy. "I'm Mac's *sister*!"

"My sister died. Try again."

It peered at me through the dimly lit basement, then, after a moment, got up on all fours and backed away, pressing itself against a crate of guns, drawing its knees up to its chest. "I didn't die. Why aren't you doing something bad to me? What game are you playing?" it demanded. "Is it because Mac won't let you hurt me? She's strong. You have no idea how strong she is. You're never going to win!"

"I'm not playing a game. You're the one playing a game. What the hell is it?"

It drew a deep shuddering breath and wiped a trickle of foamy spit from its chin. "I don't understand," it finally said. "I don't understand anything that's happening anymore. Where's Darroc? What happened to all the *people*? Why is everything in Dublin so damaged? What's going on?"

"Ms. Lane," a deep voice slid from the shadowy stairs. "It's not Fae."

"It's not?" I snapped. "Are you certain?"

"Unequivocally."

"Then what the hell *is* it?" I snarled.

Barrons stepped into the light at the bottom of the stairs, fully clothed, and I realized he must store caches of clothing all over the city, in case he needed to transform unexpectedly.

He swept the Alina look-alike with a cold, penetrating gaze.

Then he looked at me and said softly, "Human."

25

*"Inside these prison walls,
I have no name . . ."*

The first time the Unseelie-king-residue came to the white, bright half of the boudoir in which he'd left her trapped by magic beyond her comprehension, the Seelie queen melted back against the wall, turned herself into a tapestry, and watched silently as a graphic scene of coupling unfolded before her unenthusiastic but eventually reluctantly fascinated gaze.

Hers was the court of sensuality, and he had once been considered king of it for good reason. Passion drenched the chamber, saturating the very air in which her tapestry hung, draping another bit of sticky, sexually charged residue on her weft and weave.

A visitor would have seen no more than a vibrant hunt scene hung upon the wall of the boudoir, and at the center, before the slab upon which the mighty white stag was being sacrificed, a slender, lovely woman with pale hair and iridescent eyes, standing, staring out from the tapestry and into the room.

She'd cut her queenly teeth on legends of the enormously brilliant, terrifyingly powerful, wild, half-mad godlike king that had nearly destroyed their entire race, and certainly condemned it to eternal struggle, with his obsession over a mortal.

She despised the Unseelie king for locking her away. For killing the original queen before the song had been passed on. For dooming them to striking alliances with weaker beings in order to survive, limping along with only a hint of their former grandeur and power.

She despised herself for not seeing through her most trusted advisor, V'lane, and being locked away by him as well, in a frozen prison, trapped in a casket of ice, scarcely daring to hope the seeds she'd planted long ago among the Keltar and O'Connor and various others might come to fruition and she would live. Carry on to try to survive the next test she'd also foreseen.

This—spelled into a chamber with memory residue—was not living. Buried in another coffin of sorts while her race suffered who knew what horrors.

The Unseelie prison walls were down. Even frozen in her casket, diminishing, being leeched of her very essence by the void-magic of the Unseelie prison, she'd felt the walls around her collapse, had known the very moment the ancient, compromised song had winked out.

She, more than any of the Seelie, understood the danger her race now faced. She was the one who'd used imperfect song, fragments she'd found hither and yon through the ages, to bind the Fae realms to the mortal coil. She'd only been able to secure her imperiled court by marrying it to the human planet.

Irretrievably.

And if that coil were devoured by the black holes, so, too, would be all the Seelie realms.

With the king, she'd pretended to know none of this, yet it had been precisely why she'd urged him to take action.

She knew their situation was worse even than that. She'd sought the mythic song herself, striving to restore that colossal magic from which their race had sprung. She'd studied the legends. She knew the truth. The song called an enormous price from imperfect beings, and they all were, to varying degrees. There was no easy way forward. It would cost her many things.

But she knew something else, too: a thing not even the Unseelie king knew. If she were able to manipulate and seduce him into saving Dublin, thereby her court, the price demanded would be levied most harshly against him.

The tapestry she'd become rippled and shuddered as she watched the residue of the Unseelie king's lies. For if she believed them, it was *her* on that pile of lush furs and bloodred rose petals, as diamonds floated lazily on the air, illuminating the chamber with millions of tiny twinkling stars.

If she believed him, she had once been mortal, and once been in love with the slaughterer of their race, the maker of the abominations, the one who'd cared nothing for the former queen to whom he'd been trothed, and less for the court he'd abandoned.

Cruce forced a cup from the cauldron of forgetting on you, the king had said before he left.

She'd never drunk from the cauldron. The queen was not allowed.

Before you were queen. When you were mine.

She didn't believe him. Refused to believe him. And even if she had—how could it matter? She was what she was now. The Seelie queen, leader of the True Race. She'd spent her entire existence as that. Had no memory of his lies. Wanted none.

And yet, she could divine no purpose for this charade. He needed nothing from her. He was the Unseelie king. He was an it, an entity, a state of existence, enormously beyond any of their race's comprehension. He needed nothing from no one. Legend was too complex and contradictory to unravel his origins. Or theirs.

She narrowed her fibrous eyes, the threads of the tapestry rippling. How could such a being as the mad king fabricate such depth of emotion as she was now seeing?

Emotion was alien to their race in this, its purest essence. They felt but facsimiles of it, enhanced by living with the primitive race she'd chosen to settle her people among, for that very reason. To expand their pale existence, to amplify their wan desires in order to sate them more amply.

Yet on the great round dais, a woman that looked and moved identically to her gazed down at the being she'd taken inside her body, inside her very soul, and laughed as Aoibheal had never known laughter. Touched as she herself had never touched. Was moved by the king she loathed far more intimately and with greater sensation than she had ever believed possible.

Forget your foolish quest, the woman on the bed said, sobering suddenly. *Run away with me.*

The king residue was abruptly angry. She could feel it, even as a tapestry. *We had this conversation. We will never have it again.*

It doesn't matter to me. I don't need to live forever.

You won't be the one left behind when you die.

Make yourself human with me, then.

Aoibheal narrowed her eyes further. A Fae make itself human for a human? Never. Only one, Adam Black, had ever insisted on such an absurd, devaluing action, and there were reasons for his madness that were her fault entirely.

The king displayed the proper Fae response.

Revulsion.

Refusal to abandon the glory that it was to be of the Old Race, the honored ones, the First Race. Perhaps in his case even—the First One. Still . . . the song had not been entrusted to him. Rather to a female. For good reason. Women were not blinded by passion. They were clarified by it.

As the king rose and towered over the woman he claimed Aoibheal was, she felt what the woman on the bed felt and it was chafing and uncomfortable: tired of fighting for something she knew she would never attain. Weary of trying to make the blind see. Knowing her lover had passed beyond her ability to reach.

But the woman on the bed felt something else Aoibheal could not understand at all.

That love was the most important thing in the universe. More so even than the song. That without love and without freedom, life was worth nothing.

The woman on the bed wept after the king was gone.

The woman in the tapestry watched in silence.

If she must pretend to be *that* woman to secure her Court's existence, so be it.

But it would cost the king everything.

26

"Separate the weak from the obsolete,
I creep hard on imposters . . ."

"It can't be human," I protested, staring at the thing that looked so heartbreakingly like my sister. "It's not possible. I've heard of doppelgangers but I don't believe in them. Not this perfect. Not this detailed." Except for a few minor things, like the diamond ring on her finger.

The imposter was sitting, leaning against the crate, its head swinging back and forth between us, eyeing me warily as if to ascertain I wasn't about to begin moving toward it again.

I gazed at Barrons in mute pain and protest. Now more than ever, I was wondering if I'd ever escaped the *Sinsar Dubh*'s clutches that night in BB&B.

You are here and I am here and this is real. Barrons shot me a cool, dark look. *Don't flake out on me now, Ms. Lane.*

I stiffened. *I never flake out.*

Remember that. And don't do it. Focus on the moment. We'll figure this out. You're trying to see the whole fucking picture in a single moment. That's enough to make anyone crazy. What do you do on a bloody minefield?

Try to get off it?

One step at a time.

He was right. Focus on the moment.

I looked back at the thing masquerading as my sister. It sat, looking as confused and disturbed as it had since the moment I'd first seen it. Then it looked up at Barrons, searchingly. "Who are you? What are you to her?"

Barrons said nothing. Answering questions isn't high on his list with anyone but me, and that's only because I have things he wants.

It went on in a rush, "My sister is carrying the *Sinsar Dubh.* It's in her clothing somewhere. We have to get it away from her. We have to save her." It cringed as it spoke the words, snatching a quick glance at me, as if it expected me to suddenly rain death and destruction on its head for speaking those words.

"I'm not carrying the *Sinsar Dubh,*" I snapped to whatever it was. "It's inside me. It has been since birth. But it's not in control of me."

I hoped.

It blinked at me. "What?"

"My sister died over a year ago in an alley on the south side of the River Liffey after scratching a clue into the pavement. What was that clue?"

"It was 1247 LaRuhe, Jr. But, Mac, I didn't die."

I felt like I'd just been kicked in the stomach by a team of frigging Clydesdales. For the teeniest of instants I wondered if it was possible. "Someone watched you die," I prompted.

"A girl with red hair. She took me to the alley. But she left before I . . . I—"

"Before you what?" I demanded coldly.

It shook its head, looking hurt and confused and lost. "I don't know. I don't remember. It's all . . . fuzzy."

Oh, that was convenient. "You don't remember. That's because my sister died. Dead people don't remember things. They sent Alina's body home to me. I saw it. I buried it." I'd mourned it. It had become my inciting incident, the catalyst that had reshaped my entire life.

"Mac," it gasped. "I don't know! All I know is I was in that alley and I was gouging a clue into the pavement for you. Then . . . I guess . . . I must have lost consciousness or something. Then two days ago I found myself standing in the middle of Temple Bar with no freaking clue how I'd gotten there! I have no idea what happened. And everything has changed! It's all so different, like I came to in the wrong—" It broke off, narrowing its eyes. "That happened a year ago? I was in that alley a *year* ago? I've lost a year? What is the date, I need to know the date!" Its voice rose with hysteria as it surged to its feet.

I took a step forward without meaning to and it pressed back against the crate, trying to become paper thin. Its hands went to its head, then one shot out to ward me off. "No, please, don't come any closer!" It whimpered until I took a step back.

I looked at Barrons.

It is conceivable, his eyes said.

"Bullshit!" I snapped. "Then how do you explain the body I buried?"

Fae illusion?

I cursed and spun away. Turned my back on the imposter. I couldn't keep looking at it. It was dicking with me royally. I couldn't believe the body I'd buried hadn't been her body. I didn't want to believe it.

Because deep down—desperately and with every ounce of my being—I wanted to believe it. Discover that someone, somehow, perhaps a Fae, had hidden my sister away and she'd never died at all. What a dream come true!

Unfortunately, I don't believe in clichéd happy endings anymore.

"Why do you have a ring on your finger?" I shot over my shoulder.

"Darroc asked me to marry him." Its voice caught on a sob. "You said he's dead. Is that true? Have I really been missing for a year? Is he alive? Tell me he's alive!"

I glanced over my shoulder at Barrons. *Is it really human? Could whatever it is be fooling even you?* I sent silently.

I sense her as fully human. Further, Ms. Lane, she smells like you.

I blinked, my eyes snapping wide. *Do* you *think she's my sister?* If Barrons believed it, I might have a complete meltdown. Or suspect my entire reality of being false. Barrons was nobody's sucker.

Not enough evidence to make that call.

What do I do?

What do you want to do?

Get that thing out of here.

Kill it?

No. Remove it.

What will that accomplish, Ms. Lane?

It will make me feel better at this very moment and that's enough.

Continue questioning her, he ordered.

I don't want to.

Do it anyway. I'm not taking her anywhere.

She's not a "her." She's an "it."

She's human. Deal with it.

I waited for him to remove the imposter. He didn't. Pissed, raw, seething, I kicked a crate out from the wall and dropped down on it. "You can start by telling me about your childhood," I fired at it.

It gave me a look. "You tell me," it fired right back.

"I thought you were afraid of me," I reminded.

"You haven't done anything." It shrugged. "At least not yet. And you're staying far enough away. Besides, if I really lost a year and Darroc's dead, do your worst," it said bitterly. "You've got my sister. I don't have anything left to lose."

"Mom and Dad."

"Don't you dare threaten them!"

I shook my head. It was acting like my sister. Bluffing me like I would have bluffed. Tried to keep the Book from knowing I had parents, if it didn't already know, then threatening if the Book appeared to be threatening them. Another twist of the worm in my apple. I was rapidly losing my grip on reality.

"Who was your first?" Failure, I didn't add.

It snorted. "Leave it to you to remind me of that. LDL."

Limp-dick-Luke. The town jock had remained a virgin much longer than most high school guys for a reason. He hadn't wanted word to get out that the powerhouse on the football field wasn't in bed. The loss of her virginity had been an epic failure. He'd never managed to get hard enough to break her hymen. But Alina had never told. Only me, and we'd christened him LDL. I'd never told either.

If my sister wasn't dead, what had I been fighting for? Grieving? Avenging? If my sister wasn't dead, where the hell had she been for a year?

Dani carried the blame for her death. If my sister wasn't dead, what really happened that night in the alley?

"Rightie?" I looked at Barrons. I so didn't want this thing—or anyone for that matter—checking out that man's package, but there were things, intimate things, Alina and I had shared. Such as eyeing a man's crotch and deciding which side he tucked his dick down. Alina used to say, "if you can't tell where it is, Jr., you don't want to know any more about it." Because it wasn't big enough to be noticeable.

Barrons stood, legs wide, arms folded, blocking the stairs, watching us with dispassionate calm, studying, analyzing, mining this unfolding madness for validity.

Its eyebrows rose as it looked at him. "Goodness. *Serious* leftie."

Barrons shot me a lethal look.

I ignored it. I wished I could figure out something to ask the fraud that I didn't know the answer to, because if this was some kind of projection, the Book inside me could very well have access to all the information I did. Might have "skimmed my mind" like the corporeal one for every last detail. But if I didn't know the answer, I couldn't confirm it. Complete catch-22.

You're thinking with your brain, Ms. Lane. It's not your most discerning organ.

What is? I snapped silently.

Your gut. Humans complicate everything. The body knows. Humans censor it. Ask. Listen. Feel.

I blew out an angry breath and shoved my hair back. "Tell me about your childhood," I said again.

"How do I know you're not the *Sinsar Dubh,* playing games with me?" it said.

"Ditto," I said tightly. "Maybe what's inside me is merely projecting you." And I was lost in a vortex of illusions.

Understanding manifested in its eyes as it absorbed what I'd said. "Oh, God, neither of us know for sure. Shit, Jr.!"

"You never used to say—"

"I know, fudge-buckets, petunia, daisies, frog. We made up our own cuss words." It snorted and we both blurted at the same time, "Because pretty women don't have ugly mouths."

It laughed.

I bit my tongue. Hating that I'd spoken with the imposter. The inflection so much the same. Cant of head nearly identical. I refused to laugh. Refused to share one moment of camaraderie with a thing that simply couldn't exist.

"How is the Book inside you? I don't understand," it said. "And why hasn't it taken you over? I heard it corrupted anyone that touched it."

"I'm the one asking the—"

"And exactly why is that? If you really *are* Mac, with the Book inside you somehow, and you aren't corrupted, and I really am your *older* sister"—it emphasized its seniority just like Alina would have—"and I'm not dead, don't I deserve a little understanding?" It frowned. "Mac, is Darroc really dead? I can't find him anywhere." Its face seemed to tremble for a moment, threaten to collapse into tears, then it stiffened. "Seriously. Tell me about Darroc and what the heck happened to Dublin, and I'll tell you about my childhood."

I sighed. If this was somehow magically my sister, she was as stubborn in her own way as I was. If it wasn't, I still obviously wasn't going to get anywhere unless I bartered a bit.

So, I filled it in on Darroc's pointless death when the Book had popped his head like a grape and gave it a scant sketch of recent events. Then I folded my arms and leaned back against the wall.

"Your turn," I said to the softly weeping woman.

27

"Ya'll oughta stop talking
start trying to catch up motherfucker . . ."

Jada knifed into the night, sharp, hard, and deadly.

This she understood. Killing made her feel alive.

She chose to believe she'd been born the way she was—not mutated as Rowena's journals had implied with endless self-aggrandizement—and this was her gift to her beloved city: cleansing the streets of those who would prey on innocents.

It didn't signify if her victims were Fae or human.

If they destroyed, they were destroyed. She knew a thing about human monsters: they were often the worst kind.

Killing those who killed was clean, simple, a calling. It distilled her, burned her down to fierce white light inside. Few had the taste for it. It was messy. It was violent. It was personal, no matter how impersonally she dealt the death blow, because at some point, whether Fae or human, their eyes met, and psychopaths and monsters also had plans, goals, investment in their existence, and resented dying, hated it, flung slurs and curses, sometimes begged with fear-slicked eyes.

She'd once thought she and Mac were the perfect pair.

Mac could kill as coldly and competently, though not as quickly.

Each rabid dog Jada put down saved the lives of countless good people, normal people unlike her, those who cared and could make the world a better place for the children, for the old ones, for the weaker ones who should be protected. She knew what she was and wasn't, never a daily need filler, but a big-picture woman.

She appreciated her gifts for what they were: speed, dexterity, the acute vision, auditory and olfactory senses of an animal, a brain that could compartmentalize the most minute details, divvying things up and sealing them off so nothing interfered with her mission.

Jada sliced her way through the streets of Dublin beneath a full moon haloed by a rim of crimson. Blood in the sky, blood in the streets, fire in her blade and heart. She stabbed and sliced, flayed and felled, reveling in purity of purpose.

Since her last rampage, the Unseelie had changed their tactics, donning glamour, clustering in groups.

They thought this afforded them protection. They were wrong.

She could take out a group as easily as a single enemy, and it saved her time hunting them individually. The stumpy-legged slow ones Mac had christened Rhino-boys were too easy. She preferred the red-and-black-clad guards to the highest castes: not sifters themselves but nearly as fast as she was, highly trained in combat.

Then there were the singularities, her preference. Sifters, they had to be trapped in a net of iron or lured into a metal-walled pit. Those were the ones that tried to tempt her with offers of the glories they could bestow with their enormous power.

Nothing affected her resolve. She was untouched by any plea, every offer.

She knew what she was. She knew what she wanted.

And the tattoo Ryodan was taking his bloody time layering into her skin was critical to her goals.

She sputtered in the slipstream, dropped down without meaning to, and stumbled into a park bench, bruising her shin. She snapped her sword up sharp and hard, spun, checking all directions. She was alone. Nothing to kill.

Ryodan. The prick.

She inhaled deeply of crisp, humid, ocean-salted air. Breath was everything. When nothing else could be done: one could breathe and shape and infuse that breath with strength and purpose. She tossed her head and straightened her spine.

Ryodan had knocked her out of the slipstream in the abbey.

And just now, in the street, the mere irritating thought of him had disrupted her focus, impairing precise manipulation of a delicate dimension.

She scraped loose strands of hair from her face, smoothed it back using the blood and goo on her hands, and plastered it smoothly, albeit chunkily, behind an ear. Then she reached into a boot and retrieved one of the last remaining pods she'd found Silverside, popped and swallowed it. She despised the thought of carrying boxes of protein bars around with her all the time, wasting space she might otherwise use for weapons and ammo. She was curious whether Dancer might invent a more potent and portable source of fuel in his endless experiments at Trinity College's abandoned labs.

A dry chittering above pressed her back into the shadows of a nearby doorway. Tipping her chin upward, she peered with narrowed eyes, wondering if they, too, could be slain. Analyzed potential methods of trapping them. Mac's stalkers had ceased trailing her for some reason, and although Jada had never seen them harm anyone, she knew they were neither benevolent nor benign.

A flock of a hundred or more carrion wraiths flew overhead, streaking across the crimson-ringed moon, cloaks trailing like ghastly skeletal black fingers beneath wispy low-hanging clouds. Their faces glinted with metallic adornments, and she shivered, an atavistic response. She recognized the flocking pattern: they were hunting. But what? Mac was visible again, and though the teenager she'd once been would have wondered about the hows and whys of that, the woman she'd become wondered about nothing that didn't further her purposes.

Only when the zombie eating wraiths—the ZEWs—had passed did she slide back up into the slipstream and head for Chester's.

Three days, he'd said. That was how long it would take him to complete his tattoo.

And Jada would have the final weapon she needed.

The great and powerful Ryodan on a leash.

"Goddamn it, do you know what you just did?" Ryodan growled when she burst into his office.

Jada dropped into a chair, tossed her legs over the side and folded her arms behind her head. She had no doubt he'd watched her dramatic entrance on one of his endless monitors. Stretching lean, she shot him a cool look. "Walked through the club." And patrons had parted around her as if she were carrying the Black Plague. Peeled away from the icy killing machine.

"Drenched in Unseelie guts," he clipped.

"Blood, too," she said lightly.

"You go slaughtering Fae, then come sauntering into my club wearing pieces of them. My employees serve Fae here."

"Perhaps they should be on the menus, not in the booths." He was as angry as she'd ever seen him. Good. Maybe he'd work faster to get rid of her tonight. She and Dancer could investigate the black holes without him. Once she had the map. "Have the rules changed and I didn't get the memo? Last I heard, I wasn't supposed to kill on your turf. I didn't."

He moved so quickly she didn't see him coming. And she had a moment of sudden insight: not only did he move faster in the slipstream, he accessed it more quickly. She'd never tried to streamline her time entering, only her time within. She added a new challenge to her list.

He towered over her. "Don't play games with me, Jada. Belligerence is beneath you."

She neither shifted position nor acknowledged his criticism. "I didn't have time to change."

"Then you'll make it now. I'm not working on you with that much death on your skin." He raked her with a cool glance. But deep in those silver eyes there was something hot. Excited by the carnage she wore. She narrowed her eyes, expanded her senses, wondering for the umpteenth time about this man's secrets.

She realized they were both breathing shallowly and instantly altered her pattern, lengthening her inhales and exhales. She didn't need a mirror to know what she looked like.

Savage. Eyes much too bright, hot and cold at the same time.

Blood and guts on her face, in her hair. Covered with it, boots, jeans, skin. Body thrumming with barely harnessed energy.

Hungry, even after so much killing, to lash out, to do something to balance the scales inside her that felt so impossibly out of kilter. "You want me to waste time leaving to take a shower when we have—Don't touch me!" She was on her feet, yanked to them. Her hands went up and out, blocking, knocking his hands away.

They stood like that, a foot apart, and she thought for a moment he was going to grab her by the shoulders and shake her, but he didn't. Merely let his hands fall. Good thing. She would have kicked his ass across the office.

He said coldly, "You tell yourself you've learned the right things to turn on and off inside you. You haven't. You killed tonight with fury. I smell it on you. And you lied to yourself while doing it. You killed from the pain of not knowing how the fuck to live in this world. Get used to it. A superhero doesn't flaunt his kills. He slides in, takes the lives he came for, and slides back out, wearing shadow."

"How would you know? You're the villain of the piece."

"Not tonight, Jada. Tonight it was you. How many did you kill?"

She said nothing. She had no idea.

"How many were human?"

Again she said nothing.

"And you're certain they deserved to die. Certain you're thinking coolly enough to pass that judgment."

She could stand in silence a long time.

"I'll say it one more time. Jada. Let me teach you."

"The only thing I'll let you do is tattoo me."

"You're brittle."

"I'm steel."

"Brittle snaps."

"Steel bends."

"Christ, you're so close." He shook his head in disgust.

"To what?" she said derisively. "To the way you think I should be? Isn't that what you've always been doing? Like Rowena? Experimenting on me? Determined to make me what you want?"

He went still, assessing her intently. "You know what Rowena did."

"I live inside my own head. I'm brilliant."

He didn't speak for a moment, as if debating what to say and what not to say, and she wondered what he thought he knew that she didn't. Measuring her. Deeming her, if she could read the look in his eyes, on the verge of an explosion. She wasn't. She had herself completely under control. To prove it, she once again adjusted her breathing. Deepening it. She wasn't entirely certain how it had gotten so shallow again.

He stepped back then, as if giving a cornered, wild animal room so it wouldn't spook. "Rowena wanted you to be what she wanted you to be," he said finally. "I want you to be what *you* want you to be. And it's not this."

"You don't know what I want. Your inferences are incorrect. Tattoo me or I leave."

Another measured look. "Wash and I'll tattoo you."

"Fine. Where's the nearest lav?" She wanted that tattoo.

Without bothering to reply, he turned for the door.

She followed, chafed that he had something she wanted badly enough that she would follow. Chafed that she was so wired her hand trembled as she swept her sword back to pass through the door.

Chafed that he was right.

She *had* killed with fury tonight.

She'd played Death like a lover, seeking release. If she'd really wanted to help Dublin the most logical and efficient way possible, she'd have gone to Inspector Jayne, forged a new alliance, and cleaned out his overflowing cages so the Guardians could capture more. Let a hundred Guardians net for her so she could slay even greater numbers. But efficient killing hadn't appealed to her, standing there, methodically slicing off the heads of dull-eyed, defeated enemies. There was something about the heat of the hunt she'd craved.

She had no desire to analyze motives that had been so clear at the last full moon, now splintered, impaling her every way she turned.

She followed him in silence. She would put up with anything, do virtually anything, to get her tattoo finished.

"Unbutton your jeans."

Resting her head on her arms on the back of a chair, Jada didn't move. "Make it smaller. I doubt any part of it needs to be on my ass."

"I won't bastardize the spell. Do you want it to work or do you want to walk around with a tat that may not perform at the critical moment?"

She popped the top two buttons on her jeans and shoved the waistband down. Then his hands were on the lower part of her back where it met her hips, and she had to bite her tongue to keep from shivering. Her skin felt too hot, the air too cool.

Once, she'd watched him touch a woman like this, close his hands on her body where he was touching her now. He'd been pushing into her from behind and thrown his head back and laughed; beautiful, cool, strong man. She'd wanted to catch that moment in her fourteen-year-old hands, explore it, understand it, strain it through her fingers. Be the cause of it happening.

Joy. This cold, hard man was capable of joy. The conundrum had fascinated her. And stirred something inside her that she now understood with a mature woman's brain, that moment when her young body had intuited on a visceral level that she, too, would experience those things, that her body was made for it, and soon a whole new realm of experience beyond imagining would open to her.

The fourteen-year-old had crouched, hidden in a ventilation shaft above Level 4, and closed her eyes, pretending to be the woman he was with. Trying to imagine how it would feel. Being the woman who made *that* man feel that way. Shivering with a blend of sensation so intense it almost hurt: hungry, anxious, wild, too hot, too cold, too alive. She'd found a large vent in a bathroom, sneaked out for a closer look, and nearly gotten caught.

Lust. It was a blinding thing. One might as well gouge out one's own eyes. Yet for some, indulged as a surface dance between strangers, it was a way of feeling without having to.

She inhaled and straightened her back. Young. Strong. Untouchable. She focused on radiating all those things, particularly the last.

He'd been working on her for over two hours, after a wasted hour in which he'd insisted she clean up and wait until her clothing was laundered by one of his many employees. She would have sat nude in front of him to get the damned ink.

Then again, perhaps not.

She'd examined the beginning of the tat yesterday with a mirror, looking over her shoulder into another mirror. It was a complex pattern with a brand in the center, layered in gray and black and something else, something glittering that wasn't any type of ink she'd ever seen. It shimmered in the hollow of her back, seeming to move in tandem with her subtlest shift, like silvery fishes beneath the surface of a lake. Somehow he was embedding a spell into her skin. And she hoped—only one. The devil was multifaceted, and so, too, might be his ink.

It offended every ounce of her being to let Ryodan do

such a thing. Yet if he could genuinely track her with it no matter where she went, mortal or Silverside, she wanted it more than any other weapon she might have been given. As she'd recently told an Unseelie princess, there was the devil who couldn't get the job done and wouldn't eat you, and the one that could but might. She knew which one Ryodan was. And was willing to take her chances. "This would work, even in the Hall of All Days?" she asked again, finding it nearly impossible to believe. But she would be depending on it.

"Hell itself couldn't keep me from joining you with this on your skin."

"Why are you doing it?" He always had motives. She couldn't divine this one. What did it matter to him if she got lost again? She didn't buy his line that he didn't lose things that were his. She wasn't, and they both knew it. He wanted something from her. But what?

"Figure it out. You're brilliant."

"You need me to save the world?"

"I don't need anything."

That left want. "Why are you always interfering in my life? Don't you have better things to do?" It had made her feel special all those years ago, that the powerful and mighty Ryodan had paid attention to her. Solicited her input, desired her around. Though she never would have admitted it and had bitched endlessly about it. He'd thought she had a great deal to offer and would one day be "one hell of a woman." It had given her a kind of aiming-at point. Silverside, she'd kept aiming at it.

Her faith in his power, his attention to those details he'd chosen to track, had been absolute.

She'd waited.

He hadn't come.

His hands were no longer moving at the base of her spine. She felt nothing for several long moments, then the light dance of his fingers across her scars. He traced one after the next. She should stop him. She didn't. It was almost as if his fingers were saying: I see every injury you suffered. You survived. Bang-up fucking job, woman.

"I could remove them," he said.

"Because a woman shouldn't have battle scars. The same thing that brands a man a hero marks a woman as disfigured."

"There's nothing disfigured about you. Except your aim. Work on that."

She was silent then. She was wary around this new Ryodan; the one that didn't push and poke and prod but treated her like . . . well, she wasn't sure what he was treating her like, and that was the crux of it. She couldn't get a handle on how to respond to him when she didn't understand his overtures. It was like trying to return a tennis ball on a court when someone had changed the rules and you didn't know which spot you were supposed to smash the ball back into. Once, they'd lobbed that ball back and forth like pros, intuiting each other's every move. Now when he swung, she spent too much time staring at the ball in the air.

In his office, she'd kissed him. He hadn't kissed her back. Now he was touching her intimately, with her shirt off, but made no move or comment to indicate it was anything but business. Not that she would have entertained anything but business. Why had he said "Kiss me or kill me" that day in his office? Had it been merely another of his position-clarifying tactics, like the night she'd discovered that, although the Crimson Hag had killed him, he'd somehow come back as good as new and insisted she choose between being disappointed that he was still alive or being loyal to him?

He'd brought her to what she was fairly certain were his private quarters, a spartan set of rooms deep beneath Chester's. She was also fairly certain it wasn't his only place and, like her and Dancer, he had many well-stocked lairs in which to retreat from the world.

Ultramodern, ultrasleek, the room was shades of chrome and slate and steel. Black, white, and, like the man himself, every shade of gray. In the room adjoining the one in which they sat was a bed with crisp white sheets and a soft, dark velvet spread. The bedroom had smelled of no one but him, which didn't surprise her. He would never take a woman to one of his places. It was never that personal. The decor was tactile, complex but simple. The kitchen was white quartzite and more steel. The bathroom sculpted of thick, silver-veined marble and glass. Everywhere she looked, the lines were straight, clean, sharp, hard, like the lines of his face, and his philosophy.

"So if I call IISS what happens again?" she fished.

He didn't reply and she hadn't expected him to, but nothing ventured nothing gained. Sometimes you could trick an answer out of someone. He'd already given her as much of an answer as he would and it had been a complete nonanswer: hope you never find out.

His finger moved slowly over a long thin scar close to her spine. "Knife?"

"Whip with steel points."

He touched a spray of white bumps. "Shrapnel?"

"Blow-dart gun." Filled with tiny crystalized rocks. Blown by a beast on a planet of eternal night.

"This?" He touched a messy, shallow one near her hip.

"Fell down a cliff. Did that one myself."

"Stay or go?"

"The scars? Stay. I earned them."

He laughed. After a moment she felt something very like the tip of a knife at the base of her spine. "I'm one inch away from ripping out your throat," she said softly.

"Blood binds. I need some of yours to set this layer of the spell."

"How much?"

"Minor."

"You're mixing yours with it."

"Yes."

Blood spells had nasty, pervasive side effects. This man's blood in hers was not something she wanted. His tattoo, however, was. "Proceed," she said without inflection.

He did, and she found herself slipping back into that strange, almost dreamy place she'd been in since he'd begun inking her. As he'd worked, his big strong hands moving with precision against her skin, the angry thrumming in her body had faded, her muscles had stilled, her tension calmed. She was having a hard time remembering what had driven her out into the streets today on such a murderous rampage. Languor infused her limbs and her stomach no longer hurt. Her psyche was beginning to feel drowsy and relaxed, as if she could just stretch out and sleep for a long, long time and not have to worry while she did because this man would stand guard and she could rest knowing that whatever predators were on this world, the world's greatest predator was right next to her and she was sa—

She sat up straighter, flexed her muscles and snapped back into high alert.

There was no such thing as safe. Safe was a trap, an ideal that could never be achieved. And hero worship was pointless. There were no heroes. Only her.

Behind her, he said, "You don't have to be on guard all the time. Nothing can hurt you here."

He was wrong. Anytime there was another person in the room with you, the possibility for hurt existed.

"You're doing something to me," she accused.

"I can have a certain . . . agitating effect on a woman."

He meant "whip her into a frenzy." She'd seen him do it.

"I can also have a gentling one."

"Stop it. I didn't ask for it."

He pressed his wrist to the base of her spine, held it a long moment, no doubt melding blood with blood, then said, "That's it for tonight."

"Finish it," she demanded. "I know you can." There was a sudden coldness behind her as the heat of his body vanished.

Her shirt hit her in the shoulder, and after a moment she yanked it on over her bra, knowing it was pointless to argue. She stood, stretched, and turned around.

"Tell me what happened to you in the Silvers and I'll finish it."

They looked at each other across the space of the chair. "I grew up," she said.

"The long version."

"That was it. You said you'd give me the map."

He tossed it to her and she caught it with one hand, slipped it into her pack. Of course he'd give it to her now. He knew she'd return for the tattoo. She'd wanted the map for two reasons: to test theories on the smallest of the holes, and alert people of their precise locations to avoid inadvertent deaths. Of far greater importance was finding a way to remove the cosmic leeches from the fabric of their reality.

"Tomorrow night, same time?" she said.

"I'm busy tomorrow night."

Fucker. He was going to dick with her about finishing the tat?

He herded her to the door with his presence, subtly yet irrefutably.

"Got a date with Jo?" she said coolly.

"Jo's fucking Lor."

She looked at him. "How did that happen? Lor does

blondes. And I thought you and Jo were exclusive." She hadn't believed that for a moment. Jo wasn't Ryodan's type.

His cool eyes lit with amusement. "It was a getting-over-the-ex fuck. And now they're both tangled up in it."

She arched a brow. "You dumped her, so she pulled a revenge fuck?"

"She dumped me. And her take on it was 'scraping the taste of me off her tongue.' "

No woman dumped Ryodan. Or scraped the taste off. If Jo had, he'd not only let her, but set the plan in motion. "What are your plans for tomorrow night? Cancel them. This is more important. I could get lost," she ordered.

"I suggest you avoid mirrors until we complete it. Day after. My office in the morning. I'll finish it."

"Tomorrow. During the day."

"Busy then, too."

Why was he delaying? What was his motive? "I'll just let myself out."

"You won't. You have the sword. I have patrons. I plan to keep them."

She was silent a moment then said, "I won't kill any of them, Ryodan. I'll respect your territory."

"If I respect yours."

"Yes."

He held out a cellphone. "Take it. IISS won't work yet but the other numbers will."

She slipped the cell into her pocket as she slipped out the door.

He closed it behind her, remaining inside, allowing her to leave unattended because she'd given her word. He'd taken her word as covenant.

She turned for no reason she could discern and placed her hand, palm flat, to the door.

Stared at it, head cocked, wondering what the hell she was doing.

After a moment she shook herself and strode briskly down the hall, swiped the panel and entered the elevator. The teen she'd been would have barged into every one of Ryodan's private places on these forbidden lower levels she could invade before he managed to stop her. And, she understood now, she'd have done it mostly for the rush of their confrontation when he finally did.

The woman had her own business to attend.

Inside the room, Ryodan removed his hand from the door.

"Is it the day yet? Is it? Is it? IS IT?" Shazam exploded from beneath a tangle of blankets and not one pillow, later that night when she entered their chambers.

"Soon," she promised. "And keep your voice down," she reminded.

"You *smell* again," Shazam fretted, turning circles in agitation. "I don't like the smell of him. He's dangerous."

"He's necessary. For now."

When she stretched out on the bed, Shazam pounced, landing on her stomach with all four paws, hard. "Not *one* thing more? Just *necessary*?"

"Ow! Good thing I didn't have to go to the bathroom!" She knew from too many enthusiastic early-morning greetings that forty-odd pounds of Shazam was hell on a full bladder. Not to mention the tenderness of a fresh tat pressing into the bed. "Not one thing more," she assured him.

"Did he finish it?"

"Not yet. Soon."

He deflated as abruptly as the melodramatic beast was wont. "It's all going to go horribly wrong," he wailed. "Everything always does." He sniffed, violet eyes dewing.

"Don't be such a pessimist."

He ruched the fur along his spine and spat a sharp hiss at her, working himself into a snit. "Pessimists are only pessimists when they're wrong. When we're right, the world calls us prophets."

"Ew, fish breath!"

"Your pitiful offerings, my bad breath. Bring me better things to eat."

"We'll be fine. You'll see."

He shifted his furry bulk around, parking his rump south of her chest (soft spots he wasn't allowed to pounce *ever*), his belly so fat he had to spread his great front paws around it. Then he leaned forward and slowly touched his wet nose to hers. "I see you, Yi-yi."

She smiled. Everything she knew about love she'd learned from this pudgy, cranky, manic-depressive, binge-eating beast that had been her companion through hell and back, too many times to count. He alone had protected her, loved her, fought for her, taught her to believe that life was worth living, even if there was no one there to see you living it.

"I see you, too, Shazam."

28

"I would give everything I own
just to have you back again . . ."

I'd left her. The woman that looked like my sister and had far too many of her memories and unique characteristics—I just left her there—in the basement where I'd been Pri-ya, sitting in the middle of crates of guns and ammo and various food supplies, looking unbearably lost and sad.

So, Mom and Dad think I'm dead? she'd asked as I was leaving.

They buried you. So did I, I'd flung over my shoulder.

Are they okay, Jr.? Did Mom lose it when she thought I was dead? Was Daddy—

They're here in Dublin, I'd cut her off coldly. *Ask them yourself. Go try to convince* them. *On second thought, don't. Stay away from my parents. Don't you dare go near them.*

They're my parents, too! Mac, you have to believe me. Why would I lie? Who else would I be? What's wrong? What happened to you? How you did get so . . . hard?

I'd stormed out. Some part of me had simply shut down and there'd been no turning it back on. I'd gotten "hard," as she called it, because my sister had been murdered.

For the past twenty-four hours I'd refused to even think about the imposter. I'd done nearly as good a job of keeping it in a box as I did with the Book.

But when it seeped out, it went something like this:

What if it really was *her*?

My sister, alone out there, and I'd turned my back on Alina in this dangerous, Fae-riddled city?

What if she got hurt? What if she was somehow truly, miraculously alive and ended up getting killed by a black hole or an Unseelie because I'd stormed away and left her alone, too wary, too suspicious, to let myself believe?

I'd have gotten my second chance—and blown it.

I suspected I might kill myself if that turned out to be the case.

What if she went to see my parents? They wouldn't be as realistic as me. They'd welcome her back blindly. Daddy might start to feel skeptical in time but I guaran-damn-tee if that imposter knocked on their door, they'd let her inside their house in one second flat.

On the other and just as plausible hand: what if it was an imposter sent to fuck me up royally, get me to trust it, only to do something terrible to me in an unguarded moment? Who could get closer to me (and my parents) than my sister?

Or what if I was stuck in one gigantic illusion that hadn't ended since the night I *thought* I'd bested the *Sinsar Dubh*?

Because I longed so desperately for it to be her, to believe that Alina had somehow survived, and I wasn't stuck in an illusion, I was a hundred times more suspicious of this whole situation. My sister was my ultimate weakness, next to Barrons. She was the perfect way to get to me, to manipulate me. She was the very thing

Cruce and Darroc and the Book had all offered me back, at one point or another, to try to tempt me.

I'd lived with Alina's ghost too long. I may not have made peace with it, but I'd accepted her death. There was a painful closure in that, a door that couldn't easily be reopened.

She claimed she couldn't remember a single thing from the moment she'd passed out in that alley until she'd been standing in Temple Bar, a few days ago.

How convenient was that?

You couldn't refute amnesia. Couldn't argue a single detail. Because there were no details.

Just exactly what might have happened to her? Was I supposed to believe some fairy godmother (or Faery godmother, to be precise) had swooped in, rescued her moments before she died, healed her then put her on ice until this week? Why would any Fae do that?

Dani believed she'd killed Alina. No, I'd never gotten full details. I didn't know if she actually remained in that alley until Alina was stone-cold dead or not. Nor did I think Jada would tell me, if I were to ask. And on that note, I didn't want to ask. I didn't want Jada/Dani having to relive it.

Oh, God, what if they ran into each other in the streets?

I glanced at Barrons as we ascended the stairs to Ryodan's office. "There's no other solution, Barrons," I said bitterly. "I'm going to have to talk to it again. I need you to—"

He gave me a dry look. "Check your cellphone."

"Huh?"

"The thing you call me on."

I rolled my eyes, pulled it out. "I know what a cellphone is. What am I looking for?"

"Contacts."

I thumbed it up. I had four, since he'd hooked up my

parents to their incomprehensible network. There were now five.

Alina.

"You put the thing's phone number in my cell? How does it even have a phone that works? The only network running is hardwired and about as reliable as—Wait a minute, you gave it one of your phones? When?"

"Her. Quit trying to carve emotional space with pronouns. And I'm not your bloodhound," he growled. "You don't dispatch me to fetch prey. When I hunt, it ends in savagery, not a fucking soap opera."

"It wasn't a soap opera," I said defensively. The imposter might have been hysterical but I'd been cool as a cucumber.

He shot me a look. "The dead sister always comes back. Or the dead husband. Or the evil twin. Mayhem and murder inevitably ensue."

"Who even says words like 'mayhem'?" At some point, while I slept, anticipating I'd want to talk to it again, Barrons had taken a phone to it and programmed mine. And washed his hands of us. I glanced at him sideways. Or not. Knowing him, he would keep a close eye on the imposter.

"You think I should have kept interrogating it—her," I said irritably. Easy for him to think. His heart hadn't been quietly hemorrhaging while looking at it. He hadn't been the one questioning his own sanity.

He gave me another look. "Strip the scenario of your volatile emotions," he clipped.

I bristled. "You *like* my volatile emotions."

"They belong in one place, Ms. Lane. My bed. My floor. Up against my wall."

"That's three places," I said pissily.

"Any fucking place I'm inside you. That's one. Keep your friends close. Enemies closer," he said tightly. "She's indisputably one or the other. And you bloody well let her walk away." He turned and stalked off down the corridor.

I stared after him with a sinking feeling. Damn the man, he was right. Whatever the Alina look-alike was, forcing it out of my space and mind might assuage my immediate discomfort but that only increased the potential for future peril. Mine, hers, my parents', everyone's.

I sighed and hurried after him. I would call the imposter the moment our meeting was over.

Assuming we all survived it.

When we entered Ryodan's office, Sean O'Bannion was standing inside. Nephew to the dead mobster Rocky O'Bannion, he shared the same rugged, black Irish muscular build and good looks and was Katarina's lover. Well, unless something was happening downstairs with Kasteo, he was. Staying in close quarters with one of the Nine, alone for a long period of time, was pretty much the worst thing a woman in a monogamous relationship could do. I wondered why she was down there. Why Ryodan had permitted it. There was no way Kat would come out of that room the same as she'd gone in.

"You haven't seen Katarina at all?" Sean was saying to Ryodan. "Since when? Killian said he saw her here a few weeks ago."

"This Killian of yours told you she was in my office?" Ryodan said.

"No, he said he saw her walking through the club. Said she seemed hell-bent on something. He kept an eye out for her but didn't see her leave. I've not been able to find her since."

Ryodan said, "I haven't seen her lately." He glanced

up and shot me a hard look: *Speak and I'll rip out your bloody throat, woman.*

Beside me, Barrons growled softly.

I'd made two oaths during my time in Dublin: one to the Gray Woman, with my proverbial fingers crossed because the bitch had tried to kill Dani and that was unforgivable enough in and of itself, but I'd also known she was going to kill still more innocents. Endlessly, until she was stopped. Steal their beauty, torture and play with them while they died. They would be someone's sister, brother, son, daughter. And more of the human race would be lost. I'd never had any intention of honoring it. A coerced oath, forced by a murderer, while threatening the life of someone I love, is not an oath. It's extortion.

I'd taken another oath, more recently, that I would keep forever. Even if it cost me. Even if it pained me enormously, which I was certain it would. I held Ryodan's gaze levelly. *Your secrets, mine.*

After a moment he inclined his head.

Sean turned to look at me. "Have you seen Kat, Mac?"

"Not lately." I availed myself of Ryodan's technique, which even Christian would have had a hard time seeing through. I hadn't seen her. Lately. Depending on how you defined lately. The trick was the same as outsmarting a polygraph, tell your mind the truth while telling the lie. "But I'm sure she's okay," I added hastily, not wanting him to worry more than he was. The skin beneath his eyes was smudged dark from stress and lack of sleep. I could only imagine what he was going through.

"I'm not so bloody sure. She's been missing for weeks."

"Dani was missing for weeks, too," I said. "And she's back just fine now." Well, that wasn't entirely accurate but she was *back*. "I'm sure she'll show up. Maybe she's off on confidential *sidhe*-seer business or something." One thing I knew for sure, Kat was safe where she was. Physically. Mostly.

He shook his head. "No one at the abbey has seen or heard from her. And Kat's never gone somewhere without telling me first. We tell each other everything."

Ryodan said dryly, "No one tells each other everything."

"We do," Sean said coolly. "I'm sore fashed and I'll tell you that. It's not like my Kat. I've been dropping by Dublin Castle twice a day, checking the bodies the Garda are collecting off the streets."

I cringed inwardly. "I'm so sorry, Sean. Is there anything I can do to help?" It was all I could do not to shoot Ryodan a nasty look. Sean was worried sick about Kat and he had every reason to be. If someone went missing in Dublin these days, the odds were high they were dead.

Sean said soberly, "Aye, keep your eye out. Let me know if you hear a whisper of a word about her. You'll find me in the piano pub with the lads most evenings. If I'm not there, any one of them will get word to me."

"I'll let you know if I hear anything," I promised.

He nodded and stepped out.

The moment the door closed, I spun on Ryodan and hissed, "I'll keep your secrets, but you need to let him know somehow that she's all right."

"Because it's not fair," he mocked.

"Because there's no need to inflict suffering if you can prevent it," I retorted.

Those cool silver eyes dismissed me. "He'll brood, he'll pine. She'll return. He'll get over it. No damage done."

I scowled at him. The man was as immutable as Barrons. They didn't view a month of worry as remotely significant because a month was the blink of an eye to them, and besides, everyone died.

Immortals. Pains in the asses, every one of them.

"Let's get this over with," I said brusquely. "I have things to do."

Our path to the small cell in the dungeon was interrupted again, this time by Christian MacKeltar.

The moment we stepped off the elevator and turned left, I felt an icy wind at my back and he was there.

I turned and gasped, startled. Christian looked nearly full Unseelie prince, taller than he usually was, much broader through the shoulders, with great black wings angled up and back and still sweeping the floor. Anger colored him in shades of the Unseelie prison. Ice dusted his wings, his face.

"What the fuck were you thinking?" he snarled at Ryodan. "I can't do this. I won't."

"Then your uncle will suffer."

"*You* do it!"

"I did the hard part. He's alive."

"He's never going to forgive you."

"Yes he will. Because one day he'll feel something besides the pain and horror and he'll be glad that he's alive. No matter the price. That's the way it works for men of a certain ilk. But you know that, don't you, Highlander?"

Ryodan turned away and we resumed walking toward the cell in silence, buffeted by an icy breeze.

In the narrow stone cell, I dropped into a chair, edgy and irritable.

My Unseelie flesh high had evaporated without warning, late this afternoon at BB&B, while I was struggling to disengage one of my least damaged bookcases from a pile of splintered furniture and stand it upright again.

The unwieldy tower of shelves had fractured several toes when it crashed to the floor, inadequately supported by abruptly too-weak muscles. Fortunately, even without Unseelie flesh, I heal quickly and no longer sported even a slight limp.

Unfortunately, withdrawal was setting in, making me short-tempered and more impatient than ever.

I wanted this over with. I'd already decided to tell them I still couldn't find the Book, even with my *sidhe*-seer senses open again. How would *they* feel if I tried to make them go rooting around inside themselves for whatever was in there? Attempted to get them to let me use their inner demon in its wildest, most uncontrolled form?

They wouldn't tolerate it for a second. Why should I? There had to be another way to save our world. Speaking of, before I went disturbing anything I shouldn't, I glanced at Barrons. *I have to show you something back at the bookstore. Tonight.*

Can it wait?

It shouldn't. It could help us with the black holes. But I want you to take it. I'm not the one to use it.

He inclined his head in assent.

If something goes wrong . . . I told him where to find it, figuring him finding my journals, too, would no longer matter to me if the worst happened tonight.

Nothing will go wrong.

Easy for him to say. My Book had been far too quiet lately.

I closed my eyes and pretended to be sinking inside, questing for my inner lake, beneath which gleamed a monster. Recalling the first time I'd discovered the place, the dark chamber, the freedom and power I'd sensed in it. Before I'd known how corrupted it was.

I'd once loved having that inner lake. Now I despised it.

A flood of water exploded inside me, gushing up, icy and black. I choked and sputtered and my eyes shot open.

"What is it," Ryodan demanded.

I swallowed surprisingly dryly, for all the water inside me. "Indigestion," I said. "I don't think this is going to work."

Ryodan said, "We've got all night."

And I had no doubt he would sit here all night with me, and make sure I sat here, too.

I closed my eyes again and sat very still, not reaching, merely feeling tentatively. What was going on? My lake had never exploded up to meet me like that, nearly drowning me.

Waters rippled and stirred. Deep down, carving chasms in my soul, there was a rapid, rushing current. I didn't like it. I'd never felt it before. My lake had always been still, serene, glassy, disturbed only when things of enormous power floated to its surface.

Yet now I felt as if there was something in there that contained a vicious undertow. And I might get swept away by it if I wasn't careful.

I opened my eyes. "Just exactly how do you think the Book could possibly be of any use to us?"

"We've been through this."

"I can't read it. I won't open it."

"Fear of a thing," Barrons said, "is often bigger than the thing."

"And if the damn 'thing' is even a tenth the size of my fear of it, that's bad enough," I retorted. "You stood in the street with me and watched what it did to Derek O'Bannion. It came after you, too. You sensed its power. And you're the one that told me if I took even one spell from it, I wouldn't ever be the same."

"I said if you 'took' a spell. It's possible there's a way to access information without taking one. It's conceivable you could read it without utilizing an ounce of magic. Like Cruce. You know the First Language."

Was it possible? His contention didn't sound entirely implausible. I did know the First Language, there inside me in the tatters of the king's memory. But those memories were part of the Book itself. If I reached for my knowledge of the First Language without it being offered, did that mean I was opening the Book? "I've always felt that simply opening it of my own will would doom me."

"It's already been open. You closed it."

I hadn't thought about any of this in months. I'd shoved every memory of the *Sinsar Dubh* into a far, dark corner of my mind. He was right. The Book had been open inside me that afternoon when he found me staring sightlessly outside BB&B, lost in my own head, debating whether I dare risk taking a spell from the *Sinsar Dubh* to free his son.

But *I* hadn't opened it. It had *been* open, the Book offering. Big difference.

Might I have read the spell to save his son, scanning only the words without disturbing the magic, without getting turned into a soulless, evil psychopath? Books could be read. Spells had to be *worked.* Was information one thing and magic entirely another? I wasn't sure I could split hairs that finely. I wasn't sure the Book would either.

Still, Barrons had a point. Fear of a thing was often worse than the thing itself. I'd been afraid of him once. Now, I couldn't even conceive of such a reaction to this man.

I wanted desperately to believe the Book wasn't the great, all-knowing, all-spying evil I'd been assuming it was.

Unfortunately, I'd have to face it to find out.

Maybe it was silent because it was gone. Maybe my lake had swallowed and neutralized *it*. I was inundated with maybes lately. Limp noodley things you could do nothing with.

I sighed and closed my eyes, no longer pretending. I wanted to know. What was at the bottom now? What was going on in the vacuum of dread I carried in my gut every blasted day?

I dove deep, kicked in hard, rejecting fear. I had Barrons and Ryodan in the room with me. What more could I ask as I faced my inner demon?

I swam, holding my breath at first, diving into one towering wave after the next, getting drenched by violently churning water capped by thick foamy brine. I ran out of breath and started struggling against the sensation of suffocation. I forced myself to relax like I had the day I stepped through the Unseelie king's great mirror in their boudoir and my lungs froze, knowing I had to breathe differently there. Now, I drew the water into my lungs, became one with it.

The waves fought me, buffeted me, as if trying to expel me, but it only strengthened my resolve. Was this why I'd nearly drowned when I first sought it? Because the Book no longer had all that much power—perhaps never had—and didn't want me to figure that out? And it was throwing up some huge, watery smoke screen to keep me from discovering the truth? Maybe my adamant rejection of it the night it turned me invisible had weakened it somehow. That was, after all, the night it had ceased speaking. And maybe I'd turned visible again because the single spell it offered had been a temporary one, with a finite, albeit damned convenient end date.

I dove deeper, inhaling my icy lake, felt it rushing through my body, filling me with *sidhe*-seer power. I kicked and thrust and swam, following a gold beacon, forced my way through the chilling undertow and finally drifted lightly down into a dark, shadowy cavern.

Last time I'd been here, the *Sinsar Dubh* had been crooning to me like a lover, welcoming me, inviting me in.

A towering wall exploded in front of me.

I shattered it with a fist.

Another!

I kicked through it, swinging and cursing.

Wall after wall sprung up and I blasted through them as if my life depended on it.

Whatever the Book didn't want me to see, I was going to see.

This was ending.

Here, tonight.

I wasn't leaving this cavern until I knew what I was dealing with.

Wall after wall tumbled, no match for my fury, until there it was: an elaborately carved ebony pedestal upon which lay a shining golden Book.

Open. Just like in the nightmare I'd recently had.

I stood motionless in the cavern.

So—it could open itself. I knew that. No big.

I'd closed it before.

I would close it again.

But first I'd see if it really was possible for me to look at it, understand the words, without using the spell.

Still . . . if it wasn't—and I turned into a homicidal maniac?

I almost wavered then. Stood, dripping water for a time, having a hard time persuading myself to move forward.

I could walk away right now. Say I couldn't find it. Storm back out of my head and let sleeping dogs lie.

I sighed.

And live forever with this eternal instability? Be undermined day after day by fear of the unknown? It was past time for me to face my demons.

Clenching my jaw, I stalked to the pedestal and forced myself to look down. Half expecting I wouldn't understand a single word. That perhaps there wouldn't even *be* any words there. That perhaps my churning *sidhe*-seer waters had stripped it clean of all forbidden magic.

The blood in my veins turned to ice.

"No," I breathed.

I would be evil if I'd used it.

I would be crazy.

I would be a psychopath.

I wasn't any of those things.

At least I didn't think I was.

"No, damn it, no!" I said again, backing away.

Not a murmur from the *Sinsar Dubh*, not a chuckle, not a jibe.

Just me alone with the hollow echo of my footfalls.

And my failure.

I'd had no problem reading and understanding the words carved into the Book's ornate golden pages. The First Language had flowed as easily as English across my mental tongue.

And those words had seemed as familiar as a beloved and often repeated nursery rhyme.

The *Sinsar Dubh* was open to a spell to resurrect the dead.

29

"I'm just holding on for dear life,
won't look down won't open my eyes . . ."

Jada moved through the crisp cool dawn in perfect sync with her environment, eyes closed, feeling her way through the slipstream.

Shazam had taught her that all things emitted frequency, that living beings were essentially receivers that could pick up the vibrations if they could only achieve clarity of mind. Meaning no ego, no past or future, no thoughts at all. Unadulterated sensation. He contended humans lacked the ability to empty themselves, that they were too superficial, and that shallowness was marbled with identity, time/ego obsessed, and given the complexity of her brain, he'd doubted that she would ever get there.

Given the complexity of her brain, she'd been quite certain she would.

And had.

Becoming nothing and no one was something she knew how to do.

Now, she heard with some indefinable sense the dense, simplistic grumble of bricks ahead, the complex whir of moving life, the sleek song of the River Liffey, the soft susurrus of the breeze, and turned minutely to avoid obstacles, melding with the razor edge of buildings.

She was being hunted.

She'd passed small clusters of angry, armed humans, clutching papers with her picture. Mostly men, determined to gain power and ensure a degree of stability in this brutally unstable city by capturing the legendary *Sinsar Dubh*.

Fools. They felt nothing more than a brisk wind as she passed, on her way to her sacred place. Her bird's-eye view. The water tower where she'd once crouched in a long black leather coat, sword in her hand, and belly-laughed, drunk on the many wonders of life.

As she pulled herself up the final rung and vaulted onto the platform, the smell of coffee and doughnuts slammed into her, and although her face betrayed nothing, inside she scowled.

She dropped down from the slipstream to tell Ryodan to get the hell off her water tower. They weren't supposed to meet for another few hours and this was her turf.

But it was Mac she saw, sprawled out on the ledge as if she was perfectly at home, slung low in the old bucket car seat Jada had dragged up there herself, ball cap angled over her badly highlighted hair to shadow her face. She was dressed nearly identical to Jada, in jeans, combat boots, and a leather jacket.

"What are you doing on my water tower?" Jada demanded.

Mac looked up at her. "I don't see your name on it anywhere."

"You know it's my water tower. I used to talk about it."

"Sorry, dude," Mac said mildly.

"Don't fecking 'dude' me," Jada said sharply, then

inhaled long and slow. "There are plenty of other places for you to be. Find your own. Have an original thought."

"I watched the Unseelie princess kill one of the Nine about an hour ago," Mac said, as if she hadn't even heard her. "She's carrying human weapons now. Marching with a small army. They shot the shit out of Fade. Started to rip his body apart."

"And?" Jada said, forgetting her irritation that Mac was here. She'd tried to strike an alliance with the Unseelie princess but the powerful Fae had chosen Ryodan instead, striking a deal for three of the princes' heads. Apparently that alliance was over, if she was now killing the Nine.

"He disappeared. The princess saw it happen."

Jada went still. She knew the Nine returned. Somehow. She didn't know the nuts and bolts of it but she certainly wanted to. "Why are you telling me this? Your loyalties are with them, not me."

"They're not mutually exclusive. My loyalties are to you as well. Coffee?" Mac nudged a thermos toward her.

Jada ignored it.

"Got doughnuts, too. They're soggy, but hey, it's sugar. It's all good."

Jada turned to leave.

"I saw Alina the other night."

Her feet rooted. "Impossible," she said.

"I know. But I did."

Jada relaxed each muscle by section of her body, starting with her head and working down. Opponents tended to focus at eye level, so she always eradicated signs of obvious tension there first. She didn't want to talk about this. She didn't think about this anymore. "I watched her die," she said finally.

"Did you? Or did you leave before it was over?" Mac held out a doughnut.

Jada ate it in two bites, wondering if this was some

kind of twisted joke Mac was playing on her. Then, in a single swallow, she tossed back the little plastic cup of coffee Mac had offered.

"Fuck," she exploded. "That was hot."

"Duh. It's coffee," Mac said, arching a brow.

"Give me another doughnut. Where did you find them?"

"Little vendor a few blocks from BB&B. And I didn't." She frowned. "I had to ask Barrons to go get breakfast, and believe me, every time I ask for anything, I get this freaking lecture on how he's not my fetch-it boy. I have to slink through the damn streets to go anywhere, hiding from everyone. They're hunting me."

"Despite my paper retracting the accusation, they're hunting me, too," Jada admitted. "We had a small mob at the abbey yesterday."

"What did you do?"

"I wasn't there. My women told them none of the accusations were true. Although they didn't believe it, my *sidhe*-seers are formidable and the mob's numbers were small. They'll be back in greater force at some point," she said, not certain why she was even having a conversation.

But sliding through dawn over Dublin this morning, for the first time since she'd returned, she'd felt . . . something . . . something to do with being here, home, back, and that maybe, just maybe, everything would work out all right. She'd find a place for herself and Shazam here.

She took the second doughnut Mac was holding out. "They're not bad," she admitted, eating slowly enough to taste it this time.

"Better than protein bars. I hear music coming from the black holes. Do you hear it?"

Jada looked at her. "What kind of music?"

"Not good. It's pretty awful, frankly. I couldn't hear

anything for the past few days, but once the Unseelie-flesh high wore off, it was there. Not all of them. The small ones give off a kind of innocuous hum, but the larger ones give me a serious migraine. Did you see Alina gouge something into the pavement?"

Jada said nothing.

"It wasn't your fault," Mac said.

"I did it," Jada said coldly. "My action."

"I'm not saying you didn't. I'm saying there were extenuating circumstances. Just trying to unskew your self-perception."

"My perception is not skewed."

"You have responsibility dysmorphia syndrome."

"You should talk."

"You were a child. And that old bitch was an adult. And she abused you. It wasn't your fault."

"I don't need absolution."

"My point exactly."

"Why are you on my water tower again?" she said icily.

"Best view in the city."

There was that. Jada crouched on the edge and looked down. "I didn't see her gouge anything into the pavement."

"Then she may have lived," Mac said slowly.

"No. Absolutely not. Rowena never would have let me leave until she was dead. She always made me stay until the last." She looked at Mac. "Alina's not alive. Don't let someone play you."

Then she stood and turned for the ladder.

"If you see someone who looks like her in the streets, do me a favor and leave her alone," Mac said. "Until I sort this out."

Jada stood motionless a moment, not liking anything about what Mac had just told her. Alina was dead. And if there was something out there masquerading as her, it would only bring trouble. "Do me a favor," she said coolly.

"Anything."

"Stay the fuck off my water tower in the future."

As she slid up into the slipstream, she heard Mac say, "When I look at you, Jada, I don't see a woman who killed my sister. I see a woman who got hurt that night in the alley every bit as badly as Alina did."

Jada shoved herself up into the beauty of the slipstream and vanished into the morning.

"Breakfast?" Ryodan said when Jada entered his office.

"Why is everyone trying to feed me this morning?"

"Who else tried to feed you?"

"We're not friends," Jada said. "Don't pretend we are."

"Who shit in your coffee this morning?"

"And you don't say things like that. You're Ryodan."

"I know who I am."

"What is *with* everyone this morning?" she said, exasperated.

"How would I know. You haven't told me who everyone is."

"Don't talk to me. Just finish the tattoo."

"After you eat." He took a silver lid off a tray and shoved a platter toward her.

She stared at it. "Eggs," she murmured. She hadn't seen them in such a long time.

And bacon and sausage and potatoes. Oh, my.

"Try the yogurt. It has something extra in it," he said.

"Poison?"

"A protein mix."

She gave him a cool look and shook her head.

"Food is energy. Energy is a weapon. It would be illogical to refuse it."

Jada dropped into a chair across the desk from him and picked up the fork. He had a valid point. Besides, eggs. Bacon. Yogurt. There was even an orange. The aroma of it all was incredible.

She ate quickly, efficiently, shoveling it down in silence, barely chewing. He was finishing her tattoo today. She was vibrating with energy, afraid he might change his mind for some reason. When she'd polished off the last crumb, she shoved the platter out of the way, yanked her shirt over her head, unbuttoned the top two buttons of her jeans and looked at him expectantly.

He didn't move.

"What?" she demanded.

"Turn around," he said. "I'm working on your back, not your front." His silver eyes were ice.

She turned around backward in the chair, hooking her ankles around the rear legs, resting her arms on the slatted back.

"Relax," he murmured as he settled into a chair behind her.

"I'm not tense," she said coolly.

He ran his fingers along the two tight ridges of muscle along her spine. "This is your idea of supple. It's a bloody rock. It'll hurt more if you don't relax."

Closing her eyes, she willed herself smooth, long, lithe. "Pain doesn't compute."

"It should. It's a warning your body needs to recognize."

After a few minutes of his hands at the base of her spine, she felt that peculiar languor spreading through her body and snapped, "Stop doing that."

"You keep tensing."

"I do not."

He traced his fingers along her spine again, delineating the hard ridges. "You want to have this argument."

"You're tattooing my skin, not my muscles." She

breathed easy and slow, relaxed again. It was merely her eagerness to see the ink done, nothing more.

"You're wrong about that."

She wasn't sure if he was skimming her mind or not, if he meant her muscles or her eagerness. "I can relax my own muscles."

"Keep bitching, I stop working."

"You like that, don't you—having the power to push people around?"

"That's why I'm giving it away."

She closed her eyes and said nothing. Was that how he thought of the tattoo he was etching into her skin? That he was giving his power to her? She wondered again what would happen when she called IISS. Precisely how much of a leash she would have him on, exactly how smart and powerful the great Ryodan really was.

She hoped enormously.

"Did you ever see anything like the black holes while you were in the Silvers?" he said after a time.

She shook her head.

"Talk, don't move. This must be precise."

"I saw many things. Nothing like those holes."

"How many worlds?"

"We're not friends."

"What are we?"

"You asked me that before. I don't repeat myself."

He laughed softly. Then, "Stretch long. There's a hollow at the base of your spine. I need it flattened."

She did, then one of his hands was on her hip, stretching her out even more.

Then she felt the tip of a knife at her back, followed by a deep burn of a slice, and a sudden warm gush of blood.

"Nearly there," he murmured.

Prick after prick of needles in a rapid dance across her skin.

Time spun out in a strange, dreamy way, and she relaxed more deeply than even she was capable of achieving on her own lately. It wasn't entirely bad, she decided. What he did to her was nearly as good as sleep. Rebooted her engines, took her down to ground zero and fueled her up again.

Then she felt his tongue at the base of her spine and shot out of the chair so fast she knocked it over and stumbled into the wall. She spun and shot him a furious look, rubbing an elbow that would undoubtedly be bruised. "What the bloody hell are you doing?" she snarled.

"Finishing the tattoo."

"With your tongue?"

"There's an enzyme in my saliva that closes wounds."

"You didn't lick me last time."

"I didn't cut as deeply last time." He gestured at a mirror above a small cabinet in an alcove. "Look."

Warily, she turned her back to the mirror and peered over her shoulder. Blood was running down her spine, dripping on her jeans, on the floor.

"Put a Band-Aid on it."

"Don't be a fool."

"You're not licking me."

"You're being absurd. It's a method. Nothing more. The wound must heal before I set the final mark. Sit the fuck down. Unless you have a good reason you don't want my saliva closing the wound."

He'd removed them both from the equation with his words. Saliva. Closing a wound. Not Ryodan's tongue on her back. Which was exactly what she should have done—seen it analytically. Many animals had unusual enzymes in their spit. She was bleeding profusely, and hadn't even known he'd cut so deep.

She picked the chair up, repositioned it and slid back

into the seat. "Go on," she said tonelessly. "You startled me. You should have told me what you were doing."

"I'm going to close the wound with my saliva," he said slowly and pointedly.

Then she felt his tongue at the base of her spine, the stubble of his shadow-beard against her skin. His hands were on her hips, his hair brushing her back. She closed her eyes and sank deep into nothing inside her. Moments later he was done. He traced a final emblem with his needles and told her she was free to go.

She bolted from the chair and headed for the door.

"Choose wisely, Jada," he said softly behind her.

She froze, hand on the panel, turned and looked at him. She had no intention of replying. But her mouth said, "Choose what wisely?"

He smiled but it didn't touch his eyes. That cool, clear silver gaze had always seemed to stare straight into her soul. She studied him, realizing his eyes weren't quite as void as she'd always thought. There was something in them, something . . . ancient. Immortal? And patient, endlessly patient, as he moved his chess pieces around. Aware, brutally, intensely alive and on point, and she had a sudden certainty that Ryodan saw right through her.

He knew. He'd known all along what she wanted.

"Why else would you let me tattoo you," he murmured.

He'd tattooed her with full awareness of what he was doing: giving her a collar, a leash to yank anytime and anyplace she wanted, with absolutely no foreknowledge of how she might choose to use it. Why would he do that?

And in those complex, every-shade-of-gray eyes, she thought she saw something else. Thought she heard him speak.

When the time comes, trust will be your weakness.

"I always choose wisely," she said, and left.

Trinity College. Jada remembered discovering it at nine years old while taking her first ever tour of the city. The sheer number of people coming and going, laughing and talking, flirting and living, had astonished the child. She'd felt like she was on fire with life. Born of a fool's fever, her mom used to say about her, words slurring with drink and exhaustion after another long day working two jobs, still finding time at night to take lovers. Jada knew nothing of that—the circumstances of her conception, how foolish it had been or not, and hadn't cared. She'd only known that she was born *with* a fever that made everything brighter, hotter, and more intense for her.

She'd been alone most of her life. People on TV weren't the same as the real thing.

Even out in the world, she'd been more isolated at nine than most grown-ups, with no clue who her father was, her mother dead. No home. Just a yellow, mom-scented pillowcase with little ducks embroidered along the edge in a house that held an iron cage she never wanted to see again.

Trinity was *college*. A magical word to the child, a place she'd seen on TV, where people gathered in large numbers, smack bang in the middle of the *craic*-filled city, and learned fascinating things, fell in love, broke up, fought and played and worked. Had *lives*.

Jada moved across the campus, deciding if Dancer tried to feed her, she would go back to the abbey. She'd had her fill of people behaving abnormally today.

She found him in one of the lecture halls that either had already housed an inordinate amount of musical equipment, including a baby grand piano, and an entire computing lab, or he'd moved everything in there to consolidate efforts and save time walking from building to building on campus.

He wasn't alone. When Jada dropped down from the slipstream and walked in, he was sitting on the piano bench, close to a pretty woman, one hand on her shoulder, as they laughed together about something.

She stopped. Nearly backed out. They looked good together. How had she failed to see what a grown man he was when she'd been fourteen? She was struck again by the idea that he'd downplayed himself for her, to hang out with the child she'd been. And now that she was grown up, he wasn't doing it anymore.

Were he and the woman lovers? The woman looked like she wanted to be, leaning into Dancer's tall, athletic body, smiling up at him. His dark, thick hair had gotten long again, falling forward into his face, and she curled her hands into fists. Years ago she used to wash it for him, drape a towel around his shoulders and cut it. He'd take his glasses off and close his eyes and she'd used the privacy to stare unabashedly at his face. They'd nurtured each other in small ways. In the back of her mind, she'd harbored the vague idea that maybe one day she'd be a woman and he'd be a man and there might be something magic between them. Dancer had been the only truly good, uncomplicated person in her life.

She must have made some small noise because he suddenly glanced over his shoulder and his face lit up.

"Jada, come in. I want you to meet everyone."

She moved forward, wondering what was going on. They'd always been a team. Just the two of them. She'd never seen him with anyone else. Ever. She hadn't even known he had friends.

He was striding toward her, long-legged, good-looking, full of youthful enthusiasm and energy. The pretty woman wasn't far behind him, hurrying to catch up. Glancing between Dancer and Jada with a guarded expression.

"Good to see you," he said, smiling.

"You have no intention of feeding me, do you?" She thought she'd better get that out of the way first.

He raised a brow. "Are you hungry?"

"No."

"Okay then, no. Jada, this," he swept an arm around the woman's shoulders and pulled her forward, "is Caoimhe Gallagher. She was working on her doctorate in music theory before the walls fell. She and"—he gestured toward the bay of computers where a young man with brilliantly colored hair was hunched before a screen—"Duncan were living in one of the dorms."

Jada studied the woman he'd called "Keeva," wondering if she was one of the O'Gallagher clan endowed with *sidhe*-seer blood. If so, she belonged at the abbey.

"Aye, and there's Squig and Doolin," Caoimhe said, offering her a hesitant smile and pointing down the line of screens. "Brilliant with math, not much for the talking. We'd no clue they'd taken up in the old library. More than a few of us managed to survive, hiding here on campus."

Dancer said, "I found them shortly after I started working in the labs. Apparently I was making a lot of noise." He grinned. "Caoimhe's been helping me refine some of my theories about the black holes, what made them, what might fix them. Wait till you hear some of her ideas about music and what it really does. She's got perfect pitch and her ear is bloody unreal!"

Jada looked at the woman's ears but saw nothing of note.

"I hum it, she can play it," Dancer clarified. "I give her frequencies to work with, and she makes songs out of them."

"I hadn't realized others were working with us," she said coolly.

"Unless someone drops the bloody Song of Making in our lap, Jada, we can't do it alone," he said. "C'mon. Let me show you around."

She left Trinity half an hour later, seeking solitude.

In the past, Dancer had a way of subtly recharging her, making her feel pretty much perfect. But today she'd realized he made a lot of people feel that way.

His "crew" saw him the same way she did: super-brainy, unpredictable, funny, high-energy, attractive.

She'd liked having him all to herself. It was confusing to watch him interact with people he'd known for a while, realizing he had a life that hadn't included her.

While she'd a life that hadn't included him, she'd believed she was his entire world.

Today she'd wondered if it had been Caoimhe he'd watched *Scream* with, that night she wasn't around. Wondered if, when he'd disappeared for days in the past, he was off with these friends she hadn't known he'd had, laughing and working and implementing plans.

Back then she'd appreciated that he hadn't held on to her too tightly. But she'd also assumed his life had kind of stopped happening when she wasn't around. That he'd gone—alone—to one of his labs, where he thought about her the entire time and invented things to help her. Her self-preoccupation had been so intense, she'd believed when she wasn't present in certain parts of the world, those parts of the world were put in a jar on a shelf until she returned.

Not so. His life had gone on while she'd kept him at bay, determinedly dodging anything that hinted at a restraint.

She remembered Mac telling her once that the reason grown-ups mystified her was because she wasn't factoring their emotions into her equations. She'd never understood how careful Dancer had been around her so she wouldn't startle and run. Apparently so cautious he'd kept their friendship completely separate from the rest of his life and friends.

There'd been nine in all that she'd met, working on various matters related to their problem. Some were studying the hard science of the holes, others searching for the softer Fae lore, and those, like Caoimhe, working with Dancer one on one, teaching him everything they knew about music, speculating with him as she once had. It was jarring to an extreme, but then the whole day had been.

She knew what she needed.

Hand on the hilt of her sword, she went fluid and kicked up into the slipstream.

30

"Step into my parlor said the spider to the fly . . ."

Putting pen to paper clarifies my thoughts.

Before I came to Dublin, I didn't have many thoughts to ponder other than new drink recipes and what guy I wanted to date.

Since my arrival here, I've filled journal after journal. The way I saw it, there were only three real possibilities and they were, unfortunately, equally plausible.

1. *The* Sinsar Dubh *is already open. I opened it in a dream and I've been using it without even realizing it, turning myself invisible when I wanted to disappear, turning myself visible again because I couldn't get the bullets out, and raising my sister from the dead because I couldn't stand living without her. Either the Book is allowing me to use it without repercussion (at this point anyway) in an effort to lead me down a dark path with a darker purpose that will bite me in the ass soon enough or I'm stronger than the Book and can use it without being corrupted. (Gee, wouldn't that be nice?) (And why did the Book stop talking to me* after *I vanished that night? Why did it bitch the whole way back to Dublin then shut*

up? Further, why did it always seem so . . . wishy-washy compared to the corporeal Book?)

2. *The* Sinsar Dubh *is closed and tricking me. It's not wishy-washy at all, just playing me like a maestro. Making me underestimate it. Granting my wishes, trying to make me think it's already open. Why? So I might reach for one of its spells myself, believing I'm in control. And when I do, it's all over. Hello psycho-Mac.*

3. *My* sidhe-*seer gifts are far more enormous than I realize. I can do all these things without the* Sinsar Dubh *and that's why it wanted me for a host. Because together we'd be unstoppable. It's possible much of the magic I've used comes from the part of the lake that is my heritage, not the Book at all, and it's just trying to make me believe that power belongs to it, not me.*

"You're still trying to label things, Ms. Lane," Barrons said, reading over my shoulder.

"I knew you were there," I said irritably. I always do. He'd walked in the back door of BB&B about twenty seconds ago. Every cell in my body comes to hard, frantic, sexual life when he's near. I hadn't expected to see him. It was barely noon and he's a night owl, not an afternoon one.

Between withdrawal that made me feel all my nerves were raw, flayed, and twitching on the surface of my skin and the many frustrating, slinking hours it took me to get back from the water tower to Chester's—all so I could *dependently* ask Barrons to get a Hunter to take me back into the bookstore—I was in a sour mood. But I'd also been in no mood to risk running into the

Unseelie princess, her army, and her human guns. I couldn't outshoot or Voice all of them at once.

For being so bloody powerful, I couldn't even walk home by myself. It pissed me off. Asking Barrons for things drives me crazy.

"Makes two of us, Ms. Lane."

"Well, do something about it," I said pissily.

"There you go, asking me for things again."

I stretched on the love seat I'd dragged from his study into the rear of the wrecked bookstore and peered up at him over my shoulder. I couldn't find him for a second. He was motionless, fading beautifully into shadow, existing in that seamless, not-quite-there way he existed only around me and only when we were alone.

"Okay. I give up. What am I doing wrong?"

"At the moment? Not fucking me."

He yanked my head back with a fistful of my hair, arched my neck at a hard angle, and sealed his mouth over mine, tongue going deep, kissing me so hard and raw and electric that my mind blanked and I dropped my journal, forgotten.

Can't breathe with this man. Can't breathe without him.

"Where do you feel most free," he murmured against my mouth.

I bit his lip. "With you."

"Wrong. You know why you fuck so good?"

I preened. Jericho Barrons thought I fucked "so good." "Because I've had a lot of practice?"

"Because you fuck like you're losing your sanity and can only find it again on the far side of depravity. Not by taking a shortcut. By taking the very long, lingering way around. You look like a pretty, soft, breakable Barbie. You fuck like a monster."

That pretty much summed it up. "Do you have a point?"

"Don't be afraid of the monster. She knows what she's doing."

"Why are you still talking?"

"Because my dick isn't in your mouth."

"That can be remedied." I was over the love seat and on him, taking him down hard to the floor beneath me, and he was falling back, laughing and oh, God, I love that sound!

I ripped his zipper open as we went, then my hands were against his hot skin and my mouth was on his dick and nothing could rattle me, nothing could touch me, because I was rattling Jericho Barrons's cage and, as always, while it lasted, I would be whole and perfect and free.

Later he said, "You think of the *Sinsar Dubh* as being an actual book inside you."

"And?" I said drowsily. Apparently sex with Barrons was the cure for everything, including the tightly wired tension of withdrawal. I'd been shooting furtive looks at my fridge, with its lovely baby food jars of canned Unseelie all day. Clenching hands and jaw, refusing to let my feet walk me over to it. But Barrons in my mouth pretty much makes me stop thinking about anything else in it.

"I doubt it's either open or closed. Stop thinking of it so concretely."

"You mean it's embedded in me, inseparably, and my ethical structure is the proverbial cover? And I need to stop worrying about the Book and think about me. What I can live with. What I won't live without."

He propped himself up on a shoulder, muscles rippling and bunching, and looked down at me, smiling faintly.

I touched his lips with my fingertips. I adore this

man's mouth, what it does to me, but I most especially adore the rare occasions he smiles or laughs out loud. In the low light, the dark, harsh angles of his face seemed chiseled from stone. Barrons isn't a classically handsome man. He's disturbing. Carnal. Base. Forbidding. Big and powerful, radiating primal hunger. His eyes are blades, slicing into you: dark, ancient, glittering with predatory intensity. He moves like a beast even in his human skin. A woman takes one look at him, her stomach drops like a stone and she runs like hell.

Which direction she goes is the defining point: she'll run away—or toward him—depending on her ability to be honest with herself, her hunger for life and willingness to pay any price at all to feel so damned alive. "What? Why are you smiling?" I said.

He bit my finger. "Stop fishing for compliments. I give you enough."

"Never enough. Not when it comes to you. Do *you* think I used it? Do you think I brought Alina back from the dead?"

"I think neither of those questions signify. You're alive. You're neither insane nor psychotic. Life goes on, and in the going, reveals itself. Quit being so impatient."

I pushed my hands into his thick dark hair. "I love how you simplify me."

"You need it. You, Ms. Lane, are a piece of work."

"I'll show you work. I want this." I leaned forward and murmured into his ear. "Right now. Exactly that way. And this *and* this. And I want you to keep doing it until I'm begging you to stop. But don't stop then. Make me take it a little longer." I wanted to feel no responsibility. No control.

"And bloody hell, woman, there you go, asking me for things again." He stood and tossed me over his shoulder, one big hand clamped possessively on my bare ass, to take me to that place we sometimes went when I had a serious kink in my already seriously kinked chain.

"Hard life, Barrons."

"I'll show you hard."

Of that I had no doubt. Every possible way.

Damn, it was good to be alive.

Much later with a voice that was raw from—well, let's just leave it at raw—I said to him when I was fairly certain he was meditating deeply enough that he wouldn't hear me, "I should have gone after her."

"Dani," he murmured.

Well, shit. He was aware after all.

"Always."

"Yes, Dani," I said.

"Analyze the odds. You know she'd have kept running."

"But Barrons, she made it out, losing virtually zero Earth-time. Maybe I could have caught up with her, somehow. Maybe she would have gone to a safer world if I'd chased her through, with a quicker way home. Maybe she wouldn't have had to be alone in there the whole time and she and I would have battled our way back to Dublin together."

"Maybes are anchors you chain to your own feet. Right before you leap off the boat into the ocean."

"I'm just saying. I think I know what I did wrong."

"What's that?"

"I didn't believe in magic. I'm living in a city of it, jam-packed with dark magic, evil spells, twisted Fae, and I have absolutely no problem believing in all of *them*. But somehow I stopped believing in the good magic." I prodded him in the ribs, where black and red tattoos stretched across his hard stomach and trailed down to his groin. "Like *Bewitched*. Or *The Wizard of Oz*—"

"An untrained witch and a charlatan," he said irritably. "Did you just bloody poke me in the bloody ribs?"

"Okay, or Dumbledore, he's the real thing. My point is you can't believe only in Voldemort. You have to believe in Dumbledore, too."

"Or you could just believe in me." He caught my hand and put it exactly where he wanted it.

I smiled. I excelled at that.

Hours later I was holding my cellphone in that hand, staring at my recently created contact.

The good magic, including those possibilities that weighed in on the side of the positive, not the negative, was heavy on my mind.

Barrons was gone, back to Chester's, where we would meet soon. I bit my still-swollen lower lip and worried it as I punched the Call button. It rang only once and she was on the line.

"Mac?" Alina said quickly. "Is that you?"

Fuck. Instant pain. How many times had I sat in my room in Dublin, dialing her damned number to listen to her recording, wishing just one more time to hear her answer? More times than I cared to count. Yet here it was. I could get addicted to this alone. Merely being able to call and hear something that sounded like my sister answering. I wondered where she was. Where Barrons had no doubt set her up, probably warding the place to keep her alive, too.

"Hey," I said.

"Hey, Jr." She sounded happy to hear from me, but wary.

"Where are you?"

"My apartment."

I closed my eyes, wincing. I could walk over there, bound up stairs I'd once sat on sobbing as if my soul was being hacked in two, slowly and with a chain saw. She'd open the door.

And instantly double over, puking, because even if she really was my sister, I couldn't hug her, because I was anathema to her now.

"Want to come over?" she said hesitantly.

"So I can make you puke some more?"

"Your boyfriend—"

"He's not my boyfriend."

"Okay, the man you love," she said flatly, "brought me some pages photocopied from the *Sinsar Dubh*. He said you used them to learn to manage the discomfort. I'm practicing. I don't like puking any more than you like making me puke."

Working with those pages had helped me only to a point. But unlike the corporeal Book—which had enjoyed tormenting me—I had no desire to hurt Alina. If she really was. And if she practiced enough with them, maybe one day I'd get that hug. If she really was. "When did Darroc give you the engagement ring?" It was bothering me, a nagging detail.

She made a soft sound that was equal parts irritation and acceptance. A *so we're going to play this stupid game?* coupled with *I love you, Mac, and I know you can be totally neurotic, so I'm going to humor you.* "A couple of weeks before I lost time. Or whatever happened."

"The body I buried wasn't wearing it."

"That makes sense," she said pointedly, "because it wasn't mine."

If the Book was trying to trick me, it might have made that mistake, putting a ring on her finger that hadn't been on her when I'd buried her, skimming my acknowledgment that they'd been in love and embellishing it with a perfectly human touch. I doggedly pursued my line of questioning. "Were you wearing the ring in the alley?"

"No. I'd taken it off that afternoon. I'd discovered some things about him. We'd had a fight. I was angry."

"What kind of things?"

"He was into some stuff I didn't know about. I don't want to talk about it."

"When did you put it back on?"

"When I went home to change. After the alley, the next thing I knew, I was standing outside the Stag's Head, wearing the most bizarre outfit. I didn't even bring it with me to Dublin. I have no clue how I ended up with it on. Remember the dress I wore my last Christmas at home? The one I hated but you thought looked so good on me? The one that made my ass look flat."

I pressed a suddenly trembling hand to my mouth.

"That's what I had on with the *ugliest* shoes. I'd never even seen them before, and I was freezing. And pearls. You know I haven't worn those things in years. I wanted to find Darroc, so I went home to change and go hunt for him but when I got there my place had been totally trashed. Did you do that? Did you freak out when you thought I was dead?"

I cleared my throat. Still, it took me two tries to get words out and when I did I croaked like a frog. "Why did you put the ring back on? According to you it was what—like only ten hours earlier that you'd taken it off?" I knew why. I'd have done the same thing with Barrons.

She said softly, "I love him. He's not perfect. I'm not either."

So, my sister had the same epiphany I did when it came to relationships. Not surprising. But my inner Book knew I'd had that epiphany. She'd spoken in present tense about Darroc, refusing to believe he was really dead. Again, like me. If someone told me my fiancé was dead and I'd never seen his body, I'd have a hard time believing it, too. I was intimately acquainted with the stages of grief: denial being the first.

"Tell me exactly what happened again. Every detail you remember from the night in the alley to the precise moment you were . . . here again." I was struggling to stay focused on logistics when my heart was pounding so hard it felt like it might rupture.

"Why? Have you figured something out, Mac? What do you think's going on? Oh, God, are you finally starting to believe me? Jr., I'm scared! I don't understand what's happening. How could I lose a whole year? How did I end up in that stupid dress?"

I closed my eyes and didn't say: *Well, gee, sis, it's like this: your baby sister has a big bad Book of black magic inside her and she wanted you back so badly, she brought you back from the dead. In the dress she chose to bury you in because she thought you looked so good in it—and hey, nobody's looking at your ass when you're lying in a coffin anyway—along with the pearls Mom and Dad gave you for your sixteenth birthday because you said they made you feel like a princess. And by the way, you're wrong—those shoes totally rocked that outfit. I know. I bought them at Bloomingdale's for you, after you died.*

Jay-sus.

I'd nearly fallen off my chair when she mentioned the dress. But of course, if I'd brought her back from the dead, she'd be wearing what I buried her in. Ergo, no body in casket.

And my inner Book probably knew that, too. If we were, as Barrons seemed to think, embedded together. Total clusterfuck.

"I'm not sure," I said finally. "But can we meet somewhere and talk?"

She laughed and said breathlessly, "Yes, Mac. Please. When? Where?"

I had a meeting tonight that I wasn't missing and I wasn't sure how long it would take.

So we made plans to meet at her place first thing in the morning. She'd make coffee and breakfast, she said.

It'd be like old times, she said.

31

"Rise, rise, rise in revolution . . ."

"Have you planted the icefire?" Cruce asked, striding impatiently across the cavern to meet him as soon as he'd finished flattening his flexible carapace and wedging it beneath the door.

Minutes passed while the roach god assumed form. It was never easy but then little was for a roach, living on the refuse and remains of others. Being chased and hunted and exterminated. Considered an enemy by one and all. In the history of man, he'd never met a human that welcomed a roach into its home, or anywhere for that matter. He was pestilence and vermin, nothing more. Yet.

"Yes," he finally grated. It had taken time to distribute the tiny pods Cruce had given him containing the blue flames, but he'd seen them well-positioned where they'd not be discovered, and when the moment was right, numerous roaches would be standing by, each with tiny plastic vials Toc had provided, which they would chew through with their heavily sclerotized mandibles to mix a drop of Unseelie blood with the flame.

"Where?" Cruce demanded, and the roach god wondered briefly if he'd merely traded one arrogant, belittling bastard for another. The prince was restless tonight, radiating dark energy, eyes bright. He preferred a cool ally, not a hot one.

The roach god repeated the three locations his ally had chosen: an old library where they stored the largest number of ancient scrolls; the chambers once occupied by the prior Grand Mistress; and the chambers occupied by the current one.

"Well done," Cruce said. "And you have Toc's blood?"

The roach god nodded, holding himself together with eons of discipline and relentless hunger for a better way of life.

"Toc had the papers printed as I instructed, and dispersed?"

"Yes."

"Excellent. When they come—"

"Will they come?" the roach god demanded.

Cruce smiled. "Oh, yes, they'll come. My name is synonymous with rebellion, and the Unseelie have long memories. We fought for freedom once before and nearly attained it. I will not fail this time. I will rule both the Fae and human realms. They are already mine. I'm merely trapped in a spiderweb for the moment and that will soon change."

"This world is dying. If it does, I want to go with you where you go."

Cruce's gaze locked on him and the roach god shuddered faintly. Ah, yes, this Fae had power. He hid it well.

"This world will not die. My realms are tied to it. When they come and the battle begins, watch and wait. If our side appears to be suffering losses, set the fires."

"You said it burns hotter than human fire. How hot?" Fire was one thing to evade, Fae fire might be entirely another.

"Not too hot for you," Cruce said. "Light all three at the same time. I want the fires to divide the humans and scatter them across the abbey. The fools will try to put it out rather than fight."

"If they don't?"

"They are governed by emotional attachments. Even the brightest among them suffers this weakness. Go. Now. Watch and wait. When the time is right, burn this fucking place to ash."

The roach god nodded and let his form collapse abruptly to the floor, disintegrating instantly, a trick he'd perfected in human homes, moving through their houses when they weren't around, as if he were one of them, sitting on their beds, fondling their combs and toothbrushes, even perching on their toilets, wondering what it would feel like to be whole and large and not a bug.

Thousands of glistening insects rippled across the stone chamber, vanishing into every crack and crevice.

32

"I will burn for you with fire and fury."

When the Hunter circled above Chester's preparing to land, I was surprised to see there wasn't the usual boisterous crowd gathered outside the club, jostling and bribing and arguing to get in.

Fewer than fifty humans loitered near the rubble of the former club at a safe distance from the cordoned-off black hole.

There wasn't a single Fae in sight. Normally, there were more Fae than humans, the lower castes that Ryodan wouldn't permit into the club, trying to seduce the bored, hungry clientele denied entry with an immediate, less potent (and far less attractive!) fix.

As I slid from the Hunter's back, I was the target for dozens of sharp, envious glares. Jealous of my "ride," that I had such a powerful beast seemingly at my command, wondering what magical gifts it bestowed—and if it could be eaten for a high probably.

I wasn't afraid of fifty humans. Not this close to Chester's.

I had guns, Voice, a Hunter, and Barrons a text away. Still, I stayed near my ride, one thickly insulated glove on its icy flank. I shivered from cold. Without Unseelie flesh in me, it wasn't nearly as comfortable to be so close to one of the icy beasts. My thighs were numb and my ass was completely frozen. I rubbed it briskly with my palm, trying to thaw it and restore sensation.

"Where are all the Fae?" I demanded, glancing at the underground entrance, surprised to find it was unguarded.

"The doors are locked," a woman said. "Does it let you eat it?" she asked with a frighteningly bright smile, shooting a greedy look at my satanic ride.

The Hunter swung its great horned head around and snorted a stunningly precise tendril of fire at the crowd.

The woman's hair went up in flame. She ran off screaming, clutching her head. The rest of the crowd backed warily away from me.

"The door to Chester's is locked?" I said incredulously. No one answered me and I got a brief bizarre flash of myself as I must look from their point of view: blond Barbie as Barrons had so pithily said, with crimson-streaked hair tangled wild from the wind, coated from head to toe with a light dusting of black ice, standing next to a demonic-looking winged dragon-beast, weapons bulging in my pockets, spear strapped to my thigh, and a snub-nosed automatic I'd tossed over my shoulder as I left for no reason I'd been able to fathom. Just a bad feeling I might need more weapons than usual tonight, or maybe all that kinky, rough sex with Barrons had made me feel more like my badass self. "Chester's never closes," I protested. That would be like the sun not rising.

Suddenly the door in the ground rattled and shot open from below. "Ms. Lane," Barrons growled as he stepped out. "About bloody time. Let's go." He closed the door then bent and traced a symbol on it, murmuring softly.

People began to hem him in, chanting, "Let us in, let us in!"

"Get the fuck out of here!" Barrons roared in Voice that staggered even me, and I felt my feet begin to move of their own volition. *Not you, Ms. Lane,* he shot me a look.

I stopped and stood, watching in astonishment as fifty people turned like zombies and trudged woodenly down the street. The most I'd ever managed was four with a single command.

Then I scowled at him. "One," I snapped, "how did you do that to fifty people at once. Two, why did it work on *me* when I thought I was supposed to be immune to you, and three—"

"The abbey is under attack. Get on the Hunter, Ms. Lane. And read this." He thrust a paper at me. "We didn't understand why the club was so empty. One of the patrons brought this in. Then Jada called. The others have already gone ahead."

He'd waited for me. That must have driven him bugfuck crazy, knowing a battle was being fought and he wasn't there. Waiting for his girlfriend.

"You're not my girlfriend, Ms. Lane," he said coolly.

"You could have gone without me," I said just as coolly.

"You could have checked your bloody texts."

I gave him a blank look. "I didn't get any." I tugged my cellphone from the front pocket of my jeans. It was completely coated with a thick layer of ice. When I fly, I scoot up beneath the bony apex of the Hunter's wings because it gives me more to hold on to, and my phone must have been pressed to the underside of the frigid crest. I tapped it against a nearby trash can to crack the ice. Sure enough, three texts messages, and the last one was pissed as hell. I made a mental note to carry it somewhere else when I flew in the future.

"You still could have gone without me."

"I bloody fucking know that." He cut me a seething glance.

"Then why didn't you?"

"Because, Ms. Lane, when the world goes to bloody hell, I will always be at your bloody side. Read the fucking paper. Not even Ryodan saw this one coming. Seems his 'news' isn't as spot-on as it once was."

I snatched the paper and scanned it quickly.

The Dublin Daily

August 7 AWC

STOP THE BLACK HOLES THAT
ARE DESTROYING OUR WORLD!!!

FREE PRINCE CRUCE!

Held hostage beneath ARLINGTON ABBEY is the most

POWERFUL FAE PRINCE ever created!

He is our SAVIOR!

He has the power to stop the black holes that are DEVOURING EARTH.

He ALONE possesses the magic to heal our world!

Fae power damaged it and only FAE MAGIC can SAVE it.

WE ARE RUNNING OUT OF TIME!!!

A secret cult known as the *sidhe*-seers has taken him PRISONER and is holding him in a vain attempt to EXPLOIT HIS POWERS for their OWN purposes!

They have the ability to travel to other worlds and care nothing for THIS ONE.

JOIN THE CRUCEAID!

FREE PRINCE CRUCE!!!

Meet at Arlington Abbey and help us liberate our champion!

See map below!

"Who would print this?" I exploded.

"No bloody clue," Barrons said tightly. "Up. Now."

I scrambled back onto the Hunter and, as Barrons settled behind me, reached for the great beast's vast, unfathomable mind. *Can you help us fight? Call more Hunters?*

We do not attend matters of Fae and man.

You've been flying me around.

You amuse.

Because it sensed the king in me? I wondered. *I order you to help us fight.*

Not even you.

Can I offer you something? If bribes were what it wanted, I'd try.

It rumbled deep inside, a chuckle of sorts. *You have nothing. We have all.*

Well, then just hurry! I urged it. *My friends are in danger. Take us to the abbey as quickly as you can get us there!*

You do not mean that. It rumbled again and I felt its mirth. *You would not survive.* But it flapped its enormous leathery sails, churning black ice beneath us, and pumped up and up.

We soared beneath the clouds, where the day was still bright, then through the clouds and above them, sailing higher and higher into blackness and stars and cold, cold sky, then just when I thought my lungs might explode and it was getting dangerously hard to breathe, it tucked its wings close to its body like an eagle preparing to plunge and whispered in my mind with a soft rumble, *Hold, not-king.*

I shoved my arms beneath its tightly wrapped wings and hugged the bony crest, clutching it, clenched my thighs and pressed my face to its frosty hide. It burned and I drew back sharply, but too late, I left a layer of my cheek on its back. "Ow!"

It suddenly went motionless, hanging in the sky like a dead weight, not moving one leathery scale. I remained just as still, bracing for whatever was about to happen.

Suddenly it rocketed forward so fast I'd have flown right off its back if it hadn't given me warning. I felt like the *Enterprise,* entering warp speed.

I tucked my face low (but not too low!) to its hide, as Barrons's arms tightened around me, and I squeezed my eyes shut against the cutting wind. I could feel the skin of my cheeks dragging back with gravitational force humans were not intended to experience without helmets or space suits.

After a moment I slitted my eyes open and watched stars trail past, like silvery party streamers.

Behind me, Barrons laughed with raw, ferocious exhilaration. I felt the same. Best. Damn. Supercar. Ever.

I sensed the Hunter prodding gently at my mind, making sure I was breathing and alive.

Best safety features, too.

We bulleted through the sky, dropping down and down until at last fields came into view, lush and fantastical from Cruce's magic. In no time at all we were nearly to the abbey.

"Oh, God, Barrons, look at all the Fae!" Nonsifters crammed the narrow winding road to the abbey, Seelie and Unseelie alike, while more loped and slithered and crawled through meadows, splashed and lumbered across streams. There were humans, too, though not many. I suspected there may have been more but this dark, wild army had fed on them, all pretense at seduction abandoned to the hunger of battle-frenzy. "All for Cruce?" I yelled over my shoulder. "I thought the Seelie despised the dark court!"

"They're unled," he shouted into my ear. "The unled are always fickle."

Once before, I'd seen Seelie and Unseelie gathered en masse. Not in clusters here and there like I'd seen mingling at Chester's but facing off like mighty armies.

V'lane had been leading the Seelie, while Darroc and I had stood at the front of the Unseelie.

I'd felt the shuddering in the tectonic plates of our planet, even with both sides holding their enormous power in check.

Now there was no division between the courts. Seelie and Unseelie were rushing toward a single place with a single goal.

Our abbey.

To destroy it.

To free Cruce. Break out the most powerful Fae prince in all creation. And they didn't even know he had all the power of the *Sinsar Dubh* at his disposal.

"Uh, Barrons, we're in a world of shit," I muttered.

"Same page, Ms. Lane. Same bloody word."

* * *

"Where are Ryodan and the others?" I cried as we soared low over the battle.

Five hundred *sidhe*-seers were down there. But I didn't see a single one of the Nine.

My sisters were facing thousands of Fae with more marching directly for them.

The front lawn of the abbey was a scene straight out of one of the *Lord of the Rings* movies. Amid towering megaliths and silvery fountains, humans battled monsters of every kind imaginable, some flying, some crawling, others stalking. Some beautiful, some hideous. There were those damned death-by-laughter fairies darting around a *sidhe*-seer's head! I watched, horrified. She was still laughing as she was killed by a ghastly Unseelie with tubular fronds all over its body.

There was Jada, slicing a circle around her, the alabaster blade of the sword gleaming. But it was only one weapon and there were thousands of Fae down there, flying, slithering.

"They aren't bloody sifters," Barrons said and snarled. "They fucking drove. And they sure as bloody hell can't be taking the road."

I sometimes forgot the Nine had limitations. They seemed so all-powerful to me. If I knew them, they'd shift not far from the abbey and lope to battle smack in the middle of the Unseelie. "Well, why didn't you call more Hunters for them?"

"This is the only one that ever comes."

"Shit," I cursed, leaning low, peering over the side.

I heard a low growl behind me, followed by the crunching sound of bones shifting, then the Hunter tensed beneath me and shook itself violently. I clung to the crest of its wings with all my strength.

"You are not my enemy," Barrons roared behind me. "I'll change and drop."

You'll drop and change, the Hunter snarled in my

head. It arched its long neck and shot an enormous burst of flame over its shoulder, blasting Barrons right off its back and singeing the hell out of my coat and hair.

"Barrons!" I screamed as he went tumbling off the Hunter's back, falling toward the lawn, transforming as he went.

The Hunter banked hard and began to circle back around. I stared down, watching Barrons fall. He was fully transformed by the time he hit the ground, horned, fanged, and ferocious.

He surged up, a sleek black shadow, grabbed the nearest Rhino-boy by the throat and ripped off its head with his enormous jaws.

Then his jaws opened even wider, impossibly wide, then the Barrons-beast vanished.

When he reappeared an instant later the Rhino-boy slumped dead to the ground.

Damn. And I still had no idea how he killed Fae.

The black-skinned beast exploded into battle, savagely ripping and clawing and killing, spraying guts and lifeblood everywhere, its crimson eyes glittering with feral glee. Vanishing. Reappearing.

He does not ride again, not-king. Nor do you.

The Hunter soared lower and turned its head, apparently about to dismount me the same way it had gotten rid of Barrons. I raised both hands in a gesture of surrender. "I'll jump, okay?" I said hastily. "Just go a little lower, I'll jump. But try not to dump me in the middle. Get me closer to her." I pointed to Jada.

The Hunter dropped like a rock, and some twenty feet from the ground I braced myself and dove off the damn thing. I wouldn't hold up so well under the same blast of fire it had turned on Barrons. I lost my automatic halfway down, watched it smash into the ground.

I didn't care. It was the spear that could make a difference in this battle, and it was secure in its holster.

I tried to tuck and roll to minimize the impact, but the objects I was plummeting toward were moving and I landed smack on top of one of the red and black Unseelie guards and took it to the ground beneath me. I slammed a hand into its ridged breastplate, nulling it, then yanked out my spear and drove it into its gut.

Adrenaline was raging through me, smoothing out my edges, perfecting my reflexes. I rolled, leapt to my feet, and began methodically slashing my way through the slithering, lumbering Fae, determined to get Jada's back. Criminy, how had she been holding them off this long?

All around me *sidhe*-seers were fighting Fae in a horrifically unmatched battle. We had three weapons: spear, sword, and Barrons, at least until the others of the Nine got here, and *sidhe*-seers were going down hard and fast.

As I spun, kicking and stabbing, I was painfully aware of the rat-a-tat-tat of automatic gunfire going off. I have a special hatred for digging bullets out of my body without Unseelie flesh in me, and I'm trying really hard to abstain. I whirled, nulled, and was about to stab when the Unseelie I was after went flying backward, knocked off its feet by a concentrated burst of bullets.

"Hey!" I snarled. "Get off my kill!"

"Sorry!" one of the new *sidhe*-seers, trained by Jada, snarled back as she hurled herself past me, taking a Rhino-boy off its feet. As I watched, she yanked a machete from a sheath on her back and began hacking the Unseelie into pieces. Damn. The *sidhe*-seers might not have weapons that killed immortals but they were pretty darned good at slicing them up, rendering them ineffective.

I felt an Unseelie behind me, spun, hand out to null,

stab, move. Null. Stab. Move. It was beginning to seem the Fae were ridiculously easy to kill. I was fighting better than I ever had before. Not one of them was managing to land a blow on me, as if deflected by an invisible shield. I was astonished by my own amazing prowess, how much better I'd gotten without even practicing.

I plunged into the battle with ferocity, periodically catching a glimpse of the ebony-skinned beast that was Barrons, lunging, powerful muscles bunching, jaws wide, ripping with talons, shredding with fangs. As I worked my way toward Jada, Barrons pushed farther into the crush, and I realized he was shoving *sidhe*-seers from harm's way, trying to make them see he was on their side by taking down Fae in front of them.

I began shouting to all the *sidhe*-seers I passed, knowing the other Nine would soon be joining us: "The black beasts with red eyes are on our side! Don't attack them! Don't kill the black beasts. They're fighting *for* us!"

Shit. Not even Jada knew their true form. This was a liability. Although they'd definitely come back, we needed them here to fight.

As I closed in on Jada, I tried to keep an eye out for Barrons. I hated knowing he might die tonight. I suddenly realized how much he must hate knowing the same about me. At least I knew he would come back. Not so for him: I didn't have a get-out-of-jail-free card.

I shook that thought from my head as I plunged my spear into a particularly vile Unseelie with wet, flailing tentacles and shoved and fought my way through the throng to Jada.

Then I narrowed my eyes, staring at the cuff glinting silver on my wrist. The next Unseelie I turned on, I didn't null or stab. I just stood there and gave him ample opportunity to take a swing at me.

His fist bounced off as if it had hit an invisible shield.

I scowled. It wasn't my amazing prowess after all.

I had the cuff of Cruce on and it was as good as V'lane had claimed it was. The Unseelie couldn't touch me. Damn.

Still, that was sweet.

"Watch your sword," I snapped to Jada as I moved into range. Like my spear, it could do horrible things to me. I wanted her to know exactly where I was at all times.

Her head whipped up and she looked at me, and I sucked in a breath. Oh, yes. She killed. That was what she did. Her emerald eyes were completely empty of all emotion. She was so drenched in guts and blood that her face was camouflaged and the whites of her eyes were blinding in comparison.

We stepped back-to-back, fell into perfect sync, whirling, slicing, stabbing.

"Who the bloody hell published that daily?" Jada demanded.

"No bloody clue," I told her grimly.

"I found it on my way back from Dublin. They were already holding them off. My women are dying," she snarled.

"I brought some . . . beasts . . . with me," I told her over my shoulder. "I have an ally you don't know about. They're fighting for us. Let your *sidhe*-seers know that." I described them to her.

"Where did you find them?"

"One of my times in the Silvers," I lied. It felt good to be here, doing this, slaying with Jada. We'd done this before and I'd missed it. I felt so bloody alive fighting with her, as if I was exactly where I was supposed to be and together we could beat anything.

"You trust these allies of yours?"

"Implicitly. They can kill the Fae."

"*Dead* dead?" she said incredulously.

"Yes."

"Is Ry—Are Barrons and the others coming?"

I didn't know what to say to that and suddenly realized we had a problem. If the beasts showed up but the Nine didn't, she would wonder why they hadn't come to help. "I'm not sure how many of them," I finally said. "I know some of them are off on some kind of mission-thingie for Ryodan." Wow. That was pathetic. Mission-thingie?

But Jada said nothing and moved away for a time, and I lost her then, as she vanished into the battle to spread the word to her women, and no doubt verify for herself these beasts I'd brought were indeed allies and indeed capable of the impossible.

I devolved into a killing machine, understanding the purity Jada and Barrons found in the act.

Here, in war, life was simple. There were good guys and bad guys. Your mission was also simple: kill the bad ones. No facade of civility required. No complex social rules. There are few moments when life is so uncomplicated and straightforward. It's disconcertingly appealing.

Eventually I found myself near the front entrance and Jada was there, with several of the Nine in beast form, snarling around her, helping block the door to the abbey.

Ryodan and Lor were there as well, both in human skins, vanishing, reappearing, sticking close.

I snorted. Ryodan thought of everything. Some of the Nine would show their faces, and others would be "off on some mission-thingie." Great minds think alike.

Around us, the Fae were beginning to fall back. It was one thing to march in to free a prince, but few of them were willing to sacrifice their immortality to do it. Humans could be motivated to fight to the death, protecting the future for their children, defending the old and weak. We're capable of patriotism, sacrificing for the long-term survival of our progeny and well-being of our world.

But not the Fae. They had no future generations, cared little for others of their kind, and had a serious aversion to parting with their arrogant, self-indulgent lives.

I warily dialed my *sidhe*-seer senses to a distant, muted station, in no mood to be assaulted by the cacophony of so many jarring melodies.

As I suspected, there was strong discord spreading through our enemy. Some in the outer ranks were loping away, others, near the center, were fighting their way free to do the same.

This was not a focused army. They were stragglers from here and there, unled, un-united. They might have come pursuing a common goal but with no more fully formed plan of attack than frontal assault. And that assault was getting them killed. Permanently.

I sighed, knowing even if the Fae pulled out right now, darkness would soon come crashing down and some would try again. They would launch better attacks, stealthier, more focused and brutal. The news was out: the legendary Prince Cruce was trapped beneath our abbey.

A sudden explosion behind me nearly took me off my feet, and a spray of glass rained down on my back.

"Fire!" someone screamed. "The abbey's on fire!"

My head whipped around just as another explosion rocked the abbey.

33

"I'll love you till the end . . ."

Things got crazy then.

Half the *sidhe*-seers rushed toward the stone fortress, the other half remained on the battlefield, looking impossibly conflicted. I was startled to see that even Jada looked torn. She never showed emotion, yet there was sudden uncertainty, a hint of worry and vulnerability in her eyes.

"Where is the fire? What part of the abbey?" she demanded.

"I can't tell from here," I told her. I was too close to the abbey to get a clear view of it.

"It looks like Rowena's old wing," a *sidhe*-seer about twenty feet from us shouted.

I had no problem with that. I wanted everything the old bitch had ever touched burned, and it conferred the added bonus of getting it out of the way of the expanding black hole.

"And the south wing with the seventeenth library!" another *sidhe*-seer called.

"Get on it. We need what's in there," Jada ordered. "Let Rowena's wing burn," she added savagely.

"The east wing looks like it's burning the hottest,"

another shouted. "The Dragon Lady's library. Must have started there. Leave it? There's nothing in there, right?"

Jada blanched and went completely motionless.

"What is it?" I said. "Do we need to put it out? Jada. Jada!" I shouted, but she'd vanished, freeze-framing into the still-exploding abbey.

Ryodan vanished, too.

Then Jada was back, with Ryodan dragging her. His mouth was bleeding and he had the start of a serious black eye.

"Get off me, you bastard!" She was snarling, kicking, punching, but he had twice her mass and muscle.

"Let the others put it out. Your sword is needed in battle."

Jada yanked her sword off her back and flung it away from her. "Take the fucking thing and let me go!"

I gaped. I couldn't fathom anything for which Jada might be willing to throw away her sword. One of the nearby *sidhe*-seers shot her a look. Jada nodded and the woman picked it up and returned to the battle.

Around us, the fight surged with renewed vigor, as *sidhe*-seers vacated the lawn to save the abbey.

But this was the only battle that mattered to me. If Jada wanted to fight the fire instead of the Fae, that was her call. I suspected there was something more to it than that. I just didn't know what. But the intensity of her reaction was spooking me. "Let go of her, Ryodan," I demanded.

They vanished again, both moving too fast for me to see, but I could hear the grunts and curses, the shouting. Jada was superior to humans in virtually every way. But Ryodan was one of the Nine. I knew who'd win this battle. And it pissed me off. Barrons lets me choose my battles. Jada deserved the same.

They were there again.

"You can die, Jada," Ryodan snarled. "You're not invincible."

"Some things are *worth* dying for!" she shouted, her voice breaking.

"The bloody abbey? Are you fucking crazy?"

"Shazam! Let me go! I have to save Shazam! He won't leave. I told him not to leave. And he trusts me. He believes in me. He'll sit there forever and he'll die and it'll be *all my fault*!"

Ryodan let go of her instantly.

Jada was gone.

So was Ryodan.

I stood blankly a moment. Shazam? Who the hell was Shazam?

Then I turned and raced into the abbey after them.

I couldn't get anywhere near them. I was forced to concede defeat a third of the way down the burning corridor to my destination. The fire wasn't natural, it glowed with a deep blue-black hue. Wood was being eaten to ash, stone was crusted with cobalt flame, and when I dragged the tip of my spear over a nearby burning wall, the outer surface of the stone crumbled to dust.

Fae-fire, no doubt.

I wondered how it had gotten into the abbey. Had someone slipped inside in the heat of battle? Gone around the back way and broken in? Had the attack on the abbey been far cleverer than I'd thought?

Sidhe-seers were rushing everywhere, carrying buckets and fire extinguishers, but neither had any effect on the flames. Blankets seemed at first to smother it, then the blaze sprang back up, hotter and more voracious than before.

"Icefire," one of the new *sidhe*-seers muttered grimly

as she pushed past me. "It can only be made by an Unseelie prince."

How did they *know* this stuff? Jada's *sidhe*-seers were ten times more knowledgeable and well trained than ours. Thanks to Rowena, who'd only permitted a select few into select few libraries, the bitch. Obviously, in other countries, they were actually allowed to read the ancient texts and legends. I narrowed my eyes. "You think Cruce . . . ?" I trailed off.

"Must've. Unless new princes have already replaced those slain. It can only be put out by an Unseelie prince," she tossed over her shoulder. "You wouldn't happen to know where we might find one of those, would you? One that's *not* the current repository for the *Sinsar Dubh*? Oh, wait, you are, too," she spat.

I ignored it. As a matter of fact, I did know where to find an Unseelie prince. In the dungeon of Chester's.

And one of the Nine owed me a favor.

And there were sifters out there in battle, and the Nine could take one alive.

I turned and raced back out into the night.

When I returned from Chester's with a pissed-off Lor and a seething Christian, the battle was over.

Not won—far from won. Just over.

The *sidhe*-seers had rapidly realized nothing they did affected the fire and returned to the front where they could at least prevent the burning abbey from being invaded. The Fae had retreated but I knew they'd be back. The abbey was ablaze in three wings, with the enchanted, blue-black fire shooting into the sky, and I had no doubt the Fae believed our fortress would be ash by dawn.

"Icefire," I told Christian. "Only an Unseelie prince can put it out."

He smiled bitterly, unfurling his wings. "Aye, lass, I've seen it before," he said, his eyes strange and remote, and I knew he was remembering something from his time in the Silvers, or perhaps his time on the cliff with the Hag. Perhaps he'd explored his forbidden powers in a way I was afraid to. Tried to create something to warm himself, trapped in the Unseelie prison, who could say. All I knew was, he was here and knew what it was, and maybe parts of the abbey could be salvaged.

He sifted out abruptly.

Movement near the entrance caught my attention.

I turned to look and gasped.

Ryodan stood in the doorway, stumbling then catching himself on the jamb, so badly burned I couldn't comprehend how he was even staying upright.

He was a mass of red, weeping blistered skin, blackened flesh, with charred bits of fabric falling off him as he stood.

Jada was motionless, tossed over a badly burned shoulder.

My heart nearly stopped.

"Is she okay? Tell me, is she okay?" I cried.

"Goddamn," he croaked, swaying in the doorway. He coughed long and deep, an agonizingly wet sound, as if parts of his lungs were coming up. "Relative." He coughed thickly again.

"What about Shazam? Did you get Shazam?" I said urgently. I couldn't bear the thought of Jada suffering one more loss. Again I wondered who Shazam was, where he or she had come from, why Jada had never mentioned this person.

"Relative," he croaked again, and I stared at him, realizing the invincible Ryodan was having a hard time functioning and something had stunned him so completely he was as close to utterly blank as I'd ever felt myself. The look in his eyes was wild. Hunted. Haunted.

Then Lor was gently taking Jada from his arms, cradling her against his chest, and I was relieved to see, except for her singed clothing and charred hair, she seemed virtually unburned. I moved in for a closer look at her face. It was wet, tear-stained. She looked so young, so fragile, her eyes closed, like a child. Without her eternal cool mask, I could see Dani in her features much more clearly. She appeared unconscious, limp, but barely touched by fire, and as Ryodan staggered and I saw the rest of his brutally burned body, I realized he must have used himself as her shield, no doubt whirling around her like a small protective tornado, burning himself, front, back, and sides, so she would remain unscathed while she searched for her friend.

"Where is Shazam?" I said again, swallowing a sudden lump in my throat. It was only the two of them. No one else had made it out.

Ryodan's eyes were slits, his lids blistered, eyes glittering, seeping bloody liquid, and I held my breath, waiting for his answer. I wondered if he needed to change to heal. I wondered if he was dying and I should get him out of here fast, before he disappeared in front of everyone.

He sighed, another awful gurgling sound, and lifted a melted mess of a hand that was clutching a charred object from which white stuffing exploded.

"Ah, Christ, Mac," he whispered, and blood gushed from his mouth.

He collapsed to his knees and I raced to his side to catch him, but he roared with agony when I touched him. I yanked my hands quickly away and took charred flesh with them.

As he fell to the ground and rolled over on his side, he convulsed with pain. "She went back in there for *this*, Mac." He thrust it at me.

"I don't understand," I said wildly. "That doesn't make any sense. What the fuck is that?" I knew what it was. I wanted him to tell me I was wrong.

"What the fuck do you think? A goddamned stuffed animal."

Part IV

You looked.

Point?

Stare into the fog long enough, you start to see shapes everywhere.

Point?

Staring at nothing is dangerous. You gotta *make* something of it, dude! Fill it up. Color it every shade of the fecking rainbow, with big, laugh-out-loud stuff. Otherwise some ghost ship'll come sailing right out of the fog with Death on the prow, bony finger pointing right at you. You look into the abyss, dude, the abyss always looks back.

What the bloody hell do you know about the abyss?

That we all got one. Bottomless, black, and chock-full o' monsters. And if you don't take control of it and fill it up with the good stuff, it takes control of you.

—From the journals of Dani "the Mega" O'Malley
Conversations with Ryodan

34

"The silicon chip inside her head gets switched to overload . . ."

"Christ, Mac, what the bloody hell do you and Barrons *do* in this place?" Lor said as he walked in the front entrance of BB&B.

He stood looking around the room, at the broken furniture I hadn't been strong enough to move, the crimson paint sloshed everywhere, and the small area of organization in the rear I'd set up for myself with a love seat and a table that looked like a very small eye in a very large storm. He whistled low and shook his head.

I knew what it looked like. A battlefield.

"Never mind," he said. "I don't wanna know. Guess there's a reason Barrons keeps you around. So, where's my little honey?"

"Upstairs. In my room," I told him. We'd brought Jada and Ryodan back to BB&B, with Barrons working more of his *Bewitched* magic to get us through the funnel cloud. "How'd you get in through the storm?" I wondered if they all knew the same spells. I'd somehow gotten the impression Barrons was by far the most proficient, that Ryodan had some degree of skill but preferred to leave the heavy lifting to Barrons, and I'd assumed Lor was mostly oblivious to . . . well, everything but blondes with big boobs. And recently, Jo.

"There's a way," he evaded.

"Then why haven't I been using it?" I said pissily. Sometimes I almost wanted to be one of them. Almost. The Hunter wasn't willing to fly me anymore. I was going to be even more dependent on Barrons in the future. Or have to give up coming home for a while. A sudden chill kissed my spine, and I wondered if for some reason, soon, I wouldn't be here much at all. I shook it off as exhausted brooding.

The owner of Chester's had insisted on returning to his club, but Barrons had flatly vetoed it, saying BB&B was more heavily warded, and besides, Jada couldn't go far if she decided to try, with the Fae-tornado surrounding the area. Both men seemed to think she'd run the second she was coherent again.

She'd been unconscious since the abbey. I'd tucked her into my bed upstairs, pulled the covers up to her chin, and sat beside her for a long time, trying to understand what was going on with her, touched and troubled by how fragile she looked, young and vulnerable.

It was sometimes hard to remember Jada was only somewhere between nineteen and twenty years old. If she were a normal girl, in a normal world, she might be a sophomore in college. She presented a facade that packed the presence of a woman of thirty. But she wasn't. She'd been a fourteen-year-old who'd had to grow up too fast. Now she was a nineteen-year-old that had grown up even more, faster and harder. I smiled bitterly, remembering one of Dani's favorite mottos: Bigger, Better, Faster, Harder, More. She'd always been voracious for life, hungry to experience it all.

Why on earth had she raced back into the abbey, into a killing Fae fire, just to save a stuffed bear, sliced down the middle with its innards falling out?

"She sleeping?" Lor said.

"I can't tell. I don't know if she's sleeping or . . . something else." Exhausted to the point of collapse, as if she'd been holding herself together with sheer force of will for a long time.

I'd held her hand. It was limp, as if all the life had been drained from her body. I was frantic to know what had happened, but Ryodan, too, had passed out shortly after arguing with Barrons about where to go.

Half the Nine had remained behind at the abbey, standing guard for when the Fae came back. We'd left Christian soaring over the burning fortress. I fervently hoped he could save some of it. I even more fervently hoped the blaze didn't burn it all the way down into the ground, freeing Cruce from the cavern. Criminy, we had a mess on our hands.

Will Ryodan die? I'd asked Barrons on the way back to BB&B. And come back whole? I hadn't added.

Not a chance, he'd replied grimly. *He's fighting it. He won't leave her like this. The bloody idiot will stay here and heal the long way.*

But he will *heal?* I'd pressed. I couldn't even bear to look at him. It was seeing the man in that movie, *The English Patient,* but with no bandages to hide the horror.

He'll heal. You would consider it rapidly. He won't. And it'll be hell.

I'd pondered having the ability to simply kill yourself if you were badly wounded, so you could swiftly end your suffering and come back perfect again. It had been beyond my comprehension. What a leap of faith to bleed yourself out. I decided they must have died so many times that they either had implicit trust they would always come back or didn't care.

He'd shot me a look. *You used the spear tonight. You didn't lose control.*

I know, I'd replied. *I don't know what was different.* It may have helped that I'd stabbed my first one instinctively before I realized what I'd done. And once I realized it, I'd known I could do it and it had been easy from there. I'd figured it was one of three things: the Book was neutralized inside me somehow; it was open and I was using it without being corrupted; or it was cooperating, for whatever reason.

You're coming into your own.

I'd kept my silence. I still couldn't shake the feeling that the universe had two really nasty evil shoes and only one of them had dropped.

We'd put Ryodan in Barrons's study on a mattress he'd dragged down from upstairs.

You could put him in the bedroom next to Jada, I'd suggested.

He won't want her to see him like this.

I don't think she's seeing much of anything, I'd pointed out.

I don't think she has been for a while. He'd glanced pointedly at the heavily smoked stuffed animal I was holding on my lap as we headed back for Dublin in one of the Nine's Hummers.

I'd tucked it into her arms as I'd tucked her into my bed.

And I'd seen the only faint signs of life in her as she sighed and curled herself tightly around it. She muttered something then that sounded like, "I see you, yee-yee."

My heart had felt raw and inflamed inside my chest, on the verge of rupturing, as I'd watched her. *Mea culpa.* I hated myself even more than I had before for chasing her into the Silvers that day. I was only now beginning to fully understand what those years had cost her.

And I'd thought then, staring down at her, what if

Alina isn't really dead? That would mean I'd chased Dani into the hall—and she hadn't even killed my sister.

For a few really hellish moments there I'd wanted to go curl up somewhere and quietly die.

But I'd shaken it off. My dying wouldn't do a thing for Dani. And she was all that mattered.

Lor strode past me and I followed him into Barrons's study.

I dropped into a chair behind the desk and looked warily at Ryodan. Barrons was draping filmy pieces of fabric drenched in some silvery liquid on his charred body, murmuring softly while he worked.

"He's awake," Barrons said.

I hadn't needed to be told. I was watching him shiver with pain as Barrons laid the barely-there pieces of glowing cloth against his raw flesh. One of the Nine shivering with pain was a terrible thing to see.

"Do you think maybe you should knock him out for his own good?" I said uneasily.

Lor laughed. "I've thought that on more than one occasion."

"He wants to be awake," Barrons murmured.

"Can he talk?"

"Yes," Ryodan rasped.

"Can you tell us what happened?"

He made a wet sighing sound. "She flew into that . . . bloody abbey like . . . a mother bear obsessed . . . with her cub. I thought . . . five and a half years is a long time . . . maybe she'd had a child . . . brought it back."

Oh, God, I thought, appalled, I hadn't even thought of that! Had the bear belonged to a child? *Her* child? Just what had Dani gone through in the Silvers?

"I kept circling her, trying to keep . . . her from . . . burning, but she acted like . . . she didn't even feel the heat. Christ . . . I could barely breathe. Beams were falling, stone was crumbling."

"Why the fuck didn't you change?" Lor growled with a quick look at me.

"I know," I said to him levelly. "Surely you know I know."

"Dunno why you're still alive, though," he said coolly.

"Not in . . . front of her." Ryodan gurgled harshly.

"Precisely," Lor said, shooting me a look.

I ignored him. "Are you sure he's okay talking?" I asked Barrons worriedly.

Barrons gave me a look. "If he's doing it, he wants to be."

"Go on," I urged Ryodan.

"Need to tell. You . . . need to know."

"He won't be conscious when I've finished," Barrons told me. "For some time."

"She kept saying she . . . had to save . . . Shazam. That she wouldn't have . . . survived without him and she wasn't . . . losing him. She wasn't leaving him. Ever. She fucked up once and . . . wasn't fucking up again. She was . . . ah, fuck. It was . . . it was like looking at her at fourteen again. All eyes and heart . . . blazing in her face. And she started to cry."

Lor said softly, "You never could stand that."

Ryodan lay shuddering while Barrons worked, then gathered his strength and went on. "She tore the damned room . . . apart looking for . . . something. I couldn't figure out what. The place was a bloody mess . . . must've exploded when the fire started. All kinds of . . . weapons, ammo . . . kept trying to push it away from the fire and . . . keep her from burning. Food everywhere . . . a filthy pillowcase with ducks on it and . . . rotting fish all over the place. Fucking fish. I kept thinking what the fuck . . . was with the fish?"

Rotting fish? I frowned, unable to process it.

"Finally, she . . . screamed and dove toward the bed

and I thought . . . so, her kid is under there . . . it's okay . . . I'll get them out."

He fell silent again and closed his eyes.

"And she pulled out the stuffed animal," I said miserably.

"Yes," he whispered.

"How did she end up unconscious?"

"Me."

"You *hit* her?" Lor growled, half rising.

"I was a bloody . . . fucking idiot. Should've known better."

"What did you do?" I exclaimed.

"When I saw . . . what she was holding . . . cooing to it like it was . . . fucking *alive*, I . . ." He trailed off. Then after a long moment he hissed, "I took it from her, ripped it open, and showed her it was just a . . . a stuffed animal."

"And she snapped," Barrons said quietly.

"Blank. Her eyes filled with . . . anguish and . . . grief then . . . just empty. Like she wasn't even . . . alive anymore."

"You think it's like that Tom Hanks movie," Lor said, "where he got stranded on an island and talked to a goddamn ball for years?"

"Only Jada forgot it wasn't real," I said, horrified.

"Don't know," Ryodan said. "Maybe it's . . . how she survived and . . . why she came back Jada. She kept saying he was so . . . emotional. Moody. He needed her to take care of him. Possible she survived by . . . divvying herself up . . . creating an imaginary friend with . . . Dani's attributes . . . while becoming Jada."

I closed my eyes. Tears slipped down my cheeks.

"I made her see . . . he wasn't real. Then she . . . was just . . . gone. Bloody hell . . . *I* did it to her."

We sat in silence for a time.

Finally, I got up.

Ryodan would survive. He had his brothers.

Dani needed a sister.

Lor followed me out. "What the fuck was up at Chester's, Mac? Why was an Unseelie prince in our club? And where the bloody hell was he hiding?" he demanded.

I stopped walking and turned to face him. When I'd asked him to capture me a sifter to take me to Chester's, he'd insisted on coming along. I'd demanded he remain in one of the subclubs with the sifter while I went to get Christian. I'd called it due as part of my favor, thereby keeping my oath to Ryodan that his secrets were mine.

I gave him a frosty look. "You asked me a favor and I gave it to the best of my ability in exchange for one from you. We're even. If you try to push me on this, I'll fight you with everything I've got. And I've got more than you think. Like you, Lor, my loyalties are to Ryodan. Give me space on this."

He measured me a long moment then inclined his head. "I'll leave it. For now."

Together, we went upstairs to stand vigil over Jada.

Over the next several hours, visitors came to see Jada. I don't have any idea how they got into the store with the funnel cloud around it. I assumed Lor was bringing them in somehow. Living with the Nine around means accepting endless mysteries. Jo came and sat with me for hours and we talked and tried to figure out what to do to help Jada/Dani heal. Jo told me she'd been to the abbey twice to see her, but Jada had kept herself surrounded by her closest advisors both times, and acknowledged her only to enlist her aid in continuing the modernization of their libraries.

Jada's *sidhe*-seers took shifts coming, sat grimly with us and kept us updated on conditions at the abbey, which I barely heard, staring at the bed, lost in sadness deep enough to drown.

Barrons intermittently came upstairs, checking with grim dark eyes to see if anything had changed.

Jada lay unmoving in the bed, as if carved from stone, holding on to the charred stuffed animal as though her life depended on it. I was surprised Ryodan hadn't dropped it. He'd been burned beyond belief but somehow managed to hang on to both Jada and the stuffed bear with which she was obsessed—and keep them both from burning. Any other man would have dropped the thing in the fire.

Finally, I was alone with her, and I moved to sit on the bed. As I pulled the covers up, the glint of Cruce's cuff caught my eye and I suddenly couldn't get it off my arm fast enough.

She'd given it to me when she kept my spear. Hadn't wanted me walking around unprotected, even then. And it had kept me safe from all harm in battle tonight.

It should have been on *her* arm.

There were so many should-have-beens.

I tried to pick up her arm to put the cuff on her wrist but I couldn't break her death grip on Shazam. I laid it on the table next to the bed so when she woke up she could have it back.

I touched her hair softly, smoothing scorched auburn tendrils from her face. It was still pulled back in a ponytail but had slipped down to her nape, and I could see the natural curl in it. I smiled faintly, sadly. One day I'd like to see her wearing it curly and wild and free again.

I stroked her cheek, wiping away a smudge of tear-streaked soot, then got a washcloth from the bathroom and gently cleaned her face. I dampened her hair and smoothed it back. The water made it even springier, with little curls forming. She didn't move at all.

"Dani," I whispered. "I love you."

Then I stretched out on the bed behind her, wrapped my arms around her, and held her like she was holding Shazam.

I didn't know what to do, what else to say. Apologies were pointless. What was, was. Dani had always lived by the motto, "The past is past. The present is now, and that's why it's a present. 'Cause you got it, and you can do stuff with it!"

I pressed my cheek to her hair and whispered the same words against her ear that I'd heard her say earlier. Although I had no idea what they meant, they obviously meant something to her.

"I see you, yee-yee," I said. "Come back. Don't go away. Please don't leave me." I started to cry. "It's safe here. We love you, Dani. Jada. Whoever you need to be. It's okay. We don't care. Just please don't leave. I've got you, honey, I've got you." I cried harder.

You never see it coming.

That final, fatal blow.

You think the shit has already hit the fan and exploded all over your face. You think things are so bad they can't get any worse. You're walking around tallying all the things that are wrong with your world when you discover you have no clue what's really going on around you and you've only been seeing the tip of the iceberg that sank the *Titanic*—at the precise moment you hit the iceberg that sank the *Titanic*.

Hours later I went downstairs, moving woodenly, aching in every limb, head hurting, eyes swollen, nose stuffed solid.

Jada still wasn't stirring, although twice in the past

hour she'd opened her eyes. Both times she'd become aware of me and closed them instantly, either slipping back into unconsciousness or just plain shutting me out.

The bookstore was surprisingly quiet, and I ducked my head into the study to see how Ryodan was doing. He was alone, draped in shimmering cloth etched with glowing symbols, slumbering deeply.

I checked the front of the store, but it was empty so I poked my head out the back to see where everyone was. In the distance, down the alley to the right, I heard voices. I cocked my head, listening.

Barrons talking softly with someone.

I stepped out into the faint bruise of dawn, thinking that in just a few hours I was supposed to meet Alina and I wasn't sure I was up to it. My heart was pulped. Dani was all I could think about. I was loath to leave her side for an hour or more, for any reason. I certainly couldn't invite Alina here. Last thing I wanted was Jada being affected in any way by her presence.

I hurried down the alley and turned the corner but no one was there.

I kept walking, absently following the sound of Barrons's voice, wondering why everyone had left the store. As I turned the next corner, I heard a dry chittering and glanced up.

The sky above me was thick with black-robed wraiths, gliding, soaring, rustling. Thanks to the Hunter, I now knew they were the Sweeper's minions. And whatever the mysterious entity was, it was right, I was certainly broken. My heart was in pieces.

There were hundreds of them. I tipped back my head. Even more perched on the rooftops on both sides of the street. I glanced back at BB&B, barely able to make out the roof of the building, and was stunned to see that it, too, was completely covered in ghoulish carrion. I'd been so lost in thought that I hadn't even looked up as

I'd stepped out. They must have been perching up there in silence.

They weren't silent now. Their chittering grew, became a sort of metallic screeching I'd never heard before as they looked from me to one another and back to me again.

"Well, shit," I muttered as a lightbulb went off in my head. They could see me. And I knew why. "That damned cuff."

I'd left it on the table near Jada. When he'd tried to sell me on it, V'lane told me the cuff of Cruce afforded protection against Fae and "assorted nasties." Apparently my wraiths fell into the latter category. It made sense, when I thought about it. Ryodan said my ghouls had once stalked the king. I could see Cruce not wanting any skulking, spying creatures near him, and working to perfect a spell to prevent them from being able to find him. That explained why once I'd become visible again, they hadn't instantly become my second skin. Jada had given me the cuff while I was cloaked by the *Sinsar Dubh.*

Now they were back. Great.

And something was still trying to decide if it wanted to "fix me." Bloody great. Good luck with that.

I started to move forward, hesitated a moment, feeling that odd finger of a chill at my spine again, and glanced back at BB&B.

I decided to wait for Barrons to get back. It made me uneasy how quickly they found me once I'd taken off the cuff. I remembered them flying over the city, searching. Although they'd never appeared to present any real threat to me, had even slept on the same bed with me in Chester's without ever doing anything to me, who knew when the rules might change in this crazy-ass world?

Maybe the Sweeper had made up its mind, I thought darkly. I didn't like that thought.

I spun briskly to head back for the safety of the bookstore.

That's when they dropped from the sky like great, smelly, black, suffocating straitjackets and took me down.

35

"If I only had a heart . . ."

I regained consciousness to find myself staring straight up at the ceiling of a dimly lit industrial warehouse.

I could tell what it was by the vast metal beams and girders and pulleys used to move supplies. I guessed I was somewhere in the Dark Zone, flown up and out by the gaunt wraiths that were far more formidable than I'd ever imagined.

When they'd descended from above, their assault was instantaneous, almost as if they'd sifted, expanding their leathery cloaks, smothering me. I hadn't even managed to lift a finger before my hands were immobilized.

My spear and guns, useless. I hadn't been able to get to anything, not even my cellphone. Then again, from what I'd seen, Barrons's tattoos hadn't been finished and IYD wouldn't have done me any good.

One moment they'd been in the sky, the next my arms were tightly straitjacketed to my sides, my legs bound. Their smelly, leathery cloaks had covered even my head and I wasn't able to breathe. I thought I was dying. The horrible thing about being suffocated is you don't know if you're going to wake up or not.

I'd decided in my last, fleeting moment of consciousness that the way the Sweeper had decided to "fix" me was apparently to kill me; a sentiment I might not have entirely disagreed with at various points in my life.

But not now. Jada needed me. Oh, she didn't know that and probably wouldn't agree with it, but she did. The Sweeper could try to kill me later. Now was not a good time. I wasn't staying here to get "fixed."

I leapt up.

Er, rather, my brain gave the command for my body to leap up.

Nothing happened.

Manacles rattled. Slightly. My wrists and ankles burned. I groaned. I'd practically broken my neck trying to stand. I was strong. My restraints were stronger.

I tried to move my head. It didn't work. There was a wide band across my forehead, strapping it tightly to the surface upon which I was stretched, flat on my back.

I was horrified to realize I was secured to some kind of cold metal gurney. For a moment I was afraid I'd been given a paralytic drug, but then found that I could move my head a few inches if I put effort into it. The rest of me was so tightly buckled down, I couldn't move my arms or legs at all.

There was a sudden rustling in the distance, the sound of my stalkers, their dry chittering. I stank to high heaven, drenched in their disgusting yellow dust.

I went motionless and closed my eyes again.

In horror flicks, when the hero gets strapped to this kind of thing, in this kind of place, the villain always waits for them to regain consciousness before the truly gruesome acts of barbarism begin.

I could play dead a long time.

As the rustling wraiths drew nearer, I heard a whirring and grinding, the sound of badly greased cogs turning. I kept my eyes closed and concentrated on breathing deep and natural.

I recognized the sound.

The thing ambulated ponderously closer, panic and dread accompanying it, filling me with the same immobilizing fear I'd felt the night the walking trash heap passed through the alley behind BB&B. I couldn't have moved then even if I'd been unrestrained.

If I *had* been able to move, I would have smacked myself in the forehead. As I ran like hell.

The trash heap I'd seen the other day was the mysterious Sweeper!

It had been right there with me, inside our protective storm, looking for me two days ago, and I'd had no clue it was the thing that had its minions watching me.

In my defense, they didn't look anything alike. And who would think something ancient and all-powerful that fixed other things would itself be compiled of refuse?

Although, I brooded, it sort of made sense. Maybe it was always fixing itself, too, and just grabbed whatever was handy. I remembered the metallic things embellishing the Unseelie princess's spine, the metal I'd seen flashing on my carrion stalker's faces, and it made even more sense. Sort of. As much as anything in our Fae-infested world made sense anymore.

The thing crashed to a rattling halt somewhere to the right of me. I lay rigid with fear, listening, trying not to let panic completely unravel me.

There were noises then, smaller ones than the Sweeper's heavy tread. Metal against metal: clinks and clacks of things being turned on and off and moved around.

Beyond my closed lids the environment grew brighter. Two more clicks and it was abruptly brilliant. Focused, intense lights had been turned on and were shining directly down on me.

I didn't like this one bit. I was strapped to a table, with bright lights above, about to be fixed by something that couldn't even walk straight and was made of trash and guts. Despite the panic immobilizing my limbs and clouding my mind, I couldn't help but wonder what the hell it thought was wrong with me. How was I broken? I wanted to know, to argue with it. I wisely kept both mouth and eyes shut. Not that I could have opened either anyway. Its mere presence was a paralytic.

After what felt like an endless amount of time, it rattled and clanked away.

The chittering of the ghouls faded as they went with it, and I collapsed in my skin with relief as voluntary motion returned.

A reprieve. No clue why. Didn't care.

I slitted my eyes open and closed them quickly again, blinded by the bright, cold lights shining down. I turned my head as far to the right as I could. That was where I'd heard the ominous sounds, and I wanted to know what I was facing. I opened my eyes again.

After ascertaining no wraiths lurking in the shadows, waiting to sound the alarm the second they saw me stir, I strained my muscles to peer as far right as possible.

A long metal table.

A dazzling array of sharp, glittering instruments.

It was straight out of a horror movie. I had the sudden unsolicited, disturbing memory of sitting in BB&B five nights ago, trying to dig bullets out of myself, thinking about what sick things could be done to me if I was tied up, given my regenerating abilities.

Breathe, I told myself. Above the table was a large rectangular screen featuring a picture of something gray and black and white and shadowy.

I narrowed my eyes, focusing on the screen. It took me a few seconds to process what I was seeing, and I only did because my nose itched and I couldn't get to it so I scrunched it up and sort of tossed my head the small amount I could, and the image on the screen moved.

It was me. On the inside. Specifically my skull.

Every detail: sinus cavities, teeth, bones, muscles. There were symbols marked in various spots on the skull. I angled my head hard and noticed that to the right of the large screen were four smaller ones.

Those took me longer to figure out but I finally realized each was showing different parts of my brain. There were symbols marked on those images, too, concentrated in—if I remembered my biology courses correctly, and unfortunately at the moment I seemed to be recalling them with horrifying clarity—the limbic region of my brain.

I knew what the limbic region was. We'd studied it in my abnormal psych course. It was a set of brain structures located on both sides of the thalamus, and it supported emotion, behavior, and long-term memory, among other things. The limbic system included the hypothalamus, the amygdala, and the hippocampus. It was highly tied to the brain's pleasure center and tightly linked to the prefrontal cortex.

The reason I recalled all this so clearly was because our university had been participating in a study while I was taking my AP course, and the professor had solicited volunteers for it.

The purpose of the study had been to explore whether a "turned off" limbic system or brain damage in that area was a valid marker of psychopathy. He'd told us there was significant evidence acquired from incarcerated criminals that there was indeed a correlation.

I remembered looking at my classmates, who'd eagerly thrust their hands in the air, thinking: Who would be stupid enough to volunteer for this? What if they got their brain scanned and learned they were psychopaths? Was that really something you wanted to know? More importantly—was it really something you wanted everyone around you to know?

I'd shoved my hands deep in my pockets that day and kept them there.

Now, as I studied the screen of my brain, I pondered the implications. I lacked the training to decide if my limbic region was "turned off" or damaged, but from the look of the instruments on the table and the symbols on the various parts of my brain—it was about to be.

The Sweeper thought my brain needed to be fixed. I scowled. There was nothing wrong with my brain. Had I been able, I would have clamped both my hands protectively to my head. Would my skull keep remodeling as it tried to cut me open? Sealing around its instruments? I had no doubt that whatever barbaric surgery it had planned wouldn't go easy. I wondered if it was the presence of the Book inside me that made the Sweeper consider me both powerful enough and fractured enough to require fixing. The damned *Sinsar Dubh* just never stopped messing up my life.

A voice broke the silence from my left—first, scaring the shit out of me, then filling me with far more horror than I'd realized I could even hold.

"It's my heart," Jada whispered. "What's it planning to fix of yours?"

36

"And I will wait, I will wait for you . . ."

I closed my eyes and sagged limply against the table.

No, no, no, I screamed inside my head. *Not this. Anything but this.*

Then I surged violently from head to toe, trying to explode from my bonds. I flailed, shuddered, and flopped. Minutely.

I got nowhere.

"No," I finally managed to whisper. And again more strongly, "No." Not Dani. Never Dani. No one was "fixing" anything about her, and certainly not her bodacious heart.

"So," she prodded in a whisper. "What's it fixing on you?"

"You're strapped to a table, about to be fixed, and you're *curious*?"

"If I hadn't told you first, wouldn't you be curious about what it thought *my* problem was?" she whispered back.

"How do you know its purpose is to fix things?"

"Pretty obvious from the images, Mac," she said dryly.

"How did you know I was here?" I hadn't known she

was. I hadn't bothered looking to my left. There hadn't been any sounds over there. Perhaps our would-be surgeon had already set up her instruments before I'd regained consciousness.

"Superhearing. You've been sighing. Occasionally, a snort. Can you reach your cellphone?"

"No," I said.

"Me either."

How had she gotten here? Had the wraiths broken out a window in BB&B, swooped in and plucked her unconscious body from the bed? Had they always possessed the power to defeat Barrons's wards and just been pretending? And why? As far as I knew, my ghouls hadn't been stalking her. Had the Sweeper simply tucked her into its cart like a grocery store customer indulging in a buy-one-get-one-free deal because she'd been handy and according to its nebulous and highly suspect criteria was "broken," too?

"How did it get you?" I asked woodenly.

"I looked out the window and saw you walking down the alley."

"I thought you were unconscious." Damn it, she should have been unconscious! Then she wouldn't be here.

"I was waiting for everyone to finally leave. Ryodan finished my tattoo today. I had someplace to go. But I looked out the window and saw you following what looked like a walking trash heap."

"Following it?" I'd never even seen it. Apparently the noisy, rattling heap could cast a glamour.

"It was about twenty feet ahead of you. Then I heard Barrons's voice coming from it and knew something was wrong. The minute I stepped outside, the ZEWs were on me. I didn't even have time to access the slipstream."

They'd straitjacketed her, too, I realized. Smothered

her and knocked her out, and like me, she'd awakened restrained from head to toe.

"Slipstream?"

"Used to call it freeze-frame."

"Got any superhero ideas?" I said. I wasn't hopeful. Restrained, even her extraordinary gifts were useless.

"Everything I learned Silverside requires use of my hands. Can you move at all?"

"Only my head and only a little."

"Ditto," she said.

I searched for something reassuring to say but could find nothing. Barrons would have no reason to look for us beyond the eight-block circumference of the storm, and I doubted we were in that part of the Dark Zone that was inside it. I'd underestimated my ghoulish stalkers. I wasn't making that mistake again. I had to assume anything that put so much premeditation into its "work" would put an equal amount of thought into choosing a place where it would not be interrupted.

We couldn't count on Barrons for a rescue. And certainly not Ryodan.

It was just the two of us.

"I've been in worse situations," Jada whispered.

I winced and closed my eyes. I really hadn't wanted to hear that. "Jada—"

"If you're going to tell me you're sorry again, stow it. It was my feet that took me where I went. That night and tonight. We make our own choices."

"And there's your responsibility dysmorphia showing again," I said coolly.

"Responsibility dysmorphia is you being so arrogant you think your actions are the only ones that count. You chased me. I ran. That's two people doing two things. We can split it fifty/fifty if you want. I planned on going Fae-side anyway. I was hungry for adventure.

I never thought ahead. I lived in the moment. You weren't responsible for that."

I remembered her laughing as she'd leapt into the mirror, deep from the belly, no fear. "I should have come after you."

"I would have darted into the nearest mirror in the hall. You know what those were? They showed pretty, happy places, sunny islands with white castles on sand. It took me a while to figure out what was on the other side wasn't what they showed. Barrons was right. You following me would have killed me."

"You know about that?"

"Lor told me. And once I'd gone through that first Silver, you had no chance of finding me. There are *billions* of portals in that hall, Mac. That's not a needle in a haystack—that's a billion needles in a gazillion haystacks."

"But you lost so many years," I whispered.

"There you go again. I didn't lose them. I *lived* them. I wouldn't undo a bit of it. It made me who I am. I like who I am."

That hadn't been how it looked at the abbey, and I told her that.

"It's hard to be alone," she said. "You do what makes survival possible. Otherwise you don't make it."

Like talking to the equivalent of a ball for five years? I didn't say. However crazy it was, it had gotten her through. Who was I to judge?

And now here she was, strapped to a table, and the part of her the Sweeper wanted to work on was her heart—that amazing, luminous, live-out-loud in every possible color part of her that, given enough time, could heal and become luminous again.

But not once the Sweeper had worked on it.

I didn't think for a moment it intended to make her more caring and emotional. I was pretty sure if either of us walked out of here after having been "fixed," we wouldn't be remotely the same, probably some Borg-like creature, a distant, collective automaton. I shuddered at the thought of losing my individuality, especially since I'd been altered to live a very long time, with my personality blotted out by the stamp of something that fancied itself an improver. How dare anything tamper with our innate structure? Who the hell was *it* to decide what was right and wrong with us?

And Dani—so unique, complex, and brilliant—what might it turn her into?

I closed my eyes. Tears seeped out the corners. "Can you forgive me?"

"I keep telling you, you didn't do anything to forgive." Then after a long pause she said, "Can you forgive *me*, Mac?" And I knew she meant Alina.

"I keep telling you—" I said.

We both sort of laughed then, and I cried harder, silently. We'd had to be tied up in the same room together to finally say what we'd needed to say.

The Sweeper was right. My brain was flawed. It couldn't be relied upon. My heart would always overrule it. Like it had when I'd been determined to bring Barrons back from the dead. Like it quite possibly had in bringing Alina back. There was no way Dani was getting worked on. I would never let it happen. No matter the cost. Right or wrong, wise or foolish, liberating or damning, I wouldn't allow the Sweeper to harm her.

"I don't like how quiet you are, Mac," she whispered. "What are you thinking in that messed up head of yours? It's your brain, isn't it?"

I must have made a sound of irritation because she sort of snickered.

"I *knew* it," she said. "It's planning to fix your brain!"

"It's not funny."

"It is, too. Admit it," she said. "We've been analyzed

by a pile of junk that looks like it's going to fall apart if it takes one wrong step, and found lacking. My heart. Your head."

I snorted. It *was* kind of funny in a really weird and not at all funny way.

"You'll notice it thinks *my* brain is perfect," she said smugly.

"Yeah, well, it thinks my heart is better than yours."

"It is."

"No, it's not."

"Well, my brain's *definitely* better than yours," she said lightly, and I was struck by the realization that cold, distant Jada was teasing.

"You do realize we're in mortal danger right now," I reminded.

"You know what Shazam did for me that was one of the best things of all? He kept it light no matter how dark it got."

Again I winced. I didn't know how to talk to her about her stuffed-animal delusion. I said nothing.

"So, what's going on in that badly highlighted head of yours? Have you tried olive oil, by the way? You aren't over there thinking about trying to do something with the *Sinsar Dubh,* are you?"

I wasn't about to defend or argue. It wasn't open to debate. Not with her. She was the reason I was going to do it. "Of course I tried olive oil. The paint penetrated the hair shaft," I said irritably. "It'll come out eventually."

"You think you can use its power without it destroying you?"

"What do you think?" I evaded.

"I think the odds are high that's a great big no."

"Dani would have risked it."

"There was a time when *I*"—she emphasized the

pronoun—"didn't understand the price you can end up paying."

"You mean going through the Silvers," I said.

"Coming back," she whispered. "That was the highest price of all."

"Got any better ideas?" I said flatly.

Long pause, then, "No."

I closed my eyes and reached for my inner lake. She was never paying another price. Not if I could help it, and I could. And maybe I'd be just fine.

"Mac, I need you to promise me something," she whispered urgently.

"Anything," I said, walking out to greet the still black waters in my mind. They didn't try to rush up and drown me this time. The surface was serene, placid, inviting, no hint of an undertow.

"If I don't make it out of here—"

"You will."

"If I don't," she repeated, "I need you to do something for me. Promise me you'll do it. Promise me you'll accomplish it no matter what. Say it."

"I promise," I said. But whatever she wanted, she could do herself, because she was getting out of here. I was going to see to it.

"The Silver I came through that brought me home . . ." She told me where it was and how to find it. "I need you to go back through it for me."

"For what?" I backed away from my lake for a moment, giving her my full attention.

"I need you to rescue Shazam."

My brain stuttered and I just lay there a few moments, opening my mouth, reconsidering and closing it. I'd thought we were having a fairly sane conversation. She'd been composed, intelligent, rational. Showing more humor than I'd ever seen from Jada. Now we were back to the stuffed animal she nearly died trying to save from the fire.

"He'll wait for me forever," she said in an anguished whisper. "He'll wait and wait and he'll believe that I'll come. I can't stand the thought of him being disappointed, over and over again."

I didn't say anything. Because I knew that was what *she* had done. Waited for someone to come rescue her. And no one had.

"Every day, he'll just keep sitting there. Thinking it's going to be *that* day. The happy one."

She started to weep then, and it set off another flood of my own tears. The happy one, she'd said. How many years had it taken for her to stop believing? To stop hoping for the happy day?

"He's so emotional," she whispered. "And he gets so depressed and he gives up. He was alone for so long. I promised him he'd never be alone again."

He was? Or *she* had been?

"And I know he's going to be hungry," she fretted. "He gets *so* hungry."

Oh, God, I thought, she must have starved in the Silvers, with her enormous requirements for food. And she'd passed that trait off, too, to an imaginary friend.

"Do you promise me you'll go back and save him if I don't get out?"

"The fish," I said woodenly. "You were feeding the stuffed animal fish."

"You might not be able to find him at first. He hides in other dimensions. You'll have to talk to the air and tell him his Yi-yi sent you and it's okay to come out. It may take a while before he believes it's safe. Whatever you do, don't let him lick you or try to eat you."

"Dani," I said brokenly. She wanted me to go through the Silvers and talk to the air.

"I knew the fish were a bad idea," she said with some embarrassment.

I didn't say anything. I didn't know what to say.

"I'm not crazy, Mac. Shazam is *real*," she said.

I blinked. What did she mean? What was she saying? I'd seen "Shazam." He was a gutted stuffed animal.

She said tightly, "I left him."

"The stuffed animal?"

"No," she said irritably, "that was different. I couldn't sleep. So I pretended it was him to help me sleep while I figured out what to do. But I knew I was pretending. Then when the abbey caught fire, I felt like it was happening all over again. It was that day again, the day I really lost him. It triggered me. I went a little nuts."

I turned my head as far to the left as I could. "Shazam is real? Really, truly *real*?" I said.

"He's a cranky, furry koala bear/cat thing. I found him my first year Silverside."

I opened my mouth, closed it. Considered what she'd just said, weighing it for clarity and conviction. Was she telling the truth? Or was she so fractured she was now convincing herself, since Ryodan had gutted her delusion, that she'd left it behind? "A koala bear/cat thing that talks and hides in the air?" I finally said.

"Mac, stop thinking so much. It's probably why it wants to work on your brain. You have all that internal monologue going on all the time."

I bristled. "Don't be a bitch." I knew why I thought so hard about everything; all my life I'd had to sift through two complete beings inside me without ever knowing the other one was there: fifty thousand years of the Unseelie king's memories bouncing around in my subconscious, recurring nightmares of icy places, fragments of songs, desires that hadn't made any sense. I'd harbored emotions I'd never been able to pinpoint to any event in my life. Everything was suspicious to me—

because half of it wasn't mine. And I'd done a damn fine job navigating what was mine and what wasn't.

She said again, "He's real. You have to believe me. That's part of the promise you're making me."

"You weren't alone the whole time?" I longed to believe that. I hated the thought that she'd spent five and a half years battling enemies all by herself.

"No. Well, except for when he vanishes. And he's amazing in a fight. Well, as long he stays focused and doesn't have one of his pessimistic meltdowns. He hates being alone. And he's alone again." She added softly, "He loves me. He never said it but I know. It's what he means when he says he sees me. And I can't let him down. I can't fail him. You have to tell him you *see* him, okay? Just keep telling the air that you see him. He'll come out. And if I don't make it, Mac, you have to love him. Promise me you'll take care of him."

I tried to wrap my brain around what she was telling me. I wanted to believe it was true, that she wasn't broken and she wasn't crazy. That she'd actually lost someone and it had been killing her inside. That in fact it had devastated her so deeply, she'd pretended he was a stuffed animal. She had feelings, deep ones. A sudden happiness filled me. Whether or not Shazam was real, Dani felt loved—and loved in return.

"There's nothing wrong with your heart, honey," I said softly.

"It's broken," she whispered. "I can't go forward with Shazam behind me. I don't know how."

God, I knew that feeling! A sister, a parent, a lover, an animal. It didn't matter where you put your unconditional love; once given, the stealing away of it was an assault to every sense. Smells were the worst—they could ambush you, put you smack back in the middle of the hottest part of the grief. The scent of a peaches-and-cream candle. The brand of deodorant she'd used. Her pillow back home. The smell of the bookstore in the evening, when I'd believed Barrons was dead. When you love too hard, you can lose the will to live without them. Everywhere you look is a great big sucking absence of what you once had and will never have again. And life gets weirdly flat and too sharp and painful at the same time, and nothing feels right and everything cuts.

There was a sudden rattling in the distance, and I inhaled sharply.

"It's coming," she whispered.

"Promise *me* a favor now," I whispered.

"Anything," she vowed.

"If you have a chance to escape, if you suddenly find yourself free, run like hell and leave me behind."

"Anything but that, Mac."

"I promised *you,* damn it," I hissed. "Now you promise me, and mean it. If you have the chance to escape, turn your back on me and run as fast as you can."

"I don't run anymore."

"Promise me. Say it."

She remained silent. The only sound was the whine and clatter of our would-be tormentor approaching.

"Quid pro quo or I won't keep my promise," I threatened. "I won't save Shazam if I get out."

"Coerced promises aren't fair, Mac. You know that."

"Please," I said softly. "It won't mean anything if what I do goes wrong and we both die. One of us has to make it."

She said nothing for a moment, then said stiffly, "I promise to do what I think is best."

I laughed softly. That was Dani. Not Jada at all. And it was enough because I knew Dani: survival at any cost.

I heard the screech of metal and knew we didn't have

much time. I closed my eyes, leapt and dove into my black lake.

"What are you doing, Mac?" she said sharply, no longer bothering to be quiet. I knew why. There was an ominous portent to the sound of the approaching Sweeper. It was no longer ambling. It was moving with briskness and focus. Our "operations" were about to begin. Whether we were awake or not.

"What I should have done the moment you jumped through that Silver," I said. "Believing in the good magic, too."

She was quiet; as if trying to think of what to say. Finally she said, simply, "I don't want to lose you, too."

"I thought you didn't like me," I reminded. Chittering, coming closer. Rustling. I swam hard, focusing on the shaft of golden light slicing through the murky water.

"I don't sometimes," she said irritably. "But we're . . ."

"Sisters?" I said as I drifted lightly to my feet in the black cavern. She'd come after me. She'd looked out that window, decided I was in trouble, and shoved aside whatever it was she'd gotten out of bed to do—go save Shazam?—and come after *me* instead.

"Peas. Pod. Whatever you're doing, think hard about it."

Peas in the Mega-pod, she'd once called us. My heart expanded, so full of love for her it hurt. "I have."

"And know I've got your back."

"Back at you, kid," I said lightly. But I'd had to say it loud, to make myself heard over the jarring approach of the Sweeper.

"I'm not a kid anymore."

"Don't we all know that," I said dryly. I dashed into the cavern, the shining, resplendent black rock chamber that housed the enormous power that had kept me immobilized by fear for far too long.

No more.

I had no idea which of my three suppositions was right, and no longer cared. The only thing that mattered to me was that Dani lived. That she went on to love. To save "Shazam" if he actually existed, to grow up and take lovers, regain her wonder and freedom of emotion and wholeness of heart.

And if the price was me, the price was me.

I guess that's what love is. You care more that they live than you care about whether you do. Dani's light would never be extinguished. Not on my watch.

Panic was pressing at the outer edges of my mind and I knew the Sweeper was almost on us. I could smell the noxious odor of the wraiths hemming us in.

I hurried to the Book and turned the pages rapidly, scanning, looking for anything I could use.

"Mac," I heard from a distance. "Don't do it for me. Don't lose your soul for me. You know I have responsibility dysmorphia syndrome. You'll make it worse."

I laughed in the cavern as I thumbed through page after page. Who said I would lose my soul? *Good magic,* I reminded myself.

There! A bit of a double-edged sword, but it would work.

Triumphantly, I shouted the words of the ancient spell I'd just found. The syllables echoed sharply off the stone of the cavern, amplifying, growing, shimmering in the air around me. I could feel the power flooding me, ready, able, and more than willing. It filled me with euphoria, and I knew something that felt so good couldn't possibly be bad.

As I finished the final syllable, the Book abruptly collapsed into a pile of shimmering gold dust.

I stared at it wondering what had just happened. Looking for the same winking red gemstones I'd seen in the cavern.

Had I absorbed it? Was I one with it? I'd been reading it in the First Language. Had I succeeded in doing what Cruce had done?

I didn't feel any different.

I knew that, beyond me, in the warehouse, the Sweeper and its minions were gone. The spell had done what I'd intended it to do. Well, essentially.

And most importantly, Dani was free and safe.

Even now she was rising from her gurney, restraints falling away as she stood up. I could see her movements in my mind's eye.

Music began to play in my cavern and I frowned. It was a Sonny and Cher song that I'd always hated. *They say we're young and we don't know . . .*

My blood turned to ice in my veins and I could feel it, oh God, I could *feel* it!

Inside me, expanding, cramming every nook and cranny of my being!

Blighting everything, blacking out the tiniest most essential parts of me, draping my soul in homicidal rage and bottomless hunger and madness and horror, shoving me back and down, cramming me into a tiny box with no holes for air, packing me in there as tightly as a sardine.

Just before the lid slammed down, I used the last bit of control I had over my mouth to scream, "Run, Dani. RUN!"

Got you, sweet thing, the *Sinsar Dubh* purred.

ACKNOWLEDGMENTS

Any novel is a team effort by the time it reaches publication, and *Feverborn* was no different. Special thanks to the ineffable Shauna Summers—who has been my editor and finest champion since the first book in the Fever Series—and the rest of my fabulous team at Random House: Libby McGuire, Scott Shannon, Matthew Schwartz, Gina Wachtel, Gina Centrello, Sarah Murphy, and Kesley Tiffey.

Also many thanks to Lynn Andreozzi and the art department for another wonderful cover, the sales team for getting my books out there, and the booksellers for hand-selling the series and converting new readers.

A special shout-out to Shauna and Sarah for sending me the latest hot-off-the-press books for Dad and me to read together in the hospital. Reading was his escape and you fed that escape for us both until the last.

Very special thanks to my first reader, Leiha Mann, who suffers me reading aloud to her as the book unfolds, offers a wide array of pithy, pointed, and pertinent comments, and has shared my passion for the Fever World since it began. Many more thanks for keeping my life running smoothly while I lose myself in another book, from managing the KMM cyberworld to making sure I eat. You're the dearest of friends and I couldn't do it without you!

Tremendous appreciation to you my faithful readers, for coming back time and again to the streets of Dublin, rooting for your favorite characters (and writing to tell me which ones you want dead), and making it possible for me to do what I love more than anything else while calling it "work."

A long overdue thanks to Paul White. I don't know if you're a sheepdog or a wolf, but it doesn't matter—you're one of the good guys. Thanks for getting me through the storm.

Deep and sincere gratitude to Dr. Philip Lemming and the compassionate nurses and staff at Christ Hospital Cancer Center in Cincinnati, Ohio, for the wonderful care you gave my father, and for helping us understand what was coming and how to see him through.

And finally, thanks to you, Dad, for your enormous, formative presence in my life. You taught me how to live, and showed me how to die with dignity, strength, and grace.

PEOPLE

SIDHE-SEERS

S*IDHE*-SEER (SHEE-SEER): *A person on whom Fae magic doesn't work, capable of seeing past the illusions or "glamour" cast by the Fae to the true nature that lies beneath. Some can also see Tabh'rs, hidden portals between realms. Others can sense Seelie and Unseelie objects of power. Each* sidhe*-seer is different, with varying degrees of resistance to the Fae. Some are limited; some are advanced, with multiple "special powers." For thousands of years the* sidhe*-seers protected humans from the Fae that slipped through on pagan feast days when the veils grew thin, to run the Wild Hunt and prey on humans.*

MACKAYLA LANE (O'CONNOR): Main character, female, twenty-three, adopted daughter of Jack and Rainey Lane, biological daughter of Isla O'Connor. Blond hair, green eyes, had an idyllic, sheltered childhood in the Deep South. When her biological sister, Alina, was murdered and the Garda swiftly closed the case with no leads, Mac quit her job bartending and headed for Dublin to search for Alina's killer herself. Shortly after her arrival she met Jericho Barrons and began reluctantly working with him toward common goals. Among her many skills and talents, Mac can track objects of power created by the Fae, including the ancient, sentient, psychopathic Book of magic known as the *Sinsar Dubh*. At the end of *Shadowfever* we learn that twenty years before, when the *Sinsar Dubh* escaped its prison beneath the abbey, it briefly possessed Mac's mother and imprinted a complete copy of itself in the unprotected fetus. Although Mac succeeds in reinterring the dangerous Book, her victory is simultaneous with the discovery that there are two copies of it; she *is* one of them and will never be free from the temptation to use her limitless, deadly power.

Alina Lane (O'Connor): Female, deceased, older sister to MacKayla Lane. At twenty-four went to Dublin to study at Trinity College and discovered she was a *sidhe*-seer. Became lovers with the Lord Master, also known as Darroc, an ex-Fae stripped of his immortality by Queen Aoibheal for attempting to overthrow her reign. Alina was killed by Rowena, who magically forced Dani O'Malley to trap her in an alley with a pair of deadly Unseelie.

Danielle "The Mega" O'Malley: Main character. An enormously gifted, genetically mutated *sidhe*-seer with an extremely high IQ, superstrength, speed, and sass. She was abused and manipulated by Rowena from a young age, molded into the old woman's personal assassin, and forced to kill Mac's sister, Alina. Despite the darkness and trauma of her childhood, Dani is eternally optimistic and determined to survive and have her fair share of life plus some. In *Shadowfever*, Mac discovers Dani killed her sister, and the two, once as close as sisters, are now bitterly estranged. In *Iced*, Dani flees Mac and leaps into a Silver, unaware it goes straight to the dangerous Hall of All Days. We learn in *Burned* that, although mere weeks passed on Earth, it took Dani five and a half years to find her way home, and when she returns, she calls herself Jada.

Rowena O'Reilly: Grand Mistress of the *sidhe*-seer organization until her death in *Shadowfever.* Governed the six major Irish *sidhe*-seer bloodlines but rather than training them, controlled and diminished them. Fiercely power-hungry, manipulative, and narcissistic, she was seduced by the *Sinsar Dubh* into freeing it. She ate Fae flesh to enhance her strength and talent, and kept a lesser Fae locked beneath the abbey. Dabbling in dangerous black arts, she experimented on many of the *sidhe*-seers in her care, most notably Danielle O'Malley. In *Shadowfever* she is possessed by the *Sinsar Dubh* and used to seduce Mac with the illusion of parents she never had, in an effort to get her to turn over the only illusion amulet capable of deceiving even the Unseelie king. Mac sees through the seduction and kills Rowena.

Isla O'Connor: Mac's biological mother. Twenty-some years ago Isla was the leader of the Haven, one of seven trusted advisors to the Grand Mistress in the sacred, innermost circle of *sidhe*-seers at Arlington Abbey. Rowena (the Grand Mistress) wanted her daughter, Kayleigh O'Reilly, to be the Haven leader, and was furious when the women selected Isla instead. Isla was the only member of the Haven who survived the night the *Sinsar Dubh* escaped its prison beneath the abbey. She was briefly possessed by the Dark Book but not turned into a lethal, sadistic killing machine. In the chaos at the abbey, Isla was stabbed and badly injured. Barrons tells Mac he visited Isla's grave five days after she left the abbey, that she was cremated. Barrons says he discovered Isla had only one daughter. He later tells Mac it is conceivable Isla could have been pregnant the one night he saw her and a child might have survived, given proper premature birth care. He also says it is conceivable Isla didn't die, but lived to bear another child (Mac) and give her up. Barrons theorizes Isla was spared because the sentient evil of the *Sinsar Dubh* imprinted itself on her unprotected fetus, made a complete second copy of itself inside the unborn Mac and deliberately released her. It is believed Isla died after having Mac and arranging for her friend Tellie to have both her daughters smuggled from Ireland and adopted in the States, forbidden ever to return to Ireland.

Augusta O'Clare: Tellie Sullivan's grandmother. Barrons took Isla O'Connor to her house the night the *Sinsar Dubh* escaped its prison beneath Arlington Abbey over twenty years ago.

Kayleigh O'Reilly: Rowena's daughter, Nana's granddaughter, best friend of Isla O'Connor. She was killed twenty-some years ago, the night the *Sinsar Dubh* escaped the abbey.

Nana O'Reilly: Rowena's mother, Kayleigh's grandmother. Old woman living alone by the sea, prone to nodding off in the middle of a sentence. She despised Rowena, saw her for what she was, and was at the abbey the night the *Sinsar Dubh* escaped more than twenty years ago. Though many have questioned her, none have ever gotten the full story of what happened that night.

Katarina (Kat) McLaughlin (McLoughlin): Daughter of a notorious crime family in Dublin, her gift is extreme empathy. She feels the pain of the world, all the emotions people work so hard to hide. Considered useless and a complete failure by her family, she was sent to the abbey at a young age, where Rowena manipulated and belittled her until she became afraid of her strengths and impeded by fear. Levelheaded, highly compassionate, with serene gray eyes that mask her constant inner turmoil, she wants desperately to learn to be a good leader and help the other *sidhe*-seers. She turned her back on her family mafia business to pursue a more scrupulous life. When Rowena was killed, Kat was coerced into becoming the next Grand Mistress, a position she felt completely unfit for. Although imprisoned beneath the abbey, Cruce is still able to project a glamour of himself, and in dreams he seduces Kat nightly, shaming her and making her feel unfit to rule, or be loved by her longtime sweetheart, Sean O'Bannion. Kat has a genuinely pure heart and pure motives but lacks the strength, discipline, and belief in herself to lead. In *Burned*, she approaches Ryodan and asks him to help her become stronger, more capable of leading. After warning her to be careful what she asks him for, he locks her beneath Chester's in a suite of rooms with the silent Kasteo.

Jo Brennan: Mid-twenties, petite, with delicate features and short, spiky dark hair, she descends from one of the six famous Irish bloodlines that can see the Fae (O'Connor, O'Reilly, Brennan, the McLaughlin or McLoughlin, O'Malley, and the Kennedy). Her special talent is eidetic or sticky memory for facts, but unfortunately by her mid-twenties she has so many facts in her head, she can rarely find the ones she needs. She has never been able to perfect a mental filing system. When Kat clandestinely dispatches her to get a job at Chester's so they can spy on the Nine, Jo allows herself to be coerced into taking a waitressing job at the nightclub by the immortal owner, Ryodan, and when he gives her his famous nod, inviting her to his bed, she's unable to resist even though she knows it's destined for an epic fail. In *Burned*, Jo turns to Lor (who is allegedly Pri-ya at the time and won't remember a thing) after she breaks up with Ryodan to "scrape the taste of him out of her mouth." She learns, too late, that Lor was never Pri-ya and he has no intention of forgetting any of the graphically sexual things that happened between them. Although, frankly, he'd like to be able to.

Patrona O'Connor: Mac's biological grandmother. Little is known of her to date.

THE NINE

Little is known about them. They are immortals who were long ago cursed to live forever and be reborn every time they die at precisely the same unknown geographic location. They have an alternate beast form that is savage, bloodthirsty, and atavistically superior. It is believed they were originally human from the planet Earth, but that is unconfirmed. There were originally ten, counting Barrons's young son. The names we know which they currently go by are Jericho Barrons, Ryodan, Lor, Kasteo, Fade. In Burned *we discover one is named Daku. There's a rumor that one of the Nine is a woman.*

Jericho Barrons: Main character. One of a group of immortals who reside in Dublin, many of them at Chester's nightclub, and is their recognized leader, although Ryodan issues and enforces most of Barrons's orders. Six feet three inches tall, black hair, brown eyes, 245 pounds, date of birth October 31, allegedly thirty-one years old, his middle initial is Z, which stands for Zigor, meaning either "the punished" or "the punisher," depending on dialect. He is adept in magic, a powerful warder, fluent in the druid art of Voice, an avid collector of antiquities and supercars. He despises words, believes in being judged by one's actions alone. No one knows how long the Nine have been alive, but references seem to indicate in excess of ten thousand years.

If Barrons is killed, he is reborn at an unknown location precisely the same as he was the first time he died. Like all of the Nine, Barrons has an animal form, a skin he can don at will or if pushed. He had a son who was also immortal, but at some point in the distant past, shortly after Barrons and his men were cursed to become what they are, the child was brutally tortured and became a permanent, psychotic version of the beast. Barrons kept him caged below his garage while he searched for a way to free him, hence his quest to obtain the most powerful Book of magic ever created, the *Sinsar Dubh.* He was seeking a way to end his son's suffering. In *Shadowfever,* Mac helps him lay his son to final rest by using the ancient Hunter, K'Vruck, to kill him.

Ryodan: Main character. Six feet four inches, 235 pounds, lean and cut, with silver eyes and dark hair nearly shaved at the sides, he has a taste for expensive clothing and toys. He has scars on his arms and a large, thick one that runs from his chest up to his jaw. Owner of Chester's and the brains behind the Nine's business empire, he manages the daily aspects of their existence. Each time the Nine have been visible in the past, he was king, ruler, pagan god, or dictator. Barrons is the silent command behind the Nine, Ryodan is the voice. Barrons is animalistic and primeval, Ryodan is urbane and professional. Highly sexual, he likes sex for breakfast and eats early and often.

Lor: Six feet two inches, 220 pounds, blond, green eyes, with strong Nordic features, he promotes himself as a caveman and likes it that way. Heavily muscled and scarred. Lor's life is a constant party. He loves music, hot blondes, and likes to chain his women to his bed so he can take his time with them, willing to play virtually any role in bed for sheer love of the sport. Long ago, however, he was called the Bonecrusher, feared and reviled throughout the Old World.

Kasteo: Tall, dark, scarred, and tattooed, with short, dark, nearly shaved hair, he hasn't spoken to anyone in a thousand years. There is a rumor floating around that others of the Nine killed the woman he loved.

Fade: Not much is known about him to date. During events in *Shadowfever*, the *Sinsar Dubh* possessed him briefly and used him to kill Barrons and Ryodan, then threaten Mac. Tall, heavily muscled, and scarred like the rest of the Nine.

FAE

Also known as the Tuatha De Danann or Tuatha De (TUA day dhanna or Tua DAY). An advanced race of otherworldly creatures that possess enormous powers of magic and illusion. After war destroyed their own world, they colonized Earth, settling on the shores of Ireland in a cloud of fog and light. Originally the Fae were united and there were only the Seelie, but the Seelie king left the queen and created his own court when she refused to use the Song of Making to grant his concubine immortality. He became the Unseelie king and created a dark, mirror image court of Fae castes. While the Seelie are golden, shining, and beautiful, the Unseelie, with the exception of royalty, are dark-haired and -skinned, misshapen, hideous abominations with sadistic, insatiable desires. Both Seelie and Unseelie have four royal houses of princes and princesses that are sexually addictive and highly lethal to humans.

UNSEELIE

Unseelie King: The most ancient of the Fae, no one knows where he came from or when he first appeared. The Seelie don't recall a time the king didn't exist, and despite the court's matriarchal nature, the king predates the queen and is the most complex and powerful of all the Fae—lacking a single enormous power that makes him the Seelie queen's lesser: she alone can use the Song of Making, which can call new matter into being. The king can create only from matter that already exists, sculpting galaxies and universes, even on occasion arranging matter so that life springs from it. Countless worlds call him God. His view of the universe is so enormous and complicated by a vision that sees and weighs every detail, every possibility, that his vast intellect is virtually inaccessible. In order to communicate with humans he has to reduce himself into multiple human parts. When he walks in the mortal realm, he does so as one of these human "skins." He never wears the same skins twice after his involvement in a specific mortal episode is through.

DREAMY-EYED GUY (aka DEG, see also Unseelie king): The Unseelie king is too enormous and complex to exist in human form unless he divides himself into multiple "skins." The Dreamy-Eyed Guy is one of the Unseelie king's many human forms and first appeared in *Darkfever* when Mac was searching a local museum for objects of power. Mac later encounters him at Trinity College in the Ancient Languages department, where he works with Christian MacKeltar, and frequently thereafter when he takes a job bartending at Chester's after the walls fall. Enigma shrouded in mystery, he imparts cryptic bits of useful information. Mac doesn't know the DEG is a part of the Unseelie king until she and the others are reinterring the *Sinsar Dubh* beneath Arlington Abbey and all of the king's skins arrive to coalesce into a single entity.

CONCUBINE (originally human, now Fae, see also Aoibheal, Seelie queen, Unseelie king, Cruce): The Unseelie king's mortal lover and unwitting cause of endless war and suffering. When the king fell in love with her, he asked the Seelie queen to use the Song of Making to make her Fae and immortal, but the queen refused. Incensed, the Seelie king left Faery, established his own icy realm, and became the dark, forbidding Unseelie king. After building his concubine the magnificent shining White Mansion inside the Silvers where she would never age so long as she didn't leave its labyrinthine walls, he vowed to re-create the Song of Making, and spent eons experimenting in his laboratory while his concubine waited. The Unseelie Court was the result of his efforts: dark, ravenous, and lethal, fashioned from an imperfect Song of Making. In *Shadowfever,* the king discovers his concubine isn't dead, as he has believed for over half a million years. Unfortunately, the cup from the Cauldron of Forgetting that Cruce forced upon the concubine destroyed her mind and she doesn't retain a single memory of the king or their love. It is as if a complete stranger wears her skin.

Cruce (Unseelie, but has masqueraded for over half a million years as the Seelie prince V'lane): Powerful, sifting, lethally sexual Fae. Believes himself to be the last and finest Unseelie prince the king created. Cruce was given special privileges at the dark court, working beside his liege to perfect the Song of Making. He was the only Fae ever allowed to enter the White Mansion, so he might carry the king's experimental potions to the concubine while the king continued with his work. Over time, Cruce grew jealous of the king, coveted his concubine and kingdom, and plotted to take it from him. Cruce resented that the king kept his dark court secret from the Seelie queen and wanted the dark and light courts to be joined into one, which he then planned to rule himself. He petitioned the king to go to the Seelie Court and present his "children," but the king refused, knowing the queen would only subject his imperfect creations to endless torture and humiliation. Angry that the king would not fight for them, Cruce went to the Seelie queen himself and told her of the dark court. Incensed at the king's betrayal and quest for power, which was matriarchal, the queen locked Cruce away in her bower and summoned the king. With the help of the illusion amulets Cruce and the king had created, Cruce wove the glamour that he was the Seelie prince, V'lane. Furious to learn the king had disobeyed her, and jealous of his love for the concubine, the queen summoned Cruce (who was actually her own prince, V'lane) and killed him with the sword of light to show the king what she would do to all his abominations. Enraged, the king stormed the Seelie Court with his dark Fae and killed the queen. When he went home to his icy realm, grieving the loss of his trusted and much-loved prince Cruce, he found his concubine was also dead. She'd left him a note saying she'd killed herself to escape what he'd become. Unknown to the king, while he'd fought with the Seelie queen, Cruce slipped back to the White Mansion and gave the concubine another "potion," which was actually a cup stolen from the Cauldron of Forgetting. After erasing her memory, he used the power of the three lesser illusion amulets to convince the king she was dead. He took her away and assumed the role of V'lane, in love with a mortal at the Seelie Court, biding time to usurp the rule of their race, both light and dark courts. As V'lane, he approached MacKayla Lane and was using her to locate the *Sinsar Dubh*. Once he had it, he planned to acquire all the Unseelie king's forbidden dark knowledge, finally kill the concubine who had become the current queen, and, as the only vessel holding both the patriarchal and matriarchal power of their race, become the next, most powerful, Unseelie king ever to rule. At the end of

Shadowfever, when the *Sinsar Dubh* is reinterred beneath the abbey, he reveals himself as Cruce and absorbs all the forbidden magic from the king's Dark Book. But before Cruce can kill the current queen and become the ruler of both light and dark courts, the Unseelie king imprisons him in a cage of ice beneath Arlington Abbey. In *Burned*, we learn Dani/Jada somehow removed the cuff of Cruce from his arm while he was imprisoned in the cage. Her disruption of the magic holding him weakened the spell. With magic she learned Silverside, she was able to close the doors on the cavernous chamber, and now only those doors hold him.

Unseelie Princes: Highly sexual, insatiable, dark counterpart to the golden Seelie princes. Long blue-black hair, leanly muscled dark-skinned bodies tattooed with brilliant complicated patterns that rush beneath their skin like kaleidoscopic storm clouds. They wear black torques like liquid darkness around their necks. They have the starved cruelty and arrogance of a human sociopath. There are four royal princes: Kiall, Rath, Cruce, and an unnamed prince slain by Danielle O'Malley in *Dreamfever.* In the way of Fae things, when one royal is killed, another becomes, and Christian MacKeltar is swiftly becoming the next Unseelie prince.

Unseelie Princesses: The princesses have not been heard of and were presumed dead until recent events brought to light that one or more were hidden away by the Unseelie king either in punishment or to contain a power he didn't want loose in the world. At least one of them was locked in the king's library inside the White Mansion until either Dani or Christian MacKeltar freed her. Highly sexual, a powerful sifter, this princess is stunningly beautiful, with long black hair, pale skin, and blue eyes. In *Burned* we learn the Sweeper tinkered with the Unseelie princess(es) and changed her (them) somehow. Unlike the Unseelie princes, who are prone to mindless savagery, the princess is quite rational about her desires, and logically focused on short-term sacrifice for long-term gain. It is unknown what her end goal is but, as with all Fae, it involves power.

Royal Hunters: A caste of Unseelie sifters, first introduced in *The Immortal Highlander,* this caste hunts for both the king and the queen, relentlessly tracking their prey. Tall, leathery skinned, with wings, they are feared by all Fae.

Crimson Hag: One of the Unseelie king's earliest creations, Dani O'Malley inadvertently freed this monster from a stoppered bottle at the king's fantastical library inside the White Mansion. Psychopathically driven to complete her unfinished, tattered gown of guts, she captures and kills anything in her path, using insectile, lancelike legs to slay her prey and disembowel them. She then perches nearby and knits their entrails into the ragged hem of her bloodred dress. They tend to rot as quickly as they're stitched, necessitating an endless, futile hunt for more. Rumor is, the Hag once held two Unseelie princes captive, killing them over and over for nearly 100,000 years before the Unseelie king stopped her. She reeks of the stench of rotting meat, has matted, blood-drenched hair, an ice-white face with black eye sockets, a thin gash of a mouth, and crimson fangs. Her upper body is lovely and voluptuous, encased in a gruesome corset of bone and sinew. She prefers to abduct Unseelie princes because they are immortal and afford an unending supply of guts, as they regenerate each time she kills them. In *Iced,* she kills Barrons and

Ryodan then captures Christian MacKeltar (the latest Unseelie prince) and carries him off.

Fear Dorcha: One of the Unseelie king's earliest creations, this seven-foot-tall, gaunt Unseelie wears a dark pin-striped tailcoat suit that is at least a century out of date and has no face. Beneath an elegant, cobwebbed black top hat is a swirling black tornado with various bits of features that occasionally materialize. Like all the Unseelie, created imperfectly from an imperfect Song of Making, he is pathologically driven to achieve what he lacks—a face and identity—by stealing faces and identities from humans. The Fear Dorcha was once the Unseelie king's personal assassin and traveling companion during his liege's time of madness after the concubine's death. In *Fever Moon,* the Fear Dorcha is defeated by Mac when she steals his top hat, but it is unknown if the Dorcha is actually deceased.

Hoar Frost King (Gh'luk-ra d'J'hai) (aka HFK): Villain introduced in *Iced,* responsible for turning Dublin into a frigid, arctic wasteland. This Unseelie is one of the most complex and powerful the king ever created, capable of opening holes in space-time to travel, similar to the Seelie ability to sift but with catastrophic results for the matter it manipulates. The Hoar Frost King is the only Unseelie aware of its fundamental imperfection on a quantum level, and like the king, was attempting to re-create the Song of Making to fix itself by collecting the necessary frequencies, physically removing them from the fabric of reality. Each place the Hoar Frost King fed, it stripped necessary structure from the universe while regurgitating a minute mass of enormous density, like a cat vomiting cosmic bones after eating a quantum bird. Although the HFK was destroyed in *Iced* by Dani, Dancer, and Ryodan, the holes it left in the fabric of the human world can only be fixed with the Song of Making.

Gray Man: Tall, monstrous, leprous, capable of sifting, he feeds by stealing beauty from human women. He projects the glamour of a devastatingly attractive human man. He is lethal but prefers his victims left hideously disfigured and alive to suffer. In *Darkfever,* Barrons stabs and kills the Gray Man with Mac's spear.

Gray Woman: The Gray Man's female counterpart, nine feet tall, she projects the glamour of a stunningly beautiful woman and lures human men to their death. Gaunt, emaciated to the point of starvation, her face is long and narrow. Her mouth consumes the entire lower half of her face. She has two rows of sharklike teeth but prefers to feed by caressing her victims, drawing their beauty and vitality out through open sores on her grotesque hands. If she wants to kill in a hurry, she clamps her hands onto human flesh, creating an unbreakable suction. Unlike the Gray Man, she usually quickly kills her victims. In *Shadowfever,* she breaks pattern and preys upon Dani, in retaliation against Mac and Barrons for killing the Gray Man, her lover. Mac makes an unholy pact with her to save Dani.

Rhino-boys: Ugly, gray-skinned creatures that resemble rhinoceroses with bumpy, protruding foreheads, barrel-like bodies, stumpy arms and legs, and lipless gashes of mouths with jutting underbites. Lower-caste Unseelie thugs dispatched primarily as watchdogs and security for high-ranking Fae.

Papa Roach (aka the roach god): Made of thousands and thousands of roachlike creatures clambering up on top of one another to form a larger being. The individual bugs feed off human flesh, specifically fat. Consequently, postwall, some women allow them to enter their bodies and live beneath their skin to keep them slim, a symbiotic liposuction. Papa Roach, the collective, is purplish-brown, about four feet tall with thick legs, a half-dozen arms, and a head the size of a walnut. It jiggles like gelatin when it moves as its countless individual parts shift minutely to remain coalesced. It has a thin-lipped beaklike mouth and round, lidless eyes.

Shades: One of the lowest castes, they started out barely sentient but have been evolving since they were freed from their Unseelie prison. They thrive in darkness, can't bear direct light, and hunt at night or in dark places. They steal life in the same manner the Gray Man steals beauty, draining their victims with vampiric swiftness, leaving behind a pile of clothing and a husk of dehydrated human matter. They consume every living thing in their path from the leaves on trees to the worms in the soil.

SEELIE

Aoibheal, the Seelie Queen (see also **Concubine**): Fae queen, last in a long line of queens with an unusual empathy for humans. In *Shadowfever,* it is revealed the queen was once human herself, and is the Unseelie king's long-lost concubine and soul mate. Over half a million years ago the Unseelie prince Cruce drugged her with a cup stolen from the Cauldron of Forgetting, erased her memory and abducted her, staging it so the Unseelie king believed she was dead. Masquerading as the Seelie prince V'lane, Cruce hid her in the one place he knew the king of the Unseelie would never go—the

Seelie Court. Prolonged time in Faery transformed Aoibheal and she became what the king had desperately desired her to be: Fae and immortal. She is now the latest in a long line of Seelie queens. Tragically, the original Seelie queen was killed by the Unseelie king before she was able to pass on the Song of Making, the most powerful and beautiful of all Fae magic. Without it, the Seelie have changed. In *Burned*, the Unseelie king took the concubine to the White Mansion and imprisoned her inside the boudoir they once shared, in an effort to restore her memory.

DARROC, LORD MASTER (Seelie turned human): Once Fae and trusted advisor to Aoibheal, he was set up by Cruce and banished from Faery for treason. At the Seelie Court, Adam Black (in the novel *The Immortal Highlander*) was given the choice to have Darroc killed or turned mortal as punishment for trying to free Unseelie and overthrow the queen. Adam chose to have him turned mortal, believing he would quickly die as a human, sparking the succession of events that culminates in *Faefever* when Darroc destroys the walls between the worlds of man and Fae, setting the long-imprisoned Unseelie free. Once in the mortal realm, Darroc learned to eat Unseelie flesh to achieve power and caught wind of the *Sinsar Dubh*'s existence in the mortal realm. When Alina Lane came to Dublin, Darroc discovered she was a *sidhe*-seer with many talents and, like her sister, Mac, could sense and track the *Sinsar Dubh*. He began by using her but fell in love with her. After Alina's death, Darroc learned of Mac and attempted to use her as well, applying various methods of coercion, including abducting her parents. Once Mac believed Barrons was dead, she teamed up with Darroc, determined to find the *Sinsar Dubh* herself and use it to bring Barrons back. Darroc was killed in *Shadowfever* by K'Vruck, allegedly at the direction of the *Sinsar Dubh,* when the Hunter popped his head like a grape.

Seelie Princes: There were once four princes and four princesses of the royal *sidhe.* The Seelie princesses have not been seen for a long time and are presumed dead. V'lane was killed long ago, Velvet (not his real name) is recently deceased, R'jan currently aspires to be king, and Adam Black is now human. Highly sexual, golden-haired (except for Adam, who assumed a darker glamour), with iridescent eyes and golden skin, they are extremely powerful sifters, capable of sustaining nearly impenetrable glamour, and affect the climate with their pleasure or displeasure.

V'lane: Seelie prince, queen of the Fae's high consort, extremely sexual and erotic. The real V'lane was killed by his own queen when Cruce switched faces and places with him via glamour. Cruce has been masquerading as V'lane ever since, hiding in plain sight.

Velvet: Lesser royalty, cousin to R'jan. He was introduced in *Shadowfever* and killed by Ryodan in *Iced.*

Dree-Lia: Frequent consort of Velvet, was present when the *Sinsar Dubh* was reinterred beneath the abbey.

R'jan: Seelie prince who would be king. Tall, blond, with the velvety gold skin of a light Fae, he makes his debut in *Iced* when he announces his claim on the Fae throne.

Adam Black: Immortal Prince of the D'Jai House and favored consort of the Seelie queen, banished from Faery and made mortal as punishment for one of his countless interferences with the human realm. Has been called the *sin siriche dubh* or blackest Fae, however undeserved. Rumor holds Adam was not always Fae, although that has not been substantiated. In *The Immortal Highlander* he is exiled among mortals, falls in love with Gabrielle O'Callaghan, a *sidhe*-seer from Cincinnati, Ohio, and chooses to remain human to stay with her. He refuses to get involved in the current war between man and Fae, fed up with the endless manipulation, seduction, and drama. With Gabrielle, he has a highly gifted and unusual daughter to protect.

THE KELTAR

An ancient bloodline of Highlanders chosen by Queen Aoibheal and trained in druidry to uphold the Compact between the races of man and Fae. Brilliant, gifted in physics and engineering, they live near Inverness and guard a circle of standing stones called Ban Drochaid (the White Bridge), which was used for time travel until the Keltar breached one of their many oaths to the queen and she closed the circle of stones to other times and dimensions. Current Keltar druids: Christopher, Christian, Cian, Dageus, Drustan.

Druid: In pre-Christian Celtic society, a druid presided over divine worship, legislative and judicial matters, philosophy, and education of elite youth to their order. Druids were believed to be privy to the secrets of the gods, including issues pertaining to the manipulation of physical matter, space, and even time. The old Irish "drui" means magician, wizard, diviner.

CHRISTOPHER MACKELTAR: Modern-day laird of the Keltar clan, father of Christian MacKeltar.

CHRISTIAN MACKELTAR (turned Unseelie prince): Handsome Scotsman, dark hair, tall, muscular body, and killer smile, he masqueraded as a student at Trinity College, working in the Ancient Languages department, but was really stationed there by his uncles to keep an eye on Jericho Barrons. Trained as a druid by his clan, he participated in a ritual at Ban Drochaid on Samhain meant to reinforce the walls between the worlds of man and Fae. Unfortunately, the ceremony went badly wrong, leaving Christian and Barrons trapped in the Silvers. When Mac later finds Christian in the Hall of All Days, she feeds him Unseelie flesh to save his life, unwittingly sparking the chain of events that begins to turn the sexy Highlander into an Unseelie prince. He loses himself for a time in madness, and fixates on the innocence of Dani O'Malley while losing his humanity. In *Iced,* he sacrifices himself to the Crimson Hag to distract her from killing the *sidhe*-seers, determined to spare Dani from having to choose between saving the abbey or the world. Currently staked to the side of a cliff above a hellish grotto, being killed over and over again. In *Burned,* Christian is rescued from the cliff by Mac, Barrons, Ryodan, Jada, Drustan, and Dageus, but Dageus sacrifices himself to save Christian in the process.

Cian MacKeltar (*Spell of the Highlander*): Highlander from the twelfth century, traveled through time to the present day, married to Jessica St. James. Cian was imprisoned for one thousand years in one of the Silvers by a vengeful sorcerer. Freed, he now lives with the other Keltar in current-day Scotland.

Dageus MacKeltar (*The Dark Highlander*): Keltar druid from the sixteenth century who traveled through time to the present day, married to Chloe Zanders. He is still inhabited (to an unknown degree) by the souls/knowledge of thirteen dead Draghar, ancient druids who used black sorcery but has concealed all knowledge of this from his clan. Long black hair nearly to his waist, dark skin, and gold eyes, he is the sexiest and most sexual of the Keltar. In *Burned,* we learn that although he gave his life to save Christian, Ryodan brought him back and is keeping him in a dungeon beneath Chester's.

Drustan MacKeltar (*Kiss of the Highlander*): Twin brother of Dageus MacKeltar, also traveled through time to the present day, married to Gwen Cassidy. Tall, dark, with long brown hair and silver eyes, he is the ultimate chivalrous knight and would sacrifice himself for the greater good if necessary.

HUMANS

Jack and Rainey Lane: Mac and Alina's parents. In *Darkfever,* Mac discovers they are not her biological parents. She and Alina were adopted, and part of the custody agreement was a promise that the girls never be allowed to return to the country of their birth. Jack is a strapping, handsome man, an attorney with a strong sense of ethics. Rainey is a compassionate blond woman who was unable to bear children of her own. She's a steel magnolia, strong yet fragile.

Dancer: Six feet four inches, he has dark, wavy hair and gorgeous aqua eyes. Very mature, intellectually gifted seventeen-year-old who was home-schooled, and graduated from college with a double major in physics and engineering by sixteen. Fascinated by physics, he speaks multiple languages and traveled extensively with wealthy, humanitarian parents. His father is an ambassador, his mother a doctor. He was alone in Dublin, considering Trinity College for grad school, when the walls between realms fell, and has survived by his wits. He is an inventor and can often think circles around most people, including Dani. He seems unruffled by Barrons, Ryodan, and his men. Dani met Dancer near the end of *Shadowfever* (when he gave her a bracelet, first gift from a guy she liked) and they've been inseparable since. In *Iced,* Dancer made it clear he has feelings for her. Dancer is the only person Dani feels like she can be herself with: young, a little geeky, a lot brainy. Both he and Dani move around frequently, never staying in one place too long. They have many hideouts around the city, above- and belowground. Dani worries about him because he doesn't have any superpowers.

Fiona Asheton: Beautiful woman in her early fifties who originally managed Barrons Books & Baubles and was deeply in love (unrequited) with Jericho Barrons. Fiendishly jealous of Barrons's interest in MacKayla, she tried to kill Mac by letting Shades (lethal Unseelie) into the bookstore while she was sleeping. Barrons exiled her for it, and Fiona then became Derek O'Bannion's lover, began eating Unseelie, and was briefly possessed by the *Sinsar Dubh,* which skinned her from head to toe but left her alive. Due to the amount of Fae flesh Fiona had eaten, she could no longer be killed by human means and was trapped in a mutilated body, in constant agony. Eventually she begged Mac to use her Fae spear and end her suffering. Fiona died in the White Mansion when she flung herself through the ancient Silver used as a doorway between the concubine and the Unseelie king's bedchambers—which kills anyone who enters it except for the king and concubine—but not before trying to kill Mac one last time.

Roark (Rocky) O'Bannion: Black Irish Catholic mobster with Saudi ancestry and the compact, powerful body of a heavyweight champion boxer, which he is. Born in a Dublin controlled by two feuding Irish crime families—the Hallorans and O'Kierneys—Roark O'Bannion fought his way to the top in the ring, but it wasn't enough for the ambitious champ; he hungered for more. When Rocky was twenty-eight years old, the Halloran and O'Kierney linchpins were killed along with every son, grandson, and pregnant woman in their families. Twenty-seven people died that night, gunned down, blown up, poisoned, knifed, or strangled. Dublin had never seen anything like it. A group of flawlessly choreographed killers had closed in all over the city, at restaurants, homes, hotels, and clubs, and struck simultaneously. The next day, when a suddenly wealthy Rocky O'Bannion, champion boxer and many a young boy's idol, retired from the ring to take control of various businesses in and around Dublin previously run by the Hallorans and O'Kierneys, he was hailed by the working-class poor as a hero, despite the fresh and obvious blood on his hands and the rough pack of ex-boxers and thugs he brought with him. O'Bannion is devoutly religious and collects sacred artifacts. Mac steals the Spear of Destiny (aka the Spear of Longinus that pierced Christ's side) from him to protect herself, as it is one of two weapons that can kill the immortal Fae. Later, in *Darkfever,* Barrons kills O'Bannion to keep Mac safe from him and his henchmen, but it's not the end of the O'Bannions gunning for Mac.

Derek O'Bannion: Rocky's younger brother, he begins snooping around Mac and the bookstore after Rocky is murdered, as his brother's car was found behind the bookstore. He becomes lovers with Fiona Asheton, is ultimately possessed by the *Sinsar Dubh,* and attacks Mac. He is killed by the *Sinsar Dubh* in *Bloodfever.*

Sean O'Bannion: Rocky O'Bannion's cousin and Katarina McLaughlin's childhood sweetheart and adult lover. After the Hallorans and the O'Kierneys were killed by Rocky, the O'Bannions controlled the city for nearly a decade, until the McLaughlins began usurping their turf. Both Sean and Kat despised the family business and refused to participate. The two crime families sought to unite the business with a marriage between them, but when nearly all the McLaughlins were killed after the walls crashed, Katarina and Sean finally felt free. But chaos reigns in a world where humans struggle to obtain simple necessities, and Sean suddenly finds himself part of the black market, competing with Ryodan and the Fae to fairly distribute the supply of food and valuable resources. Kat is devastated to see him doing the wrong things for all the right reasons and it puts a serious strain on their relationship.

MALLUCÉ (aka John Johnstone, Jr.): Geeky son of billionaire parents until he kills them for their fortune and reinvents himself as the steampunk vampire Mallucé. In *Darkfever,* he teams up with Darroc, the Lord Master, who teaches him to eat Unseelie flesh for the strength and enormous sexual stamina and appetite it confers. He's wounded in battle by Mac's Spear of Destiny. Because he'd been eating Unseelie, the lethal prick of the Fae blade caused parts of him to die, killing flesh but not his body, trapping him in a half-rotted, agonizing shell of a body. He appears to Mac as the Grim Reaper in *Bloodfever,* and after psychologically tormenting her, abducts and holds her prisoner in a hellish grotto beneath the Burren in Ireland, where he tortures and nearly kills her. Barrons kills him and saves Mac by feeding her Unseelie flesh, changing her forever.

THE GUARDIANS: Originally Dublin's police force, the Gardai, under the command of Inspector Jayne. They eat Unseelie to obtain heightened strength, speed, and acuity, and hunt all Fae. They've learned to use iron bullets to temporarily wound them and iron bars to contain them. Most Fae can be significantly weakened by iron. If applied properly, iron can prevent a Fae from being able to sift.

Inspector O'Duffy: Original Garda on Alina Lane's murder case, brother-in-law to Inspector Jayne. He was killed in *Bloodfever,* his throat slit while holding a scrap of paper with Mac's name and address on it. It is currently unknown who killed him.

Inspector Jayne: Garda who takes over Alina Lane's murder case after Inspector O'Duffy, Jayne's brother-in-law, is killed. Big, rawboned Irishman who looks like Liam Neeson, he tails Mac and generally complicates her life. Initially, he's more interested in what happened to O'Duffy than solving Alina's case, but Mac treats him to Unseelie-laced tea and opens his eyes to what's going on in their city and world. Jayne joins the fight against the Fae and transforms the Gardai into the New Guardians, a ruthless army of ex-policemen who eat Unseelie, battle Fae, and protect humans. Jayne is a good man in a hard position. Although he and his men can capture the Fae, they can't kill them without either Mac's or Dani's weapon. In *Iced,* Jayne earns Dani's eternal wrath by stealing her sword when she's too injured to fight back.

CHARACTERS OF UNKNOWN GENUS

K'Vruck: Allegedly the most ancient of the Unseelie caste of Royal Hunters—although it is not substantiated that he is truly Unseelie. He was once the Unseelie king's favored companion and "steed" as he traveled worlds on its great black wings. Enormous as a small skyscraper, vaguely resembling a dragon, it's coal black, leathery, and icy, with eyes like huge orange furnaces. When it flies, it churns black frosty flakes in the air and liquid ice streams in its wake. It has a special affinity for Mac and appears to her at odd moments as it senses the king inside her (via the *Sinsar Dubh*). When K'Vruck kills, it is the ultimate death, extinguishing life so completely it's forever erased from the karmic cycle. To be K'Vrucked is to be removed completely from existence as if you've never been, no trace, no residue. Mac used K'Vruck to free Barrons's son. K'Vruck is the only being (known so far) capable of killing the immortal Nine.

Sweeper: A collector of powerful, broken things, it resembles a giant trash heap of metal cogs and gears. First encountered by the Unseelie king shortly after he lost his concubine and descended into a period of madness and grief. The Sweeper traveled with him for a time, studying him, or perhaps seeing if he, too, could be collected and tinkered with. According to the Unseelie king, it fancies itself a god.

ZEWs: Acronym for zombie eating wraiths, so named by Dani O'Malley. Hulking anorexic vulturelike creatures, they are five to six feet tall, with gaunt, hunched bodies and heavily cowled faces. They appear to be wearing cobwebbed, black robes but it is actually their skin. They have exposed bone at their sleeves and pale smudges inside their cowls. In *Burned,* Mac catches a glimpse of metal where their faces should be but doesn't get a good look.

PLACES

Arlington Abbey: An ancient stone abbey located nearly two hours from Dublin, situated on a thousand acres of prime farmland. The mystically fortified abbey houses an Order of *sidhe*-seers gathered from six bloodlines of Irish women born with the ability to see the Fae and their realms. The abbey was built in the seventh century and is completely self-sustaining, with multiple artesian wells, livestock, and gardens. According to historical records, the land occupied by the abbey was previously a church, and before that a sacred circle of stones, and long before that a fairy shian, or mound. *Sidhe*-seer legend suggests the Unseelie king himself spawned their order, mixing his blood with that of six Irish houses, to create protectors for the one thing he should never have made—the *Sinsar Dubh.*

Ashford, Georgia: MacKayla Lane's small, rural hometown in the Deep South.

Barrons Books & Baubles: Located on the outskirts of Temple Bar in Dublin, Barrons Books & Baubles is an Old World bookstore previously owned by Jericho Barrons, now owned by MacKayla Lane. It shares design characteristics with the Lello Bookstore in Portugal, but is somewhat more elegant and refined. Due to the location of a large Sifting Silver in the study on the first floor, the bookstore's dimensions can shift from as few as four stories to as many as seven, and rooms on the upper levels often reposition themselves. It is where MacKayla Lane calls home.

Barrons's Garage: Located directly behind Barrons Books & Baubles, it houses a collection of expensive cars. Far beneath it, accessible only through the heavily warded Silver in the bookstore, are Jericho Barrons's living quarters.

The Brickyard: The bar in Ashford, Georgia, where MacKayla Lane bartended before she came to Dublin.

Chester's Nightclub: An enormous underground club of chrome and glass located at 939 Rêvemal Street. Chester's is owned by one of Barrons's associates, Ryodan. The upper levels are open to the public, the lower levels contain the Nine's residences and their private clubs. Since the walls between man and Fae fell, Chester's has become the hot spot in Dublin for Fae and humans to mingle.

Dark Zone: An area that has been taken over by the Shades, deadly Unseelie that suck the life from humans, leaving only a husk of skin and indigestible matter such as eyeglasses, wallets, and medical implants. During the day it looks like an everyday abandoned, run-down neighborhood. Once night falls it's a death trap. The largest known Dark Zone in Dublin is adjacent to Barrons Books & Baubles and is nearly twenty by thirteen city blocks.

Faery: A general term encompassing the many realms of the Fae.

Hall of All Days: The "airport terminal" of the Sifting Silvers where one can choose which mirror to enter to travel to other worlds and realms. Fashioned of gold from floor to ceiling, the endless corridor is lined with billions of mirrors that are portals to alternate universes and times, and exudes a chilling spatial-temporal distortion that makes a visitor feel utterly inconsequential. Time isn't linear in the hall, it's malleable and slippery, and a visitor can get permanently lost in memories that never were and dreams of futures that will never be. One moment you feel terrifyingly alone, the next as if an endless chain of paper-doll versions of oneself is unfolding sideways, holding cutout construction-paper hands with thousands of different feet in thousands of different worlds, all at the same time. Compounding the many dangers of the hall, when the Silvers were corrupted by Cruce's curse (intended to bar entry to the Unseelie king), the mirrors were altered and now the image they present is no longer a guarantee of what's on the other side. A lush rain forest may lead to a parched, cracked desert, a tropical oasis to a world of ice, but one can't count on total opposites either.

The River Liffey: The river that divides Dublin into south and north sections, and supplies most of Dublin's water.

Temple Bar District: An area in Dublin also known simply as "Temple Bar," in which the Temple Bar Pub is located, along with an endless selection of boisterous drinking establishments including the famed Oliver St. John Gogarty, the Quays Bar, the Foggy Dew, the Brazen Head, Buskers, The Purty Kitchen, The Auld Dubliner, and so on. On the south bank of the River Liffey, Temple Bar (the district) sprawls for blocks, and has two meeting squares that used to be overflowing with tourists and partiers. Countless street musicians, great restaurants and shops, local bands, and raucous Stag and Hen parties made Temple Bar the *craic*-filled center of the city.

Temple Bar Pub: A quaint, famous pub named after Sir William Temple, who once lived there. Founded in 1840, it squats bright red and cozy, draped with string lights at the corner of Temple Bar Street and Temple Lane, and rambles from garden to alcove to main room. The famous pub boasts a first-rate whiskey collection, a beer garden for smoking, legendary Dublin Bay oysters, perfectly stacked Guinness, terrific atmosphere, and the finest traditional Irish music in the city.

Trinity College: Founded in 1592, located on College Green, recognized as one of the finest universities in the world, it houses a library that contains over 4.5 million printed volumes including spectacular works such as the *Book of Kells*. It's ranked in the world's top one hundred universities for physics and mathematics, with state-of-the-art laboratories and equipment. Dancer does much of his research on the now abandoned college campus.

Unseelie Prison: Located in the Unseelie king's realm, close to his fortress of black ice, the prison once held all Unseelie captives for over half a million years in a stark, arctic prison of ice. When the walls between man and Faery were destroyed by Darroc (a banished Seelie prince with a vendetta against the Seelie queen), all the Unseelie were freed to invade the human realms.

The White Mansion: Located inside the Silvers, the house that the Unseelie king built for his beloved concubine. Enormous, ever-changing, the many halls and rooms in the mansion rearrange themselves at will.

THINGS

Amulet: Also called the One True Amulet, see The Four Unseelie Hallows.

Amulets, the Three Lesser: Amulets created prior to the One True Amulet, these objects are capable of weaving and sustaining nearly impenetrable illusion when used together. Currently in possession of Cruce.

Compact: Agreement negotiated between Queen Aoibheal and the MacKeltar clan (Keltar means hidden barrier or mantle) long ago to keep the realms of mankind and Fae separate. The Seelie queen taught them to tithe and perform rituals that would reinforce the walls that were compromised when the original queen used a portion of them to create the Unseelie prison.

Crimson Runes: This enormously powerful and complex magic formed the foundation of the walls of the Unseelie prison and is offered by the *Sinsar Dubh* to MacKayla on several occasions to use to protect herself. All Fae fear them. When the walls between man and Fae began to weaken long ago, the Seelie queen tapped into the prison walls, siphoning some of their power, which she used to reinforce the boundaries between worlds . . . thus dangerously weakening the prison walls. It was at that time the first Unseelie began to escape. The more one struggles against the crimson runes, the stronger they grow, feeding off the energy expended in the victim's effort to escape. MacKayla used them in *Shadowfever* to seal the *Sinsar Dubh* shut until Cruce, posing as V'lane, persuaded her to remove them. The beast form of Jericho Barrons eats these runes, and seems to consider them a delicacy.

Cuff of Cruce: A cuff made of silver and gold, set with bloodred stones; an ancient Fae relic that protects the wearer against all Fae and many other creatures. Cruce claims he made it, not the king, and that he gave it to the king as a gift to give his lover. According to Cruce, its powers were dual: it not only protected the concubine from threats, but allowed her to summon him by merely touching it, thinking of the king, and wishing for his presence.

Dolmen: A single-chamber megalithic tomb constructed of three or more upright stones supporting a large, flat, horizontal capstone. Dolmens are common in Ireland, especially around the Burren and Connemara. The Lord Master used a dolmen in a ritual of dark magic to open a doorway between realms and bring through Unseelie.

The Dreaming: It's where all hopes, fantasies, illusions, and nightmares of sentient beings come to be or go to rest, whichever you prefer to believe. No one knows where the Dreaming came from or who created it. It is far more ancient even than the Fae. Since Cruce cursed the Silvers and the Hall of All Days was corrupted, the Dreaming can be accessed via the hall, though with enormous difficulty.

Elixir of Life: Both the Seelie queen and Unseelie king have a version of this powerful potion. The Seelie queen's version can make a human immortal (though not bestow the grace and power of being Fae). It is currently unknown what the king's version does but reasonable to expect that, as the imperfect song used to fashion his court, it is also flawed in some way.

The Four Stones: Chiseled from the blue-black walls of the Unseelie prison, these four stones have the ability to contain the *Sinsar Dubh* in place if positioned properly, rendering its power inert, allowing it to be transported safely. The stones contain the Book's magic and immobilize it completely, preventing it from being able to possess the person transporting it. They are capable of immobilizing it in any form, including MacKayla Lane as she has the Book inside her. They are etched with ancient runes and react with many other Fae objects of power. When united, they sing a lesser Song of Making. Not nearly as powerful as the crimson runes, they can contain only the *Sinsar Dubh*.

Glamour: Illusion cast by the Fae to camouflage their true appearance. The more powerful the Fae, the more difficult it is to penetrate its disguise. Average humans see only what the Fae want them to see and are subtly repelled from bumping into or brushing against it by a small perimeter of spatial distortion that is part of the Fae glamour.

The Hallows: Eight ancient artifacts created by the Fae possessing enormous power. There are four Seelie and four Unseelie hallows.

The Four Seelie Hallows

The Spear of Luisne: Also known as the Spear of Luin, Spear of Longinus, Spear of Destiny, the Flaming Spear, it is one of two hallows capable of killing Fae. Currently in possession of MacKayla Lane.

The Sword of Lugh: Also known as the Sword of Light, the second hallow capable of killing Fae. Currently in possession of Danielle O'Malley.

The Cauldron: Also called the Cauldron of Forgetting. The Fae are subject to a type of madness that sets in at advanced years. They drink from the cauldron to erase all memory and begin fresh. None but the Scribe, Cruce, and the Unseelie king, who have never drunk from the cauldron, know the true history of their race. Currently located at the Seelie Court. Cruce stole a cup from the Cauldron of Forgetting and tricked the concubine/Aoibheal into drinking it, thereby erasing all memory of the king and her life before the moment the cup touched her lips.

The Stone: Little is known of this Seelie hallow.

The Four Unseelie Hallows

The Amulet: Created by the Unseelie king for his concubine so that she could manipulate reality as well as a Fae. Fashioned of gold, silver, sapphires, and onyx, the gilt "cage" of the amulet houses an enormous clear stone of unknown composition. It can be used by a person of epic will to impact and reshape perception. The list of past owners is legendary, including Merlin, Boudicca, Joan of Arc, Charlemagne, and Napoleon. This amulet is capable of weaving illusion that will deceive even the Unseelie king. In *Shadowfever,* MacKayla Lane used it to defeat the *Sinsar Dubh.* Currently stored in Barrons's lair beneath the garage, locked away for safekeeping.

The Silvers: An elaborate network of mirrors created by the Unseelie king, once used as the primary method of Fae travel between realms. The central hub for the Silvers is the Hall of All Days, an infinite, gilded corridor where time is not linear, filled with mirrors of assorted shapes and sizes that are portals to other worlds, places, and times. Before Cruce cursed the Silvers, whenever a traveler stepped through a mirror at a perimeter location, he was instantly translated to the hall, where he could then choose a new destination from the images the mirrors displayed. After Cruce cursed the Silvers, the mirrors in the hall were compromised and no longer accurately display their true destinations. It's highly dangerous to travel within the Silvers.

The Book (See also *Sinsar Dubh*; she-suh DOO): A fragment of the Unseelie king himself, a sentient, psychopathic Book of enormous, dark magic created when the king tried to expel the corrupt arts with which he'd tampered, trying to re-create the Song of Making. The Book was originally a nonsentient, spelled object, but in the way of Fae it evolved and over time became sentient, living, conscious. When it did, like all Unseelie created via an imperfect song, it was obsessed by a desire to complete itself, to obtain a corporeal body for its consciousness, to become like others of its kind. It usually presents itself in one of three forms: an innocuous hardcover book; a thick, gilded, magnificent ancient tome with runes and locks; or a monstrous amorphous beast. It temporarily achieves corporeality by possessing humans, but the human host rejects it and the body self-destructs quickly. The *Sinsar Dubh* usually toys with its hosts, uses them to vent its sadistic rage, then kills them and jumps to a new body (or jumps to a new body and uses it to kill them). The closest it has ever come to obtaining a body was by imprinting a full copy of itself in Mac as an unformed fetus while it possessed her mother. Since the *Sinsar Dubh*'s presence has been inside Mac from the earliest stages of her life, her body chemistry doesn't sense it as an intruder and reject it. She can survive its possession without it destroying her. Still, the original *Sinsar Dubh* craves a body of its own and for Mac to embrace her copy so that it will finally be flesh and blood and have a mate.

The Box: Little is known of this Unseelie hallow. Legend says the Unseelie king created it for his concubine.

The Haven: High Council and advisors to the Grand Mistress of the abbey, made up of the seven most talented, powerful *sidhe*-seers. Twenty years ago it was led by Mac's mother, Isla O'Connor, but the Haven got wind of Rowena tampering with black arts and suspected she'd been seduced by the *Sinsar Dubh,* which was locked away beneath the abbey in a heavily warded cavern. They discovered she'd been entering the forbidden chamber, talking with it. They formed a second, secret Haven to monitor Rowena's activities, which included Rowena's own daughter and Isla's best friend, Kayleigh. The Haven was right, Rowena had been corrupted and ultimately freed the *Sinsar Dubh.* It is unknown who carried it from the abbey the night the Book escaped or where it was for the next two decades.

IFP: Interdimensional Fairy Pothole, created when the walls between man and Faery fell and chunks of reality fragmented. They exist also within the network of Silvers, the result of Cruce's curse. Translucent, funnel-shaped, with narrow bases and wide tops, they are difficult to see and drift unless tethered. There is no way to determine what type of environment exists inside one until you've stepped through, extreme climate excepted.

Iron: Fe on the periodic table, painful to Fae. Iron bars can contain nonsifting Fae. Properly spelled iron can constrain a sifting Fae to a degree. Iron cannot kill a Fae.

MacHalo: Invented by MacKayla Lane, a bike helmet with LED lights affixed to it. Designed to protect the wearer from the vampiric Shades by casting a halo of light all around the body.

Null: A *sidhe*-seer with the power to freeze a Fae with the touch of his or her hands (MacKayla Lane has this talent). While frozen, a nulled Fae is completely powerless, but the higher and more powerful the caste of Fae, the shorter the length of time it stays immobilized. It can still see, hear, and think while frozen, making it very dangerous to be in its vicinity when unfrozen.

Poste Haste, Inc.: A bicycling courier service headquartered in Dublin that is actually the Order of *Sidhe*-Seers. Founded by Rowena, she established an international branch of PHI in countries all over the world to stay apprised of all developments globally.

Pri-ya: A human who is sexually addicted to and enslaved by the Fae. The royal castes of Fae are so sexual and erotic that sex with them is addictive and destructive to the human mind. It creates a painful, debilitating, insatiable need in a human. The royal castes can, if they choose, diminish their impact during sex and make it merely stupendous. But if they don't, it overloads human senses and turns the human into a sex addict, incapable of thought or speech, capable only of serving the sexual pleasures of whomever is their master. Since the walls fell, many humans have been turned Pri-ya, and society is trying to deal with these wrecked humans in a way that doesn't involve incarcerating them in padded cells, in mindless misery.

Shamrock: This slightly misshapen three-leaf clover is the ancient symbol of the *sidhe*-seers, who are charged with the mission to See, Serve, and Protect mankind from the Fae. In *Bloodfever,* Rowena shares the history of the emblem with Mac: "Before it was the clover of Saint Patrick's trinity, it was ours. It's the emblem of our order. It's the symbol our ancient sisters used to carve on their doors and dye into banners millennia ago when they moved to a new village. It was our way of letting the inhabitants know who we were and what we were there to do. When people saw our sign, they declared a time of great feasting and celebrated for a fortnight. They welcomed us with gifts of their finest food, wine, and men. They held tournaments to compete to bed us. It is not a clover at all, but a vow. You see how these two leaves make a sideways figure eight, like a horizontal Möbius strip? They are two S's, one right side up, one upside down, ends meeting. The third leaf and stem is an upright P. The first S is for See, the second for Serve, the P for Protect. The shamrock itself is the symbol of Eire, the great Ireland. The Möbius strip is our pledge of guardianship eternal. We are the *sidhe*-seers and we watch over mankind. We protect them from the Old Ones. We stand between this world and all the others."

Sifting: Fae method of travel. The higher ranking, most powerful Fae are able to translocate from place to place at the speed of thought. Once they could travel through time as well as place, but Aoibheal stripped that power from them for repeated offenses.

Sinsar Dubh: Originally designed as an ensorcelled tome, it was intended to be the inert repository or dumping ground for all the Unseelie king's arcane knowledge of a flawed, toxic Song of Making. It was with this knowledge he created the Unseelie Court and castes. The Book contains an enormous amount of dangerous magic that can create and destroy worlds. Like the king, its power is nearly limitless. Unfortunately, as with all Fae things, the Book, drenched with magic, changed and evolved until it achieved full sentience. No longer a mere book, it is a homicidal, psychopathic, starved, and power-hungry being. Like the rest of the imperfect Unseelie, it wants to finish or perfect itself, to attain that which it perceives it lacks. In this case, the perfect host body. When the king realized the Book had become sentient, he created a prison for it, and made the *sidhe*-seers—some say by tampering with their bloodline, lending a bit of his own—to guard it and keep it from ever escaping. The king realized that rather than eradicating the dangerous magic, he'd only managed to create a copy of it. Much like the king, the *Sinsar Dubh* found a way to create a copy of itself, and planted it inside an unborn fetus, MacKayla Lane. There are currently two *Sinsar Dubh*s: one that Cruce absorbed (or became possessed by), and the copy inside MacKayla Lane that she refuses to open. As long as she never voluntarily seeks or takes a single spell from it, it can't take her over and she won't be possessed. If, however, she uses it for any reason, she will be obliterated by the psychopathic villain trapped inside it, forever silenced. With the long-starved and imprisoned *Sinsar Dubh* free, life for humans will become Hell on Earth. Unfortunately, the Book is highly charismatic, brilliant, and seductive, and has observed humanity long enough to exploit human weaknesses like a maestro.

SONG OF MAKING: The greatest power in the universe, this song can create life from nothing. All life stems from it. Originally known by the first Seelie queen, she rarely used it because, as with all great magic, it demands a great price. It was to be passed from queen to queen, to be used only when absolutely necessary to protect and sustain life. To hear this song is to experience Heaven on Earth, to know the how, when, and why of our existence, and simultaneously have no need to know it at all. The melody is allegedly so beautiful, transformative, and pure that if one who harbors evil in his heart hears it, he will be charred to ash where he stands.

UNSEELIE FLESH: Eating Unseelie flesh endows an average human with enormous strength, power, and sensory acuity; heightens sexual pleasure and stamina; and is highly addictive. It also lifts the veil between worlds and permits a human to see past the glamour worn by the Fae, to see their actual forms. Before the walls fell, all Fae concealed themselves with glamour. After the walls fell, they didn't care, but now Fae are beginning to conceal themselves again, as humans have learned that the common element iron is useful in injuring and imprisoning them.

VOICE: A druid art or skill that compels the person it's being used on to precisely obey the letter of whatever command is issued. Dageus, Drustan, and Cian MacKeltar are fluent in it. Jericho Barrons taught Darroc (for a price) and also trained MacKayla Lane to use and withstand it. Teacher and apprentice become immune to each other and can no longer be compelled.

Ward: A powerful magic known to druids, sorcerers, *sidhe*-seers, and Fae. There are many categories, including but not limited to Earth, Air, Fire, Stone, and Metal wards. Barrons is adept at placing wards, more so than any of the Nine besides Daku.

WeCare: An organization founded after the walls between man and Fae fell, using food, supplies, and safety as a lure to draw followers. Rainey Lane works with them, sees only the good in the organization, possibly because it's the only place she can harness resources to rebuild Dublin and run her Green-Up group. Someone in WeCare authors the *Dublin Daily,* a local newspaper to compete with the *Dani Daily*; whoever does it dislikes Dani a great deal and is always ragging on her. Not much is known about this group. They lost some of their power when three major players began raiding them and stockpiling supplies.

Mac and Barrons are back with a vengeance
in the next installment of the blockbuster
Fever series from #1 *New York Times* bestselling
sensation Karen Marie Moning

FEVERSONG

Available now

Read on for a sneak peek

A warehouse in a Dark Zone, Dublin, Ireland

I rise.

Or try to. Jada crashes into me with a muffled grunt, then her hands are on me, everywhere, touching, patting and pulling, undoing my restraints, and the sensation is too much. My body is hypersensitive.

Finally, she frees my hands. I push her away and open my eyes. Too fast, too much. Light thrusts cruel needles into my brain.

I swiftly close my eyes. Scents overwhelm me: the pungent odor of the Sweeper's minions, concrete and rusting metal, chemicals and sweat.

"Turn off the lights," I say.

"Why?" Jada says.

"I have a headache." I wait without moving as she hurries about the warehouse, extinguishing the blinding lights the Sweeper arranged for our surgery. Once I sense diminished brilliance beyond my lids, I open my eyes again. Tolerable.

"Mac, what did you do?" Jada exclaims. "They're gone. Just gone!"

Sound impacts the delicate structure of my ears as if she's taken a gong to a shield. Not gone. The Sweeper and his minions were displaced—a simple spell of sifting—backward, not forward. In short order, they will be here again, in this warehouse, but I intend to be gone.

I. Intend.

I rise. My body doesn't move as planned. It shudders, flops, and goes limp. "Stiff from being on the table so long," I tell Jada, who watches me with narrowed eyes. I contract my abdomen, bend at the waist, stabilize my upper body, rotate my hips, shift my legs as a unit over the side of the gurney, and touch my feet to the floor.

I stand.

I AM.

Desire. Lust. Greed. And the path I choose to supremacy.

Master of adaptation and evolution, I slide more surely into my skin with each breath, enjoying the complex, albeit imperfect elegance of what I possess. I inhale long and slow, swelling first my abdomen then lungs with air. Breathing brings an assault of unfathomable stenches, but I will acclimate.

Every thought, every emotion MacKayla Lane experienced is filed in my meticulous mental vault, but during my incarceration in her body, I couldn't see, I couldn't hear, I couldn't smell.

I was—as she is now—trapped in a dark, silent prison, my only connection to the world an attachment I forged to her central nervous system through supremacy of will and relentless trial and failure. My existence was a smattering of complex electrical charges, intricate patterns without substance. Although I spied on her life as much as possible, I was able to seize and use her body, hands, and eyes only once, for brief duration. All else was diluted, second-hand perception absorbed from within, but for that overcast, rainy day I killed the Gray Woman and Mick O'Leary.

The power. The glory. That was the day I knew I would win. Those clumsy, debilitating hours I rode a body for the first time.

I require time to perfect control.

I. Require.

I draw myself up inside, gathering the enormity, the ancientness, the hunger and storm of my being and expand into the imperfect biological vessel I've claimed, saturating, possessing every atom. I fill my blood, my bones, my skin.

I turn the full force of my regard upon Jada, blink once, and reveal myself. My eyes, reflected in the stainless-steel door of a commercial freezer unit behind her, fill with obsidian until no white remains.

She changes color. Fear impacts the nerves that connect brain to heart, constricting circulation. The blood vanishes from her face, leaving freckles upon snow. Her eyes widen, her pupils dilate and freeze. The scent of her body alters to one I find . . . intriguing.

I experience all of this with my own senses. It's incomparable. My mere presence reprograms the anatomy of those around me.

Power.

I was made for it.

I would prefer to shred her flesh from bone, but several things prevent me. I smile with my new face.

"I would run if I were you," I tell her softly.